3 AND A HALF MURDERS

Salil Desai is the author of the much-acclaimed Inspector Saralkar Mystery Series. The books are currently being adapted into a web series by Jio Studios.

An alumnus of Film & Television Institute of India (FTII), Salil also conducts intensive workshops in creative fiction writing, story and scenario design, screenplay writing and film-making at leading liberal arts institutions and media & communication colleges across India.

He is a seasoned newspaper columnist, with over 400 articles, op-ed pieces, features and travelogues in leading dailies. Salil's books have been reviewed in *The Hindu*, *New Indian Express*, *The Pioneer*, *Bangalore Mirror*, *DNA*, *First City* and *The Tribune* among others. His work has been praised by veteran authors Dr Shashi Tharoor, Shobhaa De and film-makers Sriram Raghavan and Sujoy Ghosh.

Salil was one of the four international authors worldwide, selected for the HALD International Writers' Residency in Denmark, hosted by the Danish Centre for Writers & Translators in June 2016. He was also invited to Gullkistan Centre for Creativity, Iceland, and spent the month of June 2023 there as a Resident.

Know more about him at www.salildesai.com

OTHER TITLES BY SALIL DESAI

The Kid Killer (2023)
Murder Milestone (2020)
The Sane Psychopath (2018)
The Murder of Sonia Raikkonen (2015)
Killing Ashish Karve (2014)
Lost Libido and Other Gulp Fiction (2012)
Murder on a Side Street (2011)

3 AND A HALF MURDERS

SALIL DESAI

AN INSPECTOR
SARALKAR MYSTERY

First published by Fingerprint, an imprint of Prakash Books India Pvt. Ltd, in 2017

No. 269/2B, First Floor, 'Irai Arul', Vimalraj Street, Nethaji Nagar, Alapakkam Main Road, Maduravoyal, Chennai 600095

Westland and the Westland logo are the trademarks of Nasadiya Technologies Private Limited, or its affiliates.

Copyright © Salil Desai, 2017

Salil Desai asserts the moral right to be identified as the author of this work.

ISBN: 9789360454326

10 9 8 7 6 5 4 3 2

This is a work of fiction. Names, characters, organisations, places, events and incidents are either products of the author's imagination or used fictitiously.

All rights reserved

Typeset by R. Ajith Kumar, Delhi

Printed at Saurabh Printers Pvt. Ltd

No part of this book may be reproduced, or stored in a retrieval system, or transmitted in any form or by any means, electronic, mechanical, photocopying, recording, or otherwise, without express written permission of the publisher.

To
Ravi Kaka
(1947–2015)
uncle, writer, sparring partner

1

TWO CORPSES OCCUPIED THE ONE-BEDROOM FLAT. THE WOMAN lay sprawled on the bed, her torso sunk into the soft mattress while her legs, folded at the knees, dangled over the side of the bed. A pillow covered her face. Outside, in the drawing room, the man's body swung lifelessly from a noose of nylon rope, fastened to a ceiling hook. He obviously wasn't watching the programme playing on the sports channel, but the television was on. And so were the lights. The windows of the flat, however, were shut and the doors were closed.

If no one bothered to check, the dead couple could well have remained entombed in the flat, like pharaohs in their pyramids. But that was not to be.

'Has Doshi madam left the house key with you?' Surekhabai asked Mrs Seema Tambe, as she put off the cooking gas and dumped the cooking utensils into the sink.

'Have you counted the chapatis?' Mrs Tambe counter-questioned pointedly. 'You often make one or two less, Surekha!'

'Yes, tai, I've made twelve,' Surekhabai replied, wiping her hands clean.

Mrs Tambe briefly considered counting the chapatis herself, then realised it would be an affront to the cook. You never knew what rubbed them the wrong way. 'Okay,' she said finally. 'No, Doshi madam hasn't left the key with me. Isn't she at home?'

'No, I rang the bell several times.'

'That's strange,' Mrs Tambe said. 'I would've sworn it's their television blaring away since morning.' She opened the balcony door ever so slightly to make her point and immediately the strains of an ad jingle could be heard floating out from the neighbouring flat.

Surekhabai shrugged. 'I'll try once more,' she said, making her way into Mrs Tambe's drawing room and out to the front door. Seema Tambe followed her and stood watching as the cook rang the bell of the Doshi flat, across the landing.

Seconds passed but neither Anushka Doshi nor her husband Sanjay opened the door. Surekhabai's puzzled expression intensified and she rang the bell a few more times in rapid succession.

'Maybe they went out and forgot to switch off the TV,' Mrs Tambe reasoned. 'I'll tell Anushka you had come.'

'Okay, tai. Also, ask Doshi madam to call if she wants me to come and cook in the evening. If not, tell her to leave my wages with you,' Surekhabai replied and skipped away to other houses that awaited her culinary skills, such as they were.

Little did the maid know that she was going to be deprived of her wages, simply because her employers lay dead inside, her last-cooked meal for them lying undigested in their stomachs.

'Don't you have a medical check-up every year in the department?' Dr Kanade asked, peering at Saralkar, who lay irritably on the examination table.

'Yes ... but I don't need an elaborate check-up. I just require this certificate for private purposes,' Saralkar replied, exasperated.

'What private purposes?' Dr Kanade asked, once again pumping the bulb-shaped rubber balloon to tighten the inflatable cuff of the sphygmomanometer around Saralkar's upper arm.

Saralkar felt cornered. Dr Kanade was a general physician he visited sometimes for minor ailments. He was not too keen on telling the doctor that the medical certificate was required for the child adoption application Jyoti had talked him into making.

'Must I tell you, Dr Kanade?' Saralkar snapped as gently as he could.

Dr Kanade looked at the recordings, then at Saralkar. 'Whether you tell me or not, I must tell you that your BP readings are pretty high.'

'What?' Saralkar asked with agitation.

'There, it's shot up again,' Dr Kanade quipped. 'What's your age?'

'Forty-seven,' Saralkar replied, still trying to absorb the information.

'When was the last time you had a complete medical?'

Saralkar pondered briefly. 'About three years ago, I think,' he lied.

'Hmm,' Dr Kanade murmured. 'I think it's time for another. Right now, I'll give you some pills for three days. Come back for a check-up on the fourth day. We'll take a reading again.'

'What's the reading now?'

'160/110. Not good. Have you been under stress lately?'

Saralkar ignored the doctor's question and put one of his own. 'What's supposed to be normal?'

'120/80,' Dr Kanade said absently, scribbling a prescription. 'It's been revised to 110/70 these days, so yours is way above.'

Saralkar grunted, feeling a trifle disturbed. 'But isn't one supposed to feel dizzy or have a headache or something? I feel perfectly okay.'

'Well, many patients have no symptoms at all,' Dr Kanade replied cheerfully. He just stopped himself from observing that this was precisely why hypertension was known as the silent killer.

'I am not a patient,' Saralkar said petulantly. 'Maybe your BP instrument is faulty.'

Dr Kanade's mild manner didn't change but his reply was as acerbic as they come. 'No, the instrument is fine. I just like to scare my patients so that they keep coming back for treatment.'

Saralkar hadn't expected the sharp retort. 'All I meant was that maybe it's just a ...'

'Look, Saralkar, if you want that medical certificate for private purposes, take the pills and come back to me after three days,' Dr Kanade said. 'Now don't waste my time. Other patients are waiting.'

Senior Inspector Saralkar grabbed the prescription, paid the doctor and stomped off. He couldn't remember the last time he had been so roundly ticked off by anyone other than his boss or his wife. The list of people he couldn't bellow back at was growing!

'That's the one that needs to be removed,' Shailendra Vyas, secretary of Atharva Apartments, said, pointing to the rather substantial beehive clinging to a parapet above the third floor of the building.

The beehive remover squinted at the swarming, dark brown mass and played his opening gambit. 'That's very big, sahib.'

Vyas was no mean negotiator himself. 'Much smaller than the last one ...'

'No, no, much bigger!' the beehive remover said, shaking his head vehemently. 'And it's at a much more difficult spot, too.'

'Why difficult?'

'Sahib, last time it was in one corner next to the second-floor balcony. This hive is in the middle of nowhere, below the chhajja above the third floor ... much more risky,' the man replied, articulating the building blocks for driving a hard bargain.

'So, are you going to be able to do it or not?' Vyas asked, feigning impatience.

The hive remover nodded and quoted a fee. They haggled vigorously for a few minutes and then struck a deal.

'I'll have to access from that third-floor flat balcony,' the hive remover said finally.

'Are you going to burn the hive or disperse it by removing the queen bee?' Vyas inquired, trying to show off his knowledge. 'I want a permanent solution. It shouldn't be that another hive is formed in a few months.'

'I need to take a closer look first,' the hive remover replied.

'Come,' Vyas beckoned him towards the staircase at the front of the building. They trudged up to the third floor and rang the bell of the Doshi flat.

No one answered. Vyas, like Surekhabai, tried a few more times and then began searching for Sanjay Doshi's number on his mobile.

'Where could they have gone?' Vyas muttered.

'I can hear the TV inside,' the hive remover remarked.

Vyas frowned and nodded distractedly, then began dialling Sanjay Doshi's number. The rings passed but no one picked up the phone. Momentarily, Vyas wondered whether he should check with Doshi's next-door neighbours, but he wasn't on particularly cordial terms with the Tambes and the other flat was locked.

The beehive remover was now glancing impatiently at his watch, as if he had a hundred other hives destroying appointments that very day.

'Can you come back later?' Vyas asked tentatively.

'Is the common terrace open?' the hive remover asked, pointing upstairs. 'I can climb down into their balcony from above and take a look at the hive.'

'Without ropes or anything?' Vyas hesitated. It was one of those twenty-five to thirty-year-old buildings that did not require Spidermanly skills to clamber around or scale. The secretary shrugged. 'I have no problem but do it at your own risk or come later.'

The hive remover smirked at this typical middle-class caveat. 'My risk only, sahib! I am not asking you to come along, am I?'

Vyas ignored the jibe and both climbed up another floor and unlocked the terrace. In no time, the hive remover swiftly descended into the Doshi balcony.

'Be careful, don't break anything. I don't want any complaints from the family,' Vyas warned.

The hive remover didn't care to respond; he was busy inspecting the hive and assessing the task at hand. He looked around for the footholds he would require, making a judgement of the structural peculiarities that he would have to keep in mind.

Satisfied, he mounted the parapet of the Doshi balcony to climb back on to the terrace above. All he needed was a foothold to heave himself on to the chhajja and then the terrace, something that the old-style window grill of the flat could easily provide.

The hive remover reached out and opened the window just wide enough to put his foot comfortably on the grill and almost lost his balance by the sight and smell that greeted him from inside the house.

2

PSI MOTKAR WONDERED WHAT IN THE WORLD HAD PROMPTED him to accept a role in a three-act play being staged by the Pune Police Cultural Society. He had never acted before, except for the role of a tree in a school skit.

Perhaps it had been the sheer thrill of doing something different that had made him spontaneously agree to participate when an old colleague had approached him. And now as the rehearsals had begun in earnest, he was simultaneously petrified and excited about the whole damn thing. The drama practices would generally happen in the evenings, but today being a Sunday, the director, an overbearing cop called Walimbe, had called them all in the afternoon.

Motkar's attention wandered now as the director harangued some of the main actors about understanding the inner motivations and discovering subtle nuances of the characters they were playing. As far as Motkar could see, the project wasn't going well at all, coming off as an excruciatingly belaboured and amateurish theatrical effort that was doomed to be either stoically endured or hooted out by the audience.

But who was he to pass judgement? He, too, hadn't been able to master the few lines of dialogues of his role and had kept fumbling during rehearsals, almost always messing up his tone, expressions and delivery, even if he did manage to remember the words.

Acting was clearly not his cup of tea and the PSI had considered coming up with some excuse to withdraw, but somehow couldn't get himself to slink away. If only an out-of-the-ordinary case materialised somehow!

His prayers were about to be answered. His mobile started ringing. Avoiding the dirty looks being thrown at him by the director, Motkar scrambled out of the practice hall apologetically to take the call.

'I just want three pills. Why do I have to take the full strip?' Saralkar growled at the chemist.

The chemist would have liked to tell him sarcastically that the argument would do his BP no good, but politely forbore from doing so. 'Can't help it, sahib. These tablets come in strips of ten only. I can't sell them loose,' he replied.

'What do you mean you can't? You just don't want to. Why should I pay for ten when I want only three?' Saralkar demanded.

The chemist nodded weakly before suggesting, 'Perhaps the doctor might ask you to continue the dose. Then they won't go waste.'

It was just the kind of sentence that could've caused Saralkar to explode, but the rings of the senior inspector's mobile saved the chemist.

'Hullo.'

'Sir, Motkar here. A couple has been found dead in their house. Man seems to have hung himself, woman's been strangled.'

'Where and when?' Saralkar asked.

'Atharva Apartments, Kothrud, sir. The society secretary reported they discovered one of the bodies at about 4 p.m.'

'Young couple or old?'

'Middle-aged, sir. Sanjay and Anushka Doshi.'

'Hmm ... Are you already there?'

'No, sir, I'm on my way now,' Motkar replied.

'Okay. I'll join you in a while,' Saralkar said and hung up.

He looked at the tablet strip, then at the chemist who was attending to another customer. 'How much?'

'Fifty rupees, sahib.'

Saralkar dipped into his pocket, took out a twenty-rupee note and placed it on the counter. Then he picked up the strip, quickly tore four tablets from it, pocketed them, and stepped out of the shop, leaving the chemist gaping.

Atharva Apartments was located in a cluster of buildings in the once quiet Mahatma Society locality of Kothrud. Once famous as the fastest growing suburb in Asia, Kothrud was more Maharashtrian and even Brahminical in flavour and character than perhaps any other part of Pune city, except the old city peth areas.

Barely twelve years ago, PSI Motkar recollected, Mahatma Society had been a charming, peaceful locality with trees, bungalows and open spaces, secured on one side by a hillock. Newly married, he and his wife had scouted around for a suitable, affordable flat in the serene area then, but hadn't been lucky. Now, of course, Mahatma Society was beyond recognition and had turned into a proverbial concrete jungle, no longer charming, serene or green, or providing open vistas of the hillock. But then, Motkar reflected, which part of Pune had escaped unscathed from the construction overdrive?

The building was located in a narrow lane, not very different from all the other apartment complexes around it—possibly a cluster that had been built around the same time, fifteen to twenty years before the construction boom—solid, secure, middle-class dwellings of three to four storeys, which were strangely comforting in contrast to the spanking new multistorey gated communities springing up almost every day.

The residents of Atharva Apartments had all gathered by the parking lot, as if ready for some mass evacuation. Two police vehicles stood by the gate.

'Third floor, sir,' a constable said, recognising PSI Motkar. He nodded and entered the building, passing the onlookers. No lift! Motkar grinned to himself. Senior Inspector Saralkar wasn't going to like having to climb all the way up. But then that was going to be the least of his boss's problems, given what Motkar had heard about the state of the dead bodies.

The door of Flat 10 stood open, with another constable at the door. Foul smell had already started emanating and the moment Motkar stepped inside the flat, the familiar, disturbing odour of death and decomposition knocked his breath away. God alone knew what it would do to Saralkar then, whose tolerance for mutilated flesh was surprisingly low for a homicide investigator.

As always, Motkar's nostrils quickly acclimatised to the stench, his attention now monopolised by the sight of the man's body still suspended between the ceiling and floor. It was a classic suicide position—a convenient cushioned stool kicked away and the body limp, as if in total surrender. Motkar had always felt that in no other position did a dead body look so utterly vulnerable and abject as in a suicide by hanging.

The man appeared to be between thirty-five to forty years old, about five feet seven inches, dressed in a round-neck T-shirt and slip-on shorts. He had a moustache and a full black beard dotted with specks of white. Motkar wasn't sure if the white specks were the colour of the man's hair or dried froth that seemed to have foamed out of his mouth as he choked to death. The fingers of both his hands, liberally decked with rings, were clutched into fists as if priming himself for the task.

The crime scene photographer and forensics team were busy doing their stuff, all of them nodding a greeting to Motkar.

'Want to see the woman's body, Motkar?' PSI Sarode called out, waving out to him. 'Here, it's in the bedroom.'

Motkar crossed the small 15x10 hall and walked left into the even smaller bedroom. A shudder passed through him as he regarded the conspicuous signs of violence done to the unfortunate woman's body. She had been assaulted and choked—her throat and right temple bearing the marks of the brutality perpetrated on her. But what turned even Motkar's gutsy stomach was the horrible disfigurement of her face with some sort of acid. It had left behind a lumpy, grotesque mask of raw, bloody flesh of what had once been a human face.

'Oh, my God!' Motkar said, averting his eyes involuntarily, then forcing himself to look at the body again. 'Did you find the bottle containing the acid used?' he asked.

'No. Maybe forensics will find it,' PSI Sarode replied. 'The man's left a suicide cum confession note. It says he killed his wife because she was having an affair and that he was also taking his own life.' He beckoned a forensic assistant who came over with the note.

PSI Motkar quickly read it. His mobile rang just as he finished. It was Saralkar. 'Where is this damn Aparna Society? Nobody seems to know it.'

'Not Aparna Society, sir. I had said Atharva Apartments,' Motkar clarified. 'You probably heard it wrong ...'

'Nonsense, Aparna Society does not in the least sound like Atharva Apartments.'

Motkar refrained from arguing with his boss and quickly gave directions after checking where exactly the senior inspector was.

'Okay, I'll be there in five minutes,' Saralkar said.

'I'll come down to meet you, sir,' Motkar replied, then hesitated before putting his foot in his mouth. 'Actually, it's a ghastly sight and the stench is terrible. You need not come up if you don't wish to ...'

His clumsy effort to protect his boss was greeted with typical Saralkar disdain. 'Don't be cheeky, Motkar. I've seen more dead bodies than you have, so don't worry, I'm not going to vomit all over you.' He hung up.

PSI Motkar wished his boss wasn't always touchy and looking for malice in every spoken word. But then he wouldn't remain Saralkar, would he?

Although he wouldn't admit it, Senior Inspector Saralkar always had to brace himself for the ordeal of seeing dead bodies of victims of violence and crime. He had sufficient experience as a homicide officer to make do with photos of the corpses and visit the crime scene after the bodies had been removed.

But it wasn't just a sense of duty or the need not to appear weak that prompted him to put himself through the ritual repeatedly. Nor was it a sleuthing imperative that would provide him with greater illumination in cracking the crime.

Saralkar chose to do so because seeing victims in the state they were found in gave a personal edge to his professional motivation to solve the crime. It made the senior inspector feel a higher responsibility because, at a deeper level, the tragedy touched him first-hand.

He clicked his tongue nowwith irritation, realising that Atharva Apartments had no lift. The smell caught up with him on the second floor and by the time he reached the third, Saralkar knew it was going to require enormous willpower not to throw up.

PSI Motkar was waiting outside the flat along with Sarode and the constables, as if Saralkar were a visiting dignitary who had to be shown around. The expression on Motkar's face was almost like an advisory to him: 'Don't do it, big mouth! You might regret it.'

Saralkar felt an urge to snap at Motkar but dared not open his mouth. Chances were, words wouldn't be the only things that would fly out.

The next two minutes were probably the longest of Saralkar's life, as they stepped into the flat. The stench was like a sharp weapon that penetrated straight into his innards. At any moment, Saralkar knew, he was in danger of making a fool of himself in the presence of junior officers. He reached into his trouser pocket for his handkerchief and pressed it against his nose and mouth, biting back the bile that was threatening to surge up from his stomach. His eyes desperately tried to take in the gruesome scene and his ears the words of Motkar and Sarode, wondering if the acute distress he was experiencing due to the appalling odour had made his BP shoot up further.

By some miracle, Saralkar got through the cursory inspection and swiftly walked out of the flat. 'Let's go to the terrace and talk,' he said to Motkar and Sarode through clenched teeth, and fled up the stairs.

Even the fresh air on the terrace was not free of the stench, but Saralkar felt like collapsing with relief. It had been a close call. Motkar and Sarode were watching him. Saralkar pretended to be lost in thought as his stomach and senses took a few moments to normalise.

'Who found them and how?' he asked eventually.

'The society secretary, Shailendra Vyas, had called a person to remove a beehive on the third-floor chhajja. The hive remover climbed down from this terrace to inspect the hive. When he began climbing back up, he opened the window of the Doshi family flat to gain a foothold on the window grill and happened to see the man hanging from the fan.'

'The hive remover opened the window or was it already open?' Saralkar asked.

'No, sir, all windows of the flat were shut as you must've noticed. The lights and TV were on,' Sarode said.

'I see. What does the suicide note say? Read it out.'

Motkar took the letter and began reading.

I am ending my miserable life today after killing my wife Anushka. She had been repeatedly unfaithful to me in the past but I forgave her because I loved her. She promised not to cheat on me again but over the last several months, she's again been having an affair with Shaunak Sodhi. I couldn't take it anymore and told her to stop. She refused and said she had decided to go away with him. She mocked my impotence and so I lost my temper and decided to kill her and destroy her deceitful face. My business has also suffered considerable losses and my debtors are not going to leave me in peace. That's why this is the best solution—to kill Anushka for her betrayal and then die because my life is not worth living. Sanjay Doshi.

Saralkar had seen many suicide notes in his life. Many were rambling—pages of poignant attempts to articulate the pain and injustice suffered, almost begging for an understanding of the decision, pathetically pinpointing blame. Some had been abrupt and brief, as if the person were scared that if they paused to write, they would lose the courage to commit the act.

This one seemed lucid and almost functional, as if Sanjay Doshi didn't want anyone to puzzle over the event, briefly summarising the what, when, why, who and how of his actions.

'Hmm ... sad, familiar story. Cuckolded husband kills wife and self. Can't say I haven't seen that before,' Saralkar said. 'No children, I presume?'

'Don't think so, sir. But we haven't checked yet.'

'Any idea when the couple was last seen?'

'We've managed to speak only to the secretary and the beehive remover so far, sir,' PSI Sarode said.

Saralkar grunted, now feeling himself again, although he could sense a headache coming on, courtesy of the stench. 'Okay. Speak to all the neighbours and gather as much background information about the couple as you can. We need to talk to family and friends, if any. I want to know when Mr and Mrs Doshi were last seen, together or alone. Did anyone hear anything? If he strangled her or threw acid on her face, there's got to be some screaming and sounds of the struggle. Is there anyone who works for them? And find out who this fellow Shaunak Sodhi is and get hold of him.'

'Yes, sir,' Motkar replied. 'I'll also get the house thoroughly searched once the forensic team is done. I'll brief you first thing tomorrow morning.'

Saralkar nodded then walked towards the terrace parapet and leaned over.

'What, sir?'

The senior inspector raised a restraining hand as if concentrating on looking for or listening to something carefully. He turned around eventually and said, 'Just making sure there is a real beehive.' He began walking towards the terrace exit, then stopped and asked Motkar, 'How's the drama practice going?'

'Okay, sir,' Motkar replied, taken aback.

'What role are you playing?'

'It's a minor role, sir. A couple of dialogues,' Motkar said awkwardly.

'Well, let's hope you don't go blank on stage, Motkar,' the senior inspector said ominously, as he left the terrace.

3

'WHY HAS DR KANADE CALLED YOU AGAIN?' JYOTI SARALKAR asked her husband, still suspicious of his claim that the doctor had not issued a medical certificate right away.

Saralkar had not yet told her about the BP and the pills. 'Big rush at his clinic,' he deadpanned.

'So?'

'So, he didn't have time to fill the entire medical fitness form,' Saralkar improvised gruffly. 'Said I should collect it later.'

'Today?'

Quite uncharacteristically, Saralkar held his peace. 'He said he'll call.'

'Want me to collect it from his clinic?' Jyoti offered cunningly.

Saralkar ground his teeth. He knew why his BP was up now—twenty years of spousal nagging.

'What you are hinting at is that you don't believe I went to Dr Kanade yesterday, don't you?' he retorted.

'Nothing of that sort,' Jyoti backtracked. 'His clinic is on my way, that's all.'

Saralkar decided it was the perfect moment to make a haughty exit without replying, even though he normally left for work fifteen minutes later.

His thoughts as he rode to office were about marriage in

general. Was marriage an artificial and unnatural state to be in? What made men and women stay together for life? Was it love? Passion? Habit? Companionship? Social convention? Or was it simply convenience—the convenience of hard-earned emotional, psychological and physical equilibrium that couples were loathe to disturb or jettison despite all its attendant negatives? The same reason why people didn't change jobs or houses or cities—too scared to leave the comfort zone of familiarity.

Or maybe, as was often said in Indian society, it was the children more than any other factor that kept couples together. But then what about childless couples like Jyoti and him? What had been their glue? He realised he hadn't a clue. On the other hand, it was rather evident what had gone so wrong with the marriage of the Doshis, for instance, the consequence of which had been so bloody.

PSI Motkar would probably have gathered all the facts that could piece together the whole wretched, sordid, commonplace story that culminated in the pathetic ending of two lives.

'Good morning, sir.' Motkar had been waiting for him.

'Did your teachers ever have to scold you, Motkar?' Saralkar couldn't resist asking.

'About what, sir?'

'About doing your homework in time or such things?'

Motkar realised his boss was being fatuous. He just shrugged.

'Well, I'm sure you were too good a boy to ever give them a chance,' Saralkar continued his pinpricking. 'But do you know the dangers of denying teachers the simple, legitimate pleasure of scolding a student?'

'I wouldn't know, sir. I've never been a teacher,' PSI Motkar said dryly.

Saralkar chuckled, aware that he was getting under Motkar's skin. 'The fact is teachers start itching for an opportunity to spank good boys.'

For once, PSI Motkar thought he had the perfect comeback and hoped he wouldn't fumble while delivering it. 'You sound ... as if you speak from experience, sir,' he said with a clumsy suaveness, which nevertheless packed enough punch.

Motkar was pleased to see a slightly miffed expression on Saralkar's face, itching for a good rejoinder. But he didn't give him that chance. He swiftly changed the topic back to work. 'Sanjay and Anushka Doshi had been staying in Atharva Apartments for slightly longer than a year, sir. Most of the building's residents said they were a cordial couple, although they kept mostly to themselves. Apparently, Sanjay was a corporate consultant of some sort, though no one seems to know exactly what. Mrs Doshi had told neighbours she was an interior designer. We've found a couple of their business cards but need to verify.'

'Does the flat belong to them or were they tenants?' Saralkar queried, still annoyed he had been stumped by his otherwise meek assistant.

'Tenants, sir. The flat belongs to a person called Pardeshi, who shifted to a bigger flat about five years ago. He runs a small fabrication unit. We've spoken to him. He says the Doshi couple approached him through some broker. He's had no problem with them—rent was paid on time, and there were no issues,' Motkar replied.

'What about rent agreement and police verification?'

Motkar shook his head. 'The rent agreement is notarised, not registered, and no police verification was done. Pardeshi gave the usual lame excuses saying he didn't know it was mandatory, that there was nothing suspicious about the Doshis—a normal, middle-aged, middle-class couple. Neither were they minority community or foreigners and thus hardly the kind who could be terrorists.'

Saralkar grunted with disdain. 'Bloody stupid, wretched citizens who'll never improve! What about the deposit and rent? Cash or cheque?'

'Everything in cash, sir. It suited Pardeshi. Said the Doshis also never asked for a rent receipt.'

'Does he at least know where they were originally from? Pune itself or some other place?'

'Apparently, they had told Pardeshi that they were from Mumbai and had just shifted to Pune,' Motkar replied. 'But, sir, one of the neighbours, Mrs Tambe, said that she got the impression that the Doshis originally hailed from Bangalore.'

'Did she say whether Anushka Doshi or her husband told her that?' Saralkar asked.

'Mrs Tambe said she faintly remembers a conversation with Anushka Doshi which left her with the impression that Bangalore was her hometown,' Motkar explained.

'Have you found any identification in the house? PAN card, driving licence, passport, Aadhaar card or voter ID?' Saralkar asked.

'We've found their driving licences but no other IDs so far.'

'Hmm ... That's a little odd. Everybody has at least one or two of these IDs. Have you searched everywhere?'

'No, sir. A thorough search is still going on. We should know by this afternoon,' Motkar asserted.

'So, when was the couple last seen alive?'

'Sir, no one is quite sure, but Mrs Tambe said she spoke to Mrs

Doshi on Saturday morning. No other neighbour remembers seeing the couple on Saturday or thereafter. Mrs Tambe also said she and Mrs Doshi shared the same cook, Surekhabai, who mentioned that she had cooked at the Doshis' on Saturday afternoon. But we haven't been able to speak to Surekhabai so far.'

'If that's true, then as of Saturday afternoon, the Doshis were alive. Their bodies were found on Sunday late afternoon, which means no one saw them again for nearly twenty-four hours. Right?' Saralkar calculated.

'Yes, sir, but there seems to have been a pizza delivery at their flat, which happened on Saturday night. We've still not been able to speak to the delivery boy but the outlet has confirmed the delivery was done at 9.37 p.m. Strangely though, the pizza was not consumed by the couple. It was simply lying there on the table, unopened,' Motkar said.

'Which narrows it down even further. That means Sanjay Doshi killed his wife and hung himself sometime on Saturday night after 9.37 p.m. What do the doctors say?'

'Non-committal so far, but they think both died just before midnight.'

Saralkar chewed on his lips. 'So did any neighbour hear sounds of a scuffle or thumps or a scream or any noise at all?'

PSI Motkar paused and consulted his notes. 'The Tambe family on the third floor were out for dinner, followed by a late-night movie show, on Saturday night. The family in the flat immediately below the Doshis are very fuzzy about it. The husband and children say they heard nothing, but the wife says she was cooking in the kitchen and thinks she heard a heavy thud from upstairs, and a scream, but she thought it was from someone's television.'

Saralkar clicked his tongue. 'Why can't witnesses and neighbours be sharp and alert like in books, damn it? Isn't there another flat on the third-floor landing?'

'Yes, sir. But no one's been staying there for the last couple of weeks.'

'What about any next of kin, family or friends of the Doshis?'

'I've given Constable Shewale the task of checking contacts on the cell phones of the Doshis, recent call records and texts. We should have the information by mid-day. None of the neighbours seem to know about relatives or friends of the Doshi couple,' PSI Motkar said a little apologetically.

'Any news from forensics?' Saralkar asked grimly.

'They've dusted the flat for fingerprints, the suicide note has gone for analysis, and they've taken the bottle which contained the acid for tests,' Motkar summed up.

Saralkar brightened up. 'The acid bottle should get us somewhere. Any idea where Sanjay Doshi procured it and when?'

Motkar shook his head slightly. 'The acid was in a used liquor bottle, sir. Either Doshi purchased it illegally through the black market or transferred it from the original container into the liquor bottle. And the funny thing was that it was kept in a cabinet among other half-empty liquor bottles.'

Saralkar frowned. 'Among other half-empty bottles? Did he expect his wife to consume it by mistake or something, assuming she had alcohol? And when that didn't happen, he threw it at her face?'

Motkar's eyebrows had risen. 'Didn't think of that possibility, sir, but it sounds quite probable. That would mean Sanjay Doshi was planning to kill her for some time.'

Saralkar's expression remained unchanged. 'But after using

the acid on his wife and killing her, why would he take the trouble of putting it back in the cabinet among other bottles, as if he wanted to hide it? I mean, he was about to hang himself, so why not leave the bottle where it was?'

PSI Motkar sat down for the first time, then spoke: 'Sir, couldn't it be that putting the bottle back in the cabinet was simply an involuntary, unthinking reflex action of a neat, tidy man who'd just killed his wife?'

Saralkar rolled his eyes. 'Motkar, you've been watching too many Hollywood films. Bloody curious if that's what happened. But either way, it's as good or as bad a theory as any so let's keep it aside for the moment. What about the man Shaunak Sodhi with whom Sanjay's wife was having an affair? Have you been able to trace him?'

PSI Motkar's face became defensive. He knew his boss was not going to be happy. 'Sorry to disappoint you, sir, but there's no lead about Sodhi yet.'

Predictably, Saralkar erupted, 'Oh, come on, if this fellow was having an affair with Anushka Doshi, she's got to have his number on her mobile or sent him texts or a photo or letters hidden somewhere.'

'Believe me, sir, I've been concentrating almost entirely on getting hold of Sodhi. His name's nowhere on her phone: no texts, no photos, no letters ... nothing to make a connection. Neighbours have never seen any man frequently visiting the house in her husband's absence. Neither does Sanjay Doshi seem to have left any clue to find him.'

'Has it occurred to you that Anushka Doshi might have saved her lover's number under some phony name?' Saralkar barked.

'Yes, sir, but that will take a little longer to check. As I said,

Constable Shewale is making a list,' Motkar replied.

'Don't tell me that a simple task like this is going to hold us up,' Saralkar said. He was irate.

'Give me a few hours, sir.'

Saralkar glared at his assistant, then slumped back in his seat, sullen and angry. Silence prevailed for a few minutes and Motkar resisted the urge to fidget.

Then, as if coming out of a trance, Saralkar spoke. 'Why does a man throw acid on the face of his unfaithful wife, Motkar?'

'As revenge for being unfaithful to him, I suppose,' Motkar answered. 'Or as a punishment of sorts.'

'You are right. As a punishment. The perverse psychology behind it being: it is this face of yours that you used to bewitch another man and to be unfaithful to me. Therefore, I shall mutilate it so that you'll live with these horrible consequences forever which you deserve. Correct?'

PSI Motkar nodded slowly, trying to figure out what the senior inspector was driving at.

Saralkar was leaning forward now, his eyes intense. 'Well, if the rationale behind the act is to make his wife suffer the consequences, then why did Sanjay Doshi kill her after that? Why not let her live and lead a tortured existence? Isn't that why all these bastards throw acid on their girlfriends or ex-lovers or women they stalk?'

PSI Motkar, as always, experienced contrasting feelings—an intense irritation that the man before him was back to his favourite game of conjecturing and twisting that which looked straightforward; and yet, what Saralkar had said made sense. Human actions, especially violence, were surprisingly rational, even if sometimes inexplicable or tediously predictable.

The senior inspector had not finished. 'And if killing her was the punishment he had in mind for Anushka, then why pour acid on her face before doing so?'

Motkar thought he knew the answer. He shrugged briefly, then said in a tone that tried not to be too challenging, 'Sir, perhaps he wanted to see her suffer. I mean, isn't it also common to see victims being tortured before their murderers eventually kill them? Maybe that was Sanjay Doshi's motive in throwing acid on her face. To first watch her writhe in agony and then kill her.'

He stopped and looked steadily at his boss, who seemed ready to mock his theory.

But Saralkar looked away and said, 'I suppose you are right, Motkar. Maybe I just like to complicate things.'

It was Motkar's turn to be surprised.

4

RANGDEV BABA LOOKED AT THE MEMBERS OF HIS FLOCK GATHERED for the morning satsang and smiled his superior, all-knowing, moronic smile, which, for some reason, always charmed his devout bhakts.

The smile could be best described as a crooked smirk that sought to contrast his line of milky white teeth with the jet-black hair of his moustache and regulation saintly beard. His eyes, suitably deepened with kohl, genuinely lit up, almost as if amused at the sight of so many miserable men and women who turned to a charlatan like him for solace.

Rangdev Baba's hands emerged from the folds of his robe and he raised his palms towards the congregation in a gesture that served the dual purpose of showering blessings while also calling for the devotees to hush. The gathering looked expectantly, waiting for him to mouth some gem of spiritual wisdom that would help them cope with the day ahead.

In his earthy and soothing voice, modulated to perfection, Rangdev Baba spoke, 'Happiness is a journey. Begin that journey today. No advance reservation is required for this journey. Just board the train. Don't put it off, don't delay, don't cancel your ticket!' He paused, beaming profoundly in all directions, confident of his prowess in making the inane sound like the sublime. His devotees listened gratefully, then rose in one voice to hail him, 'Jai Rangdev Baba!'

The morning satsang was over. Most people started dispersing, while a few made a beeline towards the stage for Baba's darshan. Rangdev Baba wasn't a five-star god-man. Perhaps a two-star one at the most, operating mainly from a small 'ashram' in Pune. In industrial terms, Rangdev Baba's outfit was an MSME with a following of about ten thousand faithful who had put their spiritual wellness in his hands.

Now, as the Baba sat benignly, permitting the queue of bhakts to touch his feet, even kiss them one after the other and make small offerings, he noticed his aide, who went under the name of Akhandanath, trying to draw his attention covertly.

Rangdev clasped his hands together in salutation to his devotees, signalling an end to the morning darshan, and got up to retreat into his air-conditioned sanctum. Akhandanath and two of his other aides followed him into his chamber.

'Get me some tea,' Rangdev ordered one aide, then turned to Akhandanath. 'What's biting you?'

Akhandanath brought out the morning paper from his robe and drew Rangdev's attention to a small news item. Two black and white mug shots of a couple stared back at Rangdev under the headline 'Couple Found Dead in Kothrud Flat'. The Baba quickly read through the item, his face tensing up for a moment, then relaxing.

'What do we do?' Akhandanath blurted out impatiently.

Rangdev looked at him. 'Nothing. Sit tight. Why should anyone connect him to us?'

'Maybe his family or neighbours know he used to come here to the ashram ...'

'He had no family. At least not here in Pune. He had told me ...' Rangdev said dismissively.

'Well, other devotees must have seen him here, isn't it?'

'So what? He was a devotee and used to come here sometimes. That's all there is to it,' Rangdev said quietly. 'There's no reason to believe the police would know anything more.'

'God knows what he must've written in his suicide note,' Akhandanath remarked.

'Relax. Why are you getting so paranoid? There's nothing to worry,' Rangdev said. But Akhandanath's panic had infected him too. 'Okay, don't we have a couple of policemen among our devotees, who can find out and tell us whether the police know about our link with Sanjay Doshi?'

'I'm sure if you request PSI Dulange, he can get us inside information,' Akhandanath suggested.

'Hmmm ...' Rangdev reflected. PSI Dulange had become a devout follower of Rangdev Baba ever since the Baba's advice and blessings seemed to have brought about some improvement in the condition of his mentally challenged son. He was sufficiently in Baba's debt.

'Okay, call up PSI Dulange,' Rangdev said. 'And tell him I have summoned him for special darshan.'

'What's the progress, Shewale?' PSI Motkar asked the constable, checking the mobiles of the dead couple.

'Sir, about twenty calls were made from the dead woman's mobile on Saturday. Almost all of them were to various contacts but none of them seem to be a fake cover name for Shaunak

Sodhi.'

'You've spoken to all of them?'

'Yes, sir.'

'Anyone of them family or friends of the couple?'

'No, sir. All of them seemed to be the lady's clients with whom she was trying to fix up appointments for Sunday and Monday,' Constable Shewale replied.

'Appointments for her interior design services?' Motkar asked.

'Not interior designing, sir. Mrs Anushka Doshi offered services like tarot reading and past life regression.'

'What? Are you sure?'

'Yes, sir. She would go to their houses for tarot reading and past life regression sessions. The clients she called included five men and seven or eight women. Out of these, three had made appointments for Sunday and when she didn't turn up, they made calls to her.'

'I see. You've taken down addresses of all?'

'Yes, sir,' Shewale assured him. 'The other calls were to a pizza outlet to place an order and there's just one more unknown number that isn't answering, although I've tried several times.' He read out the number to PSI Motkar.

'When was the call made from this number?' Motkar asked.

'Mrs Doshi spoke to the number twice—once on Friday late night and then again on Saturday early morning at around 5 a.m.'

PSI Motkar scratched his chin. 'You hardly call strangers at 5 a.m., do you? And yet the number does not figure under contacts.' He paused thoughtfully. It was tantalisingly easy to get excited and assume that this number belonged to the elusive, mysterious Shaunak Sodhi. But, for some reason, he doubted it. It made no sense for a woman not to save the number of a purported lover, at least under some fictitious name.

'Okay, keep trying the number and make a note that we might need to get details of whom it belongs to, from the service provider. What about calls to and from Sanjay Doshi's mobile?'

Constable Shewale flipped to another sheet of his neat notes. 'Sir, Sanjay Doshi made and received just a few calls on Friday and Saturday. On Sunday, none at all. Of the calls made on Friday and Saturday, one was made to a person whose classified ad had appeared in a Marathi newspaper for the sale of some NA land near Mulshi. Another call was to a hospital asking for rates for different diagnostic tests—very general, nothing specific. And the third call was again in response to a classified ad of a person called Prakash Niyogi, who was looking for private investment finance for some business project. Apparently, Sanjay Doshi inquired about the amount required, the purpose and the terms. Doshi was supposed to meet Niyogi in his office on Saturday evening but didn't turn up.'

'Didn't this Niyogi call Doshi back to remind him?'

'No, sir,' Constable Shewale explained. 'Niyogi said he gets calls from several such would-be investors but most of them are just making casual inquiries. He does not follow up unless he thinks it's a serious investor and since Doshi didn't turn up, he wasn't sure.'

'I see. No other calls from anyone who sounded like a creditor of Doshi?'

'No, sir.'

Motkar felt perplexed. How come Sanjay Doshi was looking for an investment opportunity just before he committed suicide, declaring that he was in a financial mess and his creditors were going to ruin him? Was it a last, desperate bid of a man who knew he was sinking? And how come there had been no calls from creditors—something that was supposed to have pushed Sanjay Doshi over the edge to take the steps he did, alongside his wife's affair?

'What about Sanjay Doshi's contacts, Shewale? Anything interesting?'

'Very, very few contacts, sir, and not uninteresting,' Constable Shewale replied in a suggestive tone. 'Two or three of the contacts were massage parlours and escort services. Looks like Doshi was a part of their regular but infrequent clientele. Other contacts included horse-racing bookies, a few shady betting operators, and three to four real-estate agents and land brokers. All of them didn't sound very big dealers, but certainly shady. Three from Pune and one from Navi Mumbai. That's the lot, sir.'

'I see. Any calls or even missed calls from any of them?'

Shewale consulted his sheet again. 'No calls, sir, but there was a missed call to Sanjay Doshi's mobile from one of the land agents—a fellow called Somnath Gawli. This was on Saturday evening around 9 p.m. When I called him up, his reaction was quite defensive and guarded. He said he'd dialled Doshi's number by mistake while searching for another contact.'

PSI Motkar was trying hard not to look intrigued but this was certainly getting more curious. Real estate agents, massage parlours, racing bookies, and shady betting operators were hardly the kind of contacts a normal corporate consultant would be keeping company with!

'One more thing, sir,' Constable Shewale said. 'I almost forgot. Another contact of Sanjay Doshi seems to be some acolyte of a small-time holy man called Baba Rangdev, who runs an ashram in Pune, at Karvenagar.'

PSI Motkar almost chuckled to himself. He could hardly blame Saralkar for complicating the case now. His own investigations had only thrown up more questions than answers so far.

With his recently acquired internet skills, Senior Inspector Saralkar had spent the last two hours browsing sites and reading all that he could about hypertension, its causes and cures. However, he now regretted having looked up the information at all. The internet was a curse, Saralkar thought sourly; within a few hours, it had actually managed to turn him into a bloody hypochondriac.

Oh, how he wished he had not read all that stuff! Ignorance truly would have been bliss. Did he actually have to be reminded in black and white that high BP was related to strokes and heart disease? Did he have to know he would need to make lifestyle changes and remain on lifelong medication? Did the information that Indians were particularly susceptible to it do any real good to him? Did the knowledge that he would have to control his diet, cut down on salt and oily food, and start exercising provide any solace?

Who had told him to take an uneducated sneak about the condition? 'Damn it!' he hissed, thumping his table in anger, only to be reminded by some part of his brain that he would have to stop blowing his top too!

PSI Motkar walked in at the very moment and, for a second, Saralkar was almost tempted to confide in his assistant. But, of course, he didn't.

'Are we getting anywhere?' he asked gruffly instead.

PSI Motkar briefed him about the facts that had been brought to light by Shewale.

Surprisingly, Saralkar didn't seem to have anything to say in response. He simply sat there, tapping the table with the index finger of his right hand, lost in thought, as if he fancied himself to be a woodpecker.

'You said you'd summoned the pizza boy and the maid servant of the Doshis, right?' the senior inspector asked, at long last.

'Yes, sir, the pizza boy and the cook. They are there at the Kothrud Police Station right now. I just got a call and was leaving,' Motkar replied.

'I'll come along,' Saralkar said. 'And also call this Somnath Gawli fellow there.'

'Sure, sir.'

5

KURMAIYYA RAJU HAD BEEN DELIGHTED WHEN HE WAS HIRED to deliver pizzas by Pizza Drop. The bright-coloured uniform branded with the Pizza Drop logo, the scooter with the hot box, the fairly higher wages compared to his previous job, and the tips received, had all made him feel lucky initially.

However, the charms of the job had begun to wear thin a few weeks later. The number of deliveries was way too many to cope with, especially on weekends. Delayed pizzas exacted a cost—arguments with customers, even abuse, and, of course, because of those absurd company ads that promised deliveries in twenty-five minutes flat, there was the ever-present danger of claims for free pizzas by aggrieved customers. The company conveniently expected the delivery boys to fend off these by playing up the sympathy factor that they would be penalised for it. There was truth in that, too. Every unpaid bill would lead to a proportionate deduction from Kurmaiyya's wages, which was the real catch.

He had, in fact, decided to change over to a new job. And as luck would have it, he had made the delivery to the ill-fated Doshi household in the last week of his employment at Pizza Drop. Kurmaiyya Raju felt wretched at this sting in the tail by fate. Why couldn't the damned couple have killed themselves the next week, by which time he would no longer have been delivering pizzas? The worst part was, of course, why at all had the suicidal couple ordered pizza in the first place if they had decided to die? Maybe they craved for pizza as their last meal.

These hard thoughts passed through Kurmaiyya Raju's mind as he sat restlessly in the Kothrud Police Station, waiting to be questioned.

'Come along,' a constable appeared abruptly, startling him. Kurmaiyya got up and followed. His thoughts had by now become weirder still. Did the police think he had anything to do with the couple's suicide? Had the couple killed themselves by lacing the pizza with poison? He was petrified at these alarming possibilities as he entered the small cell in which two police officers were waiting for him.

'Sit down,' PSI Motkar said. 'You are Kurmaiyya Raju?'

Kurmaiyya remained standing and nodded.

'You can speak, can't you?' Saralkar asked with enough toughness to force speech.

'Yes, sir,' Kurmaiyya replied hastily.

'So, tell us about the pizza delivery you made at the Doshi residence in Atharva Apartments a few evenings ago.'

Kurmaiyya made an effort to compose himself before speaking. 'Sir, I delivered a Chicken Hawaiian Pizza at 9.37 p.m. at their flat on Saturday night.'

'How can you be so sure of the time?'

'We have to be very particular and log it in because of that free delivery offer, sir,' Kurmaiyya replied.

'Who opened the door?' Saralkar asked.

'It was a lady, sir. Mrs Doshi, I guess.'

'Describe her.'

Kurmaiyya licked his dry lips. He didn't know how to describe anyone. He looked with confusion at both officers.

PSI Motkar seemed to grasp his problem. 'Age, looks, height, frame, fat, thin, complexion, clothes she was wearing, any striking or odd features you noticed?'

Kurmaiyya was silent for a second, trying to recollect a woman he had seen once, only fleetingly.

'She was a middle-aged woman, sir, not fair, not dark, quite tall and well-built.' Kurmaiyya paused, straining to visualise more, '... I ... I think she was wearing a Punjabi dress ... light blue colour, but I am not absolutely sure, sir.'

He stopped again, wondering what else to say. Clearly more prompting was needed.

'Hair?' Motkar asked.

Kurmaiyya's brow wrinkled. 'Yes, she had hair, sir.'

Saralkar suddenly felt the urge to guffaw at the delivery boy's confused response.

'Yes, but what kind? Black, white, grey, short, long?' PSI Motkar queried.

'... didn't notice, sir, but black, I think, and short ... shoulder length.'

'Okay. Eye colour?'

'I think black, sir.'

'Shape of nose?'

Something lit up in Kurmaiyya's eyes, as if he'd suddenly remembered a unique feature. 'Flattened, sir, as if it had been pressed down hard.'

The two policemen looked at each other. This flattened nose feature, more than anything, made it clear that the pizza delivery boy was indeed talking about Mrs Doshi.

PSI Motkar took out three photos from his shirt pocket and put them in front of Kurmaiyya. 'Was it one of these women?'

Kurmaiyya took one look and tapped his finger on Anushka Doshi's photo. 'That's the lady, sir.'

Motkar took another photo from the same pocket and showed it to the pizza delivery boy.

Kurmaiyya recoiled violently at the mortal position shot of the dead body, the woman's face a ghastly mess.

'Was that the dress she was wearing?'

It took Kurmaiyya a moment to recover from the shock and answer, 'Yes, sir.' His heart was thudding and his face had gone pale.

Senior Inspector Saralkar gave him a sharp glance. 'Did you do this to her?'

Kurmaiyya looked up at the senior inspector, his face horrified. 'Why would I do it, sir? I had nothing to do with it!'

'Tell me your whereabouts after this delivery,' Saralkar continued cold-eyed.

Kurmaiyya Raju had begun to shake with fear. 'I ... uhh ... I had two more deliveries in the same locality, sir. I delivered the pizzas and returned to the outlet by around 10.15 p.m. You please check ... I didn't do anything, sir ... I didn't. I am a poor man!'

A lump arose in his throat and he gave one loud sob, looking all set to break down.

'Calm down!' Motkar stepped in quickly. 'We are just asking you questions.'

Kurmaiyya struggled to control his sobs and panic, his facial muscles pulling in all directions, his palms quickly coming to the rescue of his agitated visage.

Saralkar gave him a few seconds, then spoke. 'You may have

been the last person to see this victim alive, so think carefully and help us. Do you understand?'

Kurmaiyya Raju, still unable to trust himself to speak, nodded vigorously.

'Did the lady look disturbed or upset when you made the delivery?'

'No, sir. I—I didn't notice particularly, sir. Normally, when I deliver a pizza on time, customers smile or acknowledge or look expectantly in some way. I can't describe her demeanour but the lady seemed tense and impatient. She ... she didn't even check the order, whether I was making the right delivery,' Kurmaiyya Raju said trying to be helpful. 'She just took the pizza and thrust out the money.'

'Hmm ... did she speak to you?' Saralkar asked.

'We just exchanged a few words, sir. She handed me a five-hundred-rupee note. I said she should give me change. She replied she didn't have change. So, I requested her to at least give me seventy rupees change and I would return her three hundred rupees. She replied I should return two hundred rupees and keep the thirty-rupee difference as a tip,' Kurmaiyya paused and looked at Saralkar and Motkar. 'That's all, sir. Then I left.'

'Did you by chance see her husband or hear him speak from inside the house?' Saralkar asked.

Again, that momentary flash of something remembered showed up on Kurmaiyya's face. 'Sir, when I told her to give me seventy rupees change, she sort of turned her head to look inside the flat and impatiently called out to her husband to ask if he had change. But he refused.'

'You heard his reply?'

'No, sir. The sound of the television was quite loud. I heard her question but not the answer from inside. I presumed he had replied "no" because she turned around and said so.'

'Had she called out his name while checking with her husband for change?'

Kurmaiyya gave him an unsure look, and replied, 'I don't think so, sir.'

'Okay. You said you could hear the television. Any recollection of what kind of programme was on? Songs, movie, match, serial? English, Hindi, Marathi ...?'

Kurmaiyya shook his head apologetically. 'Can't really recollect, sir. I—I wasn't paying attention.'

Saralkar gave him a vexed look. It was not an unfamiliar sentiment. As a police officer, he had often experienced unreasonable irritation, even anger, towards witnesses for not knowing or for not having noticed some small detail that could have helped.

'Okay. Now give us details of the pizza deliveries you made after leaving the Doshi house. And mind you, if there are any discrepancies in your movements from what you have officially logged, admit them honestly right now, because we will be checking,' Saralkar said with a hint of warning.

Kurmaiyya fidgeted and looked nervous, as if weighing what to speak. He finally said, 'Sir ... I ... I—I actually first made a delivery at a regular customer's place who tips quite handsomely, whereas I logged it in after Mrs Doshi's delivery. So, actually, the 9.37 p.m. delivery is for the other customer's delivery while I reached Mrs Doshi at around 9.55 p.m., even though she had booked earlier ...'

He stopped and looked at the two policemen, guilt writ large on his face. He had started sweating and his stiff and wary body language clearly betrayed the anxiety that he was probably expecting either a tongue-lashing or a blow.

PSI Motkar also wondered how his boss was going to react, since it pushed the 'last seen alive' time of the Doshis even further.

Saralkar looked at Kurmaiyya steadily. 'Next time you think of fudging things, remember you could get suspected of murder. Okay? Now give all details of the first delivery to PSI Motkar.'

The mildness of his words did not lessen the menace of his tone and when Kurmaiyya Raju finally stepped out of the police station thirty minutes later, he almost collapsed with relief on the footpath outside.

Surekhabai had no love lost for the police. They hardly ever helped folks like her. When her good-for-nothing husband had been alive, she had complained several times to the local chowki about his violent ways. But the cops had never been sympathetic and just shooed her away most of the times, telling her not to bring 'frivolous' family fights to them. Only once had they intervened and mildly admonished her husband. The vile fellow had turned on her the moment the police left and thrashed her within an inch of her life.

Mercifully, five years ago, the maker had recalled her husband's soul but she had never forgotten the callousness of the police. What had compounded her dislike for them was that a year ago, the police had picked up her twenty-year-old son, Hrithik, while rounding up miscreants in the slum, following some skirmish in the locality. The boy had been released the next morning, but not before being at the receiving end of some casual police brutality. Worse still, probably as a direct consequence of this incident, her son had also got introduced to neighbourhood goons and his descent into bad company had started assuming alarming portents.

Surekhabai stared at the three cops—two officers and a lady constable—her hostility held up like an invisible banner.

'How long had you been working for the Doshis?' PSI Motkar began by asking.

'About a year,' Surekhabai replied grudgingly.

'What were the chores you did for them?'

'I am a cook, not a maidservant to do other chores,' Surekhabai replied testily.

She would've liked to add that just as Motkar wasn't a mere constable, her station in life too was higher than that of maid servants who washed dishes or clothes, or mopped and swept houses.

'Did you cook two times a day or just once?'

'Afternoon and evening,' Surekhabai continued to keep her answers short.

'Did you cook for them last Saturday?'

'Yes. On Saturday afternoon.' She didn't use any honorific like 'sahib' either.

'You didn't go back in the evening?'

'No, Doshi madam said they might be eating out so I needn't come and cook in the evening.'

'I see. What about Sunday morning?' PSI Motkar asked.

Surekhabai thought this was a terribly foolish question. 'I rang the bell several times but obviously no one opened the door,' she said scathingly. 'I also checked with Seema tai whether Doshi madam had left the house key with her or not.'

'Mrs Seema Tambe?' Motkar clarified, taking no notice of her irreverence.

'Yes. I also rang the bell of Doshi madam's house once more after I finished cooking at Seema tai's place. She was present. Check with her. We could only hear the TV,' Surekhabai replied in a tone that suggested Motkar should've known about all this.

'And when you left on Saturday afternoon, were both Mr and Mrs Doshi at home?'

Surekhabai's forehead wrinkled for a moment, then she replied, 'I saw only Mrs Doshi but she mentioned that Doshi sahib was taking a nap. The bedroom door was shut.'

'But you didn't see him?'

'How could I? I told you the bedroom door was shut,' Surekhabai took another swipe at PSI Motkar, who represented the entire police force to her just now.

'Was this unusual?'

'What?'

'Mr Doshi being at home on Saturday morning?' PSI Motkar asked.

'Doshi sahib was often home,' Surekhabai replied dryly. 'He didn't step out very frequently. Many a times, he would be watching TV when I went in the mornings; in the evenings, he would be watching TV and drinking.'

Middle-class men were no different than those in the working class, she seemed to imply—doing little work and getting drunk.

'He didn't work?'

Surekhabai shrugged. 'I don't know. Not that he was in the house every day but you can't be doing a job or a business if you are home so often, isn't it?' she reasoned. She seemed to open her mouth to say something further but clamped up.

'What?' PSI Motkar prompted, observing her action. 'You were going to add something.'

'Nothing,' Surekhabai said, looking away.

'Okay, tell us whether you noticed anything unusual in Mrs Doshi's behaviour that day,' PSI Motkar asked, casting a sideways glance at Senior Inspector Saralkar who had been completely silent so far. He noticed his boss's eyes seemed to be glazed over, as if he was far away.

'Like what?' Surekhabai asked Motkar.

'Well, did she appear sad or disturbed or was she behaving differently than usual? Did she look scared?'

Surekhabai shook her head slowly. 'Not that I noticed. She didn't talk much and was away from the kitchen most of the time. She seemed to be busy doing something—kept going in and out of the bedroom….'

'Did they fight much?' Senior Inspector Saralkar's voice suddenly startled her.

Surekhabai reoriented her faculties to answer Saralkar. Her hostility to Motkar, which had graduated to condescension, now took the shape of wariness. 'Well ... I did hear them fight sometimes ...'

'How often?'

'They seemed to be fighting a little more these days,' Surekhabai admitted cautiously.

'What about?'

'I don't know,' she said indignantly because of the implication of eavesdropping in the question.

'What do you mean you don't know? You must've heard something,' Saralkar snapped at her.

Surekhabai felt a little uneasy. The senior inspector was a different kettle of fish. She glanced at the lady constable who hadn't taken any active part in the questioning.

'I mean ... they never argued in Marathi, sahib, so how could I understand?' she said in a far less belligerent tone.

It was a fair point, Saralkar realised. Doshi was a Gujarati surname, certainly not Marathi. 'Hmm ...' he conceded with a grunt. 'Did you ever see Mrs Doshi hurt or bruised? Did she ever mention to you that her husband hit her or something?'

Surekhabai gave a little snigger. 'No,' she said and paused. Then almost as if unable to control herself, she blurted out, 'Seemed to me the other way around ...'

There was a little note of triumph in her voice; as if Mrs Doshi had done what she'd have liked to do to her own husband, when he had been alive.

'What are you saying? That Mrs Doshi used to hit her husband?' Saralkar asked.

Surekhabai nodded and her tone was bitter and sarcastic when she spoke. 'Well, I am not a stranger to sudden swellings and bruises on the face, sahib. I could tell ...'

Saralkar and Motkar looked at each other. It was certainly plausible. Domestic violence cases in which wives beat their husbands were no longer unheard of and both officers had come across such incidents in their careers.

'Are you just making this up or do you know for sure?' Saralkar asked sternly.

Surekhabai looked offended. 'Don't believe me if you don't want to, sahib. But I know what I am talking about!' she replied defiantly.

Saralkar regarded her. There was something about her

unflinching demeanour that told him she wasn't bluffing or exaggerating. 'Is there any particular incident you can tell us about, which gave you that impression?'

Surekhabai looked away for a few seconds, probably debating with herself or thinking back. She finally spoke, hesitant and a little flustered for the first time. 'Some weeks ago he made a pass at me, when Doshi madam had gone out somewhere. I immediately told him to back off and said I'd tell madam about it. He began apologising profusely, asking me to forgive him because he was drunk. He begged me not to tell his wife and blurted out that she would beat him up if she came to know.'

'I see ... are you sure he wasn't just fibbing about it to stop you from telling Doshi madam?' Saralkar dug deeper.

'No, sahib. I'd always suspected it from the frequency with which he would have swellings on his face and arms,' Surekhabai asserted, her face now more animated. 'In the days after the incident, I could see how terrified he was that I would tell her. The moment I would come into the house, there would be a pleading, desperate expression on his face. He certainly was afraid of Doshi madam's wrath. She was quite a fierce lady, you know. Looked a bit like one of those lady wrestlers, as Seema tai and I used to joke.'

PSI Motkar digested this information. He could make out by the way Saralkar was scratching his chin that his boss, too, was trying to do the same.

'Did any visitors come to their house frequently?' Saralkar asked.

'Sometimes there would be guests, but very rarely.'

'Doshi madam's friends?'

'More like patients, actually, but no one I would be able

to recognise. Doshi madam told me she sometimes gave some treatments to these people,' Surekhabai said, now almost completely bereft of hostility.

'What kind of treatments?' PSI Motkar asked. This was all getting intriguing.

'She didn't explain, even though I asked her. Most of the times the guests would be leaving just as I came to cook, or would arrive just as I was leaving,' Surekhabai explained.

'Would Mr Doshi be present when these patients came?'

'No, never.'

'Did only women patients come or were there men, too?'

Surekhabai scowled as if suspicious of what Motkar was trying to imply about her dead employer. 'I never saw any men.' There was reserve and disapproval in her voice, as if she was not going to be part of any salacious innuendoes Motkar might have in his dirty mind.

'What about Mr Doshi? Did any of his guests or other men come to meet him at home?'

Surekhabai again shook her head in denial.

'Okay. Did you ever hear the couple mention a person called Shaunak Sodhi?' It was Saralkar who had spoken again.

'Shaunak Sodhi?' Surekhabai remarked as if pronouncing the name of some rare, exotic item, then shook her head again. 'No.'

'Sure?'

'Sure, sahib!'

Saralkar was quiet for a few seconds, thinking perhaps of more questions to ask. 'Anything else you want to tell us? Mr Doshi seems to have killed his wife and then himself,' he said, then paused and looked at the cook. A look of distress was now evident on her face, probably because of having been reminded of the gruesome fate of her recent employers.

Saralkar continued with slow, deliberate emphasis. 'So ... any other information you may have will help. Don't hide anything or avoid telling us, thinking it is unimportant.'

Again, the same sly expression that Motkar had seen earlier appeared on Surekhabai's face and she seemed to totter on the horns of a dilemma. PSI Motkar asked, 'Surekhabai, there is something you haven't told us, isn't it?'

Surekhabai hesitated once again but then said coyly, 'You are right, sahib ... but ... I don't know if it's appropriate to talk about it.'

'About what? C'mon, out with it,' Saralkar rasped.

'It's, uhh, it's just that Doshi madam didn't pay me wages for this month. Will it be possible for you to pay the amount from any cash that madam has left behind in the house?' Surekhabai asked ingratiatingly.

It was hardly an insensitive request from someone who lived on working-class income and yet Saralkar felt a knowing cunningness in her eyes, which he could not quite decipher.

'Let's see what we can do,' he replied.

6

KUNIKA AHUJA'S SWARTHY, POCKMARKED, MIDDLE-AGED FACE had been troubled and reflective, ever since she had seen the news flash on TV that morning of the grisly fate of the Doshis. The sight of Anushka Doshi's photo had chilled her as she recollected her own unpleasant encounter with the woman. It was a chapter she would've liked to erase permanently from her memory, but the human brain was no computer in this regard and there was no recycle bin that could be completely emptied.

How could she forget Anushka Doshi's amiable, fleshy features made distinctive only by a boxer nose, which transformed into a cruel, wicked expression capable of unimaginable evil in a matter of seconds? And the gruff, husky but friendly voice that turned into a threatening, menacing, ruthless tone?

'Horrible woman!' Kunika Ahuja muttered to herself as she fed her dog, Bruno, and petted him. Bruno was too preoccupied with the food to reply. Kunika shuddered and said a silent prayer to the Almighty.

Although it had been more than two months, she still lived with the fear that Anushka Doshi would enter her life again. Kunika had felt terribly vulnerable and rarely went anywhere without Bruno, her only companion and, of course, her bodyguard—a pugnacious, black Labrador committed to his mistress. Kunika knew she would have had no qualms in ordering him to ferociously attack Anushka Doshi if she came anywhere near her, and Bruno would do it too, although he was the friendliest of creatures otherwise.

'Good dog!' she petted him again, suddenly feeling happy and relieved. Why was she worried now? Anushka Doshi was dead. No longer a danger to her! The forty-year-old spinster sighed and started getting ready to go to her gifts and cards shop, bequeathed to her by her father four years ago, knowing well that his daughter's chances of ever getting married were virtually over, given her age, plain looks and stocky, starchy frame.

Then suddenly a thought entered her mind—something that had bothered her earlier too. Wasn't it possible that Anushka Doshi had tried to ensnare other lonely, unmarried, disoriented women like her looking for solace, friendship, meaning and support? Women who had some money and property and could become easy prey—emotionally, psychologically, financially and physically. Kunika suddenly wondered whether it was her duty to inform the police about Anushka's racket.

'What difference does it make now?' she said to herself. Yet, it continued to nag her subconsciously. She had no inclination to get involved with the police needlessly. She knew it would only bring trouble her way. Yet, now that Anushka Doshi was dead, Kunika Ahuja felt a powerful need to share and get her ordeal off her chest.

As she began unlocking her door, she wondered whether she needed to take Bruno along any longer to her shop. Maybe she didn't, but Bruno was no longer used to staying all alone at home. He barked at her now as if gently reminding her that he was to be taken along too.

Of course, he was right. Kunika Ahuja untied his strap, walked him out on his leash, and locked the door. Two minutes later as they drove down the road, Kunika hit upon an idea. She would send an anonymous tip to the police so that she would've done her duty and yet not got personally involved. The only question that needed to be answered was whether to make an anonymous phone call to the police or send an anonymous letter.

Saralkar and Motkar studied Somnath Gawli who had been ushered into their presence—a six-foot, strapping, thirty-five-year-old character with close cropped hair as if he'd just returned from Tirupati. The dark, unsmiling face was bordered by a trim, salt-pepper beard. He was wearing a white half shirt, coal black trousers and polished leather shoes. A mobile stuck out from his shirt pocket while another was clutched in his hands. His neck was covered with a couple of gold chains with lockets while a gold bracelet and an assortment of rings bedecked his wrist and fingers respectively.

Almost true to type, Saralkar thought—the man in front of him had to be a real estate agent or a petty contractor of some sort, who would one day try his hand at becoming a municipal corporator to consolidate whatever money, muscle and political clout he enjoyed.

Gawli had made a deferential gesture to the policemen as he entered—his right palm going to his chest in salutation accompanied by a brisk bow of his head—an abridged version of the Maratha mujra. Not a man who was intimidated by the police but not keen to offend them either.

'Sit down. How did you know Sanjay Doshi?' Saralkar wasted no time in asking.

Somnath Gawli sat down. His mouth opened slightly to answer, then realised that he had forgotten to spit out the tobacco he had been chewing before entering. He squeezed and adjusted the plug of tobacco to one side of his mouth and spoke telegraphically, 'Land deals.' The saliva generated almost spilled out with the words, but he managed to avoid it.

'He owed you money?' Saralkar continued.

This time Gawli realised he had to do something if his words were not to be incoherent. His Adam's apple bobbed up and down as he quickly swallowed the tobacco expertly along with the accompanying saliva. His stomach protested with a little hiccough but that was it. 'Yes, he did. About ten lakhs.'

'You had a dispute with him, right?'

Somnath Gawli's face was impassive. 'What dispute, sir?'

'Perhaps he wanted more time to pay you the money he owed,' Saralkar said in an I-know-it tone.

'Why do you say that?' Gawli asked, his hand pulling at the sweaty collar sticking to his neck.

Saralkar gazed at him, quietly waiting for him to become a little shifty, then said, 'You know Sanjay Doshi committed suicide right after killing his wife?'

Gawli's body language became more wary. 'Yes ... I saw ...' His hands clasped each other.

Motkar noted that he didn't add any clichés like 'Poor man!' or 'Terrible tragedy!' which most people would have, without really feeling so.

'He left behind a suicide note,' Saralkar continued, his tone a little harsher now, 'blaming some of his creditors for hounding him.'

Somnath Gawli's right hand unclasped itself from the left and went towards his crotch this time, which he adjusted. 'I had nothing to do with it,' he replied defensively.

Saralkar got up from his chair and perched himself on the corner of the table lying between the police officers and Gawli. 'You threatened Sanjay Doshi, right?'

'I did no such thing! Asking for your money is not threatening,' Gawli replied without flinching, even though Saralkar was closer now and looming over him.

'You know you can be behind bars for driving him to suicide,' Saralkar leaned forward and growled. 'Doshi's suicide note is enough proof ...'

The defiance in Gawli's look and tenor diminished a little as he adjusted his crotch again. 'But ... but I had not spoken to him for more than a week now.'

'Should I show you the call records? You called him up on Saturday evening,' Saralkar said aggressively.

'I didn't call on my own, sir, just check. Doshi gave me a missed call and I just called back, that's all. I didn't even speak to him,' Gawli reasoned frantically.

'You are lying. There's no missed call from his side,' PSI Motkar interjected quickly. 'You had called him.'

'Believe me, sir, in any case he didn't take my call,' Gawli replied, his features beginning to look a bit ruffled now.

'Maybe you had threatened him so badly earlier that even the sight of your incoming call terrorised him!' Saralkar said, now moving in for the kill.

'No, sir, it was the other way round. It was that wife of his who threatened me not to call him again for the money,' Gawli said, sounding acutely embarrassed. 'That's why I didn't call again for some time since I wanted to think it through.'

'What do you mean? Mrs Doshi threatened you?' Saralkar scoffed. 'You expect me to believe that? What could she have said that frightened you enough to stop calling?'

Gawli looked at Saralkar with bitter reproach. 'Believe me, sir, that woman was a vicious bitch! Do you know what she said? She said she'd file a complaint of molestation and attempted rape against me if I dared confront or call her husband again for the money!'

The estate agent stopped and looked from one policeman to the other as if asking for justice. 'That's why I ... I didn't call. I was wondering how to recover the money without being put behind bars for attempted rape and molestation,' he paused and adjusted his collar again. Then, he said with a look of victimhood, 'Sir, you know what it is like these days ... even without verifying the facts your department colleagues would have arrested me if the lady had made such a bogus complaint. I mean they would've had to ... so I knew I had to be careful.'

Saralkar knew that the new law that ensured the arrest of a man on a mere sexual harassment complaint by any woman had much potential for misuse, but it had certainly proved to be an effective deterrent.

'So, tell us about your business history with Sanjay Doshi. When did you meet, what did you know about him, what deals did you do together, why did he owe you money?' Saralkar asked.

Somnath Gawli's busy fingers were now playing with his gold rings. 'I'll tell you, sir, but please tell me first if he has mentioned my name in the suicide note. Because if he has, the bastard was lying!'

He stopped and glared at both policemen. 'Please tell me, sahib, is my name there?'

Motkar looked at Saralkar, almost anticipating the latter's reply—bluffing without answering.

'How do you think we got to know about you, then?' Saralkar said with a convincing smirk.

Somnath Gawli's face darkened with anger and frustration. He let loose a volley of abuses in Sanjay Doshi's memory. 'He'll rot in hell, sir. First the swine cheats me and dupes me of my money just because he's too weak to live and pay up, and then he dares to put my name in his suicide note.'

He frothed at his mouth with some more vituperative directed at the late Sanjay Doshi as Saralkar let him vent some steam.

'Okay, that's enough,' Saralkar finally said. 'Your abuses are not going to help you. Tell me the facts I need and we might be persuaded.'

Gawli calmed down, probably assured by Saralkar's statement.

'Sir, Doshi first contacted me about a year ago about some land plots near Tamhini Ghat. He claimed to be from Mumbai and said he was looking for investment options. We met a couple of times to show him different plots. Doshi went through with one or two deals initially.'

'Which area? Give me the date, name of seller and the registry office,' PSI Motkar interrupted.

Gawli seemed to have the information at the tip of his fingers, which he gave to Motkar.

'Do you have a copy of the papers?'

'I keep copies in my office, sir.'

'Okay. Were all payments in white, or black and white?' Motkar continued.

Saralkar cast a disapproving glance in his direction, as if hinting that such details could wait.

But Gawli had already started replying albeit with great hesitation. 'I—I can't help it if Doshi wanted to pay seventy per cent in black, sir. I'm not responsible for the black economy.'

Saralkar's interest was aroused. 'Doshi paid seventy per cent in black? How the hell do you do it with all the laws?'

'There are ways, sahib. Anyway, the deals were not very large, just about twenty-five lakhs worth, so it wasn't a problem.'

'What about your commission? Was that also paid in black?'

Gawli didn't give a straight reply. 'Can't quarrel with a customer, sir!'

PSI Motkar shook his head but caught Saralkar's eye, which clearly indicated that he shut up.

'Okay. What after that?' the senior inspector hastened to ask.

'Sir, then the bastard started acting smart,' Gawli said, clearly incensed by the memory. 'He would go for plot visits and to see other properties with me but would feign no further interest. Then the slimy fellow would take the help of some associate, contact the seller or the owner directly after a few weeks, and purchase the land or property without a middleman. That is by cutting me out of the deal. Since he would offer them more than fifty per cent in black and because they didn't have to shell out agent's commission, the sellers were happy to do the deal.

'I got wind of it only by chance, because of an acquaintance in one of the registry offices. Naturally, I was furious. I began to dig around and found that Doshi had done six or seven such deals of land and properties which he'd first visited with me.'

Somnath Gawli stopped, almost too indignant now to continue without eliciting a sympathetic response from the policemen.

'Go on,' Saralkar said, instantly disappointing him.

Gawli licked his lips, a little put off by the senior inspector's apathy. 'Well, I bloody well wasn't going to let him get away with it. I confronted the bastard and told him to shell out my commission. First, he tried to evade and act smart but eventually agreed to pay me when I cornered him. That was the money I was after. My commission, sir, and he died without paying.'

'How much did the deals amount to?'

'I tracked down about five to six crores worth of deals.'

PSI Motkar raised his eyebrows. 'That's quite a bit of money and if you are saying he paid fifty to sixty per cent in cash, that amounts to three to four crores! Where could he have got that kind of cash?'

Saralkar was nodding his head slowly. 'You said he took the help of some associate. Do you know the name?'

'Some north Indian name, sir. Sodhi, I think. All the deals were made in his name,' Gawli readily replied.

Saralkar and Motkar were trained never to let a witness or suspect know that the information he had shared was important. It always became that much more difficult to extract. So, neither of them exchanged glances even though their excitement was mounting.

'Sodhi? Do you know this man? Have you ever met him?'

'No, sir. But all the documents are in his name.'

'Do you have copies of the documents?' PSI Motkar asked.

'I got copies of a couple of the deals from sources, before confronting Sanjay Doshi,' Gawli answered.

'So, the documents will have this Sodhi's photo and address, right, while registering the deal?'

'Yes, sir,' Gawli said. 'Address, yes, but I think he also had a Power of Attorney in some.'

'Okay, get me those right away and we might not need to take you into custody,' Saralkar said, as if offering a quid pro quo.

Gawli, of course, knew he had no choice. 'Yes, sir,' he replied, readjusting his crotch with great relief.

7

MRS SEEMA TAMBE SUFFERED HER FIRST PANIC ATTACK JUST after lunch on the following day. She had finished watching her post-lunch TV serial and just as she was about to enter her bedroom for a siesta, an inexplicable fear gripped her.

Her hands and legs began trembling uncontrollably, her chest began to thud against her ribcage, and she began to sweat copiously like a tap turned on, while her mouth ran dry. Seema Tambe's senses were suddenly invaded by frenzy so primal that she wanted to run out of her flat screaming. There was somebody in the bedroom waiting to murder her, slaughter her—loud voices in her brain began clamouring. 'Run, Seema ... Scream, Seema ... Run for your life.'

And yet Mrs Tambe couldn't move. Nor would any sound emanate from her mouth, as if the connection between her mind and body had been suspended. She just sank to the floor, convinced someone was going to step out of her bedroom any moment, put his arms around her neck and choke the life out of her or slash her and leave her to slowly bleed to death.

She didn't know how long she sat there, half-crazed, half-paralysed, but it was the doorbell that jolted her into action. Seema Tambe ran for her life, yanked open the door and burst into tears as she collapsed into the arms of her teenage daughter, Sapna, who had just come home from college.

Bewildered, Sapna comforted her hysterical mother, took her inside after a great deal of coaxing, gave her a glass of water when she finally let her go, and called up her father.

Back in his office again, Saralkar brooded silently. A constable had been sent to accompany Somnath Gawli to get the papers while Motkar was busy collating other information related to the investigation, after they had returned.

Theories usually sprouted in Saralkar's mind like wild grass on any patch of land after a shower. But his mind had been strangely prosaic today, as if imagination and intuition had taken the day off. Could it be because of that stupid BP medication he had taken in the morning?

Saralkar grunted with annoyance, suddenly feeling dull and tired and stale. Perhaps he ought to go home or maybe to a movie or to a play. He couldn't remember the last time he had entertained himself.

Motkar walked in before he could decide.

'Anything new?'

'Nothing much, sir, except that a key, probably the key to a bank locker, was also found in the Doshi house.'

'Which bank?'

'No idea, sir. I have asked one of the constables to check with all the banks in the locality tomorrow, either for an account or a locker held by the Doshis,' Motkar replied.

'Mmm,' Saralkar said, clicking his tongue. 'If what Gawli

says is true and Doshi was dealing in so much cash, finding their bank account might not help much.'

'I'm pinning my hopes on tracing their locker, sir. Lots of people hold cash and unaccounted money in lockers,' Motkar said.

'And secrets …' Saralkar observed pointedly. 'There's something pretty murky about all this. Shady land deals, an aggressive wife who ill-treats her husband, threatens a creditor, and has an affair with her husband's partner or associate, who also happens to be a front for the land deals …'

'In a way, doesn't it make sense, sir? The abused and cuckolded husband suddenly can't take it anymore. All his hate erupts, he goes berserk with rage, turns on his chief tormentor, his wife, kills her, and then ends his own life.'

'True, Motkar, except why doesn't he kill his wife's paramour as well who has hurt him equally grievously,' Saralkar remarked. 'Why spare him? Why just name him? I mean, why did Sanjay Doshi turn inward and not outward? Why kill yourself and not your wife's lover?'

'Maybe he didn't have the guts, sir. From what we know of Sanjay Doshi, he seems to have been a timid person, scared of his wife. Maybe it was within his capacity to kill his wife in a fit of hatred and fury, but not Shaunak Sodhi.'

'Mmm … you could be right, Motkar,' Saralkar said. 'Do you know about one of the most infamous murder cases in the history of crime? Dr Crippen?'

'No, sir.'

'Mousy little man. Not a real doctor. His wife, Cora Crippen, was a rather abusive, crude and large woman who fancied herself as a music hall singer. She would beat him up from time to time and humiliate him. Then one day, the worm turned. Crippen poisoned her, then dismembered her body, and buried it piece by piece in the basement. I wonder if Sanjay Doshi would've killed himself if he had a basement and dismemberment skills.'

Saralkar smirked and got up. 'Okay, got to go. See you tomorrow.'

Motkar nodded, silently wondering where his boss got his macabre sense of humour.

Surekhabai lay down pensively after dinner. Her son, Hrithik, had been gone for two days now. God alone knew where he would disappear for two to three days at a stretch, every now and then. It had become a habit of his over the last few months. Probably loafing around with those good-for-nothing friends of his, up to some mischief.

He had been a nice, sincere and harmless boy till that day a year ago when the police had picked him up. That experience had changed everything, especially because it had brought him into contact with the goons in the area. Was he eventually going to end up like his horrible father—drunk and idle, blowing up any money he earned?

Hrithik had already joined and left a dozen jobs—as a peon first, then as a mall employee, a delivery boy for Amazon, and so on.

Surekhabai had lost count and watched with alarm. But what had been worrying was his newfound tendency of flirting with illegal activities since he had joined the nearby 'mandal'. If her late husband had had one relative virtue, it was that he had never shown any predilection for crime. Probably he had been too lazy even for that, Surekhabai thought uncharitably.

Was her son going to go down that forbidden path, which even his late father had not trodden? There had already been disturbing signs—suddenly he seemed to be well-stocked with money, had become increasingly secretive, and whatever snatches of conversation she sometimes heard when he spoke to his friends on the mobile, sounded ominous.

The cook dialled Hrithik's mobile number now but the rings passed unanswered. Surekhabai felt sickened in her heart, trying desperately to shoo away the suspicions she wouldn't admit even to herself. Why had she been so careless?

After making a pass at her, Sanjay Doshi hadn't merely apologised profusely. Sozzled and panicky, he had offered Surekhabai a lot of cash to keep quiet. He had rushed into the bedroom and unlocked the big steel cupboard with his key. Curious, she had peeped into the room and had been aghast to see bundles of cash tumbling out as Doshi in his clumsy, drunken haste managed to dislodge them.

Surekhabai had craned her neck further and so far as she had been able to make out, there were untidy stacks of cash on every shelf in the cupboard, barely camouflaged by clothes. Doshi had put the bundles back hastily, except one wad, which he had rushed out and offered to her as compensation for his attempt to outrage her modesty.

Surekhabai had refused the wad of ten thousand rupees and the wretched man had promptly grovelled and offered two and then three wads, totalling thirty thousand rupees. She had finally relented and taken the cash home and tucked it away for a rainy day.

But Hrithik, perhaps familiar with her hiding places since childhood, had stumbled upon the cash somehow and confronted his mother. Like a fool, she had told him everything—the pass made by Doshi, the bundles tumbling out of the cupboard, and the untidy stacks of cash of a huge amount still lying there.

Her son had breathed fire, vowing to teach Doshi a lesson. Then a few days later, Hrithik's uncomfortable questions had started—about the location of the cupboard, about the layout of the Doshi flat, about security in the society, about grill doors and the routines of the Doshis.

Surekhabai had grown increasingly alarmed, sometimes rebuffing him, sometimes warning him to keep away, her uneasiness growing by the day. And now the Doshis were dead and her son hadn't come home for two days, untraceable and incommunicado. What was she to make of that? 'Oh God!' she prayed. 'Let it be just a coincidence. Let him come back today.'

Her mobile sprang to life almost immediately as if God were a telephone operator who immediately patched her through to her son.

'Hullo, where are you, Hrithik?'

'What's it?' her son replied rudely. 'Why are you calling?'

'Why haven't you come home since yesterday?' Surekhabai demanded in a shrill voice.

'Work,' Hrithik replied laconically.

'What work? Where are you? Who is with you?'

'Don't bother me, I'm busy. Can't talk now.'

'Hullo ... hullo ... Don't cut the phone!' Surekhabai shouted. 'Tell me when are you coming home? Tonight?'

'I'll come when I come,' Hrithik replied.

'What kind of work keeps you away for two or three days?' his mother asked angrily.

'Don't poke your nose into my business, okay?' Hrithik warned petulantly and ended the call, leaving Surekhabai none the wiser or calmer.

Cool down, she told herself. She was unnecessarily letting her fears get the better of her. He had sounded his usual self. There was no reason to think Hrithik was in any way involved with the death of the Doshis. How could he?

Hadn't the police said Doshi had killed his wife and then himself? So why was she freaking out and connecting the disappearance of his son to the tragedy?

Of course, perhaps she should have informed the police about the stacks of money she had seen. But chances were that the police had already found and impounded all that cash. That's why she had gently hinted about her pending wages. Surely, they wouldn't grudge her that.

PSI Motkar knew he was late for drama practice. He opened the door of the practice hall as noiselessly as he could and slunk inside. A scene rehearsal was in full progress. PSI Motkar bit his lip when he realised it was a scene featuring his character. A constable with a dialogue sheet in hand was standing in for him.

No one seemed to have noticed his entry. The dialogues between the main characters, a volatile couple, boomed. One spouse said to the other, 'Dammit! How did you become me and I become you? What's this? I feel like the man in Kafka's

Metamorphosis who wakes up to find himself turned into a cockroach.'

'Are you saying being a woman is like being a cockroach?' the other spouse thundered.

Before the scene could proceed further, one of the actors muffed his lines and the rehearsal ground to a halt. The lead actor requested a break for a quick cigarette. The rest of the cast and crew also trickled out of the hall, some of them waving or acknowledging Motkar as they passed him. Hands on his hips, the director shook his head and turned around. His eyes fell on Motkar. 'You are an hour late,' he said sourly.

'Sorry, Walimbe. I got a new case on my hands. Husband killed wife, then committed suicide,' Motkar replied, offering his excuse.

Walimbe made a face. 'So, what's new, Motkar? Come on, even we have cases. I don't understand why you have to suck up to your boss so much!'

Motkar gave a conciliatory smile in response. 'Nothing like that. Should I go over my lines with you?'

Walimbe still hadn't been placated. 'Only if you have rehearsed them at home and ironed out the mistakes you kept making yesterday.'

Motkar felt a little twinge of guilt. He hadn't made any effort to rehearse at home, but he bluffed away. 'Yes, yes. You'll notice the difference. Okay, should I start?'

Walimbe nodded grudgingly. 'Go on, he said, and sat down on a chair.

Motkar cleared his throat, glanced at the first dialogue on the sheet and began, 'Hey, please don't start fighting again.

Amruta ... er ... Yogesh, it's ... sorry ... just a twenty-four-hour transformation ... er ... metamorphosis.'

Walimbe cut him short. 'What is this, Motkar? You can't hum and haw like that, boss. I told you, first learn the lines by heart, damn it.'

Motkar squirmed, feeling like a junior artist being rebuked by some prima donna. Damn it, what had he got himself into? How was he ever going to get through this ordeal?

'Give me two minutes, Walimbe,' he said meekly, and began practising his dialogues in earnest.

8

SARALKAR OPENED HIS EYES AND IMMEDIATELY SENSED THAT he had overslept. He turned around to take a look at his mobile, resting on the bedside table. It showed 8 a.m., much later than usual. He wondered when he too, like most people, had stopped using a table clock. Mobiles had made clocks almost redundant.

The fleeting lamentation about clocks was brushed aside by the fact that his head felt slightly heavy. He shook it gingerly to make sure it wasn't too bad. Could it be a symptom of elevated BP? Saralkar felt intensely irritated with himself for thinking like that. There could be several explanations for the heaviness—acidity, oversleeping, hangover, migraine, blocked nose—all of which he had experienced some time or the other. Why then did his brain have to immediately think of BP?

He dragged himself out of bed, not wanting his mood fouled up by that stray doubt.

His wife was practising yoga asanas in the drawing room. Fitness had come to Jyoti Saralkar a year ago, just like religion gets to some people suddenly, one fine day. And with Shilpa Shetty–like gusto, she had taken to it.

Saralkar could never understand why people chose to contort and torture their bodies thus or, for that matter, jog or skip or go to the gym. He had never felt the least bit like doing any of it.

His wife had just finished another asana when she noticed him. 'I thought you were taking the day off,' she said.

'Why should I do that?' he asked with his trademark morning grumpiness.

Jyoti didn't argue. 'I'll make tea,' she said, getting up and folding her yoga mat.

'Why didn't you wake me up at my usual time?' Saralkar asked.

'You looked very tired yesterday,' she replied simply.

Saralkar grunted and retreated to the washbasin to brush his teeth. The dull grogginess above his left eyebrow had still not gone away ten minutes later, as he took his first sip of the tea.

'What are those pills Dr Kanade gave you?' Jyoti asked quietly.

Saralkar cursed himself inwardly. 'Why do you snoop around in my pockets?'

'Well, if you don't want me to stumble upon your secrets, be more careful while putting your trousers for a wash,' Jyoti retorted in a calm voice.

Saralkar glared at her, then looked away.

'Are you feeling unwell?' Jyoti persisted.

'He just gave me some headache pills.'

'I saw the prescription also. He's scribbled your BP readings on the top corner. 160/110.'

'So why are you asking me if you already know?'

'But why didn't you tell me yourself?'

Saralkar shrugged. 'What's there to tell? Dr Kanade gave me the pills and asked me to come back after three days. It's not as if I've been diagnosed with hypertension or something. It may just be a temporary spurt.'

Jyoti's palm glided across to his forearm and squeezed it. Her touch felt nice and soft and comforting, but he was damned if he was going to tell her that or put his own palm on hers. The idea of doing anything remotely romantic rebelled against his self-image.

'You should take a break,' Jyoti said.

'Nothing's wrong with me. I'm perfectly okay!' he replied, conscious even as he said it, of the heaviness on his temple. It was probably going to get worse as the day wore on, he knew.

'Investigating all these murders and being with criminals and violent people does you no good,' Jyoti said. 'I am sure that's the main cause of your stress.'

'Nonsense! I spend more time with you than with criminals,' he replied gruffly.

Jyoti didn't take the bait. She was silent for a few seconds, looking at him anxiously, caressing his hand, before saying, 'Can't someone else investigate that Doshi couple case?'

'Don't be ridiculous, Jyoti.'

'Let Motkar handle it by himself, no,' she coaxed.

'But why?' Saralkar snapped.

'So you can take rest!' Jyoti said. 'I'll also take leave for two days.'

'And do what? You also want to take rest?'

'No, I'm just bored of the daily routine. Let's go to a movie, shop a bit, eat out ... you can take a nap in the afternoon. It'll be such a change,' his wife said, suspiciously big-eyed.

Saralkar felt alarmed because the prospect of spending two whole weekdays without doing any police work was so alluring. He was just about to grunt non-committally to give himself time to think about it when she spoiled it all by speaking again.

'... and tomorrow let's get your entire check-up done.'

Saralkar looked at her scornfully. 'I knew there was a sting in the tail somewhere. No, thanks. I'm going to work.'

He began taking bigger, determined gulps of tea, which had become lukewarm by now.

'Okay, you do the check-up whenever you want. Let's just do all the other things today, at least. Come on, I'm bored,' his wife said, trying to make amends.

'No, I can't. I've got work,' he replied.

She knew that he wouldn't change his mind now. A few seconds of silence followed and just as Saralkar was about to get up and leave the table, Jyoti asked softly, 'Why did the man do it?'

She usually never displayed much curiosity about his work, so Saralkar was surprised. 'Apparently his wife was having an affair, and she also mistreated him,' he answered briefly.

Jyoti raised her eyebrows. 'Really? You mean he was a battered husband?'

'Looks like—'

'So … you think he killed her in self-defence that day and then committed suicide?'

'Could be, but it's not as straightforward as it looks. The paramour's missing,' he said. 'That's why I need to go.'

Jyoti nodded thoughtfully, and then asked, 'I wonder why men are either tyrants or weaklings.'

Saralkar grunted. 'Because they are always under siege.'

It was the perfect provocation but, yet again, Jyoti did not take the bait. Instead, she asked, 'Okay, what should I cook for lunch today?'

'Anything will do,' Saralkar replied, and went for his bath. As he turned on the shower, something about his wife's last poser reminded him of two basic questions he should've asked Doshi's cook: *'What did she usually cook for them every day?'* and *'What language did the couple use at home?'*

He made a mental note.

Constable Shrike had laid out the copies of the five property agreements provided by Somnath Gawli, turned to the page with signatures, thumb impressions and photos of the seller and buyer.

'Three different people appear as Shaunak Sodhi, sir,' Constable Shrike observed, his thick index finger jabbing on three different photos in the five documents.

Senior Inspector Saralkar and PSI Motkar studied the photos, then looked at each other. PSI Motkar was the first to speak. 'Probably one of them is the real Shaunak Sodhi. The others? Fake.'

Saralkar cast his eyes over the photos again. The documents had been photocopied not from the original agreements but from their photocopies. The photos therefore looked smudgy and patchy. While it was possible to make out that the photos were of different people, the features were not very clearly visible.

One version of Shaunak Sodhi was a bald, bespectacled, clean-shaven, middle-aged man with drawn lips and high cheekbones. The second one was a complete contrast—long hair and side locks, a full moustache and beard; he looked like a street thug. There was an earring pierced on the top half of his ear. The smudging around his eyes, nose and mouth made the features difficult to discern. The third photo was that of a washed-out Sardar—pushing seventy, eyes drooping, face wilting, wearing a much used, faded turban.

'Yes, one of them could be the real Sodhi, but which one?' Saralkar said at long last. 'And anyway, why the hell would Sanjay Doshi be purchasing and selling land in the name of his wife's paramour?'

'Sir, as Gawli said, the game was to get the best bargain directly from the seller and cut out the commission payable entirely. Sanjay would scout out the land using Gawli and then buy it in Sodhi's name so that none would be the wiser,' PSI Motkar said.

'Of course, I understand that Sodhi was a front, Motkar,' Saralkar said irritably, 'but were he and Sodhi equal partners in the land dealings? And if they were, then was Sodhi the white money component and Sanjay Doshi the black money guy? Also, if that was the case, why do we have different people impersonating as Shaunak Sodhi and signing documents at three different registration offices? Was he the mastermind or was it Sanjay Doshi? Because Sanjay and his wife are dead, and it's Shaunak Sodhi, the wife's paramour and husband's partner, who's disappeared.'

There followed a rather long pause, as if the three policemen were waiting for each other to break it. Saralkar had closed his eyes because it almost hurt to keep them open.

PSI Motkar finally spoke hesitantly. 'Sir, by any chance, do you suspect that Sanjay Doshi did not murder his wife and kill himself? That Sodhi had something to do with it?'

Saralkar massaged his forehead, his eyes still shut. The heaviness had graduated to a dull throb travelling across his skull, like a planet across its orbit. 'Yes, Motkar. I'm wondering whether this is a double murder and not a homicide cum suicide. And till we find the mysterious Shaunak Sodhi, he is on top of my suspect list.'

'But what about Sanjay Doshi's suicide note, sir?'

Saralkar gave a smirk. 'Come on, Motkar. Even if it turns out to be written by Sanjay, it could have been written under duress, if the murderer was threatening to kill him.'

'No, sir, I don't mean that. I mean the note specifically mentions Shaunak Sodhi,' Motkar said. 'If Sodhi killed the couple, why would he put his own name in the note? Would it not lead to him?'

Saralkar's eyes flashed at Motkar, angry perhaps for having his theory contradicted logically. 'Maybe he was just being too clever by half, Motkar,' the senior inspector lashed out, then suddenly stopped and changed his tone. 'No, no ... you are right. No murderer would call suspicion upon himself by putting his own name, even the most oversmart criminal.'

He paused once more then glared at Motkar again as if the brief moment of self-doubt had passed. 'But mark my words, Motkar, this is a double murder—both Sanjay and Anushka Doshi were killed. Just wait for the post-mortem results and you'll see I'm right. When are we getting it?'

'In a day or two, sir,' Motkar replied.

Saralkar grunted. 'I'll die of heart attack the day they give us a post-mortem report within twenty-four hours.'

Constable Shirke gave an involuntary chuckle while Motkar also found himself agreeing with the sentiment expressed by his boss.

'Anyway, check out the addresses of the different Sodhis mentioned in the documents. Maybe one of them will lead us to the real Sodhi's whereabouts,' Saralkar said. 'And collect the thumb impressions of the different Sodhis from the property registrar's office and check through the State and National Crime Records databases if we get any matches with known criminals.'

'Yes, sir,' Motkar replied.

'Any luck with finding the locker or possible bank account of the Doshis?' Saralkar asked.

'Not yet, sir.'

'Hurry up, Motkar,' Saralkar grumbled. 'What about tracing the acid to its source?'

PSI Motkar just shook his head this time.

'And what about the number that had called Anushka Doshi twice at odd hours? Has the caller been traced?' Saralkar asked with mounting belligerence.

'Well, Constable Shewale hasn't ...'

'Don't blame Shewale, damn it!' Saralkar suddenly flared up. 'Shewale isn't whiling away his time acting in amateur theatre, Motkar! It's you who has been doing that!'

Not for the first time in his career, PSI Motkar experienced first-hand his boss's uncanny knack of finding chinks in his armour.

PSI Dulange lay prostrate before Rangdev Baba. He was overwhelmed to have been summoned for a rare, personal darshan of the holy man.

Rangdev Baba muttered his blessings and patted the policeman's back gently.

PSI Dulange rose and sat back on his knees, his arms folded.

'How is our sweet little Anand progressing?' Rangdev Baba asked, referring to Dulange's nine-year-old, suffering from mental retardation.

'He's much better, Baba ... all due to your blessings,' Dulange replied.

'That's good. But why didn't you bring him with you?'

Dulange hesitated. 'I wanted to, but Akhandanath-ji said you wished to see me alone about something.'

Rangdev Baba threw a vexed glance at Akhandanath who was standing to one side, then smiled at PSI Dulange and said in a perfectly intoned, affectionate rebuke, 'Next time, remember you require no one's permission to bring Anand ... joy ... happiness.'

The god-man stopped and gave a little smile as if bowled over by his own pun, disguised as childlike profoundness.

PSI Dulange was duly gratified. 'Yes, Baba. Please tell me what can I do for you.'

Rangdev gave a world-weary sigh, then spoke: 'You know that my ashram is open to all. Being a man of God I can't turn anyone away, even bad people and sinners. Right ...? Because it is my duty to provide solace to all those who have lost their way ... all those who approach me.'

PSI Dulange nodded as if he understood Baba's saintly compulsions immediately.

'Well, one such depraved individual kept coming to my satsangs for several weeks and tried to take advantage of my piety and kindness ... by making some outrageous propositions and indulging in immoral activities with one or two of my junior disciples,' Rangdev Baba paused, his kohl-framed eyes trying to gauge the effect on his listener. He was gratified to find PSI Dulange's face mirroring his shock and dismay.

Baba continued. 'Naturally, the moment I learnt of it, I forbade the man from coming here again and was also going to expel the disciples who had fallen prey to his machinations. But they begged for my forgiveness, and as you know, forgiveness is second nature to me, so I let them stay.'

PSI Dulange nodded understandingly. 'Who is this person, Baba? Is he causing trouble again? Do you want me to fix him?' he asked, eager to help.

Rangdev Baba shook his head sagely. 'The miserable sinner is beyond human intervention. I am informed that he killed his wife and then himself a few days ago. His name was Sanjay Doshi.'

Recognition dawned on PSI Dulange. 'Yes, yes, the homicide cum suicide case in Kothrud.'

'Exactly. The man lived an evil life and died a sinner. May God forgive him. What I am worried about, Dulange, is that the investigation into the case is bound to bring to light his misdeeds and crimes. It might also reveal that he tried to use my ashram and one or two of my gullible disciples for his own selfish, nefarious motives.' Rangdev Baba paused and closed his eyes, as if too distressed to continue.

PSI Dulange hastened to comfort him. 'No, no, Baba. You shouldn't worry yourself unduly. Just because he was your devotee and had some links with your disciples does not mean the police will investigate you.'

'I know that, Dulange, but you know the times we live in. A whiff of a scandal is enough ... The media is always ready to pounce on all god-men because of the few charlatans in our midst. It would set my heart at rest if you can find out for me ... if any such whisperings are afloat in your department.'

PSI Dulange found the request odd. For the first time since he had become a bhakt, he found himself wondering about

Rangdev Baba. Not that his faith cracked, but why was the Baba so anxious if he had no immediate connection to Sanjay Doshi? Nevertheless, Dulange's sense of obligation asserted itself, albeit cautiously. 'I'll certainly try and find out what I can, Baba, but if you don't mind, can you tell me exactly what this man Sanjay Doshi and your two wayward disciples had been up to?'

Rangdev Baba realised that PSI Dulange had not turned out to be as gullible and unquestioningly grateful as he had hoped. Trying to fob him off would prove counterproductive. He summoned his entire acting prowess and proceeded to tell PSI Dulange a carefully crafted combination of fact and fiction, which he had fortunately prepared beforehand.

9

SENIOR INSPECTOR SARALKAR'S HEADACHE PEAKED IN THE LATE afternoon. It had already travelled halfway across his skull, and going by its trajectory, he knew it would end up where his neck met his head. It produced a sickening, nauseating feeling and all the thinking he had been doing about the Doshi case had only made matters worse.

Moreover, his mind had thrown up no promising theories or hypothesis, no startling insights or interesting little possibilities that had not already struck him before. Any further brooding and dissection of facts in the closed confines of his office was not going to get him anywhere for the moment. It was only going to intensify his suffering. Nor was there any point in getting after Motkar.

Saralkar made a decision. He got up from his seat, walked out of his office, trudged down the stairs, started his motorcycle, and was off. Every movement had been sheer agony for his fragile skull, every jerk producing a sensation of disorientation, but Saralkar knew that if he had to get through the rest of the day, his sterile office was not the place to be in.

The best option was to visit the Doshi flat and to explore the possibility of finding a proverbial needle in the haystack. Not that the Kothrud Police or PSI Motkar wouldn't have done their job thoroughly, but if there was one thing that years of policing had taught Saralkar, it was the importance of double-checking for anything that may have fallen through the cracks.

It took him about twenty-five minutes to negotiate the traffic and when he reached Atharva Apartments, the combined assault of the heat and pollution had taken its toll, but the headache, for some mysterious reasons, was a little better.

He took a deep breath at the upsetting thought of climbing the staircase, but what couldn't be avoided had to be endured. The residents of Atharva Apartments seemed to have returned to some semblance of normalcy. They appeared to have taken the murder cum suicide into their middle-class strides. A man was talking on his mobile in the parking, a maidservant was drying clothes in a balcony, a grandfather was curled up with a newspaper in the verandah of a ground-floor flat, like on any other day.

All of them noticed him but there was no wide-eyed curiosity or frowns of apprehension. A policeman prowling about the premises had been absorbed into their routine. Climbing up the staircase, Saralkar was also accosted by a couple of school-going kids, rushing down the steps, chasing each other playfully with accompanying sound effects. Even they didn't seem in awe of the sight of a police officer, making sure only that they didn't dash into him.

A lone, forlorn, bored policeman sat on a stool outside the Doshi flat, playing some game on his mobile. He scrambled to his feet as the huffing and puffing figure of Saralkar came into view, climbing up the last flight of stairs.

Saralkar's head had started pounding. 'Open the flat,' he managed to say, out of breath.

The constable dipped into his pocket, produced a key and unlocked the door. A whiff of the pungent air wafted out of the flat as fresh air rushed in. Saralkar's nostrils could still smell the faint odour of decomposition, which had combined with mustiness and staleness.

He stepped in and cast a glance around the hall. Two people had lived here and died unnatural deaths. There had to be something in this living space that explained what had gone wrong. Where was he to begin looking?

The Kothrud Police had inventoried everything tidily and tagged items of possible importance. He had studied the lists. Nothing really out of the ordinary. Nothing he could put his finger on that could be classified as odd or revelatory.

In fact, that's what had bothered him ... the items not on the list. No personal IDs except driving licences, no commonly held documents of any kind—life insurance policies, cheque books, pass books or important bills, no photographs, no cameras, no computer, no scribbled notepads, no boxes full of assorted odds and ends.

As if the Doshis had been living on an island completely unconnected to the mainland, or as if Sanjay Doshi had removed all the things that would distract from the main narrative—of him having murdered his wife and dying by suicide.

But why would anyone do that? In Saralkar's experience, human lives that ended abruptly, including by suicide, always left behind a mess—a whole load of junk to be done some other day, which never came. From the utterly trivial to the most important, cherished items from the past, to earnest desires of the distant future, from the extremely personal to the merely casual—evidence of a normal existence lived till it was unnaturally cut off. For instance, he still remembered how he had found on the table of a suicide victim, an autograph book signed by a few celebrities and friends, right next to an unused gift coupon of a nearby mall. Just two of the innumerable pieces of the poignant jigsaw puzzle of an unfortunate human being's life.

Where were such bits and pieces of the lives of the Doshis, amongst their belongings? Why were there only clothes and accessories and kitchenware and furniture and showpieces and stuff—the hardware of life but not the software.

Saralkar spent an hour examining the inventories, like a kid detective hoping to stumble over a neglected, well-hidden clue. His headache had weakened considerably by now. Saralkar paused, pondering over what was most likely to have been overlooked by the policemen handling the routine search task. Two possibilities now suggested themselves to him, as he looked around for the umpteenth time—the refrigerator and the newspapers piled up above the shoe shelves.

Yes, he was quite sure the Kothrud Police team might not have felt any compelling reason to check the contents of the refrigerator or rummage through the newspaper stack. He walked over to the refrigerator first and opened it. He bent over to peep in, then realised he would have to drop onto his haunches to have a better look.

His haunches complained as he eased his weight onto them. Saralkar wasn't sure how long they would hold up and so began to quickly examine the contents. There was a half-empty bottle of coke on the side and two lagers. A solitary bottle of water gave them company along with a bottle of ketchup. Two small bottles containing what looked like puree or some thick liquid but without any labels on them stood inconspicuously behind the bigger bottles. There were eggs in the egg compartment, butter in the butter tray, and bread in the top shelf, next to a bowl of some soup or rasam. A vessel contained a rice dish—yellow-coloured, with assorted vegetables and topped with grated coconut. An airtight container in the middle shelf had a small portion of leftover curd rice, next to a ceramic container which seemed to have a fish curry, going by the smell.

Saralkar's thighs were now definitely groaning under the stress they were being subjected to. He quickly glanced into the vegetable tray, which was more or less empty except for a few shoots of spring onion. He pushed back the tray and lumbered to his feet. Ripples of pain shot through his thighs and knee joints. The ageing process, thought Saralkar, was well and truly on its way. He grunted and opened the freezer compartment. The ice trays were full, while the rest of the freezer had ready-to-eat packs of chicken, along with an unopened pack of ice cream. There was also another plastic bottle with liquid, again without a label. What were these bottles of liquid, Saralkar wondered. He picked up the bottle, holding its neck between the first two fingers of his inverted palm to avoid touching the cap, shut the freezer, put it on the table, then took the other two small bottles out which he had earlier seen beside the beer and water bottles.

He hollered out to the constable, who came running.

'Put these in some plastic bag and give it to me.'

The constable, eager to assist, reached out to collect the bottles with his bare hands.

'Use a bloody handkerchief,' Saralkar snapped at him. 'Do I have to tell you that? Even schoolkids know this from watching TV serials. And hold them only by the cap.'

The constable winced and managed to pull out a clean

handkerchief, that itself being a minor miracle, and scrambled away to find a suitable plastic bag.

Saralkar stared thoughtfully at the refrigerator for a second, then turned his attention to the stacked newspaper raddi. He doubted there would be anything much to find, but some instinct propelled him to run through it. The preferred paper of the Doshis seemed to be the *Indian Express* and the stack dated back to about a month and a half. There seemed to be nothing of note, just neatly crease-folded papers—no marked items or ads, no annotated pages. And then, nearly at the bottom of the heap, as Saralkar lifted another issue of the *Indian Express*, pages of *Deccan Herald*, a paper almost exclusively read in Bangalore and Karnataka, stared back at him.

He skimmed through the four newspaper pages quickly, looking for any items that might suggest why the Doshis were interested in it. None of the news items seemed of any striking relevance. There were also a couple of display ads, three obit announcements, and two distress inserts—one, a missing person ad, and the other a return appeal to someone who had left home. He studied the various photos and names in the ads. Nothing aroused extraordinary curiosity or the hint of a connection to the dead couple.

Saralkar placed it aside and pondered his various discoveries. What were *Deccan Herald*, fish curry, curd rice, rasam doing in the house of the Doshis—a surname that was ostensibly Gujarati, with almost no likelihood of South Indian ancestry. Unless, of course, Sanjay Doshi had been a second- or third-generation Gujarati brought up in one of the South Indian states, or his wife Anushka had been a South Indian.

The senior inspector's memory stirred. Hadn't Motkar said a

neighbour had mentioned she thought the Doshis hailed from Bangalore? His headache had all but disappeared now as he dialled Motkar's mobile number.

'Motkar, which neighbour had said she thought the Doshis were from Bangalore?' he asked as soon as his assistant took the call.

'Mrs Seema Tambe, sir. She stays on the same floor, across the Doshi flat,' Motkar replied efficiently. 'Where are you now, sir?'

But he was speaking into emptiness, since Saralkar had already hung up.

The senior inspector put the *Deccan Herald* pages into the same plastic bag the constable had provided for the bottles and walked out of the Doshi flat. 'Lock the door,' he instructed the constable curtly, then went across and rang the doorbell of the Tambe flat.

The door did not open immediately and just as he began wondering if there was anyone at home, it opened slightly, with the chain lock in place, as if to prevent anyone rushing in. It was a young girl, looking out apprehensively. 'Papa isn't home and Mummy's resting,' she said even before Saralkar spoke.

'Oh! I need to speak to your Mummy, Mrs Seema Tambe, for a minute. May I come in?' Saralkar asked.

The girl hesitated. 'But ... uncle ... Mummy is unwell. Papa said she should rest and is not to be disturbed; that's why I have not even gone to college.'

Saralkar clicked his tongue impatiently, then asked, 'Is your Mummy down with a viral or something? Too weak to get up?'

This time the girl's face clouded further as if she would rather slam the door in his face than answer. She reflected momentarily and said, 'Uncle, can you please speak to Papa? I'll dial his number if you want.'

She produced a mobile and began dialling before Saralkar could either nod or object. 'Hullo, Papa, a police officer wants to talk to Mummy. I'll give the phone to him.' She held out the phone for Saralkar.

'Hullo, Mr Tambe, this is Senior Inspector Saralkar. I need to speak to your wife. Can you please ask your daughter to let me in?'

Tambe's voice was squeaky and timid. 'But ... er ... sir, my wife is really unwell. Can't you come later, please?'

Saralkar's tone became a lot more authoritative. 'What exactly has happened to her, Mr Tambe? She's not hospitalised, so surely if she's at home, Mrs Tambe can't be so ill that I can't speak to her for a few moments.'

Tambe's voice became squeakier still and softer, almost down to a whisper. 'Sir, the fact is Seema, my wife, has had a nervous breakdown. The doctor said it's ... it's most probably because of the Doshi ... uhh ... incident. So, he's advised complete rest and no stress. In fact, he's also asked us to go away for a few days, which we are going to do this weekend, as soon as my leave is sanctioned.'

'I see,' Saralkar said, his harshness falling away but not his exasperation. 'I understand. Have you consulted a psychiatrist?'

'Yes. Dr Dheeraj Nene. You see, Seema had a panic attack yesterday. She is afraid to be alone now. She thinks someone is going to, well, murder her ... like what happened next door with the Doshis.'

Saralkar stopped himself from giving a derisive grunt, at what he thought was a hysterical over-reaction. Not only because he couldn't deny that the human mind was a delicate, sensitive mechanism that could go to pieces at any time but also because it suddenly occurred to him that perhaps Seema Tambe may have had reason to believe that her neighbours were both murdered. Maybe she or her subconscious knew something that she hadn't told the police.

'Mr Tambe, I understand your dilemma, but I promise none of my questions will disturb or cause further shock to your wife,' he said gently, trying to sound as sincere as he could.

A less meek man would have refused but Tambe belonged to a category that wouldn't dare to defy officialdom. 'Okay ... but ... please, Inspector, I don't want my wife traumatised ...' he begged.

'Don't worry, Mr Tambe, I'm giving the phone to your daughter. Please tell her yourself.'

He returned the phone to the girl, who fastened it to her ear and listened. 'But Papa—' she mildly protested once, then said, 'Okay' and disconnected.

She threw a disgruntled, hostile glance at Saralkar as she unlocked the chain lock and let him into the house. She didn't ask him to sit nor did she say another word. The girl just went inside, to communicate with and fetch her mother.

Saralkar was sure he had just managed to lower her father's esteem in her eyes. He sat down uninvited. Now that the headache was on the wane, he was feeling hungry. If not something to munch on, tea would definitely help. He very much doubted that the girl would offer him some unless the mother told her to. But why should she? Policemen were not guests. They were unwanted, scary intruders.

The house was almost a replica of the Doshi flat structurally, but was far more lovingly decorated. Mrs Tambe was probably an old-fashioned, house-proud homemaker, as indicated by the over-furnished drawing room.

He could hear a very faint murmur from an inside room, probably the daughter coaxing her mother. Maybe Mrs Tambe was really prostrate, too weak and disturbed to meet him. Once again Saralkar realised just how inconsiderate and ruthless a man he was. Motkar, for example, wouldn't have insisted on meeting Mrs Tambe in her condition. But then Motkar had always been the good cop, whereas he, Saralkar, did not in the least mind being the good, bad or ugly cop, depending solely on whatever the situation demanded, moved the case forward and got results soon. That streak was a part of his DNA.

Saralkar waited impatiently for mother and daughter to show up, hoping he wouldn't have to deal either with the woman's hysteria or tears. The shuffling noise in the passage alerted him to the fact that the mother and daughter were making their way out.

One glance at Mrs Tambe's face was enough to see that this lady wasn't putting on an attention-seeking stunt. Her expressions were of someone who had no idea what had hit her. A debilitating fear lurked behind the superhuman effort to retain dignity and control. She was dressed simply in an everyday printed cotton saree—a genteel, pleasant-faced woman who probably laughed a lot, although she seemed to have forgotten to even smile now.

Seema Tambe looked at him anxiously for a second, shepherded along by her protective daughter, and then lowered her eyes as she sat down on the sofa. Her daughter glared at the senior inspector, sitting right next to her mum, holding her hand.

Saralkar was suddenly and uncharacteristically determined to be gentle and patient with Mrs Tambe. 'Thank you, Mrs Tambe, for meeting me,' he said, spouting words unfamiliar to his gruff tongue. 'I am very sorry for disturbing you. Are you feeling any better?'

Mrs Tambe seemed to feel reassured enough to make eye contact and nod. 'Are you sure about the way they died?' she surprised him by asking in a tremulous whisper.

Saralkar leaned forward and asked, 'Do you have any doubts about it, Mrs Tambe? You don't think Sanjay Doshi killed his wife and then himself?'

Mrs Tambe stared at him for a second, then looked at her daughter as if trying to draw comfort. 'I ... don't know. I just can't believe it. For some reason, I keep imagining that someone entered their house and killed them both. And now he's going to get me too....'

She stopped, suddenly beginning to tremble, hiding her face in her hands. Then when her daughter drew her closer, Seema Tambe embraced her. 'Oh God! I just want to go away, somewhere far ... where no one will try and murder me in my own house. I'll go crazy otherwise; I am so scared. I feel a murderer is lurking in the next room all the time.'

There was no mistaking the pounding fear in her voice, a fear that had somehow been let loose and was running amok in her mind and consciousness.

Saralkar realised he'd made a mistake. He shouldn't have barged in on her suffering by bullying her husband. Her fear might have been based on something real—facts that she knew about the Doshis' lives which she had chosen not to disclose. On the other hand, it was equally likely that her brain had conjured up a bogey, based on something she had observed at the subconscious level, or it was simply her imagination gone wild.

Or maybe it really was an irrational, unreasoning fear that

had nothing to do with reality. Either way he could see that Mrs Tambe seemed to be in no condition to be questioned.

To salvage the interview, Saralkar made one last effort. 'Mrs Tambe, please calm down. You have nothing to fear at all. A policeman is sitting just outside your door all the time. He's going to be here for the rest of the week. No one can enter your house without passing him. Calm down, please! If you don't believe me, ask your daughter.' He paused and gestured in the direction of Mrs Tambe's daughter.

For the first time, the daughter's hostility seemed to evaporate. 'Yes, Mummy,' she said, squeezing her mother's arm. 'There is a constable outside and I'm also there, no.'

Mrs Tambe looked from her daughter to the inspector and then back again, 'But ... but how long will you miss college, Sapna? And what if the murderer overpowers the constable?'

'Mrs Tambe, policemen are trained. Please do not worry. Also, tell me what makes you think that Sanjay Doshi didn't kill his wife and commit suicide? Why do you think someone killed them both? Did Mrs Doshi ever confide in you that they were threatened by someone or did you see someone come to their house and make death threats?' Saralkar asked.

Seema Tambe began sobbing. Bizarrely though, the sobs were succeeded by poignant giggles. 'It—it's hard to believe that ... thin, puny husband could've killed Anushka. He was subdued ... and scared of her,' she managed to say finally, ashamed of her outburst and giggles. But it seemed to have calmed her down a bit. 'No, she never confided in me about any threats, but I just remembered there was a man who had come a few times ... with whom they had a fight once or twice.'

'Fight ... What about? And when?' Saralkar said, leaning

forward with cautious interest.

'I—I don't remember. I heard some commotion on the landing so I opened my door. All I could hear was something about money and mother. Then they all saw me and fell silent. Anushka was looking very, very angry and her husband looked pale. The young man was standing with his hands on his hips, his back towards me. Anushka quickly said to him, "Get out and don't dare come back" and withdrew inside the house, pulling her husband too. She slammed the door. The young man was about to knock on the door hard, then caught a glimpse of me, and slunk away.'

'And you are saying this young man came more than once?'

'Yes. I saw him again, once or twice. Once in the lane outside the society, he was accosting or threatening Mr Doshi, who seemed to be pleading with him, and then he had also come last week. I was climbing up the stairs and he was descending, all red-faced and viciously furious. He averted his eyes from me and left,' Mrs Tambe said, her voice much steadier.

'Did you catch a glimpse of his face?' Saralkar asked, hopefully.

Seema Tambe nodded, and Saralkar realised that her fear seemed to be receding into the background, just a bit.

'Will you be able to describe him to my police artist? I can send him across.'

'What's a police artist?' Mrs Tambe asked doubtfully.

Her daughter answered before Saralkar could. 'Aai, a police artist will ask you the man's features—what kind of hair, colour, nose, mouth, eyes, all such things—and then he'll draw a sketch of the person, based on your description.' Sapna inadvertently looked at Saralkar for approval.

'Your daughter's right. If you are able to give a good description, police artists can come up with sketches that bear close resemblance to suspects,' Saralkar replied, then attempted some armchair psychiatry. 'It might also help you psychologically to get over your own fear, if subconsciously your mind feels this man could've harmed the Doshi couple.'

There was no basis to his assertion but Saralkar felt it would tip the scales.

Mrs Tambe reflected for a second, then said, 'Maybe you are right. Every time I saw the young man, his face was suffused with rage as if he bore a deep hatred or grudge against the Doshis,' she shuddered. 'And the most frightening part is, somehow he looked familiar, especially when he averted his gaze that day while coming down the stairs, as if he recognised me but wanted to avoid.'

'Do you think you know him?'

'No. I just had a familiar feeling as if I'd seen him earlier, not in the recent past, though,' Mrs Tambe paused. 'Maybe that's why I feel scared ... that I know the person yet don't know who he is.'

'Trust me, Mrs Tambe, the session with the police artist will make you feel better. We all need to reduce our nameless fears to something tangible or manageable, and then it starts losing its power over us,' Saralkar said, surprised at how pretentious he was sounding, yet how sincerely he had spoken.

Mrs Tambe looked at him gratefully and Saralkar almost felt ashamed of himself. He hoped the session with the police artist would turn out to be cathartic for her. Even her daughter seemed less hostile towards him now.

'I have just two or three more questions, Mrs Tambe. You told one of my colleagues that you got the impression the

Doshis were from Bangalore. Right? Can you tell me what was the reason you felt so?'

Mrs Tambe was thoughtful. 'I am not sure exactly but I think we were once just chatting and I said to her that my husband, Sapna and I were planning to go to Bangalore, Mysore, Ooty. Anushka looked at me with interest and said that the city was her hometown. I am not sure whether she said "our" or "my" but she said it. What was odd was that after that, she clamped up and when I asked her some questions to help me on the trip, she was quite evasive, as if she didn't want to discuss anything more.'

'I see ... Did she say when or how long ago she'd stayed in Bangalore?'

'No, nothing. She didn't say a word about her family or share any memories about the city or places or highlights, the way we affectionately talk about our hometown. Nothing at all.'

'And she made no other references to Bangalore any other time?'

'No, never. I broached the Bangalore topic once more after we came back from our trip, but Anushka didn't show any interest, which I thought was very guarded or very unnatural for someone who claimed to hail from Bangalore,' Mrs Tambe said and paused. 'Then I thought, maybe she had some bad memories of the city, that's why.'

She shrugged, sounding almost normal now.

'I see. And did Mrs Doshi ever mention whether they were Gujaratis?'

Mrs Tambe replied promptly. 'I had asked her once because her accent puzzled me. It sounded South Indian whereas her surname was Gujarati. Anushka only said her husband was Gujarati but did not elaborate, but I am more or less sure she was a South Indian, although I have no idea whether she was a Tamilian or Telugu or a Kannadiga or a Malayali.'

Saralkar nodded with understanding. India's mind-boggling diversity made it difficult for almost any average person to be sure of each other's exact origins, unless one was an exceptionally keen observer. 'What makes you so sure?' he asked. 'Apart from the accent.'

'Well, the aromas from her house were ... well ... very, very South Indian—fish, sambhar, that sort of thing. Besides, we have the same cook—Surekhabai. I asked her once what they cooked and she told me all kinds of South Indian and Goan dishes. Not one mention of any Gujarati cuisine.'

She was cut short in mid-sentence by the ringing of the doorbell. Startled and nervous, fear returned to Seema Tambe's face. Sapna, her daughter, got up to answer the bell. 'It must be Surekhabai,' she said reassuringly to her mother.

The next moment the cook stepped in through the door, smiling benignly at her employer. 'Feeling better today, tai?' But she froze as her eyes fell on Senior Inspector Saralkar. She began hastening towards the kitchen.

'Just a minute, Surekhabai,' Saralkar called out.

She stopped and turned reluctantly.

'Mrs Tambe was just telling me what kind of food you generally cooked for the Doshis. I'd like to hear from you.'

Surekhabai looked uneasily at Seema Tambe.

'I told Inspector Saralkar that you told me that they generally preferred South Indian and Goan dishes,' Mrs Tambe prompted before Saralkar could stop her.

'Yes ...' Surekhabai said with hesitation. 'Doshi madam employed me because I knew many South Indian and Goan dishes well.'

She rattled out the names of different dishes, none of which seemed to have any Gujarati connection.

'Were both husband and wife South Indian?' Saralkar asked her.

'I think so,' Surekhabai replied, fidgeting.

'Wasn't Sanjay Doshi a Gujarati?'

'I don't think so ... never heard him speak in the language.'

'Do you understand Gujarati, Surekhabai?'

'Just a few words, but I can recognise it,' Surekhabai replied and volunteered further. 'They always spoke to each other in English or a South Indian tongue.'

'Which language?'

'How would I know, sahib. Tamil or Malayalam, I guess.'

'Why didn't you tell me before?' Saralkar asked with some asperity.

'You never asked me, sahib! How am I to know you wanted this information?' Surekhabai said defiantly.

She was right, Saralkar knew. 'How did husband and wife address each other? Did they use first names or what?'

Surekhabai hesitated. 'I don't remember him ever calling his wife by first name, but many times she called him Krishna.'

'Krishna?' Saralkar sat up puzzled. 'Are you sure?'

'Yes.'

'You mean she never called him Sanjay or Sanju or something?'

'No, always Krishna,' Surekhabai said. 'I—I thought it's his nickname.'

'Yes ... Yes, even I heard her refer to her husband as Krishna once or twice ...' Seema Tambe suddenly interrupted.

Saralkar turned to her and stared questioningly.

'I thought it was a slip of tongue. We were talking and she said "Krishna will be back soon." So I asked her who she was referring to, and she looked at me and said that I had misheard the name. She just pretended she never uttered the name Krishna,' Seema Tambe said with excitement. 'Then another time, I was just climbing down from the terrace, when their door opened and Anushka hissed out "Krishna". I was not visible to them. Her husband had probably just stepped out and she was calling him back for some instructions. When I came down the flight of stairs on to our landing, they were just talking, but I distinctly remember her hissing out that name.'

Saralkar listened quietly, then looked at both women. The visit had been fruitful. The neighbour and the cook had certainly given him something substantial to chew over, and his headache had also been cured.

'Would you like some tea, inspector uncle?' Mrs Tambe's daughter, Sapna, suddenly asked.

For the first time since morning, Saralkar felt gratified. 'Throw in some biscuits, too, if you don't mind,' he replied with all the charm he could manage.

———

10

CONSTABLE SHEWALE ONCE AGAIN DIALLED THE UNKNOWN number from which two calls had been made to Anushka Doshi's mobile—one on Friday late night and then early on Saturday morning. He had still not received customer details from the service provider, but blaming them was hardly going to placate PSI Motkar or Senior Inspector Saralkar.

To his great surprise, the number, which had hitherto remained unanswered or switched off, was now picked up. 'Hullo?' a man came on the line.

'Hullo, this is Constable Shewale from Pune Homicide Unit. Whose number is this?'

'This is my sister Meenakshi Rao's number,' the man replied, after a pause, perhaps momentarily taken aback that it was the police calling. 'What ... what is the problem?'

'Where is your sister?'

'She's not here just now. I'll ask her to call you back, sir, but can you tell me what the problem is?' the man asked.

'What's your name?'

'Lokesh Rao. I'm Meenakshi's older brother, sir.'

'Does your sister know a lady called Anushka Doshi?'

'Anushka Doshi? I don't know, sahib. What is this about?' the man asked nervously.

'We need to speak to your sister urgently. Ask her to come to the Pune Homicide Unit.' Constable Shewale gave him the address.

'Sir, I'll ask her to call you first as soon as she is back,' Lokesh Rao replied. 'But is there anything specific to be cleared up?'

'Yes. We need to know how she knew Anushka Doshi and why she had called her up early on Saturday morning at around 5 a.m., and also the previous night at 11 p.m.,' Constable Shewale said.

'Okay, sir. I'll tell my sister to call you back as soon as she is here,' Lokesh Rao assured and rung off.

Constable Shewale heaved a sigh of relief. At least he could report some progress made to PSI Motkar.

It was an hour later that his phone rang. A husky female voice spoke. 'Sir, I am Meenakshi Rao. My brother said Pune Police wanted to speak to me about Mrs Anushka Doshi madam.'

'Yes. How did you know her?'

'She ... she ... I mean, I went to her for personal counselling, sir,' Meenakshi Rao replied hesitantly. She then asked, 'Actually it's a private matter, sir. Why do the police want to know?'

'Madam, it's very important. Can you please come to Pune Homicide Unit headquarters?'

'But, sir, I can't do that.'

'Why not? You can bring your brother or some other family member along if you wish,' Constable Shewale said. 'Or we can come to your residence if you give me your address.'

'Actually, sir, I am not in Pune just now; we are on a trip.'

'Oh! Where are you?'

'Sir, we are near Tirupati. I'll only be back after seven to eight days. Please ask me whatever you wish to, sir, but first please tell me why you want to know how I am acquainted with Mrs Anushka Doshi,' Meenakshi Rao said guardedly.

Constable Shewale sighed. 'Well, Mrs Anushka Doshi and her husband were found dead on Sunday.'

'Oh, my God!' Meenakshi Rao shrieked. 'What happened?'

'We are investigating the case. Looks like you are one of the last persons who spoke to her. Why did you make calls to her late on Friday night and then again around 5.00 a.m. early morning on Saturday?' Constable Shewale asked. 'At such odd times?'

He heard a few sniffs at the other end of the line and when Meenakshi Rao spoke, it sounded as if she had been crying quietly. 'My God, sir. She ... she helped me get over so many of my problems ... through her unique therapy. Oh, my God! What am I going to do now?' Meenakshi Rao began crying again.

'Madam, please calm down. You may have important information. What therapy are you talking about?'

'Past life regression,' Meenakshi Rao replied. 'We suffer in our present birth because of certain events and incidents and our karmas in our previous birth. Anushka madam helped people get acquainted with their lives in previous births so that they understand the root cause of their sufferings in the present birth. She helped identify specific reasons and incidents in our past life that needed to be addressed, accepted and neutralised so that we can free ourselves from suffering in this life.'

Constable Shewale had already heard something similar before, from some of the other clients of Anushka Doshi that he had spoken to. 'Okay. So since how long were you undergoing Mrs Doshi's therapy?' he inquired, taking down notes.

'About two months, sir, and there's been a great deal of improvement in my life. My negative feelings have gone,'

Meenakshi Rao replied, sounding like one of those people in TV ads who swore by miraculous talismans.

'So why had you called her so early that morning and the previous evening?'

'To activate a particular soul cleansing ritual that she had advised me to do. It was to commence at 5.30 a.m. and she had told me to call and confirm the session. If she were ready, I was to go over to her house for the early morning session,' Meenakshi Rao explained. 'But she told me that we would have to do it some other day as the cosmic vibes and impulses were not right. Also, she said she was upset and her concentration was suffering and so she would not be able to induce the state of deep hypnosis required. So, I thanked her and said I would call after I came back from the trip.'

'Did she elaborate on why she was disturbed?'

'No, sir,' Meenakshi Rao said. 'Although I knew that all was not well between Anushka madam and her husband.'

'She confided in you?'

'No, no. Just something I could make out from their behaviour with each other. I mean, I never liked the look of her husband and there always seemed to be some tension between them ...'

'I see. We require your statement. When are you coming back to Pune?'

'Seven to eight days, sir.'

'That long? Try to come back earlier and report to us as soon as you reach. In the meanwhile, if my senior wishes to speak to you, we'll call on this number,' Constable Shewale said. 'Please tell me your travel schedule over the next few days.'

'Sir, from Tirupati we are going to Hyderabad and then ...'

She continued telling him about her plans.

The constable noted down the details. 'And where will you be staying?'

'We've not done any advance bookings in hotels, sir.'

'Who's with you?'

'My brother and his family.'

'What about your own family? Husband, children?'

'I am unmarried, sir,' Meenakshi Rao replied.

'Okay, please give me the mobile number of your brother,' Shewale said.

'His phone was stolen at Shimoga ST stand, sir. We have lodged a police complaint at Shimoga and deactivated the number. But I will be available on this number, sir.'

'Okay, madam,' Constable Shewale said. 'One final question. Why weren't you answering the phone over the last two-three days?'

There was the briefest of pauses and then Meenakshi Rao explained, 'Sir ... I normally don't take calls from unknown numbers, and especially now that I am travelling. Just now also, only because my brother was there, he took the call.'

Constable Shewale again repeated that his boss might want to speak to her and then called off. All that needed to be done now was to double-check Meenakshi Rao's details with the service provider, get her address in Pune, confirm she stayed there, and that she was indeed currently out of station. Finally, he would need to ensure that her current location was really in Tirupati.

That's exactly what Motkar instructed Shewale to do when he briefed the PSI a few minutes later.

Kunika Ahuja stared at the blank sheet of paper before her. She had no idea how she was going to crisply and concisely write the anonymous note to the police. She had discarded the thought of making an anonymous phone call; she was sure the police would be able to trace it back to her. The only options she had were to call from her own mobile or landline or her shop landline. All these could be easily traceable.

If she called from the phone of a neighbour or acquaintance, that, too, would eventually lead back to her. She couldn't think of a single telephone booth that operated nearby or indeed anywhere in the city. And even if it did, anonymity was not possible because hardly anyone used PCOs these days. So, the PCO owner would definitely remember her.

Kunika had then cunningly considered requesting a stranger and calling from his or her mobile. But that, too, wasn't without risks. What she had to say to the police would be time-consuming and no stranger was likely to let her use the phone for a long call. And in any case, he or she would be hovering around, making it difficult for her to tell the police what she wished to.

Most importantly, what number would she call on? The Police Control Room number, 100, was obvious, but the thought made her uneasy. Maybe she might even lose her nerve.

That's when she decided it would have to be an anonymous note. And now the snag was how to compose one, and how exactly to word it. Was she to summarise her ordeal or just give vague tips of Anushka Doshi's wickedness? For example, would the police pay any attention if she simply wrote: *Anushka Doshi was a dangerous woman who used the gimmick of past life regression to harass and snare women for nefarious purposes. I narrowly escaped from coming to harm, because of some sixth sense. She definitely had sinister and criminal intentions. Maybe the couple's death was a result of her unscrupulous activities. Please examine this angle.?*

Kunika Ahuja thought it would suffice. She was not interested in furnishing details of what she had faced and undergone. She just wanted to alert the police about the evil side of Anushka Doshi, in case they didn't already know it. Investigating it further was their job, not hers.

She put pen to paper and began writing the note.

'I am so sorry, sir, for doing a bad job,' PSI Motkar said, his face inconsolable with embarrassment. 'All this information should really have been unearthed by me from the Doshi flat and Mrs Tambe.'

Saralkar had just finished briefing him about his visit the previous day. 'Don't be too hard on yourself, Motkar,' he responded wryly to his assistant. 'It happens. Investigation is all about going over the same ground again and again, in the hope of chancing upon something new, that had escaped us earlier.'

He had rarely known Motkar to be emotional, but as of now the PSI seemed to be almost quivering with self-loathing. 'No, sir,' Motkar said with scorn that appeared to be directed at himself. 'I just wasn't up to the mark. I had accepted it as a straightforward case of a spouse's murder followed by suicide.'

'It might still be just that,' Saralkar observed. 'The only thing is, it's much more complicated and so we need to be absolutely thorough in ascertaining it's not a double murder.'

Motkar nodded slightly, probably still unable to forgive himself. Saralkar decided it was time to shift focus. 'Are you just going to stand there kicking yourself or will you brief me about any progress at your end?'

It acted upon Motkar like a mahout's jab to the pachyderm in his charge. 'We've managed to establish contact with the person who made calls to Anushka Doshi at odd times on Friday and Saturday,' he replied, brightening up visibly.

'That's good! Who did this mysterious caller turn out to be?'

'A woman named Meenakshi Rao, one more of Anushka Doshi's past life regression clients,' Motkar said, and briefed the senior inspector about Constable Shewale's telephonic conversation with the woman.

'Hmm ... I thought you had managed to trace the elusive Shaunak Sodhi finally,' Saralkar remarked.

'No, sir, but we've also been able to identify one of the fellows who posed to be Sodhi in the land registration documents,' PSI Motkar said, now upbeat. 'A petty conman called Mobin Ghatwai, with a police record of minor offences—petty forgery, fraud, cheating, that kind of a thing. Hopefully, we will be able to nab him soon. There's someone keeping a tab on his regular hangouts and house.'

Motkar showed him the document in which the faded Sardar-ji had posed as Sodhi. Saralkar felt doubtful they would get anything out of the man in the photo, principally because old, sozzled, petty crooks rarely asked questions while taking part in petty deceptions or offences such as impersonation. Many a times, they wouldn't even have a remote idea. But then, Saralkar had been in the force long enough to know that sometimes breakthroughs came from unexpected quarters and the most unexpected people.

'Good, looks like we are finally making some headway,'

Saralkar remarked.

PSI Motkar's mobile interrupted whatever he was about to say in response, because the ringtone was unimaginably ghastly. It had a child's voice bleating shrilly, *'Papa the phone's ringing. Papa the phone's ringing.'* And it kept getting shriller with each ring.

PSI Motkar's shocked face said it all. 'I'm sorry, sir! My kid may have changed the ringtone.' Embarrassed beyond words, the PSI quickly took the call, 'Hullo? Motkar here. Yes, Shirke?' He stole an awkward glance at Saralkar, looked away, and once again turned to his boss, this time the embarrassed expression on his face turning to an alert one, as he listened. 'Hmm ... Hmm ... Mumbai. Okay. Okay ... okay. Get the manager along. Yes ... Saralkar sahib is also here.'

Motkar disconnected, his sincere little face taut with excitement. 'Sir, Shirke may probably have traced the locker, the key to which we had found in the Doshi flat!'

'Where is it? Which bank?'

'Probably the Sanpada branch of the Suburban Bank, Mumbai.'

'What? What's Shirke doing in Mumbai?'

'No, no, sir. Shirke was visiting branches of all banks in the Kothrud locality. He had gone to the Dahanukar Colony branch of the Suburban Bank also this morning and, while making inquiries, an assistant manager at the branch, Abhay Dalvi, recognised Sanjay Doshi's photograph. He had been posted in the Sanpada branch of Suburban Bank earlier and has recently been transferred to Pune in the Dahanukar Colony branch,' PSI Motkar elaborated. 'Abhay Dalvi said that Sanjay Doshi had opened an account and taken a locker in the Sanpada branch about a year and half ago. Dalvi even remembered Sanjay Doshi's name. Apparently, he visited the Sanpada branch twice or thrice during the year. Shirke is bringing Dalvi over.'

Senior Inspector Saralkar was elated enough to thump his fist on the desk. 'Looks like today's going to be our day, Motkar,' he growled. 'You and Shirke leave for Mumbai along with Dalvi. Get the details and check the goddamn locker. I'm sure we are going to find Sanjay and Anushka Doshi's secret buried in there.'

'Yes, sir. Are you also coming to Mumbai?'

'No, Motkar, I've got a doctor's appointment this evening,' Saralkar replied, almost immediately regretting the admission.

'Doctor? Anything wrong, sir?' Motkar asked with concern.

'I'm fine, Motkar,' Saralkar replied haughtily.

'But then ...?'

'C'mon, Motkar, can't a man go to a doctor, without the whole world wanting to know why?'

'I'm sorry, sir. It's just that you didn't look well yesterday, so I thought ...'

'You thought what, Motkar?' Saralkar snapped.

'Well, I mean ... these days it's advisable to get oneself checked for BP or diabetes ... after forty... so I was wondering,' Motkar faltered.

'Well, you thought wrong, Motkar. I was just going for vaccination.'

'Vaccination, sir?' the PSI exclaimed with incredulity.

'Yes, Motkar. I never got chicken pox when I was a kid. Don't want to get it now, that's why I am getting vaccinated,' Saralkar replied insouciantly. 'Want to join me?'

Motkar was too surprised to reply.

11

'WHITE COAT HYPERTENSION' WAS ONE PHRASE AMONG THE many that Saralkar had become acquainted with, during his internet research on blood pressure, a few days ago. Apparently, it referred to the phenomenon of higher BP recordings of a patient resulting from the mere presence of a doctor. The implication being that some people with otherwise normal BP got so stressed out by a visit to the doctor that it resulted in a spike in their readings.

Dr Kanade never wore a white coat, nor was he wearing one now as he pumped the sphygmomanometer again, tightening the arm cuff on Saralkar's left arm, just below his shoulder.

No, Saralkar thought to himself, he wasn't going to let the doctor's presence psychologically affect his BP. He silently willed himself to have a lower BP.

'Okay, sit up now,' the doctor said.

Saralkar began to pull at the Velcro fastening of the arm cuff.

'Wait. Who asked you to remove that?' Dr Kanade rebuked mildly, readjusting the cuff. 'We need to take one more reading sitting up.'

He pumped the sphygmomanometer as Saralkar forced himself to remain calm and not think hard thoughts about the doctor. A whole minute passed before Dr Kanade finished taking the readings and unshackled Saralkar from the instrument.

'I suppose it's normal now, isn't it?' Saralkar asked.

'Better than last time but still on the higher side,' Dr Kanade replied.

'What's the reading?'

'140/90.'

'So, it's okay, right? Last time it was 160/110,' Saralkar said, getting down from the doctor's examination table and sitting across from his side-desk.

Dr Kanade regarded him tolerantly. 'Look, it's lower because you took the tablets. Without them, the readings would probably have remained higher. And it's still above normal, which is 120/80. It appears you might need to be put on daily medication. Get all these tests done first.' He began scribbling on his prescription pad.

'But ... but ... are you saying I have chronic high BP? Why should I have it?' Saralkar protested, a frown beginning to form on his face.

Dr Kanade cocked a glance at him. 'Why wouldn't you have it? You are overweight, you are in a stressful job, you probably smoke or drink or do both—'

'I don't smoke,' Saralkar interrupted indignantly.

'So what? You don't exercise, you probably eat the wrong kind of food, you have a short temper. So, there's every bloody reason for you to have high BP,' Dr Kanade sneered and resumed his prescription writing.

Saralkar spluttered for words. 'But ... but isn't BP hereditary? Neither of my parents ever had it!'

Dr Kanade finished writing the prescription and slid it across the desk to Saralkar. 'Your parents probably didn't even know they had it. Times were different. There was little awareness, and people didn't go to doctors for routine check-ups. Anyway, get all these standard tests done. And I am referring you to another doctor, whom you should consult after getting the reports.'

'Why another doctor? Why can't you treat me?' Saralkar asked, quite rattled now.

'Well, I'm just a GP, Saralkar. It's the era of specialists! So, you need to see one,' Dr Kanade said cheerfully, then winked. 'Besides, patients like you make my blood pressure go up, so it's better I pass you on to someone else.' He bared his teeth and gave a toothy grin.

Saralkar responded with a cold look, as if the doctor was personally responsible for his condition. He paid Dr Kanade, then asked grudgingly, 'Do the tests have to be done urgently?'

The doctor had got over his fatuousness by now. 'The sooner the better, although there's no urgency. But why delay? Look, there's nothing to worry; high BP is quite common these days and the medication quite standard and reliable.'

Saralkar nodded and stepped out of the clinic. The doctor's reassurance had done nothing to make him feel better. His mobile rang just as he was about to start his bike. It was Motkar.

'Yes, Motkar.'

'Sir, Abhay Dalvi's information was correct. Sanjay Doshi had opened an account in the Sanpada branch of Suburban Bank and also had a locker in his name. The key we found in the Doshi flat is of that very locker,' Motkar said.

'Have the bank authorities permitted you to open the locker?'

'Yes, sir. We opened it and your instinct turned out to be right!'

'What did you find?' Saralkar asked impatiently.

'Sir, the locker contained fifty lakhs in cash!'

'Fifty lakhs?' Saralkar almost whistled. 'Go on, what else?'

'Sir, we also found several legal documents, some in Kannada, and other papers including two passports—one in the name of Sanjay Doshi issued last year, and another one in the name of Krishna Bhupathi from Bangalore, issued in 2002. Looks like Sanjay Doshi and Krishna Bhupathi are the same person. There are also other documents of deals in Goa and Hubli and other places.'

'Good job, Motkar! That's quite a haul. Get it all here as quickly as you can. I think all of it will help us get to the bottom of this case.'

'We hope to leave in an hour or so, sir, after the formalities are completed.'

'Good. Do you have a locker in some bank, Motkar?' Saralkar asked.

'No, sir,' Motkar said, taken aback by his boss's query.

'Never mind, Motkar; only dishonest cops keep lockers. The honest ones are only familiar with lock-ups.'

'Why are you making such a fuss about it?' Jyoti demanded as she gave final touches to the folds of her saree in front of the mirror. 'It's only a simple blood test followed by an ECG and a sonography. Won't take more than two hours.'

She threw a disapproving glance at Saralkar who didn't bother looking up at her as he tied his shoelaces. 'It's you who's making the fuss,' he retorted. 'I said I'd get it done.'

'When?'

'When I finish solving this case.'

'How long's that going to be?'

'I don't know yet. A week or two,' Saralkar said, as he got up and glanced at his watch.

'By which time another case will land on your table,' Jyoti said, a vexed expression on her face.

'If you are going to nag me about this all the way, you better go by auto,' Saralkar warned.

He'd agreed to drop her off to work, something he rarely did.

Jyoti made a face and said nothing more till they were on the way on his motorcycle. Just as Saralkar had begun to feel he'd stopped her in her tracks, she spoke. 'Are you scared?'

'*Tchah!*' he grunted much too indignantly. 'Scared of what?'

'Undergoing the medical tests because of the BP diagnosis?' Jyoti said. 'That it might show the real status of your health.'

Saralkar couldn't think of anything to say for a moment. Jyoti had an uncanny knack of putting a finger on the source of his discomfort. 'Oh, come on!' he finally managed. 'It's not as if I may have a terminal illness, you know.'

'Yes, but—'

'Will you stop talking about my health and those god damn tests, Jyoti?' he finally said, coming to a halt by the side of the road and turning around. 'Or else you take an auto from here.'

'Okay ... but I was just—'

'Not a word!' Saralkar said, firmly refusing to resume the ride till she fell silent.

Normally feisty, Jyoti would have got down and flagged an auto on any other occasion, but she stayed put this time. They continued the ride in uneasy silence and five minutes later, Saralkar dropped his wife off outside the school she worked at.

'Deliberate ignorance isn't bliss when it comes to health. It's foolishness,' Jyoti said and walked away, before Saralkar even had a chance to react.

Saralkar glared after her, hoping she would turn around and catch his glance. She didn't, and soon disappeared from sight inside the school.

Her words rankled as he drove towards his office. Of course, he needed to get the check-up done but that didn't mean he had to submit to it enthusiastically and immediately. He had a case to solve and he could do without the distraction of a pathologist sticking a needle inside him to draw blood.

Motkar greeted him with a smile, and if he had had a tail, Saralkar was sure it would've wagged a great deal; such was his assistant's excited demeanour.

'Sanjay Doshi's real name was Krishna Bhupathi, sir. He was an absconding criminal from Bangalore. Just got his identity confirmation off the National Crime Records Bureau database, sir.'

'What are the charges?'

'Bangalore Police lodged several cases against him in 2007 and then 2008, sir. Cheating, fraud, forgery. And there also seems to be a murder case. More details are awaited.'

Saralkar nodded and surveyed the contents of the bank locker, which Motkar had arranged on a side table. There were a bunch of legal agreements—in Kannada and English. Beside it were two passports and two wads of notes—samples from the fifty-lakh haul. Obviously, Motkar had processed all the material evidence as per standard procedure, including the cash. He was extremely efficient and meticulous.

Saralkar reached for the passports and opened them one

after the other. The lifeless man who had been found hanging stared back at him from both. The recently issued passport was in the name of Sanjay Doshi, with a Mumbai address. The older passport, still valid, was in the name of Krishna Bhupathi and had a Bangalore address.

There was no doubt it was the same man, but whereas Krishna Bhupathi was clean-shaven and sported a full pate of hair, Sanjay Doshi had a rapidly receding hairline, almost grey, compensated for by a moustache and beard. The eyes and the look in them had changed. While Krishna Bhupathi appeared confident, even slightly cocky, and almost respectable, Sanjay Doshi looked furtive, weary and cornered. Sanjay Doshi also seemed to have gained an injury scar, near his right-side burn.

'Both these passports look genuine. Check whether police verification was done in Mumbai or if it was managed.'

'Yes, sir. I am also getting the wads of notes analysed. The tags are intact so we might be able to trace any bundles which originated from Bangalore,' Motkar replied.

'Worth a try, but it's a long shot. Unless, of course, you are saying that Sanjay Doshi retained some bundles with which he originally absconded from Bangalore all those years ago and that this is money earned from the crimes he committed in the city,' Saralkar said.

Motkar nodded. 'Sir, as I see it, this locker has no joint signatory, so I think Anushka Doshi was unaware of it. There is no record of her having visited the branch. Sanjay Doshi, on the other hand, visited twice or thrice and the staff of the branch is more or less sure he was alone on all those occasions. I have asked them for CCTV footage for the dates of entries made by Doshi in the locker register. But they generally don't retain footage more than three months old, so it's possible we might get footage of his last visit but not the earlier ones. If Doshi was maintaining this locker and keeping money in it without his wife's knowledge, then it is probably money he earned and already possessed. Therefore, it's possible some of this money could belong to his original lot.'

Saralkar threw an approving look at him. 'Okay. Your reasoning can't be faulted, even if it's based on too many assumptions,' he remarked. 'I think there's also one more assumption we can safely make.'

'What's that, sir?'

'Well, the fact that he had kept his passports along with the money in the locker, which his wife probably didn't know about, means it's possible he was planning to flee abroad, leaving her behind. What do you say?'

'Yes, sir, that thought had crossed my mind too,' Motkar agreed.

'Which also brings us back to the original question: why would Sanjay Doshi kill his wife and himself if he had made standby arrangements to flee, even the country, on his own? Why not just abandon her and go missing either in India or abroad?'

'But the act of killing his wife could have been activated by pure jealousy and fury, sir, for being betrayed by both his wife, Anushka and his partner, Sodhi, who also had the properties in his name. It could have been a "heat of the moment" thing, sir. And then when Sanjay realised he was now a murderer, he killed himself knowing he would be caught and also made accountable for his previous crimes,' Motkar argued.

Saralkar snorted. 'Isn't that all the more reason for him to try and run away than hang himself? Secondly, if indeed he killed himself for reasons you said, then why claim in his suicide note that creditors were hounding him? Especially when he had so much money salted away in the locker. And if it was a *crime passionnel*, a murder that was not premeditated, how come Doshi had made arrangements to get the acid beforehand?'

PSI Motkar found himself unable to counter his boss's line of reasoning. 'So what should be our next step, sir?'

Saralkar rubbed his chin. It was an affectation Motkar had recently noticed him resorting to sometimes, as if measuring the extent to which his chin had graduated to a double chin.

'The answer is obvious, Motkar. We have to find Shaunak Sodhi and for that we need to travel back in time and to Bangalore, the scene of Krishna Bhupathi's original crimes.'

'I have already contacted Bangalore Police, sir. We should be getting the information in a few days.'

'If it's a 2008 case, Motkar, we can hardly expect Bangalore Police to move quickly on it. Nor is second-hand information going to be enough. We'll have to conduct our own investigation based on the leads supplied by Bangalore. And the quickest way to do that is to travel to Bangalore and meet the investigating officers who were on the case,' Saralkar asserted.

'But, sir ...' PSI Motkar said and shrugged, as if not in agreement with his boss but unable to say so.

Saralkar looked at him quizzically. 'You seem somewhat reluctant at the idea of travelling to Bangalore, Motkar. Do you also have some hidden secrets in the city?'

'No, sir ... of course, not,' Motkar replied awkwardly. 'I just thought maybe we should wait for some specific details before going all the way to Bangalore.'

Saralkar's eyes narrowed, his expression puzzled. Then

realisation seemed to dawn and consternation spread across his face. 'Has this reluctance got something to do with that damn play you are acting in?'

Motkar immediately became defensive. 'It's not like that, sir. It's just that the show is only seven days away.'

'What's wrong with your priorities, Motkar?' Saralkar scowled. 'You are a policeman, not a bloody actor to give precedence to this blasted play!'

'Of course not, sir,' PSI Motkar said, flushing red. 'I ... I know I made a mistake by accepting the role, but I can't get out of it now. So, I was wondering whether we can send someone else to Bangalore, like PSI Salunkhe went to Gorakhpur last time for the Sonia Raikkonen case. Maybe PSI Sarode of Kothrud Police Station can go in my place ...?'

Saralkar gave him a piercing look. 'PSI Sarode!' He shook his head in contempt. There were things he would have liked to say to Motkar, give him a proper dressing down. But a thought struck him. Wouldn't going to Bangalore himself be the perfect way to get Jyoti off his back about the medical tests? He made his decision instantly.

'No point sending Sarode. I'd much rather go to Bangalore myself.'

Motkar gawked at him in disbelief. He had been half expecting either to be browbeaten into going to Bangalore or his boss eventually agreeing to send Sarode. But not for a moment had he thought Saralkar would consider the option of going to Bangalore himself, knowing how much the senior inspector hated travelling. It probably showed just how important Saralkar thought the trip was.

Motkar considered thanking his boss, but knew instinctively

it was better to keep his mouth shut lest it triggered a re-think. He realised Saralkar was regarding him again and figured immediately that a sharp rap on the knuckles was on the way. He was right. It was not long in coming.

'Hope you'll not be too engrossed with your theatrical distractions to follow up on all the leads here in Pune, Motkar sahib, while I'm pounding the streets of Bangalore!'

It made Motkar cringe like never before.

12

MANY MOONS AGO, SARALKAR HAD VISITED BANGALORE AS A young police officer, to nab a crook. At that time, it had struck him as a slightly bigger version of Pune—pleasant, leisurely paced, blending the charming atmosphere of a small town with big city comforts and attractions. Where it particularly scored over Pune was that Bangalore also enjoyed the perks of being the capital city of Karnataka.

What greeted him now was a chaotic, bustling megacity that had surrendered its innocence and traded its charm for the rapacity of commerce. Much like Pune! No wonder crime had gone up proportionately, and homicide too. In fact, Bangalore now had the dubious distinction of ranking second after New Delhi in the number of serious crimes including murders, well ahead of Pune, which ranked sixth.

Saralkar remembered reading about some recent significant cases in the city—an IT professional whose body was found completely swathed in duct tape, a case which eventually turned out to be a bizarre method of suicide; a corporate executive who killed his wife then pretended to have been out jogging with a friend when he got her distress call; a retired, decorated Indian Air Force officer who was mysteriously slaughtered in his high-end villa in a high-security gated community, while his wife slept in the next room, totally oblivious to his fate.

Human nature on a hair trigger that could be squeezed any time—by the city's overpowering obsession with achieving instant gratification or the cold fury of punishing non-gratification. No different from Pune, except in the statistical degree to which the cult of hedonism led to bloodshed!

The Bangalore Homicide Squad HQ was not very different from his own lair in Pune. Cleaner perhaps, slightly brighter, yes, but unmistakably daunting for every outsider, as police premises usually are, with the ominous suggestion of being ready to swallow anyone who dared venture in.

Saralkar had had a quick protocol meeting with the squad chief, who had assured him full cooperation and then directed him to a dour-faced officer, Inspector Pai, who was apparently in charge of all cold cases that had remained unsolved for over five years. Inspector Pai had, in turn, taken him to his own desk and disappeared to get the case papers, leaving Saralkar to sweat copiously in the sweltering heat. Saralkar had tried the fan but it threatened to blow off the papers spread across Inspector Pai's desk and, therefore, had to be switched off.

Fifteen minutes passed, then twenty, and with every passing second Saralkar's irritation grew. This was a job for PSI Motkar. It was his subordinate who should have been wasting his time and perspiring buckets like that, not he. What was it that Inspector Pai was doing any way, taking so long? Wasn't he supposed to have kept the case file ready since Saralkar had already sent a detailed request before leaving Pune?

The worst part was that he couldn't even snap at the Bangalore Police officer to hurry up. He had no power over him. Saralkar cursed under his breath and continued sweating.

Pai appeared exactly thirty minutes after he had left, as if he had timed his exit and entry. 'Sorry, sir,' he mumbled without looking at Saralkar, as if he didn't think his guest reallydeserved an apology. He placed two box files on the table in front of Saralkar and settled into his own chair with no further comment, with the air of one whose work has been done.

Saralkar held back the urge to thump the table. 'Before I begin going through the files,' he said in an icily polite voice, 'can you please give me a brief summary and background of the cases against Krishna Bhupathi?'

Inspector Pai's dour features registered surprise. He shrugged very slightly and shook his head slowly. 'Sorry, sir. I have not studied the files so far because it is a 2008 case. I'm still reviewing the unsolved cases of 2005.'

Saralkar could have skinned the man alive. But he had to make do with just a click of exasperation. 'Can't I meet the investigating officers of the cases?'

Inspector Pai sighed and consulted the file. 'Sir, the investigating officers were Inspector Hegde and his assistant ASI Murgud ...' He broke off, picked up his phone, and dialled another extension.

A brief conversation in Kannada ensued with whoever was at the other end of the line. Pai kept the phone and turned to Saralkar. 'Sorry, sir, ASI Murgud is transferred to Belgaum and Inspector Hegde is on leave for his daughter's wedding.'

Saralkar was close to bursting with expletives. 'Okay, is there some meeting room or a spare cubicle where I can sit, put on a fan, and go through these files?' he asked Pai, as civilly as he could manage, wondering whether he would get another answer that began with 'Sorry, sir'.

'Oh, please come with me, sir,' Pai replied with surprising geniality and got up to lead the way.

Saralkar thanked God for small mercies and was even more delighted when he was led to a small air-conditioned meeting room.

'Hope this is okay, sir?' Pai asked.

'Thank you,' Saralkar said almost gratefully. 'By the way, there are some documents and reports in Kannada in these files. Who can help me understand the contents?'

'You can please call me, sir,' Pai replied, the dour face breaking into a deferential smile.

PSI Motkar had been determined to regain his standing with Saralkar. He was painfully aware that it was he who should've been in Bangalore instead of his boss, and that Saralkar had been perfectly right in getting pissed off and looking down upon him for using the excuse of the play for not going.

This had come on the heels of Motkar's embarrassing failure to dig out key leads from Mrs Tambe and the Doshi house, which his boss had later managed to. No wonder his stock was at an all-time low with Saralkar. The only way to change that was to slog hard and produce results on various leads by the time Saralkar was back.

Motkar had prepared a list of pending matters that needed to be pursued vigorously in the case. He cast a glance over it to make sure he had not missed out anything. It read:

1) Post-mortem and viscera results
2) Forensic and lab analysis results – fingerprints, suicide note,

fridge contents, locker cash
3) Police artist suspect sketch – Mrs Tambe
4) Sodhi impersonations – trace suspects and interrogate
5) Acid source
6) Complete final caller details verification of both victim phones
7) Follow up Mumbai passport verification of Sanjay Doshi

Motkar's mind hovered briefly over the list. Wasn't there another significant name that had cropped up in Sanjay Doshi's mobile's contact list? A name that needed to be checked? Motkar jogged his memory, then remembered—Akhandanath, the aide of that god-man, Baba Rangdev.

He quickly summoned Constable Shewale, who was taking a tea break. 'Shewale, have you finished all caller verifications on both victims' phones?' Motkar asked as soon as Shewale showed up a few minutes later.

'Sir, document and ID verifications of every caller have been received but physical verification of some is still pending,' Shewale replied.

Physical verification was always a tedious process, Motkar was well aware. 'I want it completed by this evening,' he said bluntly, and was struck at how much he had just sounded like his own boss.

Shewale nodded.

'Have you at least traced Meenakshi Rao's residence and spoken to the neighbours?' Motkar asked.

'Yes, sir. She lives in a one-room kitchen flat in Khadki area. We checked with the neighbours. She had talked of going to Tirupati. She runs a small beauty parlour from home.'

'What about her brother and his family?'

'No, the neighbours just know Meenakshi Rao lives by herself. She's probably a divorcee. One neighbour said a man sometimes visits her but they don't know if he's her brother.'

'Okay, when is she supposed to be back in Pune?'

'Another four to five days, sir. Do you want to speak to her?'

'Not now. But I hope you have confirmed that her current location is really Tirupati.'

'Yes, sir. I've put her phone on tracking.'

'Did you also verify from the tower data if the calls she made to Anushka Doshi were from her home location?'

'I'll do that, sir,' Shewale replied.

'What about Rangdev Baba's aide Akhandanath? Did you speak to him and ask about Sanjay Doshi's connection with Rangdev?'

'No, sir. There's no record of any calls made from or to his mobile by Sanjay Doshi during the week prior to his death. But there was one call about ten days ago. Akhandanath's name also appears in Sanjay Doshi's contact list, that's all.'

'We can't afford to leave it at that, Shewale. He was one of the handful of contacts on Doshi's phone,' PSI Motkar said thoughtfully. 'Call him now and say we'd like to talk to him and Rangdev Baba.'

Shewale nodded, then asked hesitantly, 'Sir, can I ask a question?'

Motkar looked up at him and raised his eyebrows.

'Sir, how come someone outside the squad knows that Rangdev Baba's involved in the case ...?'

'Who said anything about Rangdev Baba being involved in the case?' Motkar asked sharply.

'That's what I am saying, sir. Someone from outside our department wanted to know why we were training our sights on Rangdev Baba,' Shewale clarified.

'Do you mean PSI Sarode or someone else from Kothrud Police Station?' Motkar asked, feeling intrigued.

It was Shewale's turn to be wary now. 'No, sir, no one from Kothrud ...'

'Then who?'

Constable Shewale again hesitated, then decided it was better to reveal all. 'It was my old boss, PSI Dulange ... from Dattawadi Police Chowky. I bumped into him yesterday evening and we got chatting since we were meeting after a long time. Somehow the conversation turned to the Doshi case and Dulange sahib asked me whether the rumour he heard was true that the Homicide Squad was examining the role of Rangdev Baba.'

'Where did he say he heard the rumour?' Motkar asked.

'I inquired, sir, but he was very vague about it. Said he'd picked it up from the departmental grapevine.'

'Hmm,' Motkar said, tapping the tips of his fingers together. 'That's quite odd, because Rangdev Baba isn't yet even high on our priority list.'

'I know, sir, but when Dulange sahib asked me, I wondered whether you or Saralkar sahib had started some discreet inquiry on Rangdev Baba which the rest of us didn't know about and that it had leaked out ...' Shewale remarked.

PSI Motkar was silent for a few seconds, turning it over in his mind. Then he asked, 'This PSI Dulange ... did you feel he was fishing for information from you, Shewale?'

'The thought had crossed my mind, sir,' Shewale admitted, thinking back, '... but he didn't probe too much or too deeply.

Dulange sahib was casual about it. Although in hindsight he did ask one question too many.'

Motkar sighed, now cracking his fingers gently. 'Any reason PSI Dulange might be interested in Rangdev Baba's welfare?'

Shewale shrugged. 'I doubt it, but do you want me to find out, sir?'

'Yes. Better than confronting Dulange right away,' Motkar replied.

Shewale nodded and exited. He was back in less than half an hour. 'Sir!' he said his eyes twinkling with satisfaction. 'PSI Dulange is a regular visitor to Rangdev Baba's ashram. It's because of his son, who's mentally challenged. Apparently, Dulange has become something of a devotee because going to the Baba seems to have improved his child's condition.'

PSI Motkar leaned forward slowly on his desk like a sailor quietly elated at the possibility of spotting land soon.

'Okay, so something's making Rangdev Baba nervous about his Doshi connection and we need to find out what and why.'

He rapped the desk with uncharacteristic spontaneity and wondered if he was turning into a mirror image of his boss in the latter's absence!

13

SO SHAUNAK SODHI WAS FOR REAL, SARALKAR REFLECTED, AS THE contents of the case files, which he had spent nearly the whole day reading, spun around in his mind! Indeed, Shaunak Sodhi and Krishna Bhupathi alias Sanjay Doshi had been partners in Bangalore—partners in a lucrative job and immigration racket that lured thousands of foolish, gullible, desperate young men and women to beg, borrow or steal two to five lakh rupees each and deposit it with their partnership firm, Bingo Overseas Recruitment & Immigration Services (BORIS), in the hope of landing jobs in distant foreign lands.

But BORIS also had a third partner—Rahul Fernandes. Together the three partners cheated and duped youth from all over Karnataka—Bangalore, Mysore, Hubli, Dharwad, Belgaum, Davangere, Gulbarga, Mangalore, Bellary—between 2004 and 2008. And all the cash they had collected from these hapless job-seekers was promptly channelised into land deals, betting, horse racing, and high-end escort services.

With hard-edged cynicism, Saralkar read page after page of heart-wrenching stories of the scam victims who had been ruined or left in debt or those who had wiped away the life savings of their poor parents. His lips curled in contempt at the credulity of these wretched souls, blinded by the prospect of foreign jobs. As a long-serving police officer, he had seen it all before and still had not found the answer to the question of how and why people got taken in by such swindlers and trusted them with unaffordable sums that could instead have been used to build a better life in their own country. What was it that got into them? Why didn't any alarm bells ring? What inspired so much confidence in these charlatans that a man was ready to risk a sum that he knew had the power to sink him if the promised job did not materialise? Why had no inner voice or well-wishers warned them?

Eventually and inevitably, some of those duped by BORIS had filed police cases and that's how Krishna Bhupathi, Shaunak Sodhi and Rahul Fernandes had first come to the notice of the Karnataka Police. The partners had been first arrested in Gulbarga but soon released for lack of enough corroborative evidence. The complainants had paid the money in cash and all that they had to show for it were printed receipts that proved nothing. The partners produced a few candidates who had been given jobs by BORIS, demolished the contentions of complainants that any job guarantee assurance had been given, bribed policemen, and continued with their racket.

Similar arrests and releases occurred in other towns in Karnataka between 2007 and 2008, but then they came up against a more serious challenge. In early 2008, the aggrieved parents of an unemployed young man who had died by suicide in Bangalore filed a case against the trio. Their son's suicide note formed the basis of the complaint. Saralkar had requested Inspector Pai to read out the note to him, since it was written in Kannada. The young man had outlined in some detail how Bhupathi and Sodhi had systematically set up the trap, the lies, the false promises, the extraction of money, the stalling, their refusal to refund and, finally, the threats and intimidation he had suffered. The young man had written of his bewilderment and frustration, his utter helplessness and, ultimately, how it had brought about his financial downfall. He blamed them squarely for the hell his life had become and held them solely responsible for his decision to end his life.

The human tragedy had caught the fancy of the media. It was just the kind of story that sent TRPs soaring and left people outraged. The result was a huge uproar that lasted long enough for the heat to be turned on, on the police. The partners-in-crime were in real trouble this time. The Karnataka Human Rights Commission also took suo motto notice and a full-fledged police investigation into the wrongdoings began, headed by an upright senior officer.

Krishna Bhupathi and Shaunak Sodhi were taken into custody and subjected to intense interrogation. Rahul Fernandes, though, managed to get anticipatory bail, claiming he had no knowledge of his partners' nefarious activities. It, of course, helped that the young man had dealt with Bhupathi and Sodhi and therefore only named them in his note. And that laid the foundation for what was to follow.

After a two-month incarceration, Bhupathi and Sodhi were chargesheeted for the jobs racket and were released on bail. One month after their release, Fernandes's wife filed a police complaint that her husband had gone missing. Rahul Fernandes had gone out with his partners the previous evening to settle their disputes and had not come back thereafter. His wife was scared he had come to harm because he had claimed to her a few times that his life was in danger from Bhupathi and Sodhi. Preliminary inquiries revealed that Fernandes's bloodstained pullover was found in Krishna Bhupathi's car while Shaunak Sodhi was absconding.

Fernandes had last been seen getting into Bhupathi's car, completely drunk and being escorted by Sodhi. Krishna Bhupathi was taken into custody and under third-degree interrogation he had confessed that Shaunak Sodhi and he had nursed a grudge against Fernandes because while they had been in jail for two months, he had quietly liquidated a lot of properties they had purchased jointly and had double-crossed the other two. He was only ready to give them a very small sum, well below the estimated amount he had made.

There had been several heated arguments between them and Sodhi and Bhupathi had hit upon a plan to settle scores with Fernandes. They had fixed up a meeting and invited Fernandes for a final amicable settlement. They had pretended to come to terms and had plied Fernandes with liquor, then taken him to a remote place outside Bangalore city. There they tortured him and extracted all the true details of the land and property sales he had done. Thereafter, they had taken him to the place where he kept all his cash—a farmhouse near Nandi Hills, removed the cash and decided to leave Fernandes there. But he had sworn to take revenge and a scuffle had ensued.

Bhupathi claimed he was too drunk to remember what happened then but when he got up in the middle of the night, Fernandes's dead body was on the floor and Sodhi claimed that both of them had killed him. Shaken and dazed, unsure of what exactly had transpired, Bhupathi said he simply did what Sodhi instructed him to because he was unable to think properly and was scared. When Sodhi said they needed to dispose of Fernandes's body, they dumped the corpse in Bhupathi's car and drove towards Mysore. Sodhi guided him off the highway on to a side road that led into a jungle-like area. Here they severed the head and limbs of the body with a sickle and knives they had found at Fernandes's farmhouse and buried the torso in a ditch.

Then they drove to Mysore and onward to Mercara. They disposed of the head and limbs at different spots in the valley on the way up the hill road. Turning around, they drove back to Mysore where Sodhi told him it would be safer to disperse and go their separate ways. Sodhi also said they should lie low for a few days and advised Bhupathi to leave Bangalore for some time. He gave Bhupathi a small amount of the cash and took the rest with him, promising to get in touch after a month or so.

Still in a state of panic, Bhupathi drove back to Bangalore to collect his family, wind up things, and flee Bangalore for a couple of months. But just before he could abscond, the police arrested him based on Fernandes's wife's complaint. Following his confession, the Bangalore Police took Bhupathi along to retrieve Rahul Fernandes's body but he was unable to locate the spot along Mysore highway. Nor were Fernandes's head or limbs recovered despite search operations on Mercara road. In the hilly terrain near Mercara especially, the police said it was quite possible that wild animals had eaten the body parts.

The bloodied clothes of Fernandes were the only evidence now apart from Bhupathi's confession. Realising that the body was not being found, Bhupathi retracted his confession and said it had been made under duress. Sodhi, too, could not be nabbed and so in the absence of clinching evidence of murder, the Bangalore Police could not file a chargesheet within the mandatory period of ninety days.

Bhupathi thus became eligible for bail and promptly secured

it. Ten days later he disappeared, leaving behind his family, and had remained untraceable thereafter.

Saralkar shut the files. This was as far back as 2008. In 2015, Bhupathi had been found dead in Pune as Sanjay Doshi, and Shaunak Sodhi had been mentioned in his suicide note. So where had Bhupathi and Sodhi been for seven long years? What had they done? How had they successfully evaded the law? When and where had Anushka come into the picture? How had Sanjay and Anushka met? Why had Bhupathi changed his name but not Sodhi?

But before he attempted to find answers to these questions, Saralkar had a few questions relating to the three partners prior to 2008, culminating in Fernandes's murder. And for that he needed to meet Inspector Hegde who had investigated the case. An official request had been made to Hegde, and although busy with his daughter's wedding, he had promised to be available the day after. So, what was he to do for one full day, Saralkar wondered. Maybe he could try and meet the families of Fernandes, Sodhi and Bhupathi, his mind promptly provided the answer.

When was the last time she had been to a post office, Kunika Ahuja wondered. Not in the last five years, at least, she concluded. Who sent letters these days? And even if you had to send one, official or personal, couriers were so much more convenient and accessible. In the universe of modern, middle-class India—with cell phones and the internet—post offices were more or less redundant. Post offices were for the poor or lower-income groups—places where you sent your peon or driver when something had to be sent by post.

Kunika Ahuja had first thought of going to the small post office in her neighbourhood, then thought the better of it. There was always the chance of bumping into the postman on her beat or meeting some acquaintances. Anonymity would be best preserved by going to a bigger post office like the GPO or City Post or Shivajinagar PO, where she would be a stranger and one among the many visitors. She had finally decided upon GPO because you could park your car inside.

She looked at the envelope in her hands addressed to Inspector Saralkar of the Pune Homicide Squad. She had looked up the address on the net. She wasn't even sure of the value of stamps she needed to affix on it to send by ordinary post. Was it still five rupees? Nervous, she stood in the stamp counter queue. After months, she had ventured out without her dog.

'What value of stamps do I need to put on an ordinary post envelope?' she asked when her turn came.

'Five rupees for the first twenty grams,' the lady at the counter answered mechanically.

'Okay. Please give me two stamps of five rupees.'

The transaction completed, Kunika Ahuja looked around for the bottle of glue that she remembered would generally be kept in most post offices. Licking stamps had never been her thing. Whatever else had changed, the blue bottle of glue had remained exactly like earlier times—a pasty, sticky, white gruel that made you feel as yucky as licking stamps. But you chose the gruel only because you had to use your fingers, not your tongue.

Kunika Ahuja quickly pasted both stamps. She knew one five-rupee stamp would have sufficed, but why take a chance? Walking out she glanced at the post boxes and took a deep breath, still wondering if she needed to do this. She moved closer to the post box marked local and her right hand hovered by the dropping slit, still unsure.

'You can give that to me.' Kunika Ahuja froze as a postman appeared from nowhere with a sack in one hand and a key in the other. 'I am just clearing this box.'

He began unlocking the box and taking out the gathered letters, which he dropped into the sack. There were not many. He finished his task and held out a hand for her envelope. She knew it would look odd if she didn't give it to him. Kunika Ahuja's hands were shaking as she handed the envelope to the postman, with its face turned down so that he would not notice the address. But almost as a reflex action he turned it over, probably to check that stamps had been affixed.

Kunika Ahuja turned and quickly walked away, her heart beating faster. Had the postman noticed the address? What if he had? It didn't mean her anonymity was blown. The postman had seen her but he didn't know her name so it didn't matter, she told herself.

She got into her car hurriedly and glanced back at the postal employee. He wasn't standing and staring or looking at her with curiosity about why some lady was sending a letter to the Homicide Squad. In all probability, he didn't even know the meaning of homicide, she thought. He was already opening the other post box and emptying its contents into another sack.

Kunika Ahuja gave a sigh of relief, got into her car, and drove away.

14

MRS SEEMA TAMBE HAD TURNED OUT TO BE THE POLICE SKETCH artist's dream witness. Inhibited initially by extreme nervousness and fear, she had relaxed as the young, soft-spoken police artist gently asked her questions for making the sketch. He had also shown her different types of facial features and options to choose from and ferreted out details of the man she had seen arguing with Sanjay and Anushka Doshi.

Her fear forgotten, and fascinated by the police artist's work, Seema Tambe had begun recollecting and describing features and nuanced characteristics of the face, as if she had a photographic memory. Even her daughter and husband listened with awe at her level of observation.

The face soon began emerging on the screen—thick, long, coarse and unkempt hair, like that of Indian pace bowler Ishant Sharma; a narrow, pimply forehead; a hooked nose between two light brown, staring eyes; a grizzled moustache bordering a thick, upper lip pushed upward by two teeth that jutted out below just a bit; skinny cheeks sloping down to a narrow chin with a slight stubble. Red and black threads adorned his neck and a small, silver-coloured amulet dangled from the black thread. The first button of the man's shirt was open, with a goggle straddled across the second button.

Overall, it gave the impression of a scowling young man in his twenties who projected a self-image of strength and menace.

'Does it now resemble the man you saw?' the police artist asked. 'Or does any feature require alteration or does not quite fit in?'

Mrs Seema Tambe studied the image closely, trying to mentally match it with the man she had seen in flesh and blood. Everything seemed to be right but she had a feeling she was missing something—as if one little detail was creating a distortion that stopped the picture from being complete. And then she remembered. 'Just ... just one small change,' she said, her face suffused with excitement. 'One of his ears, his right ear, actually, was slightly folded and crumpled on top ... like a ... a rose that has half-opened petals.'

She paused and looked at the police artist as if apologising for her inadequate powers of description. 'Do you ... do you understand? What I mean?'

The police artist gave her a little smile, once again impressed by the middle-aged housewife. 'I think I know what you mean, Mrs Tambe.' It was such details that greatly enhanced the effectiveness of police sketches as identification tools. He quickly proceeded to make a few changes to the ear, trying out a couple of permutations then settled on one and sat back. 'Is that how it looked?' he asked her after a few minutes, turning the screen towards her again.

Seema Tame looked and gave a little gasp, 'Yes that's exactly how it was!' She suddenly seemed to feel lighter, as if the pall of fear and anxiousness were lifting. She turned and smiled at her husband and daughter, her eyes wet with tears.

Saralkar thanked the slim, middle-aged lady for the glass of water. Uneasiness was writ large on her face. Despite her prematurely grey hair, the bags under her eyes and the stamp of worry almost tattooed onto every inch of her face, Sanjay Doshi's first wife, rather Krishna Bhupathi's first wife, Latha Bhupathi, was a far better-looking woman than his second one, Anushka Doshi.

He was suddenly curious to know how and why Krishna Bhupathi had chosen to marry Anushka Doshi? What were the charms he had fallen for? Of one thing he was certain: it could not have been Anushka Doshi's looks!

It was a theory he had long held that men who had more than one woman in their lives, essentially mated a second time either with the same type of woman as their first wife or partner or girlfriend, or with someone who had exactly opposite personality traits. He wondered what similarities or dissimilarities between Latha Bhupathi and Anushka Doshi had influenced Krishna Bhupathi's choice of both spouses.

'You said you had news of my husband, Krishna Bhupathi,' Latha Bhupathi asked tonelessly, keeping the emotions zig-zagging across her face out of her voice. 'We haven't heard anything from him since the day he ... fled ... abandoned me and my son.'

'Nothing at all?' Saralkar asked.

Latha Bhupathi hesitated slightly, the fingers of her left hand rotating the single gold bangle on her right hand. 'No, nothing,' she asserted.

'Why do I find that hard to believe?'

She looked up at him and then down at the bangle again. 'Because it is your job to doubt everybody, making no distinction between a crook and his family members.'

She had suffered, Saralkar could make out, like thousands of innocent family members of hundreds of runaway criminals. Subjected to repeated interrogation, accusations, humiliation, dire warnings, threats and shaming by the police in their quest to nab fugitives and criminals who had left these soft targets behind to face the consequences of their misdeeds.

'Are you saying he hasn't tried to get in touch with you even once in all these years? By phone or letter or email or in person or through someone?'

Latha Bhupathi shook her head slightly, as if she felt no need to emphasise this simple truth.

'Why is that? Did your son and you mean so little to him?' Saralkar remarked. Sometimes taunts worked and provoked.

Latha Bhupathi shrugged. 'Perhaps,' she replied evenly.

Again, Saralkar noticed a mismatch between the tone of her voice and the expressions on her face.

'Maybe he was just too scared to take the risk,' she spoke again.

'Why? Did he think you would've reported him to the police?' Saralkar asked.

'I don't know what he thought,' she replied abruptly. 'Have you found Krishna?'

Saralkar did not answer, instead putting another question. 'What do you think? Did he murder his partner, Rahul Fernandes?'

'I don't know. Please, inspector, I have answered all these questions over and over again at that time and from time to time since then,' she replied wearily.

'Your husband had confessed to the murder, you know, although he retracted it later. But you were his wife and perhaps know the truth. He must've told you something before disappearing, when he came out on bail. Or even earlier when you were all going to abscond just before he was caught,' Saralkar said.

'I had already told the police what I knew.'

'Can you please repeat it for me?'

Latha Bhupathi's eyes flashed suddenly. 'But why? You haven't told me why you've come and what news you have about Krishna. I want to know first,' she said, looking at him defiantly.

Saralkar reached into his shirt pocket and produced a colour photocopy of Sanjay Doshi's passport. He opened the first page and thrust it in her direction.

She took the papers in her hand, closely looked at them and blinked several times. For a moment she was speechless, her attention riveted on the passport. Then she looked up at Saralkar, her eyes wide with disbelief and glistening with emotion. 'It's him,' she said in a hushed voice. 'That's what he is living as now?'

'Yes, that's the current identity since 2012 at least. We are still not sure where he was between 2008 and 2012. Are you a hundred per cent sure it's your husband Krishna Bhupathi?'

She nodded. 'Has he been arrested? Have you brought him here to Bangalore ... to face trial for the Fernandes murder?'

'No,' Saralkar replied, then cleared his throat, calculating if he could get more information by withholding the revelation of her husband's death or by telling her right away. He realised he had one more question up his sleeve to double-check whether this woman had been in touch with her husband and known his whereabouts.

'Did you know he married another woman?' he asked.

A stunned expression rocked Latha Bhupathi's face. And

Saralkar knew it was too genuine to be put on. If Latha Bhupathi had had any contact with her husband, she would certainly not remain quiet now, he was confident.

Her palm had now wrapped itself around the bangle and pressed down on the inside of her wrist. Saralkar could almost hear the angry, vindictive thoughts circling inside her mind now—*'He ran away, abandoned me and my child, ruined my life and happiness and he goes and gets married to some bitch!'*

'Now that I have told you news about your husband, can you answer my earlier question?' Saralkar asked, seizing the psychological moment. 'What did he tell you about his involvement in his partner's murder? Was he guilty?'

Latha Bhupathi did not break into tears or resort to hysterical ranting. But for once, the expressions on her face matched her tone of voice. Both were harsh. 'Krishna told me he and Sodhi confronted Fernandes for double-crossing them and thrashed and tortured him that night. But he was too drunk to remember if he had a hand in actually killing Fernandes. Krishna's gut instinct was that Sodhi killed Fernandes when he had fallen asleep for some time. He told me he was so scared and numbed by the sight of the blood and the body thereafter that he just did what Sodhi told him to. Krishna also admitted to me that he had helped Sodhi in getting rid of the body, driving to Mysore and Mercara and all that. But he kept denying he participated in Fernandes's murder.'

'And you believed him?' Saralkar could see she was biting back anger and bitterness.

'Krishna was bitten by the "get rich" bug,' she finally said. 'That's why he could be crooked, could cheat, deceive, do all such things. But I didn't think, still don't think, he was capable of murder.'

'Then why did he run away? In fact immediately after the murder also he wanted to abscond along with you and your son, but the police landed up just as you were leaving.'

'Immediately after the murder Krishna was terrified ... in absolute panic! He just wanted to disappear from Bangalore. He had no idea where we would flee, where we would hide. He just kept pleading with me to go with him. I tried to talk sense into him but he wanted to get away from the city. Our son was ill, down with a viral and very high fever, so I told Krishna it would not be wise to travel with him in such a condition. He agreed to wait for a day and said he would come back to fetch me early next morning. My son's condition improved overnight but just as we were about to leave early next morning, the police arrived and nabbed him.'

'What about later, after he was released on bail? What made him run then?' Saralkar grilled her further. 'Why did he leave you and your son behind? Why didn't you go with him?'

Latha Bhupathi flushed angrily and replied, 'Because I had committed no crime! I had a son to look after and bring up. I had a proper job. If Krishna was convicted either for the job racket or the murder or both, I knew he would be behind bars for a long time. Running away was no solution. What future would I give my son as a fugitive from law? The only sensible thing to do was to remain here in Bangalore, where I had a job, so that I could give my son a respectable future even if his father was convicted as a criminal ... Krishna spoilt his own life; I wasn't going to let him spoil my son's life because of that.'

She stopped, her face fierce and suffused with the emotions and convictions behind her choices.

'So you knew he was going to abscond after he got bail,' Saralkar remarked. 'Why didn't you try and stop him?'

Latha Bhupathi looked across at him with an inscrutable expression. 'I knew Krishna was planning to disappear. He told me he had no alternative. Sodhi had absconded, so if Fernandes's body were found, Krishna's goose would be cooked. On the other hand, he was afraid of Sodhi, having witnessed what he had done to Fernandes. Then there was also the rumour that Fernandes's family was seeking revenge—that they had put out a contract for having him killed. That's why he wanted to run away while he could, to save his own life. He kept trying to persuade me but I had made up my mind. But ... you are right; I didn't try to stop him because I realised running away was Krishna's only chance.'

'I see,' Saralkar said and paused. He knew he had to tell her about Krishna Bhupathi's fate now.

But Latha Bhupathi spoke again before he could, asking a flurry of questions. 'So ... does Krishna and his second wife have children? How did you find him? Has he committed any more crimes? Will he spend the rest of his life in jail now? Will my son have to know?'

Saralkar shook his head. 'Your husband, Krishna Bhupathi alias Sanjay Doshi, and his second wife Anushka, were found dead in their rented apartment in Pune last week.'

'What?' Latha Bhupathi looked as if she had been hit by a train.

'Yes. It seems he killed her and then committed suicide.'

'Oh, my God!' Latha Bhupathi had started trembling. A shattered look of immense hopelessness had come into her eyes, as if something inside had gone to pieces. Perhaps the distant hope that some day she would be united with her husband or that there would be a not-too-unhappy ending. Or maybe the horror of realising that her husband was indeed a killer, not once but two times over.

She sat like that, shell-shocked, as if her mind refused to deal with or process the facts she had just been told. Saralkar let her be. When she finally gathered herself, Latha Bhupathi said, 'All these years ... I told my son his father ran away because he was not a murderer ... because he couldn't prove his innocence. Now what do I tell him? That I had lied to him ... that the blood of a killer runs in his veins—a man who has killed twice?'

Saralkar felt something approaching sympathy for Latha Bhupathi. He wondered whether to tell her that there was a possibility her husband had not killed his second wife and himself.

What she asked next made it almost unavoidable.

'Why did Krishna ... do it?'

Saralkar grunted. He held out a copy of Sanjay Doshi's suicide note. 'That's what he left behind.'

She took the note and her eyes ran down the lines rapidly. Then, as if she hadn't understood the first time, her eyes again started at the top and went over the lines more slowly. Finally, she looked up from it into the far distance, her eyes moist, her shoulders slumped. 'Poor Krishna! Ultimately that beast Shaunak Sodhi ruined him! Why couldn't he have stayed away from him?'

Saralkar asked, 'Are you sure it's Krishna's handwriting?'

She nodded without any hesitation, still looking away. 'Yes. But ... but ... not a word about me or our son ... perhaps he had long forgotten us,' she paused and wiped her tears. 'How am I to believe we ... weren't in his thoughts, at least in his last moments.'

She choked, swallowing back a sob.

Saralkar waited uncomfortably. Tears always stumped him. If she was keeping any secrets, now was probably the only time she would speak.

'Inspector?' she finally said. 'It is not completely true that Krishna never got in touch.'

Saralkar sat up alert. 'Yes ...' he encouraged her gently.

'Krishna ... he ... I mean ... every year or two, I would receive a DD from him. There would be no name, no address, nothing. Just an envelope with a DD. I knew it had to be from Krishna ... for us, for my son ... but I kept it all in a separate account. I knew it was crime money, tainted with blood. I had decided to use it only if my son needed it at some time, if I could not provide the amount required from my earnings and savings.'

'When was the last time a DD came?'

'About a month ago. Of ten lakhs and ...' she hesitated, 'around the same time I also got a blank call on my land line.'

'Blank call?'

'Yes, I was sure it was Krishna calling. It has happened earlier too. He never spoke a word but I would know it was him.'

'How often did it happen?'

'Once in two years, not often ... but I could just immediately sense it was Krishna.'

She stopped and began composing herself. 'That's all I know, and nothing more.'

For all his cynicism, Saralkar thought she was telling the truth. He thanked the unfortunate Latha Bhupathi and took her leave.

15

PSI MOTKAR HAD NEVER MET PSI DULANGE IN THE COURSE of his police career. Their paths had never crossed. Motkar had made the decision to talk to him immediately after Constable Shewale told him that Rangdev Baba was conducting a health camp at his ashram that day.

Motkar had thought it prudent not to meet the god-man on a day his ashram was swarming with devotees. Instead, he had decided to ambush PSI Dulange. With Shewale in tow, Motkar had landed unannounced at the Dattawadi Police Station and requested two minutes of PSI Dulange's time—a reasonable enough request which no police officer could refuse a brother officer of the same or higher rank.

'Where did you hear that the Homicide Squad suspects Rangdev Baba's involvement in the Doshi case?' PSI Motkar asked him bluntly, without beating around the bush.

Dulange was clearly discomfited, passing his tongue over his lips while throwing an uneasy glace at Constable Shewale out of the corner of his eye. 'Departmental grapevine,' he replied tentatively.

'There is nothing on the grapevine to that effect,' Motkar said tersely. 'Look, were you making inquiries on behalf of Rangdev Baba?'

PSI Dulange went pale and tried to look offended. 'Bullshit! How can you—?'

'We know you go to his ashram with your son, that you are his devotee,' Motkar cut in.

Dulange swallowed the words of angry denial coming out of his mouth, clearly flustered. 'So—so what?' he finally stammered.

'Look, Dulange, this does not have to go any further. Just tell us what you know of Rangdev Baba's involvement in this matter. Why exactly has he asked you to find out why his name figures in the investigations?' Motkar said in a matter-of-fact tone.

PSI Dulange regarded him with a cornered expression, then gave Constable Shewale an injured look, as if he had betrayed his confidence. Inwardly, he was cursing his indiscretion. He knew the Homicide Squad could get an internal inquiry ordered about his conduct and even if nothing came of it, it would unnecessarily create complications for him and blot his record. Wisdom lay in telling Motkar everything. None of what he knew implicated him seriously in trying to help Rangdev so far.

'So, what is it going to be? Are you going to speak or do I have to do this officially?' Motkar asked, inserting a bit of impatience into his tone.

'Will you promise this won't go any further? No internal inquiry if I tell you?'

'Can't promise. But if there is no criminality involved, or there was no intention to help Rangdev escape the law, there is no reason for us to report you. Depends on how serious it is and whether you come clean. Complete disclosure.'

PSI Dulange cleared his throat and began talking. 'Look, this Rangdev Baba has been good for my son, Anand. There is great improvement in his condition ... and I—I felt obliged to him.

Believe me, Rangdev Baba is not like other god-men. That's why when he asked me to check if your investigations pointed towards him and his ashram, I agreed to try and find out. That's all.'

He paused, looking at both Motkar and Shewale nervously.

'But what's the story behind Rangdev's discomfiture? How did he know Sanjay Doshi?' Motkar asked.

'Well, apparently, Doshi used to visit the ashram as a devotee. But then he and two of Baba Rangdev's disciples started some unsavoury racket together. When Baba found out, he immediately put an end to it and debarred Doshi from visiting the ashram. He was also going to throw out the two disciples but said he had to forgive them and give another chance, when they repented and begged him to condone their behaviour,' Dulange explained anxiously. 'Baba was worried that given the circumstances of Doshi's death, his links to the ashram may surface and the police might start probing the angle. He felt such an investigation may tarnish his and his ashram's image ... that's why he wanted me to try and find out.'

PSI Motkar was appalled. He frowned, 'As a police officer, didn't you find all this fishy? Didn't you smell a rat? How could you even think of helping him?'

'Look, of course, I asked him to give me details and only after I was convinced what he said was genuine, did I agree. I could not say no to him after all that he had done for my son. He's a good man,' PSI Dulange said wretchedly.

'So, what was this racket that Doshi ran with Rangdev's disciples?'

'Apparently, Sanjay Doshi and Baba's two disciples had started a racket of siphoning off a portion of the donation cash and using it for betting purposes. The two disciples also used inside information of various devotees for blackmailing them. Rangdev Baba conducts these sessions where devotees confess to their sins and misdeeds in strict confidence. One of those two disciples was sometimes privy to such secrets, which were then misused by Doshi.'

Dulange paused again. 'That's all I know; that's what Baba told me.'

'I see,' Motkar said thoughtfully.

This information added a whole new dimension to the mystery of Sanjay and Anushka Doshi's deaths. If Sanjay Doshi was indeed using donation money for betting and had also been blackmailing some of Rangdev's devotees, then the field of suspects would be far wider. It also gave enough cause for Rangdev Baba to be worried if the nefarious activities of his devotees and Sanjay Doshi were linked to Doshi's death.

And yet, Motkar felt a sliver of doubt as if the information did not quite fit in with what they had got to know about Sanjay and Anushka Doshi so far. Given Doshi's criminal background of fraud, employment rackets and land scamming, Motkar had no problems accepting that he could've been involved in siphoning off donation money for betting with Rangdev's disciples. But somehow, the blackmailing racket hit a false note. Even criminals had comfort zones of the kind of crimes they could attempt and commit. He very much doubted if blackmail would fall into Doshi's comfort zone. It required a different set of skills and more importantly, temperament.

But then so did murder and suicide, Motkar's mind immediately countered. So, if Doshi could've committed murder, then why not blackmail.

'Did Rangdev give you the names of his two disciples who

had joined hands with Sanjay Doshi?' he asked PSI Dulange who was fidgeting anxiously.

'No, no ... actually I asked him ... but he said he would rather not tell me their names.'

'And that's all you know? You are not keeping anything at all from us, Dulange?' PSI Motkar asked with a warning note in his voice.

'I swear on my son,' PSI Dulange said, sounding suddenly desperate. 'That's all I know, Motkar. Believe me. I—I know I made a mistake ... I didn't want to do it. I wouldn't have done it if I suspected Baba's involvement even for a minute. I still think Baba is innocent. He was just worried. Believe me, I did it because he's been a miracle for my son ... You don't know how Baba has changed our lives. After all these years of sheer frustration and desperation ...' He stopped, almost embarrassed by his emotional outburst, but Motkar could see it was genuine. He believed the man had only done it out of a misplaced sense of obligation to Baba Rangdev, who had provided him an enormous relief in life.

'Please ... I've told you the truth, Motkar. Don't foist an internal inquiry on me,' Dulange pleaded.

PSI Motkar nodded. 'The final decision will be that of my boss, Senior Inspector Saralkar. But I'll try my best,' he said. 'Better pray that Rangdev Baba hasn't been fooling you too and isn't more deeply involved in Doshi's case. And, yes, you dare not let Rangdev Baba know about this conversation. If you breathe a word, I can't save you.'

Dulange nodded and then shook his head vehemently as if to say he'd never open his mouth again.

Sherly Fernandes directed a hostile, unpleasant gaze at Senior Inspector Saralkar. Her green eyes were icy. The first incongruity that struck Saralkar was that she was wearing a saree. Given her name, the senior inspector had expected someone in Western attire. Another stereotypical, stupid assumption, Saralkar realised sheepishly.

Secondly, she hardly looked like someone who had once been a model—neither good features, nor charm, nor curvaceousness. In fact, her appearance was gaunt and hard-edged, utterly lacking in softness. Maybe the years and events had taken their toll, but could they have completely erased any hint of the original spark? A fleeting thought crossed his mind. Could it be that model was a euphemism and that Sherly Fernandes had actually been a part of the escort services that the three partners had invested in, before becoming Rahul Fernandes' wife?

'Why did you want to meet me?' she asked in a sharp, throaty voice. 'It's been seven years. Can't the police leave me in peace? For God's sake, I've moved on! Don't I have a right to put all that behind me now?'

Her greenish-grey eyes were full of resentment and her teeth dug into her lower lip, as if she were biting back the urge to attack Saralkar physically.

'I'm going to smoke,' she declared defiantly, and dipped into her purse.

'Do you think Krishna Bhupathi and Shaunak Sodhi killed your husband, Rahul Fernandes?' Saralkar asked evenly.

'Of course. Who else?' she replied tersely, taking the first puff of the cigarette she had lit.

'I understand Rahul had told you earlier that he feared for his life?' Saralkar asked, shifting slightly away to get out of the path of her smoke.

A bitter smile appeared on her face, happy perhaps that her cigarette smoke was affecting Saralkar.

'Yes. Rahul told me he was afraid Bhupathi and Sodhi would try and kill him.'

'Why?'

'Obviously because he had double-crossed them while they were imprisoned in the job racket case. He had got rid of all properties, raked in the cash, and was cheating them of their fair shares,' Sherly Fernandes replied succinctly. She ran her tongue over the coat of lipstick on her lips, making it glossy, then took another puff. Unlike many women who smoked, she appeared to inhale deeply.

'You knew he had actually double-crossed them?' Saralkar asked.

'I didn't know it for a fact. I just knew Rahul well. He was a crook, out and out.'

'So, if he was feeling threatened, why did he go out with them that evening, all alone?'

'To try and come to a settlement, of course.'

'And what exactly did he tell you before leaving?'

Sherly Fernandes scowled at him for a second, then took two puffs before replying, 'You are just making me repeat everything. Rahul said I should file a police complaint if he didn't turn up by next morning. I did exactly that.'

'But it says here you lodged a complaint only the following late night.'

'They shooed me away when I went in the morning. Only after I went back with a lawyer did they file the FIR late at night,' she replied.

'Why didn't you go to Bhupathi's or Sodhi's house and confront them?'

'And get killed just like Rahul? No, thanks. I called their numbers but there was no response. Look, what's the point of all this?'

She threw down her cigarette and crushed it with her sandal. 'Are you just trying to tally what I said then and now?' she gave him a challenging look. 'Rahul's dead, Sodhi disappeared, Bhupathi confessed to the police and then he too fled. How does any of this change the facts? And why ask me?'

Saralkar regarded the woman in front of him and an idea suddenly began to form in his mind. 'So what happened to all the money that Rahul had?' he asked.

Sherly Fernandes blinked. 'Money ... I—uhh—I ... what do you mean? Sodhi and Bhupathi made Rahul reveal where he had stacked the cash ... before killing him ... that's what he said in his confession. I don't have any of it, if that's what you are implying.'

'You mean you didn't know where your husband had hidden the money or that he had no alternate hiding place where he left something behind for you?' Saralkar said in a tone loaded with deliberate disbelief.

The expressions on her face became more cunning and her mouth twisted. 'You think I would've remained in India if Rahul had left me money, or I knew where he had hidden the rest of it? All I got was the flat we were staying in and what was in his bank, which was peanuts. All the rest of his money had disappeared, taken by the other two; that's the reason they have never been found, have they?'

'I see,' Saralkar observed, searching her face for the slightest of signs she was hiding something. 'If Rahul was scared for his life, didn't he take any precautions to protect himself? No bodyguards or at least a gun for self-defence?'

'Rahul always carried a small gun,' Sherly replied, a trifle ruffled by Saralkar's questions. 'Even on that night ...'

Saralkar couldn't recollect any mention of a gun in the police report by the Bangalore Homicide Squad that he had read. This bit of news had come as a surprise. He made a mental note to check when he finally met Inspector Hegde.

'Okay. I've heard a contract was placed by Rahul's family to get Sodhi and Bhupathi eliminated. Do you know anything about that?' Saralkar asked, watching her closely.

Sherly Fernandes stared at him. 'Contract to kill! By Rahul's family? I—I have no idea what you are talking about ... I mean, Rahul had no family other than me ... and I didn't place any such contract.'

'You mean he had no family whatsoever?'

'No. Why don't you read my statements to the police? I have told all this to that officer. ASI Murgud, I think. Rahul was orphaned when he was still a kid; his father died first and then his mother, in Goa. He came to Bangalore after that.' She paused and gave him an uneasy glance. 'Can you leave me in peace now?'

Saralkar nodded but made no effort to go. 'How long were you and Rahul married?'

'Three years.'

'Were you aware he was a criminal before you married him?'

She considered the question, running her tongue over her lips again. 'Well, I knew he was no saint, but I thought he was more like a normal, dishonest businessman, not a criminal.'

'I see. How happy was your marriage with Rahul Fernandes?'

Her eyes flashed. 'How's that your business? What's that got to do with anything?'

'Well, three people stood to benefit from Rahul's death—Sodhi, Bhupathi and you. I don't see you having done any follow up with the Bangalore Police to solve the case. You didn't even ask me if I had found his killers,' Saralkar said in a mean, mocking tone. 'It makes me wonder. Not exactly the picture of a grieving wife who cared about her husband, especially one who met a gruesome fate.'

Sherly Fernandes's eyes had become as big as saucers and blazed with a seething sadness. 'Marrying Rahul was the biggest mistake of my life. Not only was he a criminal, he made life hell for me ... in ways you can't imagine, inspector. Sodhi and Bhupathi did me a big favour by killing him, although I was not involved in his death. I filed the police complaint only because Rahul had warned me to, but no one was happier than me to know when it was confirmed he was murdered. Why? Because I got my life back. I escaped from hell,' she paused and gave a harsh, mirthless laugh, before continuing. 'Why should I want to follow up for justice? Rahul wasn't a man I loved or cared for. He was a horrid pervert and a criminal who was murdered by two other criminals. What's it to me if you bring them to justice or don't?'

Sherly Fernandes stood up, shaking with anger and indignation.

Saralkar remained seated. 'Looks like you've undergone a lot. Can you tell me what hellish treatment Rahul subjected you to, to earn such hatred?'

'Are you just pretending you don't know what I have told the Bangalore Police already?' she shouted at him, completely livid now as if he had kept touching a raw nerve. 'Just get lost from here, inspector. I have nothing more to say to you.'

Saralkar was stung. Never before had he been told to 'get lost' so peremptorily. No one would have dared to dismiss him like that in Pune. But this was Bangalore, where he could wield little authority as a Maharashtra Police officer. There wasn't much he could do.

'Didn't you hear me? Get out!' Sherly Fernandes said once again. Her green eyes were glistening with scorn and bitterness.

Saralkar reddened and got up. Swallowing the insult, he tried his final gambit. 'Krishna Bhupathi was found hanging in his Pune home last week ...'

He left the sentence hanging to watch her reaction as he opened the door to let himself out.

Sherly Fernandes's belligerent expression didn't change. 'So? I hope you don't have some stupid, fancy theory that I had him hunted down and killed after seven years to avenge my dear ex-hubby, Rahul Fernandes!'

She gave another sudden, grim laugh, strode to the door, glared at Inspector Saralkar as he stepped out of her house, and slammed the door shut on his face.

16

'YOU ARE DRUNK!' SUREKHABAI COULDN'T HIDE HER DISGUST even as relief swept over her to see her son, Hrithik, at the door. She'd been worried sick, as his absence had stretched into the fourth day.

Her son gave her a glazed look as he stumbled into the house. 'Serve me dinner,' he ordered his mother.

Surekhabai wrinkled her nose as the stink of liquor and her son's unwashed self filled the two-room tenement. 'I'm not your servant. Where have you been?' she said, flaring up. Her alcoholic husband had blighted her youth and middle age. The idea of her remaining years being cursed by a drunkard son was insufferable.

'I'm hungry!' her son screamed back. 'Stop blabbering and give me food.'

'I asked you where you've been all this time. Answer me first.'

'None of your bloody business,' Hrithik replied cockily. 'Don't ask questions, you stupid old hag. Serve dinner before I count up to three.'

'Is that so? Well, you aren't getting any food till you answer my questions,' Surekhabai replied, anger and anxiety raging in her mind.

With a sudden movement, Hrithik lunged at her, one hand grabbing her left arm and the other wrapping itself around her throat. 'How dare you! I'll kill you!' he cried out in his drunken rage and began choking her.

Surekhabai was stunned, debilitated momentarily by fear and the shock of her son attacking her. His grip was strong and it was hurting her. Surekhabai's survival instinct kicked in a moment later and she began clawing at Hrithik's face. She had staved off many such attacks from her husband. But that had been when she was younger. Age had weakened her now. As she gasped for breath, she knew she had to use her legs. With a surge of strength, she kicked with all her might at her son's abdomen.

It probably hit the perfect spot, because his grip on her neck broke and he collapsed on the floor, clutching his stomach in pain, then retched and vomited.

Surekhabai, who had quickly moved away and picked up the washing bat to protect herself from further assault, surveyed the mess her son had made and knew he was spent. She controlled the urge to wallop him with the bat. 'You shameless monster! How dare you attack and abuse your own mother?' she shouted bitterly, her eyes running over the features of the son she had given birth to, loved and raised—the thick, long hair she once oiled and combed, the hooked nose and buck teeth which had never seemed ugly to her affectionate gaze, the cauliflower ear which she had kissed so often when other children had teased him about it ...

Seething at his writhing body and the mess he had created, Surekhabai suddenly became aware of the bundles of cash that had fallen out of his pocket as a result of the struggle. Her rage gave way to alarm and panic. 'Where did all this money come from?' she hissed. 'What have you been up to?'

Her son was still curled up with pain and his hands were

holding his head. Foul words flew out of his mouth.

'Hrithik, you fool! Tell me! Has this money come from the Doshis? Tell me, did you ... harm them? Did you have anything to do with ... with ... what happened to them?'

Hrithik raised himself, shaking and quivering. 'You whore, you characterless woman! Are you grieving that the bastard is dead? Did he just make passes at you or did you sleep with him? He's dead now! Serves him right. He can no longer defile you.'

He struggled to his feet, swaying, and began gathering the bundles of cash, but soon lost his balance and fell over again in a drunken stupor, clutching the money.

A cold dread swept over Surekhabai's heart. Had her son done the unthinkable? The violence she had just experienced at his hands suddenly made it all so feasible. If a man didn't have any qualms attacking his mother, would he have demurred in killing someone else?

PSI Motkar's attention had kept wandering during the drama practice. He was actually thoroughly bored with Walimbe's directorial histrionics and hysterics as well as the attitudes of all the other amateur actors. He had finally managed to mug up his dialogues and at least deliver them without having to be prompted. His intonation still left much to be desired. Motkar doubted it would get much better, but at least he had got Walimbe off his back.

As the umpteenth rehearsal of one of the scenes in which he was not required commenced, Motkar wondered if he should make a placatory call to Saralkar. They hadn't talked since his boss had left for Bangalore, fussing and fuming. It was perhaps time to ring him up to find out what his boss had dug up in Bangalore and also update him about what he himself had been doing.

Motkar stepped out of the practice hall and dialled the number, steeling himself up for some taunts, harsh words, and being taken to task. The phone kept ringing and went unanswered. Motkar glanced at his watch. It was past ten. Was it possible that Saralkar had called it a day already? He disconnected and decided he would try again the following morning.

Just as he was about to enter the hall, his mobile began ringing. Perhaps his boss was giving a call back, but the caller ID on his screen showed the number of an old police informant, Bajrang Landge.

'Yes, Bajrang.'

'Namaskar, Motkar sahib,' Bajrang greeted him exuberantly. 'Got some hot information for you.'

'About?'

'That sketch of the suspect released for the Doshi case.'

'I see. You know who it is?' Motkar asked, his pulse quickening.

'I think it's a fellow called Hrithik Dhond. Stays in Bakre chawl near Shastrinagar.'

Something stirred in Motkar's mind. The surname sounded familiar.

'Hrithik Dhond ... Is he a history-sheeter?'

'No, sahib, but I think he was booked last year for rioting and public disorder. No other crime record, as far as I know. But given the company he keeps these days, it's a matter of time before he has one,' Bajrang replied.

'So, what does this Hrithik Dhond do for a living?'

'Not much. Odd painting contracts here and there these days. Earlier he worked as a peon, then delivery boy. As I said, spends most of his time with other good-for-nothing guys in the vicinity.'

'Hmm. You are sure it's him?' Motkar asked.

'Yes, sahib. Pukka information,' Bajrang assured him.

'Okay. Good. Any idea of his current whereabouts?'

'He's usually here only. Lives with his mother. You want me to confirm tonight? I'll ask a friend to check if you want,' Bajrang offered. More information, more the remuneration, he knew.

'No. Don't bother,' Motkar said. He knew it was a task the Kothrud Police station could easily do. 'Thanks, Bajrang. Keep in touch.'

He hung up and scratched his head. Hrithik Dhond. Where had he heard the surname recently? Was it related to this case or some older one? Then suddenly it came to him. Dhond was the surname of Surekhabai, the cook of the Doshi and Tambe families. Almost immediately, the significance of the tip he had received increased manifold. So the suspect in the sketch was Surekhabai's son.

Motkar licked his lips in anticipation. There was no time to be lost. He had to get Hrithik Dhond picked up right away or first thing the next morning.

'Motkar,' someone hollered from the hall door. 'You are needed for the next scene.'

'Just a minute, I have a call to make,' Motkar replied, busy dialling the number of PSI Sarode. It took several rings before PSI Sarode's sleepy voice came on the line. 'What's up, Motkar?'

'Sarode, I just got a tip about the sketch suspect. Apparently, it's a fellow called Hrithik Dhond who stays in Bakre chawl.

He's the son of the cook, Surekhabai. I want you to pick him up tomorrow morning from his house. Can you place a watch there tonight?'

'Okay, will do. Not sure whether I have the manpower for a watch tonight but I'll pick him up tomorrow morning, if he's there in his house,' Sarode assured him.

'Okay, thanks. Just check, he might have a record. I am told he was picked up for rioting or something by you or your colleagues at Kothrud last year.'

'Sure, but it must be some minor offence, otherwise I would've recognised a goon from my area,' Sarode replied with a yawn.

He hung up and even before Motkar could put the phone back in his pocket, an incoming call began flashing and ringing. It was Saralkar. Motkar felt elated his boss wasn't cold-shouldering him. He cast a glance in the direction of the practice hall door, saw no one was waiting to beckon him impatiently, then took Saralkar's call.

'Hullo, sir. How are you?' Motkar asked, feeling awkward.

'Ah, Motkar, cracked the case, did you?' Saralkar said, his voice booming with unbridled sarcasm.

'No, sir. Just called to brief you and inquire how, er, Bangalore's treating you,' Motkar said carefully.

'Oh, so you finally found time from your grand drama practice, is it?' Saralkar said without letting up. 'Where are you right now?'

Motkar contemplated lying to him for a second. 'Just ... finishing the rehearsal for the day, sir,' he replied clumsily.

'Great! What commitment, Motkar! When you become an acting sensation and someone interviews me for a feature on you,

I'll wax eloquent on how dedicated you were to your art. His job was crime investigation, I'll say, but acting was his real passion! How's that for a quote, Motkar? Look how neatly investigation rhymes with passion,' Saralkar spoke at his scathing best.

It riled Motkar but he kept his peace. 'Come on, sir, that's a little harsh,' he replied mildly.

'Okay, so what sweet nothings do you wish me to murmur in your ears, Motkar?'

Motkar ignored the jibe again and quickly began briefing the senior inspector about Dulange and Rangdev, the sketch based on Mrs Tambe's description, and the informant's tip that pointed to Hrithik Dhond.

'I see. Not too bad, Motkar. Grill Dhond properly. Don't bloody handle him with kid gloves. If he's a first-timer, I bet he'll confess fast. A couple of blows will do the trick. Use Shewale if you have qualms,' Saralkar advised, knowing his subordinate's distaste for even the mildest form of third degree. 'And when are you questioning Rangdev Baba?'

'That's what I wanted to check with you, sir. Being a god-man and all that, should I go ahead with questioning Rangdev by myself or wait for you to return?'

'Mmm, might be a good idea to wait. Rangdev's not in the big league really as a god-man but we should be prepared for string-pulling and his devotees making a ruckus—that sort of a thing. We'll do it after I'm back.'

'How's it going in Bangalore, sir? Any big leads?'

'Lots of interesting information. Let's see where it takes us. Too much to pass on over phone,' Saralkar replied. 'Do one thing, check out with Sanjay Doshi's bank whether he made demand drafts of big amounts in the name of his first wife, Latha

Bhupathi. Apparently, he kept sending big sums to her, though she claims he never got in touch.'

'Sure, sir. So when are you going to be back?'

'Depends, Motkar. The officer who investigated the case, Inspector Hegde, is going to be available tomorrow. I'll know if I have to check anything further only after meeting him. In the meanwhile, I've decided to get a taste of Bangalore's nightlife. Don't keep me from it.'

He called off cheerfully and, for a moment, left Motkar tickled with disbelief, trying to visualise his boss moving across Bangalore's famed pubs and having a good time.

'Motkar, what the hell's wrong with you, man?' Walimbe, the director, screamed at him, hands on his hips, framed in the hall doorway. 'Who are you sucking up to this time—your wife or your boss? For God's sake, man, do you come here to practice or for timepass?'

The normally placid Motkar now flipped his lid. He strode up to Walimbe and said in a voice loud enough for other actors to hear. 'Walimbe, you and your play be stuffed, okay! I'm a police officer and I damn well have things to do. You talk to me like that once again and I'll slap you right there and quit. Understood?'

It stopped Walimbe in his tracks, Motkar was gratified to see.

17

'ARE YOU OKAY?' JYOTI'S VOICE PLEASANTLY FILLED SARALKAR'S ears as he was getting ready to leave for the Bangalore Homicide Squad office the next morning.

'Fine. What's wrong with me?' he replied jauntily. Of course, he didn't ask her how she was because he knew from experience that women used the question as the perfect pretext to talk about all that was going on in their lives at that time, including boring nuggets from their routines.

'You haven't called me up at all since you reached Bangalore,' Jyoti said.

'I sent you a text message as soon as I reached, didn't I?'

'Yes, but it's been three days ... I was getting worried.'

'I've been busy,' Saralkar replied. He wasn't about to tell her what a relief it was not to be nagged about the medical tests—part of the reason why he had come to Bangalore.

'Haven't you finished your work there? When are you coming back?' his wife asked.

'Can't say. Probably day after tomorrow.'

'Have you been taking the BP tablets without fail?'

'Yes,' Saralkar said a little too assertively, having realised he had forgotten to take it that morning. 'Okay, see you, I've got to go.'

'Okay. I miss you. Do you miss me?' Jyoti asked softly.

It caught Saralkar off guard. He felt flustered. What was a forty-seven-year-old man like him supposed to reply? 'Yes', like a lovesick teenager, or 'No', like a daft male who does not know what's good for him?

'You—your voice is breaking, Jyoti! We'll speak later.'

'You are lying. Of course, you can hear me and, of course, you miss me. Bye!' Jyoti laughed. 'And take that tablet.'

She called off, leaving Saralkar wondering again whether women had some mysterious third eye. He looked at his watch. It was time to leave.

Half an hour later, he sat facing Inspector Hegde, the man who had investigated the Rahul Fernandes murder seven years earlier. Hegde was about six to seven years senior to Saralkar; a dignified officer, dressed impeccably in his uniform. He was clean-shaven, the scant hair on his pate neatly combed. A smile played on his face as if he had come to the conclusion that investigating murder was a philosophically amusing pursuit. But there was also a toughness about him that could suddenly be revealed when the smile switched off. His thick fingers and rugged palm had held Saralkar's hand in a firm, strong grip when they had shaken hands.

'Ah, Senior Inspector Saralkar, sorry I couldn't meet you earlier. My daughter's wedding, you know,' he said with a distinct Kannada twang in his voice. They chatted a bit about this and that—first about Hegde's daughter and son-in-law, and then about their own backgrounds, careers and cases.

'Okay, tell me. I believe you've found my missing murderer, Krishna Bhupathi,' Hegde said, signalling the end of the small talk.

'Yes,' Saralkar replied, and quickly summarised all that had happened in Pune and how the trail had led to Bangalore. He also showed Hegde the photographs of Sanjay Doshi alias Krishna Bhupathi's body, which the latter carefully examined.

'It's him, all right! I guess the forensic data has also been matched, hasn't it?' Hegde observed.

'Yes, it has.'

Hegde handed back the photos. 'The bugger eluded the law for seven years,' he said, almost as if he were admiring Bhupathi's skills. 'And now he's managed to cheat justice forever.'

'True. Were you sure of his guilt in Rahul Fernandes's murder?' Saralkar asked.

'Well, you've read my case papers. Bhupathi confessed almost straightaway after we nabbed him that he and Shaunak Sodhi had done it.'

'But he retracted the confession later and said that he'd done it under duress. I understand you couldn't find sufficient corroborative evidence and so the chargesheet could not be filed, and he was let out on bail,' Saralkar said, knowing well no police officer liked being reminded of failure.

Hegde made a face. 'That does not mean the bugger didn't do it; otherwise why did he abscond as soon as he was out on bail? Because he knew some day we would get the evidence to nail him and his accomplice, Shaunak Sodhi, who had already run away immediately after the incident.'

He paused and shook his head as if ruing a lost opportunity. 'And if I had got a tip-off that Bhupathi was living in Pune with a fake identity, I would've promptly nabbed him and got him chargesheeted and tried with the fresh evidence I had.'

'Fresh evidence against Krishna Bhupathi for Rahul

Fernandes's murder?' Saralkar asked, sitting up alert.

'Yes, against both him and Sodhi,' Hegde asserted.

'But I saw no mention of any fresh evidence in the files,' Saralkar said, frowning. 'Unless I missed something. All that you had was the blood-stained pullover, Bhupathi's confession, call records that all three had been together that night, statements of witnesses who had seen them leave the bar where they had dined together, right? Since you hadn't been able to find Rahul Fernandes's body and Bhupathi had retracted his confession, there was nothing except circumstantial evidence.'

It was Hegde's turn to look mystified. 'That was in 2008. Fernandes's body was found in 2013. Didn't Pai give you that update and related documents?'

'No! I haven't seen any of that. Why don't you tell me,' Saralkar said, glad he hadn't left Bangalore without meeting Hegde.

'Well ... that is pretty tardy of Pai,' Hegde said with annoyance. 'Anyway, I am sure you already know that Bhupathi told us he and Sodhi dismembered Fernandes's body and buried the torso and limbs somewhere off the Mysore highway, deep into the woods, and threw his head amidst the valleys on the hill road from Mysore to Mercara. We took Bhupathi along to search and locate the exact spot where they had buried the body. He said it had been late at night and he had been drunk and scared of Sodhi. He showed us where they had turned off the highway onto a smaller road, but then simply couldn't locate the spot. We tried everything—threatening, cajoling. We even offered to make him a prosecution witness if he helped us recover the body. But he kept pleading he just couldn't remember where exactly they had buried it. We conducted a search operation for two days and combed the surrounding countryside, but nothing came off it. We alerted all police stations and posts in the area and hoped that someone from the nearby villages would stumble upon the remains.

'Many times, as you know, even animals dig up shallow graves. But no luck. We grilled Bhupathi again and carried out another search. No results again, so we just didn't have a body. In fact, I began wondering if Bhupathi was misleading us about the area and whether Sodhi and he had dumped Fernandes's corpse elsewhere.'

'I see. So how and where did you find it in 2013?'

'Well, Bhupathi had led us to the right area, but either deliberately or erroneously he had taken us much farther ahead and that too along the wrong road. After turning off the highway, a few kilometres ahead, the road bifurcated once again. While the main road continued straight ahead, another smaller road forked left. It was in a wooded area off that road that Fernandes's body was found in 2013 by a developer who had started a farmhouse scheme there. He immediately called in the local police when his site workers found a headless skeleton and remains. Local police called us because one of the constables posted there remembered the search.'

'But how did you establish the identity of Fernandes? DNA testing or something?' Saralkar asked, and even as he said it, he remembered that Sherly Fernandes had told him Rahul had had no kin.

Inspector Hegde confirmed the fact. 'No, Fernandes didn't have any family apart from his wife, so DNA testing was out of question. But there was his watch and his smashed mobile phone with the body. The SIM card had been thrown away but the IMEI number of the phone matched.'

'So was Fernandes's wife informed and did she come for the identification?'

'Yes, obviously we had to get her for formal identification. She identified his watch and the phone.'

'What impression do you have of Fernandes's wife?' Saralkar asked.

'Well, you know, we did have some suspicions initially whether she was involved in her husband's murder or not, conspiring with Sodhi and Bhupathi,' Hegde said with a shrug. 'There were some stray rumours picked up by informants that she and Sodhi had been lovers, but we couldn't get any proof. In fact, we kept a watch on her and also put her mobile on tracking for some time, but there was nothing suspicious. The only impression I got was she viscerally hated her husband and had no interest in pursuing the case. Why do you ask?'

'Just to get a clear picture,' Saralkar said, downplaying the point. 'Did she tell you her husband carried a gun for self-defence, even that evening?'

'Yes,' Hegde nodded. 'But we didn't find the gun with the body. So, either Sodhi took it with him or disposed it elsewhere.'

'But they didn't shoot Fernandes with his own gun?'

'No, Bhupathi said Sodhi strangled him.'

'Was that confirmed when his remains were examined?'

'The examination of the skeleton and remains was inconclusive except for the confirmation that the skeleton had been there for about five years and that the head had been sawed off. We matched the marks of the beheading with the blade heads of the tools found in Bhupathi's car. The remains had deteriorated too much for us to determine anything more other than the fact that it was the skeleton of a male in his thirties. But why do you doubt Bhupathi's version?' Hegde asked in a slightly intrigued tone.

'No, no. I was wondering that since they had a weapon, so wouldn't it have been simpler to shoot him in the head with it? Why strangle Fernandes, which is a much more arduous and terrifying way to kill, even for a murderer? The head has never been found and you only have the torso, so there's no conclusive proof he was strangled. Isn't it therefore much more likely that they shot him in the head?'

A touch of professional reserve and envy appeared in Hegde's expression, though he tried to mask it with a smile. 'Interesting theory! We'll know for sure only when we find a bullet-ridden skull in Mercara. You should write crime novels, Saralkar, like an old, retired colleague of ours does, sexing up real cases with all kinds of bizarre possibilities. The public loves it because they don't know how boring and mundane most murders are.'

Saralkar realised he had to be careful not to antagonise Inspector Hedge even subliminally by sounding superior to him. He was going to need cooperation from the officer in the future too. The Fernandes murder was not his case to solve.

'You are right; I have a weakness for theories,' he said with a self-deprecatory laugh. 'Did you find any incriminating evidence against Sodhi and Bhupathi with Fernandes's body?'

It brought Inspector Hegde back to his affable self. 'Nothing against Bhupathi that heralded his presence, but we found Sodhi's nasal inhaler and hair band with the body.'

'Inhaler and hairband?' Saralkar asked, puzzled.

'Yes. Sodhi suffered from asthma, so he always kept an inhaler. It probably slipped from his pocket while digging the grave or lowering Rahul Fernandes's body into it. Sodhi also had punk-like long hair and a ponytail, with a fancy hairband, which was also found. His parents identified it.'

Saralkar nodded. 'Pity you found the body so late. Otherwise, you'd have been able to chargesheet Bhupathi and both of them wouldn't have got away.'

'True. So you think it was Sodhi who killed Bhupathi and his second wife in Pune?' It was now Inspector Hegde's turn to ask questions.

'It seems quite likely. Sodhi and Bhupathi were doing land deals together, and Sodhi seems to also have been carrying on an affair with Bhupathi's second wife, Anushka Doshi. But we don't have a clue about his whereabouts. It's like he has disappeared into thin air. The guy seems to be a slippery customer,' Saralkar replied. 'And now that their criminal history has been unearthed, my suspicions are even more strengthened that there has been foul play.'

Inspector Hegde nodded gravely. 'The fact is even I know very little about Sodhi. The officer who had investigated the job recruitment racket case went on a CBI deputation to the central government in 2009. I spoke to him a couple of times. He told me Sodhi was an MBA dropout—a personable, charming fellow who was pathologically inclined to be a swindler. Flamboyant, unscrupulous, ready to do anything for quick money, manipulative, on the lookout for sexual conquests, all the kinds of tendencies that fast forward the descent into crime.'

'Did he have any previous convictions for violent crime?'

'No. But the officer wasn't surprised to hear about Sodhi's involvement in Fernandes's murder. He said Sodhi was a bit of a hothead. While he was in police custody during the job racket investigations, he got into frequent brawls with other prisoners and once even thrashed a convict badly. It's only when his asthma worsened in jail that he caused no further trouble,' Hedge replied.

'Sodhi's parents are still in Bangalore, aren't they?'

'Yes. Both are above seventy. The mother has been ill for a long time. We had kept a watch on both his and Bhupathi's family for some time after the murder, and we keep checking on them intermittently to find if there has been any contact. Negative so far, but you never know.'

'I see. By the way, were you aware Bhupathi had been sending money to his family at least once in two years?' Saralkar asked.

'What? No! How did you find out?' Inspector Hegde said, glaring at Saralkar as if the latter had produced a rabbit from his hat by subterfuge.

'His first wife, Latha Bhupathi, told me about it after I informed her that Bhupathi had married again and was now dead. It's possible Sodhi, too, was in touch with his parents then.'

Hegde sniffed, obviously not happy with the likelihood of such things having happened under his nose. 'Can't rule it out. Maybe I'll send my men to shake up the old couple a bit.'

'No, I think I need to meet them anyway, so I'll let you know if they admit to any contact with him,' Saralkar replied.

Inspector Hegde looked at him grudgingly. 'Okay. Tell me if you require any help.'

Saralkar smiled and held out his hand. 'Inspector Hegde, you've already been a great help. Thank you so much.'

Even as he spoke, Saralkar was puzzled by his own effusiveness. Could it be that in his middle age, he had inadvertently started learning the skills of how to win friends and influence people?

18

'MOTKAR, WE'VE PICKED UP YOUR SUSPECT, HRITHIK DHOND,' PSI Sarode informed Motkar on the mobile. 'When are you coming over?'

'Right away, Sarode. Thanks a lot,' Motkar replied.

'We found fifty thousand rupees on him,' Sarode said grimly. 'Sure doesn't look like honest earnings.'

'Oh! I'm on my way!' Motkar kept down the phone and wondered momentarily whether it would finally boil down to murder for money. He glanced at the post-mortem and viscera report he had been going through. Sanjay Doshi had met his death between 10 p.m. and midnight. Death had been due to asphyxiation caused by hanging. There was a faint possibility he could have been strangulated but if so, it was by rope and not by hand. There had been plenty of liquor in his system and just a slight likelihood that he had been taking or had been given sedatives through the day on which he died. The report of Anushka Doshi conclusively suggested death by strangulation. She had been choked with her dupatta, probably under heavy sedation. The acid had been thrown on her face moments after her death. There were no signs of torture or other injuries, but she had probably been gagged and bound for some hours prior to her death, which seemed a little odd. She too had died between

10 p.m. and midnight.

PSI Motkar kept the report back neatly in the envelope and left his office. The drive to Kothrud Police Station took about fifteen minutes and as he mulled the post-mortem reports in his mind, he couldn't escape a feeling of mild disappointment. Clearly, Anushka Doshi had been murdered, while the report did not unequivocally conclude strangulation in the case of her husband Sanjay Doshi. The conclusions seemed quite consistent with suicide by hanging, although they left room for doubt that he could have been strangulated by rope.

So, was it possible after all the investigation that Sanjay Doshi had killed his wife and then hung himself? That this was no double murder by Shaunak Sodhi or some other person, as Saralkar had suspected? Yet, there were just too many unanswered questions. With so much money in his locker, why would Sanjay Doshi have killed himself claiming debtors were hounding him? If his wife was having an affair, why kill her and himself? Why not just leave her, take the money and go elsewhere, even abroad, since he had a new identity and a passport?

And where the hell was this Shaunak Sodhi? And if Shaunak had killed Doshi and his wife, why would he incriminate himself by putting his ownname in the suicide note? Also, why did he kill Anushka if he was having an affair with her and, more importantly, would have been in a position to gain control of the other properties through her? So, was it possible that a third person was involved in the murder who knew the truth about Bhupathi and Sodhi's past? Someone who also knew Shaunak Sodhi was having an affair with Anushka, and about the land deals in which Sanjay Doshi and Shaunak Sodhi had been partners? Someone who had taken advantage of this knowledge to murder the Doshi couple and incriminate Sodhi? Some shadowy criminal associate to whom Saralkar's investigations in Bangalore might hopefully lead! Or someone like Surekhabai and her son, Hrithik, who had stumbled upon their secrets and sordid history while working for them. Or perhaps even Somnath Gawli or one of the betting bookies or escort girls and other shady contacts of Sanjay Doshi, whom they had still not investigated.

PSI Motkar clicked his tongue, reined in his speculations and shook his head. Lately, he realised, he had got into the habit of theorising and conjecturing like his boss. He was not Saralkar, he warned himself. His strength lay in sturdy common sense and detailed police work, just as Saralkar's lay in combining investigative professionalism with intuition and imagination.

Stepping into the Kothrud Police Chowki, Motkar's eyes fell on Surekhabai, who was seated in a corner in the shade of a tree, probably waiting to know the fate of her son. As soon as she saw Motkar, she hurried towards him. 'Sahib, my son is innocent! He couldn't have harmed Doshi madam and her husband. Whoever has named him is lying!' she started snivelling wretchedly. All her earlier contempt for Motkar had fallen by the wayside.

'We'll see,' Motkar replied non-commitally. He went in, had a quick word with Sarode, and then entered the small interrogation cell where Hrithik Dhond was being held.

The strong reek of vomit and liquor hit him immediately. Hrithik Dhond, he guessed, had clearly been dragged out from his bed and taken into custody. Motkar, like most policemen, had trained himself early on in his career to remain unaffected by offensive sights, sounds, smells and touches. Compared to the hideous-looking individual cringing in the cell, the sketch almost appeared a gentlemanly depiction of the young man. But there was no doubt Hrithik Dhond bore a striking resemblance to the sketch.

Motkar could see that the potent combination of a terrible hangover, shock and fear of the arrest, and the anxiety of what would happen to him now was tearing Hrithik apart. It wouldn't take long for him to confess his crimes, if any, or spill all that he knew.

'Why did you kill your mother's employers, Sanjay and Anushka Doshi?' Motkar asked point-blank.

'That's false, I didn't kill them,' Hrithik Dhond replied morosely.

'Don't lie! You were seen by witnesses.'

A flash of defiance flickered in Hrithik's eyes. 'Doing what?'

'Threatening the Doshi couple several times. Leaving their house,' PSI Motkar said in a raised voice, keeping the remark deliberately vague.

Hrithik Dhond winced. He looked away, unsteady, unsure of what to reply.

'That's ... that's not true. I—I would just go to call my mother sometimes because she used to work there.'

'Ah! You used to go there to call your mother, is it? Why? Doesn't she have a mobile?'

Hrithik Dhond passed his tongue over his dry lips. 'She does but sometimes when there is no balance in either her or my mobile ... then I have to.'

'Mmm. So when was the last time you went to the Doshi house?'

'I don't remember.'

'I see. Where were you last Saturday?'

'I never went to their house last Saturday,' Hrithik Dhond

suddenly cried vehemently.

PSI Motkar smirked. 'I asked you where you were. Anyway, prove to me that you didn't go to the Doshi residence on Saturday.'

Hrithik Dhond was breathing heavily now, and a cornered look was creeping into his eyes. 'I—I was with friends on Saturday and Sunday.'

'Doing what?'

'We all had gone to Lonavala–Khandala for some partying and enjoyment.'

'Tell me the names of all these friends of yours,' Motkar demanded.

Hrithik Dhond hesitated. 'Why? They have nothing to do with—'

'That means you are bluffing. You weren't with friends in Lonavala. You were here in Pune, at the Doshi residence.'

'No! No ... I was in Lonavala.'

'Where?'

'At someone's farmhouse.'

'Whose farmhouse?'

Hrithik Dhond lapsed into silence for a few seconds. Then he looked at Motkar and pleaded. 'My head's killing me. Can I have something to eat or drink? At least tea; I'm feeling dizzy, sahib.'

'Later. First answer my questions,' Motkar heard himself say. It almost sounded like his boss was talking. 'Where did all that cash come from?'

Hrithik Dhond massaged his head, as if it would fall apart any second if he didn't. The dishevelled, thick hair, the hooked nose were making his face look like a grotesque mask. 'I won it ... at cards in Lonavala.'

'Ah, while playing at the mysterious farmhouse with your unnamed friends! Sure you didn't loot it from the Doshis after murdering them?'

'Sahib, I swear I didn't kill them. Please!' He clasped his hands together, as if begging for mercy.

A couple of slaps and he would crumble, Motkar could see. But he resisted the temptation. 'You are lying. You were seen and heard threatening them several times. You even accosted Sanjay Doshi outside his house on a few occasions, and we know you had a strong motive to kill the couple.'

'What motive, sahib? I didn't go anywhere near them,' Hrithik Dhond croaked.

'Are you going to continue this charade? You want the truth beaten out of you?' Motkar said, raising his voice again, 'Or do you want us to put your mother behind bars too? She's waiting outside only. Should we take her into custody?'

The last shreds of Hrithik Dhond's composure gave away and his facial muscles signalled surrender. 'Sahib, why my mother, sahib? She's old. Neither I nor she have done anything. Please don't do this. She's got nothing to do with this.'

'It's got everything to do with her. Tell me the entire truth and we won't arrest her. If not, both of you are going to spend the rest of your lives in jail,' Motkar said tightening the screws.

'For what?' Hrithik Dhond wailed. 'Just because my mother cooked for them and I am her son?'

'I don't want filmy dialogues, Hrithik. I want the truth. Why did you threaten the Doshis? Do you or do you not confess to killing them? If you did not murder them, then give me proof and witnesses that you were not here in Pune on Saturday. And explain where you got all this money from, if you didn't loot it from the Doshis?'

'But—'

'Don't waste my precious time, Hrithik. If you don't start talking, I'm going to hand you over to my constables, who love nothing better than spending quality time with goons like you. And Sarode sahib will also take Surekhabai into custody,' Motkar said, his voice tingling with warning bells.

Not even fifteen seconds elapsed before Hrithik Dhond's tear ducts began overflowing and he started talking.

19

AN AIR OF MELANCHOLY WAS THE DEFINING FEATURE OF THE house in which Shaunak Sodhi's parents lived. Saralkar felt it keenly as if a heartbreaking sadness had seeped into the walls, the ceiling, the floor, and laid permanent siege.

Sodhi's father, for all his military bearing, seemed like a pale shadow of a once proud and happy man. Neatly turbaned and dressed, ramrod straight, radiating an old-world dignity, what was missing was the spark of hope and happiness. His wife had not even bothered to keep up appearances. She wore a crumpled, sloppy salwar–kameez, as if nothing really mattered. Hegde had told Saralkar she had been hospitalised and was very ill. Maybe that was what had broken her completely, compared to her husband.

Saralkar had not had the heart to refuse when Sodhi senior had asked him if he would like to have sherbet. He took a sip of the perfect lemonade the old man had quickly prepared and cleared his throat. 'Has your son been in touch with you by any chance, in all these years?'

'The last time we talked to him was 7 November 2008,' the old man said precisely, as if time had stopped for them ever since that date.

Saralkar stole a quick glance at Shaunak's mother to see her reactions. She was staring down at her feet, her face blank.

'Isn't that a little strange? Wouldn't any son be worried about his parents?'

'He knew I would immediately inform the police or advise him to surrender,' the old man said, not with the pride of an upright man but with the humility of one who had started doubting lifelong principles.

'He hasn't even contacted his mother?' Saralkar asked, addressing old Mrs Sodhi. 'Especially since you were hospitalised a few times?' But she didn't show any sign of having heard him.

The old man turned to his wife. 'Leela,' he said softly, as if to gently rouse her from her reverie.

She looked up at him, then at Saralkar. 'Shaunak would certainly have come or at least called, if he had known. But how would he?' Her voice was so soft that Saralkar had to strain to hear.

'It's been so long ...' Her eyes suddenly filled with tears. 'Sometimes I wish he's caught by the police; at least I'll get to see him before I die.' She raised her dupatta to her face and covered it, crying silently.

Her husband shuffled across to her side and put a hand around her shoulder to comfort her.

'I don't believe Shaunak has murdered anyone ... but even if he has, I don't care. I just want to see him once, hold him close ...' she said in a voice so loaded with grief that it brought a lump even to Saralkar's unaccustomed throat.

What was happening to him, Saralkar suddenly wondered. Was he going soft and mushy with age? He didn't have children, had never known what it felt to be a parent or to being separated from a child. And yet, the mother of an absconding criminal had stirred hitherto unknown emotions in his mind that were almost interfering with his job.

Sodhi senior spoke. 'Can she rest inside? I can answer all your questions.'

'No problem,' Saralkar said gruffly, trying to disguise his discomfiture.

The old man gently escorted his wife into an inside room. He came out a few minutes later, shutting the door behind him. 'Sometimes it all gets too much for her, especially since we lost our daughter too,' Sodhi senior said.

Saralkar felt another twinge. 'I'm sorry. You also had a daughter?'

'Yes. She was settled in Canada with her husband and kids. She died last year. Cervical cancer,' the old man replied. He spoke matter-of-factly, as if that was his way to stop drowning in grief. 'When Leela heard you were coming, she was hoping you would have some news about Shaunak.'

He struggled helplessly. 'The doctors have given her a year at the most. I wonder if she'll ever see him again.'

'What is your wife suffering from?' Saralkar asked.

'Abdominal cancer, clinically,' Sodhi senior replied, 'but heartbreak, really. It's just taken the form of cancer. My daughter's death has been a big blow, of course. We could not even travel for her last rites because of my wife's illness, but it's Shaunak's disappearance that has been killing Leela, little by little. I wish I can bring him back for her. I even put in an advertisement appealing to him to come back for his ailing mother.'

Something stirred in Saralkar's mind. 'In a local daily or national daily?'

'*Deccan Herald*, a local English daily, but it's circulated all over Karnataka and Delhi. I thought if Shaunak was somewhere in the state or a place like Delhi, maybe ...' Sodhi senior's voice trailed off. 'No luck.'

'Can I see the advertisement or can you tell me the date of its publication?' Saralkar asked.

The old man walked over to a chest of drawers and retrieved a small folder from it. He handed over a page of the newspaper in which a small 8x10 ad was published. It displayed the photo of Leela Sodhi with a short message underneath: *'Your Beeji is very ill. Please come back/contact me. No one will be told.'* A mobile number and address were also given.

Saralkar realised why he had failed to see the lead, even though he had seen the nebulous significance of *Deccan Herald*. He remembered seeing the ad now, but the photo bore little resemblance to the sad woman he had just met.

'I—I didn't put Shaunak's photo or name or even our names because I didn't want the police or anyone else to be alerted,' Sodhi senior said apologetically. 'And I wanted to assure him he needn't be concerned I would hand him over to the authorities or something.'

Saralkar nodded. 'So did you get any response from anyone?'

Sodhi senior hesitated. 'I just got this anonymous note by post one month later. I didn't know what to make of it.'

Saralkar took the postal envelope and a handwritten note stapled to it, which read: *Can't contact. Safe. Do you require money for treatment? If so, advertise in the same paper in the 15 February issue. Mention amount required.*

'Is this your son's handwriting?' Saralkar asked.

'No, it's not written by him. Wouldn't he at least have asked after her health?'

Saralkar looked at the note again, trying to mentally visualise Sanjay Doshi's suicide note for comparison. He was fairly sure the handwriting was the same. Whether penned by Sanjay Doshi or his killer, the suicide note and the note Sodhi senior had produced had been written by the same person.

'So did you advertise again on the given date?'

'No, I didn't.'

'Why?'

'I didn't want the money ... crime money ... and I figured that if it was indeed Shaunak who had arranged to have the note sent to me, he would get restless if he did not see the advertisement on 15 February and anyway try and contact me. Any son would be concerned whether his mother was alive or dead, or why I hadn't advertised,' Sodhi senior replied.

Saralkar marvelled at the impeccable logic and psychology. 'So did it work? Did Shaunak or this person contact you again?'

The old man shook his head. 'I've often wondered if I should've put in another advertisement saying that money was not needed but that his mother was dying. Sort of make it clear.' He faltered and was silent for a few seconds, as if gathering his thoughts.

Just as Saralkar was gauging whether to add something, the old man spoke again. 'Shaunak loves his mother ... or ... or at least he did back then. I ... I don't know how things went wrong with him; how he became a ... criminal.'

For the first time, he saw the old man's eyes moisten. The shoulders had finally slumped, as if Sodhi senior had decided to lay down the burden of being strong, at least for the time being.

Saralkar felt himself overcome with sympathy. Why did such things happen to good people? Why did they have to suffer, like this old man in front of him? 'Can you tell me how exactly Shaunak got mixed up with Bhupathi and Fernandes? I understand he was doing his MBA, but he dropped out midway ...?' he asked.

'Yes, after I retired from the Indian Air Force, I decided to settle down in Bangalore, because I got a job here. Shaunak completed his college, and then started working in a company and also applied for the armed forces. Because of his asthma, he expectedly did not get selected and decided to pursue his MBA instead. He chucked his job and enrolled for MBA at a good institute in the city. That's where he met this girl, a fellow student he fell in love with. She was from an extremely rich family ... and that's what started Shaunak's downward spiral. He got obsessed with earning money and getting rich soon so that he could marry this girl with her family's consent,' Sodhi senior said. 'I don't know how exactly he met Bhupathi and Fernandes or where, but it was probably in the course of his betting activities, which he had taken to as a way to make big money. Since I strongly disapproved of all the wrong turns he had been taking after he met that girl, Shaunak and I were not on talking terms. So I just learnt from his mother that he was starting a business with two partners. I was very uneasy the moment I heard the nature of the business—foreign employment and immigration—but there was nothing I could do.'

'Did you ever meet either Bhupathi or Fernandes? Did Shaunak bring them home or did you by chance bump into them in his office?'

'No, never.'

'Did your son ever tell you or his mother anything about them?'

The old man shook his head. 'Not really.'

'Not even after he was arrested and imprisoned in the employment racket case?' Saralkar pressed on. 'Didn't he express any kind of feelings—anger, frustration, claims of innocence, shame?'

The old man was silent for a few seconds, as if figuring things for himself. 'To be honest, in the last couple of years just before his disappearance, I hardly seemed to know my son. We lived in the same house, but his work, his life, was all out of bounds for me. Even for his mother, for that matter. Shaunak had completely withdrawn into himself after the girl broke up with him, and seemed to head further down the path of wrongdoing. He refused to discuss anything, and if his anguished mother or I tried to force a conversation upon him about his way of life or various other things, he would simply threaten to leave the house. So we just kept our peace.'

He paused, looking beyond Saralkar, as if introspecting and reflecting rather than talking to someone else. Saralkar chose to wait without prompting.

Sodhi senior spoke again. 'I didn't want to probe too much because I was sure I wouldn't be able to stop myself from doing the right thing if I got any confirmation from him that he was indulging in nefarious and illegal activities. I just prayed he would come to his senses some day and not get sucked deeper into the morass. But he did. We were not here when he was arrested. We were in Canada, visiting our daughter. We didn't even know about it for the first month or so. By the time we got information and came back to India, Shaunak had been in prison for nearly six to seven weeks. He even refused to meet us. We finally met him only when he got out on bail much later.

But even then, not a word from him. He would just sit there brooding or watching TV. Whether he was guilty or not, whether he had done anything criminal or not—he told us nothing. We never knew what was going on in his mind.'

'Did he ever talk about Rahul Fernandes or how he had cheated and double-crossed him and Bhupathi? Did he hint at taking revenge?' Saralkar asked a little more bluntly this time.

Old man Sodhi's reply was surprisingly sharp. 'I wouldn't put it past Shaunak to have killed a man! Anger, money, revenge can drive anyone to kill. Initially, I couldn't get myself to believe the worst, but over time ... I've wondered. Otherwise, why did he flee like that, if he was innocent? I have, of course, never told his mother that.'

Once again Sodhi senior's candidness impressed Saralkar. He was about to ask the next question, but Shaunak's father was not yet done.

'Mind you, there is one thing which always bothers me, though. Shaunak wasn't feeling well that day. He'd been having asthma attacks and had been coughing and wheezing quite badly. Perhaps you know how cruel the Bangalore weather can be to asthma patients. Shaunak's asthma had only got worse in prison, and it had taken a toll on his overall health. His mother even asked him why he couldn't stay home if he was feeling so unwell that evening. But he went ... and never came back.'

Saralkar nodded. 'And what bothers you is that you think in his condition he wouldn't have been able to do what he did?'

'Yes, I mean ... to think of him having the strength to kill someone while wheezing, coughing, breathing heavily ...' the old man left the sentence hanging.

'But there were two of them. Bhupathi was with Shaunak and

together they could easily have overpowered Fernandes, who was quite drunk,' Saralkar pointed out. 'In fact, as you already know, when the police finally found Fernandes's body where Bhupathi and your son had buried it, your son's inhaler and hairband were also found, which he probably dropped.'

'That too had puzzled me,' Sodhi senior replied, 'because my wife had also lamented after he left the house that evening that Shaunak had forgotten to take his inhaler and might need it later. She even tried calling on his mobile. So how could it be Shaunak's inhaler that was found with Rahul Fernandes's body? I mentioned this to the inspector. In fact, the inhaler that was found was of a different strength than the one Shaunak used regularly.'

Saralkar made a mental note of checking this discrepancy. Moving to the present, he said, 'It's possible that Shaunak might have killed again. Bhupathi and his second wife were found dead in mysterious circumstances in Pune recently,' and watched the old man's reactions carefully.

Sodhi senior seemed to stiffen a little. His palms, which had been clasped together, and were resting between his thighs, were unclasped and now clutched the edges of the diwan he was sitting on, as if to steady himself. His eyes had inadvertently strayed towards the door leading into the inside room where his wife lay, as if to check she had not suddenly materialised and chanced to hear this revelation about their son.

'He's killed his other business partner too, after so many years?' the old man asked hoarsely.

'Seems quite likely by the look of things.'

'Has Shaunak been caught?'

'Not yet.'

The old man stared at Saralkar for a few seconds, then said in a gravelly tone, 'If Shaunak's killed again, inspector, then he's beyond hope, beyond redemption. I hope my wife does not have to know.'

Saralkar nodded. 'Will you then please inform me immediately if Shaunak tries to get in touch?'

The old man spoke again. 'Of that, you have my word, inspector.'

And Saralkar believed the aged, dignified Sikh.

20

IT HAD BEEN A PARTICULARLY HECTIC DAY AND AS HE SAT MAKING his daily case report, PSI Motkar once again marvelled at how often the investigation of one case led to the unearthing of a different crime altogether.

Hrithik Dhond, for example, had been picked up as a suspect in the Doshi case, but it had instead revealed his involvement in a burglary, which would perhaps have remained undetected otherwise, if Hrithik hadn't been forced to account for his whereabouts on the day of the Doshi murder and thereafter.

Faced with the prospect of being charged with murder and his mother being dumped in jail, Hrithik Dhond had first admitted to threatening the Doshis. 'Sir, that bastard tried to molest my mother! When my mother told me, I lost it and wanted to beat Sanjay Doshi black and blue,' Hrithik had said morosely. 'Which son wouldn't?'

'Go on,' Motkar had prodded.

'I—I didn't want it to happen again. I wanted to protect my mother. So I just went to their flat and warned him,' Hrithik Dhond had replied.

'How did Sanjay Doshi react?'

'He denied the incident at first, then later he began apologising and said it wouldn't happen again.'

'So why did you go to his place again and again?'

'I didn't go again,' Hrithik Dhond had wailed.

'You mean the matter ended there with just one visit?'

'Yes.'

'So how come you were seen on other occasions, even shouting and arguing with both Sanjay Doshi and his wife, Anushka Doshi?' Motkar's voice had hardened. 'What were you doing, Hrithik? Paying the couple a courtesy call?'

'But, sir!' Hrithik had whined again.

'Quick, quick,' Motkar had said, snapping his fingers impatiently, almost enjoying his new role as the rough and ready officer. 'You were trying to extort money from Sanjay Doshi, right, for his conduct with your mother? Come on, out with it!'

Hrithik Dhond had nodded shamefacedly.

'Ah, the cat's out of the bag. And when you tried the extortion stunt too many times, Doshi told his wife and they refused to pay you any further?' Motkar had demanded. 'Right?'

'No, he had told me to come and take the money from his house one day, since his wife was going to be away. She turned up just as Sanjay Doshi was handing over some money to me, and demanded to know what was happening and who was I. The idiot panicked and gave some weird reason—of me being some creditor's man. The lady got suspicious and it led to a big argument. She snatched back the money from my hands and threatened me not to come again.'

'Is that why you decided to have your revenge by murdering the Doshis and looting their money?'

'No! Sir, I really had nothing to do with the murder. I told you I wasn't even here ...'

'Again, we are back to square one,' Motkar had sniggered.

'So where were you if not here? What were you doing? Who was with you? Where did you get all the money found on you? I want all the details of your whereabouts right from Saturday to this morning. Start talking if you want to save yourself.'

Hrithik Dhond's face had become indescribably tense, as if he knew he was walking into a trap. 'On Saturday, I and three others burgled a flat in Vishrantwadi area and immediately fled Pune. That's why I cannot have murdered the Doshis!' he blurted finally.

'What?' Motkar had been taken completely by surprise. 'Whose flat? Tell me more.'

'It's ... it's a flat where I had undertaken painting work two months ago. I—I made a duplicate of the key and bided my time. The family moved in last month and we kept a watch. Last Friday, they left for a weekend trip, so we took the opportunity and burgled it on Saturday afternoon.'

PSI Motkar had gazed at the cowering Hrithik fixedly, trying to figure out if it was just a ploy to get off the hook. 'Are you saying you are a part of some gang of burglars?'

Hrithik had nodded wretchedly and then out tumbled details of his brief criminal career and the burglary in question, all of which Motkar had immediately sent for checking to the Crime unit and the police station concerned.

That such a burglary had indeed occurred in Vishrantwadi was confirmed right away, but the rest of the story would need thorough verification, right from tracing Hrithik's accomplices to forensic evidence. Till then, Hrithik would remain in custody, but as far as Motkar was concerned, he had been effectively ruled out as a suspect from the Doshi murder case.

PSI Motkar finished his report and sat back with a yawn.

He knew he had to go for the drama practice, but felt distinctly disinclined to do so. Nor was he feeling like going home. In fact, he realised with a start, he would've liked nothing better at the moment than to discuss the case with his boss. The realisation depressed him. Was he also turning into a workaholic like Saralkar? Was his personality undergoing a change? Was he becoming a different version of himself or simply a copy of Saralkar in parts? Was he getting obsessed with cases, crimes and criminals to the exclusion of everything else?

Motkar got up from his desk. It was time to leave if he wanted to freshen up and have a bite before reaching drama practice. He put his papers into his drawer and glanced at Saralkar's desk as he walked past it. There were a couple of new documents and letters. Nothing that could not be seen tomorrow. And then his eye fell on a pink envelope. Who sent pink envelopes to policemen? It certainly couldn't be something official. Nor was it a greeting or invitation card.

It was addressed to Senior Inspector Saralkar. Motkar took a closer look. The full official address of the Homicide Unit was printed on a piece of paper pasted on the envelope. Two postal stamps neatly gummed in the corner were overlapped by a Pune postmark.

Some policemanly instinct prodded PSI Motkar to pick up the envelope and carefully open it. Inside was a short, printed, anonymous letter.

Motkar began reading Kunika Ahuja's note and immediately knew he needed to find the writer.

Saralkar took a look around his room one last time to make sure he hadn't left anything behind. Satisfied he had packed everything, he proceeded to check out of the Officer's Guesthouse. The guesthouse manager had made arrangements for a taxi, and Saralkar was soon on his way to Bangalore railway station.

He couldn't shake off a feeling of disappointment. Was he going back to Pune with anything substantive, he wondered. Certainly a lot of background information about Bhupathi and Sodhi and their crimes, as well as about their dead partner Fernandes. But did he have any leads for cracking the mystery of why Bhupathi and his second wife, Anushka, were killed in Pune?

He had to admit, he didn't. All he knew was that Bhupathi and Sodhi had fled Bangalore after killing Fernandes in 2008, and that Bhupathi had been found dead with his second wife in Pune in 2015, while Sodhi had disappeared again. But only when the events of the seven years in between were meticulously pieced together, would he be any nearer to solving the case. And that piecing together would entail horribly tedious work.

Saralkar grunted. The only alternative was inspired, intuitive hunches—letting the brain imaginatively twirl the facts and information available and spit out all kinds of wild possibilities—most of them garbled nonsense. And yet it had been his experience that when you let the brain set aside logic awhile, it could surprise you with some crazy germ of a thought that held the promise of opening some secret compartment hidden inside the forbidding wall of hard facts.

So far, Saralkar's mind had been disappointingly out of form, poking and prodding around to pick up singles but showing no appetite for big hitting or even stroke play. As he boarded his

AC train compartment and took his seat, he realised he had a twenty-hour journey ahead with nothing much to do except stretch himself on his berth and think.

There had been a time when Saralkar hadn't minded train travel, gazing out from the cocooned comfort of an AC compartment at the landscape, rhythmically speeding by, pleasantly blank-minded, or thinking runaway thoughts—serene, undisturbed, peaceful—and unknowingly dropping off to sleep.

But all that was before the advent of cell phones. For Saralkar, train bogies had never remained the same thereafter, nor had train journeys. He often wondered what was it that people incessantly yammered about? What was it that couldn't wait? Or was it that people were so utterly bored or scared of their own company even for a few hours that they had to connect with someone or the other? Perhaps a more charitable explanation was that the enforced leisure of a train journey triggered the need to catch up with friends, relatives and acquaintances.

Whatever it was, Saralkar found it mighty irritating, especially co-passengers with loudspeaker voices—a description that fitted a huge majority of Indians. Why couldn't the buggers talk softly at least, or, better still, lose their voices or cell phones!

He felt a twinge of ridiculous guilt now, as his cell phone rang.

'Caught the train?' Jyoti asked chirpily.

'Yes. Catching trains isn't half as difficult as catching criminals,' he replied.

She laughed. 'I'm sure you'll catch them too, as always. What time does the train reach Pune tomorrow?'

'Noon.'

'Okay, I'll leave lunch on the table. Don't rush off to work without eating,' Jyoti said. 'Now bye. I'll get back to the TV.'

Saralkar grunted. 'Again watching some trashy serial?'

'No, hubby dear, I am watching that old Shatrughan Sinha movie, *Kalicharan*. You know I always had a sort of crush on him, growing up,' his wife teased. 'Bye!'

'Bye,' Saralkar said, unable to resist a grin. Dev Anand, Rajesh Khanna, Amitabh Bachchan, Dharmendra, Shashi Kapoor, Vinod Khanna, yes, but whoever would have thought there were women like his wife who'd had a crush on Shatrughan Sinha, of all the heroes of the 1970s—an actor who'd started life as a stylishly menacing, screen villain. With his thundering dialogues, he was more of a male audience favourite than a female matinee idol.

But then there was no accounting for tastes. And if his wife had indeed been a Shatrughan Sinha fan, then *Kalicharan* was an obvious nostalgic 'must-see' considering that was the movie that decisively catapulted the actor from playing villain to hero roles. Saralkar sat back in his seat, still idly thinking of the movie. He too remembered having liked the film back then, although not as much for Shatrughan Sinha as for the villain played by that endearing character actor, Ajit, who had immortalised the role of the smuggler, Lion, with his trademark dialogue delivery.

Much to Saralkar's exasperation, his phone buzzed again. It was Motkar this time.

'I've started back from Bangalore, Motkar. Anything to report?'

'Two things, sir. Hrithik Dhond was busy burgling a flat in Vishrantwadi with his pals and fleeing Pune last weekend, so he might not be our culprit. Secondly, we've received an anonymous letter from a woman who claims Anushka Doshi used to dupe women through her past life regression gig and tried to entrap them for criminal and sinister purposes. The letter writer says she escaped narrowly and that the death of the Doshis could be directly a result of Anushka's nefarious actions.'

'No details or story of her personal experiences with Anushka Doshi or what she underwent?' Saralkar asked.

'No, sir, but somehow it's not like the usual crank letters we get,' Motkar said.

'Hmm! None of Anushka Doshi's other past life regression clients hinted at such issues, did they, when Salunkhe talked to them?' Saralkar asked.

'No, sir. I was thinking of speaking to them myself to double-check. I'll also see if I can get any leads from the GPO, where the letter was posted three days ago. It's a long shot, but I'll try.'

'Okay. I'll be in office in the second half tomorrow,' Saralkar replied, and switched off the mobile.

He gazed out of the window. The train was just pulling out of Bangalore's outskirts now. Soon the open country would be visible, sparsely habited and populated—sometimes lush with greenery, sometimes barren, sometimes a rocky or hilly terrain, sometimes flat lands—an existence far removed from the hurried, hectic, cramped, squalor-filled environs of city and town life. Where you could still see a bit of nature's creations as against the artificial constructs made by man.

Strangely, Saralkar's mind did not start thinking about the case, as was its wont. It was pleasantly blank as if suddenly aware that it was not obliged to generate the average of seven thousand thoughts that are supposed to flit through human minds daily.

His fellow passengers in the section of six berths were mercifully the quiet types, relatively speaking. And even though Saralkar had been allotted a side berth, no one had as yet occupied the seat opposite his. Saralkar stretched his legs and continued gazing out, aware that he was getting drowsier. Eventually, thoughts once again started trooping in, even as his blank mind resisted the onslaught. How had Sanjay Doshi or Shaunak Sodhi known about the advertisement in the *Deccan Herald*, even when the paper wasn't circulated in Pune? Could it be explained by the possibility that by some almighty coincidence, either Bhupathi or Sodhi happened to be visiting Bangalore on the very day it appeared?

Saralkar's mind instinctively rejected such a coincidence. It strained his credulity. Yes, such coincidences could happen, but wasn't it far more likely that somebody Sodhi or Bhupathi knew was a Bangalore resident and helping them—an old accomplice or criminal acquaintance. Somebody who had tipped them off about the advertisement. Who could that be?

Saralkar wished he had had the time or authority to go through all the records of the Bangalore Police in the Fernandes murder investigation, as well as the recruitment scam case. Some name was bound to surface, which had hitherto remained in the shadows, buried in the paperwork. It was probably at this point that Saralkar dozed off.

The next thing he remembered was waking up with a start, with the acute sensation of having stumbled upon an extremely significant connectionmade by his brain. That link was present in his consciousness at the precise moment of waking up but before he could firmly grasp and register it in his memory, he was distracted by the immediate demand being made on his attention by the ticket-checker asking for his ticket.

In that microsecond, the momentous clue was gone,

retreating away from his consciousness into some crevice of his mind. By the time Saralkar had finished furnishing his ticket and identity card for the ticket-checker, the breakthrough link was nothing more than a vague, elusive feeling that the discovery was in some way connected to *Kalicharan*, the movie his wife and he had spoken about just a little earlier. What in the world had the Doshi murder got to do with *Kalicharan*, Saralkar wondered, thoroughly annoyed at his impish brain.

21

IN CHOOSING TO POST THE LETTER AT THE GPO, KUNIKA AHUJA'S instincts had led her into making two errors. Firstly, she had entered the GPO and purchased stamps without realising that CCTV cameras stared down from above. Instead, she could've done well to have bought the stamps from some other post office and posted the letter at the Pune GPO, without being recorded by the CCTVs. Secondly, rather than taking an auto, she had driven her car and parked inside the GPO premises, which afforded a full view of her car registration plate to the CCTVs outside.

But neither of these two mistakes led Motkar to her doorstep, because there was no way a random check of the CCTV footage would have enabled him to deduce that she was the woman who had posted the letter.

The CCTV footage helped only by way of jogging the memory of the postal staff in identifying her as the lady who'd returned to the post office in panic half an hour later the same day, because she had, in her haste, forgotten her purse on the shelf meant for pasting stamps, where the glue bottle had been placed.

In her ensuing attempts to trace and recover her purse, Kunika Ahuja had interacted with a number of postal employees, thus inadvertently etching her distressed face and the incident in their memories. This also included the assistant postmaster, the counter clerk who had sold her the stamps, as well as the employee to whom she had handed over the letter. Because of the purse incident, this particular employee, who would otherwise have completely forgotten all about her, immediately identified Kunika Ahuja in the CCTV footage as the same lady who had handed him a letter addressed to the Pune Homicide Unit, while he was clearing the post box.

This recollection, in conjunction with the footage of the car registration number in which Kunika Ahuja was clearly seen to have driven in and out of the GPO premises, enabled Motkar to track her down deftly.

'Kunika Ahuja?' he asked as soon as the door to the address in which the car was registered, opened and revealed a middle-aged, anxious looking woman.

The guilty, flustered look Kunika Ahuja threw at him convinced Motkar that this was the lady who had written and sent the anonymous letter.

'What is it?' she managed to ask through the grill door.

PSI Motkar held up the pink envelope and letter for her to see, trying to sound non-threatening, if not friendly. 'I am PSI Motkar from Pune Homicide Unit. I think you sent us this?'

Kunika Ahuja had gone pale, as if she had sent the police a letter-bomb instead of a mere anonymous letter. Perhaps sensing her distress, Bruno, her dog started barking. It galvanised Kunika into action. 'Just give me a minute, inspector. I—I'll tie Bruno up.'

She frantically began hushing her pet, while simultaneously looking for his leash. 'Sorry,' she apologised to Motkar over her shoulder, when she couldn't find the leash after looking around.

Then she turned to the dog and began ordering him out of the room.

Bruno's barks only got louder, trying to defy his mistress's order as he growled at Motkar standing outside the grill door. But finally, the dog backed away as she rebuked him and pointed inside. When he finally retreated into the next room, Kunika Ahuja closed the door on him, turned around, and hurried to open the grill door for Motkar and the woman police constable accompanying him.

'I'm so sorry! He is very protective,' she said, ushering them in.

PSI Motkar couldn't define what it was, but she distinctly had that spinsterly look and air about her—a kind of forlorn demeanour combined with a stubborn manner peculiar to lonely women, yet to come to terms with their doubts.

'You did send us this letter, didn't you, Ms Kunika Ahuja?' Motkar asked, taking a seat like a man used to never being asked to take one.

Kunika Ahuja stared at the letter in his hands, then at the lady constable, and finally back at Motkar. 'I—I suppose there's no point denying it,' she finally sighed, half apologetically.

Motkar nodded. 'Do you live alone?'

She looked at him, unsure. 'Yes ... why?'

'Just in case you wish to have some family member with you while we talk to you,' Motkar said gently.

'No, it's okay,' Kunika Ahuja said, then hastened to add, 'Look ... I was just trying to help, but I didn't want to get involved in police and courts. I hope it's not an offence to send such a letter to the police?'

'No. You don't have to worry about that. But it will be very helpful if you can tell us more about the matter. Your letter is very brief,' Motkar replied.

Kunika Ahuja was a little less nervous now. She sat down on the opposite sofa. 'What do you wish to know?'

'Well, please tell us precisely what kind of bad experiences you had with Mrs Anushka Doshi?' Motkar asked.

Kunika Ahuja gave an involuntary shudder, then looked in the direction of the door she had shut on Bruno. The dog could still be heard barking and scratching against the closed door. 'Can I please calm Bruno down and get him in here? I'll ... I'll feel much better,' she almost implored Motkar.

The dog was probably her moral and emotional support, Motkar figured. He nodded, although apprehensive that Bruno might create more ruckus.

Kunika Ahuja gratefully walked over to the door and began talking to the dog. When it had quietened down, she opened the door, squatted beside Bruno as he wriggled in, petting him and murmuring soothingly into his ear, while he glared at the visitors. Finally, she led him to the sofa and ordered him to sit, sternly instructing Bruno to be a 'good boy' and 'no barking'. Like a chastened child, the dog obeyed his mistress, not taking his eyes off Motkar, but the hostility was gone and a gentle wagging of his tail had begun.

Kunika Ahuja sat down again, running her hand over his fur repeatedly. It seemed to have as much a calming effect on her as on the dog. She looked composed and began speaking. 'Since I lost my father about four years ago, I had been, well, lonely and sad. I just wanted peace of mind. About six to seven months ago, things got really, uhh, unbearable. I was always disturbed and crying. I'd even thought of visiting a psychiatrist but ... kept avoiding it. That's when Anushka Doshi walked into my gift shop one day.'

She suddenly paused as if overcome by distaste.

'Was she alone?' Motkar asked gently.

'Yes, she ... came in as a customer, to purchase some gift. I—I was a little upset that time because I'd just had an unpleasant argument with a girl who worked for me in the shop. As I was packing the gift for Anushka Doshi, she suddenly startled me by directly asking me why I looked unhappy. You can imagine how taken aback I was by a total stranger asking me such a question. But somehow, I got drawn into a conversation with her and soon she was telling me about how she too had grappled with unhappiness and how past life regression therapy had helped her. She told me she was now helping others using the same therapy. I was intrigued. We exchanged phone numbers and that's how my acquaintance with her began. Subsequently, she dropped in a couple of more times and she would tell me stories of other women clients of hers.

'As I mentioned, I was still having a lot of mood swings and felt very depressed at times. I would lie awake at night and just cry, feeling lonely and ... It was really bad.'

Kunika Ahuja stopped, as if she didn't want to think or talk about that phase.

Motkar gave a little nod of understanding. He knew how loneliness brought people to their knees—that feeling of utter desolation, being unloved and unwanted, with no way out.

'I was ... I was so desperate to get out of that mental state that I allowed myself to be persuaded for a past life regression session. I thought, what's the harm? Anushka Doshi seemed like a nice, respectable kind of woman. At least till then, I had got no negative and dangerous vibes from her ...'

'I see. So where was this session held?'

'Here in my house.'

'And were only you and she present?'

'Yes.'

'So take me through how Anushka Doshi conducted the session.'

Kunika Ahuja petted Bruno again and pulled him a little closer. The dog snuggled and rewarded her with a lick. Then, as if to warn Motkar that he could be both loving and fierce, Bruno directed a low growl at them.

'No, Bruno,' she chided him, then continued. 'Anushka Doshi first told me that she would induce a state of hypnosis and then guide me to open the doors of memories of my different births. She said it would all depend upon my willingness to regress into my past lives and readiness in placing my trust in her to make that journey happen. By now, I was quite impressed by her compassion and kindness, so I wasn't sceptical.'

That was always the potent weapon of tricksters—the ability to win the trust of their victims. And it wasn't just gullible folks who fell for it. All kinds of people did, when they were in some stage of emotional vulnerability. It was like even otherwise healthy people falling grievously ill when their immunity levels were low.

'Did you ask where Anushka Doshi had learnt these past life regression techniques?' Motkar queried.

'Yes, I had asked her earlier and she told me the names of some psychoanalysts in Delhi and also how she had undergone training with some well-known hypnotherapists in Bangalore and Mumbai. She also said she'd attended a workshop of some international expert in this field, some Dr Brian Weiss, when he'd come to India, in 2006.'

Motkar nodded and quickly made a note. 'Please go on about what happened thereafter.'

'Then she described the kind of experience I might undergo during the session ... how I might see vivid memories and scenes from my past lives, hear sounds and voices, even feel sensations or smell things, as if everything were happening for real. She told me to be prepared to experience distressful happenings or incidents from my previous births because these were the key to understanding some of my fears and sufferings in this life, and the only way to overcome them and heal was by understanding what my soul went through in my past lives ... So, I should not resist such sad or painful memories.'

'How did she hypnotise you? Did she make you take some drug or something?'

'No, she didn't try anything like that. She simply asked me to shut my eyes and then softly gave me step by step instructions to relax my mind and body, which I followed and felt myself slowly entering into, how shall I put it, an altered state of consciousness,' Kunika Ahuja replied, almost as if she were reliving the experience. 'Then she asked me if I could see a staircase. When I said I did, she asked me to descend the staircase. Finally, she asked me if I could see a door, which again I did. Anushka Doshi told me that it was the gateway to my past lives and all I had to do was open the door.'

'What happened next?' Motkar prompted.

'Well, I opened the door and then began seeing a bewildering array of images like in a dream ... but ... but very real, which she kept asking me to describe. At first, nothing made sense but I had this feeling of familiarity as if I had seen all this before or been there before, you know ... like a déjà vu. It was as if I was looking at some old photo album. Anushka Doshi kept asking questions and I kept answering what I saw or heard or felt.'

'What kind of questions did she ask?'

Kunika Ahuja frowned. 'Actually, it's a bit of a blur, that first session. I was just too astonished by the whole experience. I think she asked me things like where did I think I was. Who were the people I could see? What was I wearing? Did I have any idea of the period? Hundred years ago, or five hundred years ago? These kinds of things ... but it's all vague. What I do remember distinctly after that session was that for the first time in months, I felt exuberantly happy, as if my sadness had fallen away ... that my soul and existence were immortal and did not have to be pinned down to the despair and sadness of my current life.' She paused awkwardly, as if conscious of how gullible she must sound.

'I see. What did Anushka Doshi say to you at the end of the first session?'

'She told me that I had sort of seen a trailer of my previous lives, and that in the next session she would help me go deeper with the help of the notes she had made of what I had seen and heard. Anushka said everything I had told her meant something, and that she would analyse it and chart my course to reconnect with important aspects of my past lives.'

'Nothing struck you as odd, or didn't Anushka Doshi make any kind of suspicious suggestions?' Motkar asked.

'No, absolutely not. In fact, we had the second session because I was really eager and hopeful that this past life regression would help me. So, I called her back on my own in the next few days.'

'I see. So tell me about the second session. Did you find out who you were in your previous births?' Motkar asked.

Perhaps the slight, unintentional note of derision in his tone conveyed itself to Kunika Ahuja. She stopped stroking the dog and her expressions became full of deep embarrassment. 'Inspector, if—if you don't mind, I'd rather not talk about it. I ... I still haven't been able to make out if what I saw and experienced that day during the session might have been a real glimpse into my past lives or whether Anushka Doshi only played tricks with my mind ... I mean, she was an evil woman, but at least in those first two sessions did she really give me a genuine experience, or was it just a con?'

'I understand. So, when exactly and why did you start suspecting something was wrong?'

Kunika Ahuja was silent for a few moments, and then quite extraordinarily, she pulled Bruno on to her lap, clutching him closer as if he were some teddy bear from her childhood. Bruno appeared to become a little self-conscious, as if even he felt he was too grown up to sit in his mistress's lap in front of strangers. But clearly, Kunika Ahuja seemed to need his proximity to speak further.

'Actually, I started getting uncomfortable right from the time Anushka Doshi turned up for the third session. She seemed like a different woman from the one I had known so far. There was a fake, edgy geniality to her manner and an impatient calculatedness appeared in her behaviour. She was also very pushy. She started by saying that I wasn't going deep enough into a hypnotic trance, which was hindering the process of regression. She said she'd got some tonic to give me that would induce a deeper state of hypnosis. When I declined, Anushka became irritable and almost hostile, saying she was only trying to help and if I didn't trust her, it was no use.

'I was firm about not taking the tonic, but although I felt uneasy, I allowed her to hypnotise me because I hadn't felt any kind of fear yet. Throughout that session, however, there was something cold and unpleasant in the tone of her voice. Then, for some unknown reason, I suddenly snapped out of the trance midway and something about the way she was looking at me, sent a chill down my spine. There was something very, very predator-like in her eyes. It scared me!'

Kunika Ahuja gave a little grimace and perhaps sensing his mistress's discomfort, Bruno bestowed another lick on her face.

'Please go on.'

'Anushka Doshi once again remarked that I wasn't going into deep trance and that she couldn't help me get to the root of my issues if this continued. She insisted that the tonic had to be taken. I fended her off, telling her we'd see next time and that I was feeling unwell. By now, I was really alarmed because I could sense a kind of ruthless desperation in her. Somehow, she finally left but was back the next day at my shop, back to being sweet and persuasive. But there was a certain cunning I could feel behind it all. When I refused another session immediately, she suddenly started telling me I would be doomed to grief and loneliness because there was a very specific reason she had diagnosed as the root of my unhappiness from all that I had told her during the hypnosis. Luckily, a few customers came along at that time, so Anushka left, much to my relief.'

'I see. But in your letter, you've mentioned you were scared for your life and you had a narrow escape. Tell me about that incident,' Motkar asked, wanting to get to the core of the story.

Kunika Ahuja hesitated. 'Inspector, it wasn't just one particular incident. The thing is, Anushka had now started coming to my shop or calling me on my mobile almost daily. It was as if she was stalking me. She once again harped on the secret of my unhappiness in my past lives and told me an extremely perverse story. She said all indications were that in my previous life, I had been a woman ... trapped in the body of a man ... and because the issue had remained unresolved in that birth, it continued to fester in my soul and being in this birth too, even though I was born a woman in this birth. She said, even though my physical self had changed, the inner conflict and torment I had experienced in the previous birth between my male and female sides continued to persist and made me feel devastatingly lonely and desolate in this life. Anushka said the only way out of such suffering was to purge my soul of the unresolved, suppressed emotions and conflicts of the previous birth by playing them out through past life regression.'

She stopped, regarding Motkar and the lady constable anxiously, as if doubtful they would believe what she was saying.

PSI Motkar gave a sympathetic nod. 'Interesting! So did you give in to Anushka Doshi's badgering?'

'It affected me. I was quite tired of my own state of mind and wondered if what she said might be worth trying, to get rid of the negativity I regularly experienced. I thought what harm could another session do? Anushka had not really done anything bad to me and perhaps her solution might help, even though the memory of her behaviour during the previous session rankled. So, I finally agreed to one last session with her. I made her promise that she would not bother me again if the session did not provide me relief, but she replied that its success depended on me using the tonic so that I could go into a deeper trance. Initially I agreed, but when Anushka came for the session, I kept getting an extremely uneasy feeling about the tonic, as if it would put me in danger. I told her that I had changed my mind about taking the tonic. She was clearly angry but accepted my decision. That day Bruno too seemed restive and kept barking at her when I tried to lock him in the other room, as I usually did during the trance.'

Kunika Ahuja paused and lovingly stroked the dog, then looked up at Motkar, and said, 'Call it my sixth sense or Bruno's, but he saved me that day.'

'What exactly happened?'

Kunika Ahuja's eyes filled with tears and, for a moment, she was overwhelmed as they rolled down her cheeks. Bruno sensed it and shifted his position, moving out of her lap and standing on the floor, facing her and wagging his tail helplessly. He gave a little yelp as if to console his mistress, then started rubbing his mouth and head against her body.

'Can we get you some water, Ms Ahuja?' Motkar asked gently.

'No, I'm okay,' she sniffed, suddenly stronger. 'Anushka Doshi put me into hypnosis and began asking me questions. I again started seeing and experiencing scenes and visuals from what seemed my past life as a man, and then suddenly I felt a sensation of great fear and alarm overcome me ... and just about the same time, Bruno broke into a ferocious round of barking. As a result, I snapped out of my hypnotic spell. The first thing I realised was that Anushka Doshi was standing beside me, and the look in her eyes was ... murderous. In her hands was her dupatta, but somehow the way she was holding it made me feel she had just been about to slip it around my neck and squeeze.

She froze when she saw me looking at her and for a few seconds we just stared at each other, as if both of us knew precisely what was going on in the other's mind. Then her demeanour suddenly changed, and she started complaining that the dog's barks had broken my trance and that's why the tonic should have been taken. I quickly got up and opened the door for Bruno and he came in and stood growling at her.

'I told her then and there that I was not interested in any more sessions; she became furious. She ranted at me, saying she would never forget the insult and that I didn't know who she was and what she was capable of. From that day, I had always been scared she would come back, and so I never left Bruno's side. I also took him to the shop with me.'

'Are you saying Anushka Doshi intended to attack you that day?'

'Yes! Inspector, not just attack, she was planning to strangle me. I could see it in her eyes, and if my sixth sense and Bruno's barks had not snapped me out of the trance, she would've slipped that dupatta around my neck. I was that close to death, I'm sure, whether you believe me or not!' Kunika Ahuja said defiantly.

'But why do you think she would do that?' PSI Motkar asked.

'I don't know. Maybe she wanted to rob my belongings, maybe she was a psycho, maybe she had some other horrible reason in mind, I have no idea what she was after.'

PSI Motkar studied the forty-five-year-old, pockmarked, stocky spinster in front of him once again. Was she being hysterical or overreacting? That she had undergone the unpleasant experiences with Anushka Doshi, as she described, he had no doubt. From other accounts as well, that of Gawli, the real-estate agent and Surekhabai, the cook, Anushka Doshi had emerged as a vicious woman. It was, therefore, entirely likely that Kunika Ahuja was right in believing she had narrowly escaped coming to harm or being murdered. The sight of an assailant standing so close to her, with a murderous look and dupatta in her hands, was certainly powerful enough to create and leave a lasting impression on a would-be victim's mind.

But could it be that the truth was more pedestrian? That Anushka Doshi didn't have murder in mind but was hoping to use Kunika Ahuja's hypnotic state to bind and gag her and then commit robbery in the house? Or maybe she was just standing close to her client to try her damnedest to ensure the trance did not break? After all, the session was a make-or-break session for her and there was simply no evidence of her actually trying to attack Kunika Ahuja.

'You think I was imagining all this, don't you? That a foolish, middle-aged, ugly spinster like me is being hysterical and fanciful,' Kunika Ahuja suddenly spoke with bitterness. 'That's why I didn't want to be identified, because I fully expected not to be taken seriously.'

'No, no, Ms. Ahuja. I'm sorry,' PSI Motkar said, genuinely apologetic. 'I am sure you've undergone a nasty experience. It just got me thinking that if Anushka Doshi tried it with you, she must've attempted it with someone else too. But none of her other past life regression clients has revealed any such experience. I'm wondering why.'

'Because, inspector, you don't realise how humiliating and traumatic it is for people like me to talk about such ordeals. It's the fear of being the subject of scorn and pity and ridicule, more than one already encounters,' Kunika Ahuja replied, and then bit her lips. She began stroking Bruno's head, as if that was all she could do to stop bursting into tears.

22

DESPITE HIS AVERSION FOR ANY FORM OF SENTIMENTALITY, Senior Inspector Saralkar couldn't help feeling elated at being back home, even if it was just for a fraction of a second. Of course, he immediately swatted away such silly thoughts as if they were flies, although they kept buzzing back as he went about freshening up and getting ready to go to office. It bugged him no end that the general buoyancy he felt this morning had to be ascribed to the fact of being back home.

The final straw was when he found himself humming under his breath, when he finished dressing up. He frowned at himself in the mirror. This was getting out of hand. He had to get back to his usual, unsentimental self. His mobile rang. It had to be either Jyoti or Motkar, Saralkar knew, as he walked over to pick it up from the table.

'Back?' his wife asked, as soon as he took the call.

'Yes,' he replied, dismayed at feeling nice to hear her voice just when he was trying to be himself again. 'Just finished my bath.'

'Going to office?'

'Of course,' he replied petulantly. 'I already told you.'

'Okay. Don't be late in the evening,' Jyoti said. 'And eat lunch before you go. It's on the table.'

'Yes. I know. You already told me.'

Jyoti called off chirpily, as if she'd paid no attention to his brusqueness. And for once, Saralkar wondered how she had put up with his chronic grumpiness all these years.

Jyoti had neatly laid out dal, bhaji, roti and rice, in different vessels on the table, along with a cryptic note stating 'curd is in the fridge'.

He heated up the items in the microwave and served himself. From the first morsel itself, it all tasted good. He wasn't really a foodie, but was quite picky about what he ate. He hated exotic, complicated dishes or trying out new cuisine. Green vegetables and salads were also anathema. While all this had presented a mighty headache for Jyoti early on in their married life, because of the limited options, permutations and combinations she had for cooking meals, she'd learnt to manage the show deftly.

Saralkar ate his lunch thoughtfully, sifting through the impressions and information lodged in his mind about the Doshi case. By the time the meal ended, his mind was again hovering over the perplexing connection to *Kalicharan* that his brain still hadn't retrieved, but kept niggling him about. What could it possibly be? He mined his memory for bits and pieces of recollections from the film. The basic story of *Kalicharan* was about a brave, young police officer, Shatrughan Sinha, who gets bumped off by the villain, Ajit, a smuggler operating under the guise of a rich, philanthropic businessman. Before dying, the officer scribbles a clue to the villain's identity, which no one is able to decipher. The police officer's father, himself a senior cop, decides to conceal the death of his son by replacing him with a hardened convict he comes across, who is the splitting image of his dead son. The idea is to use the lookalike as a bait to get the villain to strike again, out of fear that his identity will be revealed once the police officer regains his lost memory. That was the substance of the plot of the movie, peppered with the usual thrills, fights and other staple clichés of Hindi films of the 1970s, until the villain is finally unmasked and brought to justice.

In fact, Saralkar remembered, the basic premise was almost the same as that of an iconic film released around the same time, titled *Don*, starring superstar Amitabh Bachchan, except of course that in *Don*, a mafia don who dies is replaced by a lookalike in order to ferret out the entire gang and its leaders. Both films had been huge hits. But why was he thinking about *Don*, Saralkar wondered, when his brain had only conjured up a connection with *Kalicharan*?

He got up, put his plate in the sink, and began cleaning up, simultaneously trying to draw possible parallels between the Doshi case and *Kalicharan*. Prima facie he couldn't see any, and he was certainly not about to believe that his brain was hinting at the silly possibility of a convenient double being involved in the Doshi murder case. That happened only in films. And, in any case, Saralkar knew his mind was far too refined to latch on to such hackneyed or disingenuous possibilities. Perhaps it would help if he watched the movie again on DVD. Maybe then his mind would make the connection again.

Saralkar decided it was time to leave for office and start a microscopic scrutiny of all the material gathered by him and Motkar to identify dots waiting to be connected. They just had to put their heads together.

Of the many field tasks still pending with him, Constable Shewale had set out to complete the one related to checking the current status of various property transactions of the Doshi couple. Computerised registration of all land and property transactions had, of course, made it much easier to track mutations, but all the properties concerned were spread over a radius of about thirty to forty kilometres around Pune. So, while centralised checking of updated records at Pune Land Revenue Office was possible in theory, practically speaking, it was far quicker to go to the relevant registration office in the vicinity of the property, check the records and simultaneously make a quick physical verification.

It soon became evident to Constable Shewale that almost each of the properties about which Somnath Gawli had shared information—most of them in the name of Sodhi—had been sold off within a month before the murders, as if in a planned manner. All the impersonators who had earlier appeared in lieu of Sodhi as buyers had again appeared as him at the time of the sale of the respective properties. In fact, from the dates of the sale transactions of various properties, Shewale could make out a pattern.

The sales of those properties, which had the same person as a Sodhi impersonator, were registered on consecutive days, one after the other, and the same modus operandi was repeated in the case of other impersonators as well. As if each of the different impersonators was hired for a period of two or three days, during which all transactions in which that particular impersonator figured, were disposed of, followed by the next person on another set of days.

Mobin Ghatwai had been the only impersonator they had

been able to identify so far, although he had not been tracked down yet, despite activating the informer network. Neither had any identities of the other impersonators been established.

And then an idea struck Shewale. Could it be that the other impersonators of Sodhi were petty criminals from other states, brought over just to execute the registrations? It was perfectly plausible, with the additional benefit of having minimal traceability, because the individuals concerned would have had no prior criminal record in Maharashtra. Constable Shewale decided it was worth sounding out PSI Motkar about such a possibility, when he got back to office.

'Where the hell have you been, Motkar?' Saralkar demanded with a scowl as soon as Motkar walked into the office at 4 p.m.

No pleasantries, no greetings, even though they were meeting after nearly a week. How typically brusque of his boss!

'I'd been to question Kunika Ahuja, sir; the lady who sent the anonymous letter,' Motkar replied. 'We managed to trace her.'

Saralkar glared at him, still not appeased. 'What, you met her for lunch and stayed back for tea, is it?' he asked, looking far from impressed.

PSI Motkar could've laughed. It was such a typical Saralkar remark—funny, although garnished with sarcasm.

Motkar knew that briefing his boss about what Kunika Ahuja had said was the best way to blunt his sharp tongue and immediately proceeded to do that.

'But what could Anushka Doshi have gained by trying to harm Kunika Ahuja?' Saralkar asked sceptically once Motkar had finished the narration. 'Money? Property? What?'

'Still trying to figure that out, sir,' Motkar replied. 'We know from what Somnath Gawli, Surekhabai and Hrithik Dhond have told us that Anushka Doshi was a pretty vicious woman. Plus, this thing about past life regression is quite suspicious. I am thinking of meeting all her other clients to check whether anyone else has had an experience like Kunika Ahuja's and hasn't reported it.'

Saralkar nodded, his irritability having more or less passed. 'Okay. Now tell me all that you've put together since I left and I'll brief you on what I gathered in Bangalore.'

For the next hour and more, the two policemen exchanged notes and discussed all the leads and information, threadbare.

'It's all so bloody tangled still,' Saralkar finally grunted. 'We really need to get on with it, Motkar. Set up that interrogation with Rangdev Baba right away. I'll speak to the boss to check on sensitivities.'

'Should I arrange for more men, in case we have trouble at the ashram from his devotees and disciples?' PSI Motkar asked.

'Yes, but plain clothes guys, and keep them on standby near the ashram. Only if we require them, we'll signal. Otherwise only you, I, and two constables are going there with Dulange in tow,' Saralkar replied.

Motkar's eyes almost popped out. 'Why Dulange, sir? Won't it—'

'Just do as I say, Motkar. And don't ask Rangdev or his aides if we can come. Just say we're coming in an hour's time. Tell Dulange also to come here.'

Again, Motkar hesitated. 'We're going there just now, sir?'

'Yes. Why?' Saralkar snorted unpleasantly. 'Don't tell me you can't go because you have drama practice.'

'No, sir, it's not that,' Motkar replied with a scowl. 'It's just that going there in the late evening might attract undue media attention, which a normal daytime visit won't.'

Saralkar pinched his chin, creating a non-existent cleft. 'You have a point. But from what you said he told Dulange, Rangdev is the one wary of the media spotlight on him. I think he'll behave. And unless one of us tips off the media, there is little chance reporters will get to know. Let's get this over with tonight.'

He gestured dismissively and began dialling the number of the Pune Police Commissioner's Office.

Motkar gave a silent sigh. Poor Walimbe was going to hit the ceiling if he didn't turn up for the drama practice today, with the show scheduled for the day after. But Motkar had no intention of dropping out of the Rangdev Baba interview. He sent Walimbe a text message about being delayed and then began making preparations to set up the meeting, wondering how his boss was so devoid of normal human impulses. Any other person would've felt it prudent to go home early and spend time with his wife, since he had just come back to town after several days. One day, he wouldn't be surprised if someone discovered that Saralkar was actually an alien in human form.

23

RANGDEV BABA HAD SHOWN HIMSELF TO BE A SHREWD operator. When Motkar called, not only had he immediately agreed to meet Saralkar and him but had also betrayed no signs of surprise or nervousness when he saw PSI Dulange accompanying them. It either meant Dulange had found some way to give the god-man a forewarning or that he was a man who had long mastered the art of keeping his wits about him—the hallmark of many successful crooks.

His sidekick, Akhandanath, on the other hand, looked quite a wreck, ready to go to pieces any time. Motkar was tempted to ask his boss whether he should interrogate Akhandanath separately, while Saralkar had a go at Rangdev Baba himself. But Motkar knew Saralkar himself would say so, if and when he thought it would be a good tactical move. Instead, Saralkar instructed Rangdev Baba to send Akhandanath with Constable Shewale to collect details of all the disciples in his ashram. That having been done, Saralkar directed PSI Dulange to leave the room.

Rangdev Baba sat facing them now. Whatever he might have been feeling inside, he continued to look unruffled, regarding both Saralkar and Motkar as if they were erring human beings, who knew not what injustice they were subjecting a saint like him to.

'Tell me, inspector sahib, how can I help you?' he asked Saralkar, the picture of cooperation.

Saralkar continued studying him silently for a few seconds, and then said, 'Do you perform any miracles, Rangdev Baba?'

PSI Motkar recognised his boss's favourite technique—always begin with an unexpected question. It had the desired effect of disorientation on Rangdev, if only momentarily.

'Miracles? I don't understand.'

'Miracles,' Saralkar repeated. 'You know, like producing sacred ash and prasad, and other items from thin air.'

Rangdev Baba recovered quickly, giving a restrained, tolerant smile in response. 'Inspector, I don't have to resort to such cheap tactics to impress my devotees.'

'I see. So, what's your speciality, Baba? What unique brand of spirituality and piety do you offer that your fellow babas don't?' Saralkar asked, his tone beautifully balancing scepticism and sarcasm.

Baba yet again showed no inclination to take offence. 'I just help people cleanse their hearts and minds, purge them of negative behaviour, thoughts, habits,' he replied evenly. 'I try to show all those who come here to make amends for their past, make peace with the present, and make way for the future.'

He paused, with the air of a doctoral student who'd given a brilliant summary of his thesis, and expected the panel to instantly award him his PhD.

'Ah,' Saralkar said with exaggerated acknowledgement, 'I thought you did far more colourful things, going by your name: Rangdev Baba. Are you simply being modest?'

He gave the Baba a meaningful look and unease flitted through Baba's eyes for a moment, as if bothered about how much Saralkar knew. Then, with a thin smile, he responded, 'Inspector, some of us are genuine, you know. Not everyone is a cad, although I don't blame you for thinking so.'

'So how come a genuine Baba got associated with a genuine crook like Sanjay Doshi?'

'Look, inspector, I've already told PSI Dulange what—'

'What you've told Dulange is at best a half-truth,' Saralkar suddenly hardened his voice. 'That's not enough. What I am after is the full truth, with no details left out. So, I'd like you to follow your own advice and cleanse your heart and mind and purge them of all facts related to Sanjay Doshi's links with you, your ashram and your disciples.'

'But what makes you think I've held back anything?' Rangdev Baba protested with an air of injured innocence.

Saralkar smirked. 'Let's just say that like holy men, policemen too are blessed with divine intuition and vision sometimes. In any case, didn't you refuse to reveal the names of your two disciples with whom Sanjay Doshi was engaged in illegal activities?'

Rangdev Baba frowned and his left hand began stroking his flowing beard.

Motkar felt an irresistible urge to ask him what he'd always wanted to ask all so-called god-men: Didn't they ever feel itchy and hot, keeping all those locks of long hair and beards? He cast an eye at Saralkar whose eyes refused to leave Rangdev Baba's face.

'That I still cannot do, my dear Inspector Saralkar,' Rangdev Baba spoke gravely. 'Much as I would like to assist the law, I cannot betray the confidence of my two disciples who have confessed to me. They are like my children. The made a grave error of judgement and yielded to the temptation put in their way by an evil man, but now it is my duty to protect them.'

He paused and looked at the senior inspector with a solemn expression. If it hadn't been for his ingrained distrust of babas, Motkar might have almost found it possible to believe that some finer principles did indeed move Rangdev Baba.

Saralkar was absorbing the answer. Rangdev Baba was proving more assured than what he had bargained for. He had expected either angry bluster or naked invocation of nuisance value and influence from the Baba, or shaky ingratiation and grovelling.

'Do you realise you are obstructing justice by refusing to reveal the names of your disciples who were involved in illegal activities?' Saralkar said with a hint of displeasure.

'But you are not investigating those illegal activities, are you, inspector? You are investigating the murder of Sanjay Doshi, which is a completely different case and has nothing to do with my disciples!' Rangdev Baba said vigorously.

'How do you know for sure that Sanjay Doshi's murder wasn't a fallout of those same illegal activities?' Saralkar countered.

'But, Saralkar sahib, is there any evidence to suggest such a link?' Rangdev Baba lowered his pitch once again, making him sound terribly reasonable and far from defiant. 'If you do, I urge you to share it with me and I promise you I won't stand in your way, believe me.'

Rangdev Baba was really playing it smart, Motkar realised. Instead of hostile rhetoric or in-your-face haughty threats, he was just politely refusing to cooperate, knowing fully well that the police would be shy of using force, even against a god-man with limited following or influence like him, until armed with enough evidence. And he'd slyly reckoned that at least so far, they didn't have such evidence.

If it was an ordinary person, Saralkar knew he would've

been able to ride roughshod by dismissing offhand the need to share any evidence. But this needed delicate handling. To rely on finding something incriminating in the ashram against Rangdev Baba or his cohorts would be taking too much of a risk. And it could boomerang on him and the Homicide Squad if he took the Baba into custody or ordered a search of the premises without due process. He mulled over the situation for a moment as Rangdev Baba watched him like a hawk-eyed goalkeeper awaiting a penalty shot.

Saralkar decided there was no option but to bluff. The question was would it work? It was worth trying, though. 'Rangdev Baba, I am really not obliged to share any evidence with you. But since you've taken a stance, here are the choices you can make. Either you tell us who those two disciples are who were associated with Sanjay Doshi or, on the basis of the cell records we possess, of several calls exchanged between your aide Akhandanath and Sanjay Doshi, we will pick him up for questioning right away. I'm sure in twenty-four hours he'll reveal a lot more information to us than this case requires.'

Rangdev Baba went pale, and Motkar could've sworn that panic rippled across his face for a few seconds. Just as Motkar thought he was about to throw in the towel, the Baba surprised him by showing extraordinary spunk. 'Why don't you arrest me instead of picking on my disciples?' he said with shaky aplomb, sounding martyr-like. 'I am prepared to accompany you even just now.'

Saralkar cursed the man's gall. Motkar wondered if Rangdev Baba had stumped his boss now or whether Saralkar would take him up on his offer. The senior inspector was still trying to articulate a suitable response. What kind of a democracy was this that touching leaders, politicians, babas and rabble-rousers was fraught with apprehension of violence and law and order problems created by their irrational supporters?

How had the state allowed itself to become so weak that it had emboldened even charlatans with a small following, like Rangdev Baba, to possess disproportionate nuisance value? The commissioner had already warned Saralkar beforehand to be cautious, and that he didn't want any ugliness.

'Thank you for the offer, Rangdev Baba,' Saralkar said dangerously. 'I am tempted to take it ...' he let the sentence dangle, fixing Rangdev Baba with a long, hard look as if turning the matter over in his mind.

Motkar could sense Rangdev Baba getting uneasy and fidgety, trying his best to appear calm. Suddenly, Saralkar turned towards Motkar and beckoned him to come closer. Then deliberately, he whispered into his ears: 'Just nod and go out of the room as if on an errand, send Dulange in here, and while I engage Rangdev and Dulange, whisk Akhandanath away to the squad office as unobtrusively as possible. Give me a buzz once you leave the ashram with Akhandanath.'

Motkar nodded as instructed, shot a glance at Rangdev Baba, who had been watching them anxiously, and walked out of the room, shutting the door behind him.

'Are you making arrangements to arrest me?' Rangdev Baba asked with hoarse belligerence.

Saralkar merely shook his head. Before Rangdev Baba could ask any further questions, the door opened and PSI Dulange stepped into the room. Rangdev Baba directed an unfriendly glance at him, as he walked over and stood next to Saralkar. Saralkar looked at Dulange briefly. With two pairs of eyes blazing at him, Dulange's face clearly showed he would rather be elsewhere.

'Rangdev Baba, now please repeat all that you told Dulange,' Saralkar said, turning to the god-man.

Rangdev Baba took a deep breath of relief and began speaking. Ten minutes into his narrative, Saralkar's mobile pinged with a text message from Motkar. Saralkar clicked it open, expecting to find Motkar's confirmation of having nabbed and whisked Akhandanath away from the ashram.

Instead, a minor shock awaited him. Akhandanath, Motkar reported with great dismay, had bolted away just as he was being led out of the ashram, having given him and two constables a slip!

24

NOT EVEN THE NASTY LOOKING BRUISES MOTKAR HAD RECEIVED on his temple and shoulders in his scuffle with the absconding Akhandanath could save him from Saralkar's severe dressing down. Akhandanath had meekly accompanied Motkar and two constables towards their vehicle. Then, when one of the two constables holding him detached himself to open the door and drive, Akhandanath had suddenly twisted the other constable's arm and wrenched free from his grip.

Motkar, who had been alert, had immediately stepped into Akhandanath's way. But he had been no match for the burly build and strength of Rangdev Baba's aide. Akhandanath had violently shoved him against the vehicle and Motkar had banged into the half-open door of the car, losing his footing altogether and clumsily falling to the ground. Worse still, in trying to scramble up and raise himself, he'd inadvertently hurt his shoulder against the sharp bottom corner of the open vehicle door. That had been disproportionately painful and slowed him down, by which time Akhandanath had put enough distance between him and the cops.

The two constables had given chase but Akhandanath had slipped away, diving and disappearing into a narrow lane, a short distance away from the ashram. The plainclothes policemen scattered nearby had also been just a tad late in reacting.

'Why don't you retire from the force, Motkar? Or get a transfer to some quiet posting, away from the hurly-burly of policing.' It was Saralkar's final biting remark before he sat back in a huff and dismissed the entire squad, individually and collectively, from his presence.

PSI Motkar too began shuffling away. His shoulders were drooping as if the combined weight of failure and the shoulder injury would soon turn him into a hunchback. Saralkar watched him on his way out with mixed feelings. 'I'm not done with you yet, Motkar,' he snapped.

Motkar stopped and turned around to face him. A grim frown had settled on his face. Before Saralkar could speak, the PSI said, 'Sir, if you meant what you said, I'll apply for a transfer.'

He stood there, a picture of hurt dignity, leaning on some invisible cane of self-respect.

Saralkar emitted a fierce snarl. 'Don't bloody try to emotionally blackmail me, Motkar! You deserve every word I uttered and you know it.'

Motkar cleared his throat. The frown on his face deepened, 'Sir, I admit I have made too many mistakes on this case and that's why I'm ready to leave if you think I am no good.'

'We'll look into all that after the case is solved,' Saralkar retorted waspishly. 'First, you damn well try and undo those mistakes. Start by abandoning that blasted play, which is distracting the hell out of you. It's all but changed your damn DNA!'

Motkar cringed. 'That's not true, sir. My mistakes have nothing to do with the play. Anyway, it's just two days for the final performance after which—'

Saralkar threw his hands up in exasperation. 'Yes, we have

plenty of time, don't we? Forty-eight hours is nothing. We have an absconder who can get from here to the other end of the country within that time, but that's okay. PSI Motkar is busy with his play!'

He glared at Motkar but this time the PSI had nothing to say. An uncomfortable silence hung in the air for a few seconds, then Motkar spoke: 'Sir, how did Rangdev Baba react to the news?'

'The bugger just clamped up. And boss simply wouldn't allow me to take him into custody for further investigations,' Saralkar growled, then aimed a kick at his empty garbage bin and sent it flying to the other side of the room. He glared at it malevolently as it hit the wall and landed.

'I suppose it was because of all those disciples and devotees who had started gathering, sir,' Motkar observed. 'Apparently, Rangdev Baba's aides had WhatsApp-ed them to come over to the ashram in substantial numbers to help him out of the sticky situation.'

'Of course, I know that, Motkar, but these are all tried and tested tricks of such crooks. It's we who have to call their bluff. And Rangdev's not all that big. He's comparatively just a small fry. The police commissioner had no business being ultra-cautious. Now we're supposed to interrogate Rangdev here tomorrow morning. By then he'll have had twelve hours to get his story right,' Saralkar said with disgust. 'Whereas if we had had him here just now, he wouldn't have been able to dodge. He would've belched out the truth about Akhandanath quickly—why he ran away and what his involvement with Sanjay Doshi was.'

He again looked at the dustbin moodily, as if he wished he could plant another kick on it if there had been more room.

Motkar nodded, then asked, 'Sir, you reckon Akhandanath bolted because he was one of the disciples involved with Sanjay Doshi, and when something went wrong, he killed the Doshi couple?'

Saralkar didn't react immediately. In fact, it almost seemed to Motkar that Saralkar had not heard his question at all. Then suddenly, the senior inspector bent and opened his drawer. He took out the thick file of documents he'd brought from Bangalore. Saralkar began flicking the pages feverishly, then stopped and gazed intently at one of the documents.

He looked up at Motkar, his face and eyes now like some flickering screen, broadcasting the excitement in his mind. Quickly removing the document that had riveted his attention, Saralkar handed it over to Motkar.

Motkar realised it was the printout of police mug shots of a young man. Scrawled on top of it was the name Shaunak Sodhi, along with a brief physical description. He looked up at his boss again. 'Sir, do you think that—'

Before he could complete his sentence, Saralkar spoke. 'Yes, Motkar! If we put a long, flowing beard and tresses on Shaunak Sodhi's photo, isn't it possible he would bear a close resemblance to our absconding friend Akhandanath?'

Motkar looked down at Sodhi's photo again, trying to visualise Akhandanath. He nodded slowly. 'Yes, sir, there is definitely a resemblance and if Akhandanath is indeed Shaunak Sodhi, it will answer a lot of questions about the exact nature of contact between Sanjay Doshi and Rangdev Baba.'

Saralkar broke into a chuckle but soon his face became serious and reproachful again. 'You've sent out a priority alert for Akhandanath with photographs, right?' he asked.

'Yes, sir.'

'Well, get the police sketch artist to Photoshop Akhandanath's photo and send out variations without a beard and moustache, with only a moustache, with only a beard, and so on. My guess is Akhandanath will shed his facial hair to escape detection. So don't go home tonight before you get the variations done, Motkar,' Saralkar looked at Motkar spitefully.

Motkar had always known his boss had a mean streak. But Motkar also knew this time he had only himself to blame for inviting Saralkar's wrath. He nodded, picked up Sodhi's photo print for reference, and wearily began calling up a suitable police sketch artist.

It was almost midnight by the time Saralkar reached home. He let himself in with his key. The drawing room was dark and empty, but he could see the glow of the table lamp in the bedroom. Jyoti was awake, he realised with a sudden twinge of guilt. She must've been expecting him back since evening. It's the least any wife would from a man who had been away for a week.

Saralkar tiptoed across to the bedroom and glanced inside. Jyoti looked up from her book for a second, then continued reading. He knew at once that he had hurt her deeply once again—for the umpteenth time in their married life—with his little insensitivities. An apology played on his lips but refused to leave his mouth. 'You ... shouldn't have stayed awake,' he just said gruffly.

She didn't respond or look up. He waited, then started unbuttoning his uniform, and fled into the bathroom to freshen up. Ten minutes later he stepped out but Jyoti hadn't moved, as she usually would have, to heat up and serve dinner.

'No dinner for me tonight?' he attempted to jest awkwardly, hoping she would get up at least now. But she didn't even look at him.

Taken aback and embarrassed, he went into the kitchen cum dining room and switched on the light, anticipating that the dinner would be on the table, like lunch in the afternoon, for him to heat and eat. But the table was more or less bare. He felt both a little prickly and uneasy, for it had never happened before in all these years. Saralkar felt annoyed. Was Jyoti trying to teach him a lesson? His empty stomach cried out to be filled. He walked over to the refrigerator. Maybe she'd just left the food inside, so he would have to take the additional trouble of thawing it, then heating up. A limited lesson to an incorrigible, uncaring husband.

Much to his dismay, the refrigerator, too, was devoid of fresh dinner. There were only eggs, some curd, and some milk—nothing else that was ready to eat. He slammed the refrigerator door. Jyoti really hadn't made or left him any dinner. He stood there uncertainly, hungry, angry, acutely aware that he had somehow brought it upon himself—that his wife of twenty years had one fine day decided to let him feed himself, tired of his peremptory, neglectful ways.

It was a moment of truth, as his pride grappled with the realisation that perhaps he had caused her one hurt too many. Seconds later, he drew back the curtain and his ego that stood in the bedroom doorway, and walked across towards Jyoti's side of the bed, then sat down beside her.

She pretended not to look at him. He watched her for a few

moments, his ego still making belated protests, and then for the first time in his married life said, 'I'm sorry.' It hurt as he spoke, but it wasn't so bad.

Jyoti finally looked up at him, her eyes searching for something in his face. Saralkar hoped she wouldn't cry or something. It would all be so dashed melodramatic if she did. He was already experiencing withdrawal symptoms for having behaved so uncharacteristically from his normal, irritable, bossy and gruff ways. Should he have thrown a tantrum at her instead?

But Jyoti's reply reminded him exactly why they'd stayed married for so long. 'Must keep you hungry more often,' she said with a little smile. 'Come, let me lead you to your dinner.'

'You mean it's ready? How come I couldn't find it?' he asked relieved, both because Jyoti hadn't given him the terrible time she would well have been justified to, and, of course, because he wouldn't have to go to bed on an empty stomach.

'That's because you don't know all the places to look.'

He followed her into the kitchen and was taken aback when she opened the microwave to reveal a big container of sabudana khichadi, one of his favourite dishes. It had never crossed his mind to look inside the microwave directly—a simple, effective hideaway.

Minutes later, she had heated it up and served it, along with curd from the refrigerator.

'We'll fight once you finish,' she said, sitting by the table as he tucked into the khichadi with relish, 'you uncaring man!'

But later they didn't fight. They did other things, which many in this land of the Kamasutra would have considered age inappropriate. Another reason for the longevity of their otherwise cranky conjugal life.

25

MORNING SAW A FLURRY OF REQUESTS FROM RANGDEV BABA'S lawyers for postponement of questioning, claiming he had suddenly started feeling unwell the previous night and had been advised to undergo a complete medical check-up and bed rest by the doctors.

Saralkar had shot down the all-too-familiar feints, characteristic of politicians, god-men, public officials and white-collared criminals, to duck questioning by the police. He had given a deadline of noon for Rangdev Baba to present himself at his office, and the commissioner had backed him to the hilt this time.

To a bleary-eyed Motkar, still suffering from the effects of inadequate sleep, Saralkar's mood seemed unusually chirpy, in complete contrast to the foul mood just the previous night. In fact, he had expected his head to be bitten off even this morning, considering Rangdev Baba's delaying tactics. Of course, his boss had always had a mercurial temperament and Motkar had witnessed many a drastic change in mood before. But even by those standards, Saralkar appeared abnormally exuberant.

Perhaps, Motkar concluded, it was because overnight his boss had become even more certain of cracking the case now that the possibility of Akhandanath turning out to be Shaunak Sodhi had emerged.

But then who would blame Motkar for making the wrong diagnosis when Saralkar himself barely realised why he was feeling so upbeat—whether to attribute it to having deduced Akhandanath might be the elusive Sodhi, or to the delicious dinner of sabudana khichadi, or to the age-inappropriate, after-dinner pleasures.

'Let's join a few other dots in the case till Rangdev turns up,' he said to Motkar. 'Do we have any fresh inputs or updates?'

'Sir, Shirke and Shewale have something. Shirke checked out the land sales transactions of the Doshis. About a month before they were found dead, there was a selling spree. One by one, all the lands and properties in the names of all the Sodhi impersonators were sold off, as if in a planned manner. There was a pattern to it: the transactions in which the same Sodhi impersonator was involved were completed one after the other within a period of two to three days. Then that of the next impersonator and so on,' Motkar explained. 'This got Shirke thinking. He wondered if this pattern meant that the various impersonators, except Mobin Ghatwai, belonged to neighbouring states, since they didn't have any records here. Perhaps they were brought here for a few days one by one to complete the transactions and then sent back.'

Saralkar sat up. This tied in with his own hunch that perhaps some old associate from Karnataka had indeed been helping Sodhi and Bhupathi. 'That's good thinking by Shirke. Yes, it's quite easily possible to have brought in impersonators from Goa, Telangana, Gujarat, MP or Karnataka. My guess is Karnataka because both Sodhi and Bhupathi hail from there and my gut feeling is they had a network of associates. Check with Karnataka Police first. Send them photos and thumbprints from the sale deeds.'

He slapped his palm on the desk looking terribly pleased. 'What else, Motkar?'

'Sir, the other thing is about the call records of Meenakshi Rao, the lady who spoke to Anushka Doshi late night and early morning.'

'The one who is in Tirupati now? Isn't she back yet?'

'She's supposed to be back tomorrow but we haven't been able to get in touch with her again.'

'So what about her?'

'Sir, from the detailed call records, an odd fact as emerged.'

'What's that?'

'The last call she made on Saturday early morning to Anushka Doshi ... She claims she'd called to check whether she could come over for a particular ritual.'

'Right. And that Anushka Doshi told her not to.'

'Well, the mobile tower location data shows that she was calling from the same locality in which Anushka and Sanjay Doshi stayed.'

'What?'

'Yes, sir. She wasn't calling from her own house, which is in Aundh Road-Bopodi area. In fact, Meenakshi Rao was in all probability calling from the same building in which Anushka Doshi stayed. But she didn't tell us that, so the question is: what was she doing there at such an unearthly hour, sir? And why did she claim she was calling Anushka to check whether she could come over when she was already there in her building or at least nearby?'

'That's bloody odd,' Saralkar said thoughtfully. 'How long was her phone active in that locality?'

'Sir, it was active for about thirty minutes, though no other call was made.'

'And then?'

'Sir, her mobile was switched off and remained so for several hours.'

Saralkar puzzled over the fact for a few seconds. 'If Meenakshi Rao came to Anushka Doshi's house, then obviously she must've driven there on her own if she has a two-wheeler or a car. Otherwise, at that time in the morning, the only way she could've gone is by an auto-rickshaw or radio cab.'

'Sir, she does not own any vehicle. When we'd checked her address and neighbourhood, it was one of the things we asked and found out. And I doubt whether she's the kind who uses radio cabs.'

'So, find the nearest auto stand near her house and trace the auto-rickshaw driver who took her fare that day. At such an early hour, there are not many on the road and the only ones available are generally waiting at an auto stand to pick up early morning passengers who want to catch a train or a flight. In all likelihood, such auto guys are early morning regulars, so it should be easy to make inquires and find the one who took her fare. If that doesn't work, make inquiries with radio cabs. Maybe she did use one, after all.'

'Yes, sir. We'll also reconfirm when Meenakshi Rao's getting back to Pune.'

'Had you physically verified her brother's address too? What he does and all that?' Saralkar asked sharply.

It was again one of those awkward moments for Motkar, something which every policeman encountered now and then, when they realised something elementary had slipped past them even after so many years of experience.

'No, sir. We didn't really think it necessary to verify her

brother's details once we'd got confirmation about her address and identity.' He held his breath, knowing he could well be in line for a volley.

Saralkar regarded him as if skinning Motkar alive was exactly what was on his mind. But perhaps the PSI was saved by the senior inspector's mood. 'Get it done now,' Saralkar finally rebuked in a tone that was mild by his standards.

Just then a constable knocked and came in. 'Sir, that Rangdev Baba is here.'

Saralkar reflected momentarily whether to make him wait or start the questioning right away. Generally, keeping a suspect waiting helped heighten anxiety but Saralkar felt keen to have a go at the Baba immediately.

'Come, Motkar,' he said, getting up from his desk and heading out of the room. Motkar followed him into the interrogation room. Slumped in a chair, Rangdev Baba seemed to be desperately trying to convey the impression that he was now nearing a state of collapse. A lawyer and a doctor flanked him. The lawyer wore a black coat and the doctor a white one, as if they didn't trust Saralkar to believe who they were, if not for their garments.

'You are not required here,' Saralkar said piquantly to both of them.

'But, sir, my client—' the lawyer started speaking.

'Save your breath and leave the room. There's no detention, there's no arrest, so what's the fuss about?'

The two men looked at each other and then at Rangdev Baba, who was observing the exchange with watchful anxiousness.

'Bu—but, sir ... Baba is unwell, so—' the doctor said.

'Looks hale and hearty to me! We'll call you if required,'

Saralkar said, and shooed them away.

The black and white coats looked at the Baba again, hesitant to leave.

'Come on. Don't waste my time,' Saralkar growled. His tone packed enough authority to propel them out of the room.

Even as Motkar shut the door, Saralkar was giving Rangdev Baba the once over. The Rangdev Baba of today was quite different from the one they'd spoken to the previous day. His whole demeanour was like that of a boxer who knew he was just a few punches away from a knockout, only worried how hard it would hit and when.

'Why did Akhandanath run?' Saralkar asked.

Rangdev Baba shook his head slightly. 'I don't know why. Perhaps he got scared.'

'Scared of what?'

'Of what might happen to him in police custody, of being accused or held for the murder,' Rangdev Baba said with calculated boldness.

'Oh, I see! And now you are afraid it's your turn?' Saralkar needled him.

'No, no,' Rangdev Baba said, trying to sound unfazed. 'I haven't tried to run away, have I?' He tried to give a light smile, which only served to highlight how nervous he seemed.

'No, but then you tried all kinds of stunts to avoid being questioned by us today,' Saralkar said nastily. 'Why?'

Rangdev Baba shifted uneasily. 'I ... I'm really not feeling well, inspector. Can't that happen?'

'Yes, we see it happening all the time when we summon important people. Overnight they become unwell. Somebody ought to give a medical name to this unique condition. Khakhiphobia or something,' Saralkar sniggered. 'So, has Akhandanath tried to get in touch with you?'

'No, absolutely not! Trust me, I'll immediately let you know if he does. I'll also advise him to surrender,' Rangdev Baba said hastily.

Saralkar subjected him to a cynical look for a few seconds, then asked, 'Was Akhandanath one of the two disciples who partnered with Sanjay Doshi in those illegal activities?'

Clearly, Rangdev Baba had been expecting the question and had prepared an answer for it after consultation. 'I—I have also *now* started wondering if he was involved ... after he ran away. Maybe he was hand in glove with those two, although I never suspected it.'

It was a cleverly thought-out reply. Any involvement of Akhandanath would imply Rangdev Baba himself knew. By claiming to suspect Akhandanath now, the Baba could claim he had been in the dark earlier and thus not culpable.

Saralkar gave a knowing smirk. 'Ah, so you now think your aide could have been committing irregularities behind your back?'

Rangdev Baba resorted to histrionics, suddenly closing his eyes, shaking his head as if overwhelmed by the wickedness in the world. 'Greed ... greed, Saralkar sahib, can waylay the best of people any time. I have seen it happen. Maybe Akhandanath was also not immune to it ... even after all these years with me. I blame myself for not turning Sanjay Doshi away from my ashram even when I knew he was a dodgy character. But we men of God can't shun a human being just because he was a sinner in the past.'

Motkar, who had been watching his performance, now spoke:

'What exactly did you know about Sanjay Doshi?'

Rangdev Baba's eyes darted in his direction. 'Not much except that he had committed some crimes earlier. He said he'd duped innocent people and then run away with their money.'

'That's all you knew?' Saralkar queried sarcastically. 'I thought you conducted special sessions with devotees to elicit a full confession of their sins and cleanse their souls.'

Rangdev Baba paled a bit. 'I—I don't force anyone to tell more than they want to. That's all Sanjay Doshi said. It's entirely up to the devotee to decide how to embrace spiritual cleansing.'

Motkar asked, 'We've heard you make video recordings of the confessions of your devotees. Do you have recordings of Sanjay Doshi's?'

Rangdev Baba's reaction was animated. 'No, no, that's absolutely untrue! We don't do any video recordings.' He was now visibly rattled, suddenly behaving like a mere mortal. Saralkar and Motkar exchanged a glance. It was time to take it up a notch.

'Did you know of Akhandanath's criminal past?' Saralkar asked.

Rangdev blinked, sighed, and tried reverting to his worldwise self. 'You know, Inspector Saralkar, they say every saint has a past and every sinner has a future. I knew Akhandanath had served prison time, but in the last five years he's been with me, I have hardly seen a more transformed individual,' he paused and looked pained. 'Unless, of course, Doshi managed to undo it.'

'What crime had he been to jail for?' Motkar asked curtly.

Rangdev Baba cleared his throat. 'I think he told me grievous assault; he'd lost his temper and beaten a man badly, but attempted murder charges were framed against him. He'd been found guilty of assault and sentenced for a year.'

'Where?'

'He hails from a village in Karnataka. I think he was in Bangalore jail,' Rangdev Baba said carefully.

Bangalore jail! Saralkar could have punched his fist into his palm. 'What was his real name? Surely Akhandanath is the name you gave him.'

'Yes, I gave him the name Akhandanath, but I really don't recollect his original name.'

Saralkar reached out into his shirt pocket and took out a photograph. He showed it to Rangdev Baba. 'When he first came to you, did Akhandanath look like that?'

Rangdev Baba peered at the photograph, then at Saralkar. 'Well, it does appear like him at that time but ... but I can't be absolutely sure.'

It was an unsatisfactory response and Saralkar clicked his tongue. No one knew more than him how difficult it actually was to identify people from old photographs, especially if their appearances were completely different now. Policemen, of course, developed an eye for identification, although they too made mistakes. 'Was his name Shaunak Sodhi by any chance?' he asked irritably.

There was a nearly imperceptible flash in Rangdev Baba's eyes for a fraction of a second, but he was already shaking his head. 'No, that wasn't the name he told me. I faintly recollect it was Shivappa or some such thing.'

Saralkar's face darkened and his tone became menacing. 'Rangdev Baba, I hope you are not bluffing. I thought you recognised the name Shaunak Sodhi. Don't forget you don't enjoy immunity for withholding information or lying! It's a murder case, so you better volunteer any information you have or we're not going to remain as gentlemanly and respectful as we have been in our conduct so far.'

Probably no one had spoken to Rangdev Baba like this before, for he almost seemed to lose his voice for a few seconds. When he spoke, it was a bleat. 'All I know, Saralkar sahib, is that Akhandanath knew Sanjay Doshi. Nothing more.'

'How?'

Rangdev Baba shook his head. 'He didn't tell.'

'You didn't ask him, especially when you knew both had criminal backgrounds?'

'I did, but Akhandanath said it's okay, so I trusted him despite my misgivings about Sanjay Doshi.'

Saralkar's tone became harsher. 'Don't tell me, even when you got to know about the illegalities your two disciples indulged in with Sanjay Doshi, you didn't suspect Akhandanath's involvement? And just who are those two disciples? Name them.'

Rangdev Baba's eyes dropped to the floor. His body had begun shaking. Clearly, he was now on the edge—the point at which many people subjected to sustained questioning begin to realise it might be better to lay down the burden of lies.

'Quick, Rangdev, or we might have to take you into custody for more intense interrogation,' Saralkar said with frightening softness, almost like a teacher nudging a student to admit to wrongdoing to avoid corporal punishment.

The god-man looked up, his sly aplomb in complete tatters. 'Saralkar sahib, there were no two other disciples. It was Akhandanath all along who was working with Sanjay Doshi. When I discovered what was going on, I confronted Akhandanath. He—he promised to stop at once and return all the money he had made from siphoning and betting. So, I—I expelled Doshi but forgave Akhandanath. I—I didn't want a scandal ... but it's not got anything to do with the Doshi murder.'

'If that is so, why didn't you simply throw Akhandanath out after you found out what he was up to?' Motkar asked. 'You are still hiding something.'

Rangdev Baba looked at him helplessly. 'I needed him ... for the ashram's activities,' he replied lamely.

Saralkar chuckled. 'That's nonsense. There can be only two explanations. Either you and Akhandanath both utilised Sanjay Doshi's services to put the ashram donations into betting and other illegal activities or, if Akhandanath was doing it behind your back, you couldn't simply throw him out because he knew too much about other questionable aspects of the ashram, which he could have spilled if you'd expelled him. Which one is it?'

Rangdev Baba knew the hole he was in was getting deeper. He cursed the day he'd allowed Akhandanath to bring Sanjay Doshi into the picture for multiplying his ill-gotten wealth. If only he had followed his own sermon on greed. But then he wasn't the only god-man with a wide gap between word and deed.

26

IT TOOK CONSTABLE SHEWALE A SURPRISINGLY SHORT TIME TO find the auto driver who had ferried Meenakshi Rao to Kothrud from her residence on Aundh Road on the day she had made an early morning call to Anushka Doshi. Just one inquiry at the auto stand nearest to Meenakshi Rao's house had led him to Bhau Zore—fifty-year-old, puffed-up face and belly, dressed quite unlike an auto driver in a grey safari dress. There was no sign of the regulation khaki uniform and brass badge that auto drivers were obliged to wear, but the insufferable insouciance of the typical Pune rickshaw-wallah was on full display.

Bhau Zore had kept scratching his grey stubble as if it gave him special pleasure. One look at Meenakshi Rao's photo and he had nodded. 'Yes, I remember she was my first fare of the day, early morning, about two weeks ago.'

'Sure?' Shewale asked sceptically. 'Why would you remember?'

Bhau Zore winked and grinned. 'Yes, not much to look at, but pretty stupid. She thought she knew the address but didn't; kept making me turn into the wrong lanes. Finally, she made a call to the folks she was visiting, who explained to me where to come.'

'Who did you speak to?'

'It was another lady, but a sensible one.'

'Did you get her name? Did your passenger mention it while talking to her?'

Bhau Zore stopped scratching his stubble for a few moments, as if thinking, then resumed scratching. 'No. The lady just told me the name of the society and the way there since we were going round and round those by-lanes.'

'What was the name of the society?'

'Don't remember that but I can take you there,' Bhau Zore offered. He described the vicinity perfectly.

'So, then you dropped Meenakshi Rao at the right address?' Shewale asked.

'Yes, the other woman was standing by the gate.'

'Did you see her? Can you describe her?' Shewale urged.

'It was still dark. I could hardly make out the features well. She was about twenty feet away,' Zore replied. Then after a moment's thought, he added tentatively, 'They, sort of, did look like sisters.'

'Sisters? Why do you say that?' Shewale asked.

Zore shrugged. 'You know how people from the same family have a similar frame or gait or similar hairstyle, that way.'

'Okay. What time do you think you dropped her there?'

'Can't be sure, but it was around five or quarter past five, quite early actually. I even wondered why the woman was commuting so early. Generally, at that time we only get customers who want to catch buses or trains or flights.'

'Okay, one last question, Zore. Was the woman in the auto carrying anything? And did she sound normal?'

'That's two questions,' Bhau Zore said, as if the constable needed to pay for the extra query. 'Anyway, the woman was carrying a purse and a small skybag. Don't remember the colour but I think it had the logo of some mobile company on it.'

A skybag had indeed been found in the Doshi flat, Shewale remembered. 'Sure?'

'Yes, I don't have a habit of opening my mouth just like that.'

'Any other information you can think of about her or what was spoken?' Shewale asked.

Bhau Zore's brow puckered for a second. He looked at Shewale slyly and said, 'Well, I remember the fare amount I collected from her, if that's of any help.'

Pleased at his own joke, Zore started guffawing and Constable Shewale reflected that the average Pune rickshaw-wallah really worked hard to earn the reputation of being pretty annoying.

Constable Shirke also got his break, finally. His hunch that the impersonators of Shaunak Sodhi for the land deals were petty criminals from adjoining states was proven right when the Karnataka Police confirmed the thumbprints and photos of the deal documents, matched with those of four petty criminals of the Belgaum-Hubli area of Karnataka state, which was just a few hours' drive from the Maharashtra border. At least three of the four could be rounded up for questioning if Shirke came over with an official request.

By evening, just as Constable Shirke had boarded the overnight bus to Belgaum, he got another call, this time from the Karjat Railway Police. 'You had sent out an alert for Mobin Ghatwai, right?'

'Yes. Is he in your custody?' Shirke asked.

'No. We found an unidentified dead body on the railway

tracks. The man was probably drunk, strayed on to the tracks, and got run over by a fast local. Happens all the time. He could be your man, Mobin Ghatwai, although his body is so badly mangled that it wasn't possible to visually identify. But we got your alert and had fortunately taken the prints of his right hand which was intact. It seems to be a match.'

'Is the body in the mortuary?'

'No. We had to promptly cremate him after the post-mortem. His belongings are here—some cash and stuff, including a damaged sim card, though his mobile was crushed.'

'Any possibility of foul play? Did the post-mortem indicate death before being crushed under the train?'

'No, nothing like that. It could be suicide but sounds unlikely. There's a bar and gambling den nearby, where he had been seen earlier in the evening. He lost cash heavily, had a brawl with one or two guys, then walked out completely sozzled. We've questioned some regulars but haven't been able to find out who he brawled with. The likelihood of them attacking and throwing him on the train tracks looks remote.'

Constable Shirke sighed. He had to make a decision whether to postpone his Belgaum trip, where he could question impersonators who were alive, or go to Karjat first to dig around the unnatural mishap of a dead impersonator. What promised to provide a better lead?

'Okay, thanks. One of us will be there tomorrow,' he said to the Karjat man, then hung up and called PSI Motkar's number. The rings went unanswered. PSI Motkar was busy in the dress rehearsal in preparation for the final performance the following evening.

Constable Shirke pondered whether it would be okay to call

up Senior Inspector Saralkar but decided it was better to try PSI Motkar again the next morning. He settled down for the overnight journey to Belgaum.

'Sir!'

Saralkar looked up. PSI Motkar was standing across the desk, looking subdued and awkward as if about to make a confession.

'Yes, Motkar?'

Motkar hesitated for a couple of seconds and seemed to become stiffer. His voice was almost a whisper when the words emerged from his mouth. 'Sir, I hope you are coming to watch the Police Cultural Society's play tonight?' he asked, turning red and apprehensive, as if he'd just invited his superior to some orgy.

Saralkar managed not to grimace but couldn't stop a disapproving expression from fleeting across his face. 'Tonight, is it? I, uhh, I forgot to order my passes,' he replied, then added as an afterthought. 'All the best, for your performance.'

Motkar nodded nervously, then reached into his upper pocket, removed two passes from it and held them out in front of the senior inspector. 'I'd kept two passes for you and Mrs Saralkar, sir, in case you wanted to come.'

A look of annoyance that was hard to hide momentarily clouded Saralkar's face, as if Motkar had played some dirty trick on him. 'Nice of you, Motkar, but you shouldn't have bothered,' he said, making no effort to accept the passes. Instead, he began rummaging through the papers on his table, as if engrossed in looking for something.

Motkar, who had been leaning forward with the passes in his

hand, waited for a few more seconds, then drew himself back. His awkwardness was now replaced by acute embarrassment. 'It's all right, sir, if you don't want to come ...'

Saralkar was torn between a sense of vexation and the feeling of being incredibly mean. He stopped the act of looking for papers and made eye contact with Motkar again. 'No, no. I meant ... you should use the passes for other friends or relatives who may want to watch. You don't have to spare them for me,' Saralkar said lamely.

'No, sir, I had kept these for you only,' Motkar replied. This time he made no move to offer the passes but looked at his boss expectantly.

'Okay ...' Saralkar said grudgingly and held out his hand to take the passes from Motkar. 'All the best ...'

'Thank you, sir,' Motkar said diffidently and turned to leave.

But Saralkar couldn't resist one parting shot. 'Hope you'll get the acting bug out of your system and get back to being a cop from tomorrow.'

'Yes, sir,' Motkar murmured and left.

Saralkar stared at the two passes in his hand with hostility, then thrust them into his pocket. The few Police Cultural Society programmes he had been forced to attend in the past gave him no confidence that this one was worth looking forward to.

He grunted and bridled at the thought of the imminent wastage of two to three hours of his life. But there was nothing he could do about it now. He sat listlessly for a while then looked at his watch. It was 3.30 p.m. Motkar's play was at 6 p.m., which meant that he would have to leave office at 4.30 p.m. to get back home by around 5 p.m., pick up his wife and reach the auditorium in time for the show.

He had an hour to spare, not quite enough to do anything substantial. Then it struck him. Perhaps he could use the time to flick through *Kalicharan* and try to put his finger on what connection his mind had made. He'd procured a DVD copy of the movie and brought it along. Yes, that might cheer him up and who knew, maybe unearth a subconscious perspective on the crime, which might help crack the case.

Saralkar inserted the DVD on his computer. Right from the title sequence itself, the film transported him back in time to the mid-1970s, when films were crafted as family entertainers that included a little bit of everything—romance, action, emotion, song and dance sequences, and good clearly triumphed evil. He watched as Shatrughan Sinha, playing the brave police officer Prabhakar, confronts the villain, businessman Dharamdas alias LION, who also happens to be his father's best friend. On his way back to report to his father, the IG of Police, and unmask Dharamdas, LION's men mow down Prabhakar with a truck. On his hospital deathbed, Prabhakar gains consciousness briefly and manages to scribble a clue to the identity of the villain on a piece of paper, just before he dies.

When his father, the IG, comes, he looks at the scribble the other way round and it appears to be 'NO17'. Saralkar chuckled to himself. While the entire audience knows that Prabhakar's scribble is actually not NO17 but the word 'LION', read upside down, it takes the father and the son's lookalike the better part of the film to figure this out and bring the villain to book.

The next moment, Saralkar's chuckle froze on his lips as a jaw-dropping realisation hit him. He didn't need to see *Kalicharan* further. He knew exactly what had flashed through his brain that day, when he'd woken up from his snooze in the train. He felt in awe of his subconscious mind. It was as if a far sharper and agile Saralkar existed in there. The Saralkar of flesh and bone and conscious thought was just a slothful, mentally tardy, dull version, who had failed to see a clue that had been staring him in his face all this while.

But first, it was time to confirm on paper the realisation that was echoing around in his head and flickering in his mind's eyes. He reached for a paper and quickly wrote down the letters of both names carefully.

SHAUNAK SODHI
ANUSHKA DOSHI

He stared at them repeatedly as if one of the letters would simply not match. Yes, there was no doubt any longer! Shaunak Sodhi and Anushka Doshi were perfect anagrams! Someone had deliberately constructed the name Anushka Doshi by rearranging the letters of Shaunak Sodhi's name. And Saralkar's brain had seen what his eyes hadn't. The question was: what did it signify? Why had Krishna Bhupathi, an absconding criminal, chosen to give his second wife a name that was an anagram of his partner-in-crime, Shaunak Sodhi? And if Anushka Doshi was not the real name of his second wife, what was her real name and identity? Moreover, again the question to which he seemed to come back was: where was Shaunak Sodhi? Had he been parading as Akhandanath all these years, as Saralkar had surmised?

Saralkar's head spun with incomprehension as he tried to make sense of the stunning fact that had just emerged. Of one thing he was certain, that he had probably stumbled upon the single most complexion-altering element of the case. All the facts, information and material they had gathered about the case needed to be looked at again, this time through the anagram lens—like watching a 3D movie through 3D goggles finally, without which the images so far had just been a double-visioned blur. Hopefully, the images would now come into better, sharper focus.

27

MOTKAR WAITED DEEP INSIDE THE STAGE WINGS. HE HAD truly begun experiencing what was known as stage fright; the symptoms were all there. A hot clamminess bathed his entire body, coupled with a numbing stillness of the mind. He couldn't remember a single dialogue of his, leave alone the entry cue and his opening lines. The only functioning part of his brain seemed to echo just one message: *You are going to make a fool of yourself.*

The co-actors around him also appeared to be suffering from some degree of stage fright, although many had assured him that once on stage, everything would be all right and his mind and body would function on autopilot. He had been far from convinced, but there was nothing really he could do about it, except hope that they were right.

The atmosphere in the wings was subdued because the performance didn't seem to be engaging the audience much. The acting was dull and listless for the most part, with even the humorous lines falling flat even as the lead actors fumbled on a couple of dialogues. All in all, the portents were not too good, Motkar thought. His wife and kid were sitting in the audience and to make matters worse, so was his boss.

Mechanically, he knew his entry was due in the next few minutes but he felt like dead weight, as if his astral body was expected to go on stage instead of him. The vibration of his cell phone in the trouser pocket distracted him. He drew it out to take a look. It was a text message from Saralkar. Immediately Motkar felt better, assuming it was a thoughtful 'Best of Luck' message.

It took him a few seconds to realise that this was not the case. He read the message a couple of times but his brain was slow to absorb it: *'Shaunak Sodhi and Anushka Doshi are anagrams,'* his boss had written. It continued: *'How dumb of us not to decode this earlier.'*

It took yet another reading for the significance of the message to penetrate Motkar's befuddled mind. For a moment, he couldn't decide what flabbergasted him more—the sensational revelation or the fact that his boss had chosen to send him this message in the middle of the performance, when he ought to have known Motkar would be grappling with stage fright and nervousness.

'Motkar,' someone hissed into his ear. 'It's time for your entry after the next two dialogues.'

The words acted upon Motkar like a thermal shock, sending a nervous tingling down his body. He pushed the mobile into his pocket, cursed his boss for making his state of mind even more incoherent, and walked on to the stage on cue, convinced that the thudding of his heart would reach the audience's ears, even if his dialogues failed him.

Saralkar fidgeted in his seat. The play being enacted in front of him now could only be characterised as insufferably shoddy, with no redeeming feature so far. Every minute of the performance had been sheer agony.

What made it worse was the unstoppable buzz in his brain, ever since the Shaunak Sodhi–Anushka Doshi anagram had electrified his grey cells. There had been no blinding illumination so far, but that didn't stop his mind from sparking one thought after another, which made it impossible to sit still. That restlessness was also what had prompted him to send a text to Motkar, rather unthinkingly, a few moments ago. It was only after he'd pressed 'send' that he'd wondered if it had been the right time to communicate with his colleague and whether it might unsettle him.

'That's Motkar, isn't it?' Jyoti whispered, with a gentle tap on his hand.

Saralkar scanned the actors on the stage with any real interest for the first time. 'Yes,' he replied, watching his subordinate move uncertainly into position and give the distinct impression of having forgotten his lines.

The senior inspector held his breath, almost wanting to stand up and cheer lustily for Motkar, like spectators did when their favourite batsman walked out to bat. Finally, Motkar mouthed his first dialogue—his voice diffident and just a little too loud. Saralkar breathed easy and grunted with relief. Oddly enough, he felt something approaching a corny sense of pride watching Motkar perform.

It was one of those ghastly (in Saralkar's view) experimental plays about husband–wife relationships with a fantasy element. Motkar was playing the role of one of the mutual friends of a couple with serious differences in their married life. The mutual friends try to explore various ways to save the marriage, until finally one of the friends, a scientist, gives the couple a twenty-four-hour tablet each, so that the husband and wife swap places, one becoming the other. It is this exchange of bodies and souls and the leading of each other's life for twenty-four hours that brings them back from the brink of separation. Suddenly, Saralkar was intrigued.

'You seemed to be spellbound by Motkar's acting,' Jyoti said, as they made their way out of the auditorium later.

Saralkar gave a preoccupied grunt. 'Motkar can't act for nuts, thank God!'

But he was glad he'd come for the play. For the second time in the day, fiction had given him an idea—a very weird idea!

'Don't you want to go backstage and compliment Motkar?' Jyoti chided him.

'For his lousy performance? I'm not going to fake appreciation, Jyoti.'

'Come on, you're his boss. He'll feel good!'

Saralkar grumbled but allowed her to lead him along. Ideas, as he well knew, always increased the odds of cracking a case, even if they came from experimental plays. If nothing else, he, at least, needed to be grateful to Motkar for dragging him to watch the performance.

'Sir, Akhandanath has been nabbed,' Motkar's voice said over the phone.

Saralkar glanced at his watch. It was 7.15 a.m. The call had woken him up. Motkar sounded remarkably free from any sort of 'performance' hangover—nothing to suggest he had just finished acting in a play the previous evening.

'Where? When?' Saralkar managed to ask.

'At a small lodge in Shirdi where he was holed up for a few days, sir. Apparently, Akhandanath's epileptic. He collapsed, just as he was checking out. A local constable, who happened to come for a routine round at the lodge, was present when it happened. He thought he recognised the man as our fugitive. After Akhandanath was revived, the constable questioned him and found his answers vague and suspicious. Akhandanath also had no identity proof and pretended he had memory loss. The constable decided something was fishy and detained him,' Motkar explained. 'Two of their constables were anyway coming to Pune today, so they are bringing Akhandanath along. They've started from Shirdi and should be here by 10.30 a.m.'

Saralkar felt elated. It felt good to get up to good news. 'Looks like we're finally closing in, Motkar! Our lucky breaks are coming thick and fast. What did you think of the names tangle?'

'It really startled me, sir,' Motkar replied, then added in a mild, disapproving tone, 'almost derailed my entry in yesterday's play.'

'Ah! I know, I shouldn't have sent you the text then,' Saralkar made a rare acknowledgement of his mistake. 'I guess I was just excited.'

'What does it mean, sir? I have been thinking and thinking. Why should they choose to use an anagram?'

Saralkar cleared his throat. 'Well, the faint outlines of some theories have begun tossing around in my mind, but I am still not quite sure what it's all leading up to. For the moment, let's concentrate on establishing if Akhandanath is Shaunak Sodhi. Maybe then we'll have answers by the evening.'

'Yes, sir,' Motkar said. 'And thanks for coming to the play.'

'Oh, well,' Saralkar said, but did not admit to him that the play too had given him a kinky theory.

'May I ask you something, sir?'

'Sure.'

'Was the performance okay?'

'Didn't my wife tell you yesterday night when we came backstage?' Saralkar parried.

'Yes ... but what did you think of it, sir?' Motkar persisted.

Saralkar stood at a crossroads—to hurt or to fake? He drew upon all the diplomacy he could squeeze out of himself. 'Not bad, but you are a much better cop than an actor ...'

He paused, wondering if he'd managed to soften the blow.

There was an awkward silence, indicating clearly that Motkar was probably disappointed. 'Thanks, sir,' he finally mumbled. 'I hope to be a far better cop on this case from today.'

Saralkar grunted in response. 'See you at ten.' He disconnected, wondering if he could laze around for a few more minutes. Jyoti was already up. Astonishingly, last night they'd made love again. Twice in three days—something of a record in recent times when once a week or two weeks had become the norm.

That it made him far less grumpy couldn't be denied. And then his wife spoilt it all the next moment, by bringing him tea and asking, 'When are you going for the health check-up and tests?'

28

NOT ONLY HAD AKHANDANATH GOT RID OF HIS FACIAL HAIR BUT had also gone completely bald in a bid to avoid recognition as a fugitive. It would probably have worked if it hadn't been for the epileptic fit. His choice of Shirdi as a hideout too had been clever, because the town had a huge floating population due to the lakhs of visitors who flocked there to the famous Sai Baba temple from all over the country, every single day of the year.

'Sai Baba favoured us, Akhandanath, not you,' Saralkar said, as he regarded the sullen, well-built man in front of him, who refused to make eye contact as if somehow that would save him from answering questions. 'Why did you flee that day?'

There was no answer. Saralkar repeated the question in a louder, harsher voice.

This time, Akhandanath's body twitched as if bracing for a blow. 'I thought I was being trapped.'

'What trap?'

Again, there was no answer. 'Look, I'm not going to keep repeating the questions. PSI Motkar here already nurses a grudge and bruised ego because you gave him the slip. He can repeat the questions with his fists if you want that,' Saralkar said with matter-of-fact menace.

Akhandanath's hitherto averted gaze flickered briefly in

Motkar's direction. Motkar managed to appear suitably tough and hid the surprise, triggered by his boss's remark.

'I—I thought the Baba had struck a deal with you to save his skin and make me the fall guy,' Akhandanath said.

'Well, Rangdev certainly seemed eager to strike a deal. He's laid a lot of things at your door, which he desperately wants us to believe.'

'He's a liar, a liar!'

'So, you tell us your side, then we'll decide whom to believe,' Saralkar said with expert vagueness.

Akhandanath was silent. Saralkar could almost read his mind—how best to combine minimum fact with maximum untruth and provide a well-diluted version of his involvement.

As PSI Motkar took a step ahead, Akhandanath promptly spoke, clearly discomfited by the possibility of third degree. 'Sir, my job was only to channelise the ashram's donation money for the betting activities that Sanjay Doshi arranged. This was done on Rangdev Baba's orders. I don't know anything else.'

'Why did you kill the Doshis—husband and wife?'

'I didn't kill them, sir!' Akhandanath screeched vehemently. 'I know nothing about it. Ask Rangdev Baba; he must've got them killed. I was just a minion handling the ashram's activities, not a henchman.'

His eyes darted at both Saralkar and Motkar briefly, then turned to face the wall as if prolonged eye contact might let the police read something in them that he didn't wish to disclose.

Motkar took over as Saralkar subtly gestured to him. 'Why would Rangdev have got the Doshis killed? You knew Sanjay Doshi, you introduced him to Rangdev, you were involved in the illegal activities with the ashram funds, and you ran away! That's a clear sign of guilt,' Motkar said belligerently. He had to admit he'd begun relishing the tough cop role. 'After all, Akhandanath, you have killed before, haven't you? In Bangalore?'

Fear knocked out anguish from Akhandanath's face. It was as if he had stopped breathing, his whole demeanour becoming taut, finally giving way to little ripples of trembling. 'It's a lie. I didn't kill anyone earlier and I haven't killed Doshi or his wife now,' he managed to say.

'Whom are you bluffing? We know exactly who you are.'

Akhandanath looked at Motkar with a kind of defiant fearfulness. 'Who?'

Motkar gave a smirk. 'Your name is not Akhandanath. You are a fugitive from the law,' he paused for effect and regarded the paleness slowly suffusing Akhandanath's face. 'You are Shaunak Sodhi.'

'No! No.'

'You and Krishna Bhupathi, alias Sanjay Doshi, murdered your third partner, Rahul Fernandes, in Bangalore seven years ago and fled. Bhupathi assumed the identity of Sanjay Doshi and you became Akhandanath to evade the law successfully for so many years. And now you've killed your partner, Bhupathi, as well.'

Akhandanath's eyes were now wide with alarm and he was no longer avoiding eye contact. 'That's not true. I'm not Sodhi. I did not kill Bhupathi nor did I kill their partner you are talking about. This is absurd! How can you say I am Sodhi, sir?'

He looked at both officers—scared, angry and desperate. Both Saralkar and Motkar responded with silence, watching him intently.

Akhandanath turned to Saralkar. 'Sir, I'm Akhandanath. Who told you all these lies? Was it Rangdev? That bastard! I'm not Shaunak Sodhi, I'm no murderer.'

Right from the moment they had started interrogating him, Saralkar had begun getting the uneasy feeling that his hunch about Akhandanath being Sodhi was flawed. No doubt there was more than a fleeting physical resemblance between them, but his instinct now told him he'd been mistaken. As a police officer desperate to crack the case, low on real clues and high on theory, he'd perhaps made the mistake of seeing a resemblance and a connection that probably did not quite exist in reality. It happened to policemen—a strong hunch which they mistook for the truth. It was time to test if he'd just imagined a breakthrough. He'd already sent Akhandanath's fingerprints for matching with Sodhi's.

'If you want us to believe you are not Shaunak Sodhi, then tell us exactly who you are. Tell me about your past. Tell me why you were a jailbird. Tell me what crimes you are running from. Tell me how you know Bhupathi,' Saralkar fired questions at him.

Akhandanath swallowed, as if lubricating his throat and mouth to facilitate a long answer. 'My name is Shivappa Goud. I am an ex-convict ... I served a five-year sentence for ... for rape in Bangalore jail. That's how I knew Bhupathi, when he was also there. First for the recruitment scam, and then for the murder of his partner, before he got bail and absconded.'

'Were you and Bhupathi cellmates or something?'

'No, sir. But he was one of the few prisoners I had more than a nodding acquaintance with. I knew about the cases against him.'

'Go on.'

'Later, I came to know he was absconding. After I finished serving my sentence, I left Karnataka to find employment and ... some peace. I joined Rangdev's disciples and soon became his aide, especially because I could organise minor illegalities for him,' Akhandanath said. 'About seven to eight months ago, when Bhupathi showed up at the ashram, I recognised him. When I confronted him, he was fearful and I realised he was still a fugitive, living under a different name. Knowing his background, I asked him to help channelise all the ashram money into betting and deal in other shady activities for multiplying it, of course. He grudgingly agreed, scared that if he refused, I'd inform the police.'

'So, you were blackmailing, Bhupathi?'

Akhandanath wiped the sweat on his forehead and face by rubbing both against his upper arm and shoulder. 'I—I didn't need to blackmail openly. He just assumed that and I let him think so. I had no intention of informing the police if he didn't agree, but ... I made the mistake of telling Rangdev that Sanjay Doshi's real name was Bhupathi and that he was a fugitive. Rangdev is an expert in such matters and he used the information when there were disagreements about Sanjay Doshi's share of the betting income. But then Bhupathi also turned the tables and told him he'd spill the beans about the illegal activities of the ashram if he was ever betrayed.'

'So, is that when he stopped working for you?'

'Yes.'

There was something in the manner in which he said it that Saralkar knew he was withholding important information. But he needed more facts before pinning him down to reveal it.

'I see. But why did Bhupathi start coming to the ashram in the first place?'

'Sir, I wasn't there when he first visited once or twice. Rangdev had sent me to Kolhapur and Nasik to organise pravachan camps. But apparently, Bhupathi told Rangdev that he had come seeking solace and mental peace. He was drinking heavily and said his mind was burdened with sins of the past, that he had a very troubled married life and wanted some kind of spiritual medicine. This was before I told Rangdev about his past,' Akhandanath said. 'In fact, Bhupathi certainly appeared miserable and wretched when I saw him for the first time at the ashram. He had not recognised me yet nor had I confronted him. Even then he met Rangdev briefly in my presence and again talked of wanting peace and atonement for his sins. It was not put-on. He looked like a man going to pieces and under immense stress. I, of course, realised he wasn't bluffing because I knew his past and thought it was the guilt and stress of his crimes.'

'So, are you saying Bhupathi approached Rangdev assuming he was a true spiritual guru, because he was genuinely distressed?'

'Yes, that was so. Whenever I saw him, he looked haggard, anxious and weighed down, as if he was going to have a nervous breakdown any time.'

'Did you ever ask Bhupathi about his partner's murder, either when you were in prison together in Bangalore or later now?' PSI Motkar interjected.

Akhandanath shook his head. 'In jail, I learnt never to confide or invite confidences,' he replied. 'All I remember is that Bhupathi seemed shaken and scared during the whole time he was in jail for the murder. He would often break down and get up screaming in the night. But I didn't share a cell with him, so I don't know exactly. This was jail gossip and I never broached the topic when we met later.'

'I see. You knew Shaunak Sodhi well, too, didn't you since he had also been in jail for the recruitment scam,' Saralkar asked.

Wariness crept into Akhandanath's eyes and he hesitated, peering anxiously at Saralkar, as if to ascertain if he'd asked a trick question. 'Yes,' he hissed almost inaudibly, as if ready to change it to a 'No' if need be, then added quickly, 'but ... but ... I am really not Shaunak Sodhi. I don't know why you think so. I am Shivappa Goud.'

'All right, Shivappa, but you look uncannily like Shaunak Sodhi,' Motkar said, and held out the two photos before him—one of Shaunak Sodhi and the other a shot of Akhandanath.

Akhandanath stared with disbelief. He shrunk back and said vehemently, 'There's no similarity, sir. You are imagining it. You please check my prison record, my fingerprints, those can't lie.'

'We'll know shortly,' Saralkar said. 'Anyway, tell me, did Bhupathi ever mention Shaunak Sodhi to you now or earlier?'

'Never, sir.'

'Did you ask him where Sodhi was?'

'Yes, I did ask him if he and Sodhi were in touch, and how they'd managed to evade arrest for so long? But he did not reply. I didn't press him ...'

'Didn't he ever hint Sodhi was also in Pune? Did you ever go to Doshi's house or meet his wife?'

'No, sir,'

'Don't tell me you trusted Bhupathi with so much of the ashram's money without finding out where he lived or other details?' Motkar responded.

Akhandanath didn't reply. He probably didn't want to admit that he knew where Bhupathi lived. It didn't really matter because they were sure he knew.

Saralkar decided it was time to come to the real crux. 'Okay, so now tell me, if you had nothing to do with the murder, if you are not Shaunak Sodhi, if all that you were involved in was the laundering of the ashram's funds, if you are not a fugitive from justice but a convict who has already served his sentence years ago, if you have nothing to hide ... then why did you run away that day, thinking you were being trapped?'

He had asked the question with calibrated, matter-of-fact irony that fell short of heavy sarcasm or ridicule. It was the kind of reasonable tone that in Saralkar's experience worked well with witnesses or accomplices who held secrets or information, but were scared of being implicated in the crime themselves.

Akhandanath took a few seconds to make up his mind. He threw short glances at Saralkar and Motkar, as if checking out whether he ought to trust the policemen. 'Sir, I am scared that if I tell you something, it will be turned against me.'

'You won't be made a scapegoat if you are not involved, Akhandanath,' Saralkar responded tersely.

There was an unmistakable ring of truth in it, which conveyed itself to Akhandanath. He once again rubbed his shoulder and upper arm against his forehead and face to wipe sweat. 'Sir, I—I am telling you only ... only what Rangdev told me, after he had threatened Bhupathi that he would not hesitate to inform the police in case he refused to continue laundering money. Bhupathi first gave in. Then a few days later, he asked for a private meeting with Rangdev in which he said that he was even ready to permanently join the ashram if Rangdev could help him with a problem. Rangdev was tempted because Bhupathi really knew how to multiply the money through betting, so he asked Bhupathi what help he wanted. Apparently, Bhupathi said he wanted help to get rid of his wife, who was the root cause of all his miseries ...'

Akhandanath paused to see if he had aroused the interest of the two cops sufficiently. Sure enough, he had! Saralkar and Motkar's eyes and ears were riveted on him.

'Bhupathi asked for Rangdev's help in getting rid of his wife, Anushka?' Saralkar repeated slowly. 'And what did Rangdev do?'

'He asked Bhupathi a whole lot of questions and why he couldn't do it himself. Bhupathi said he no longer had the nerve, that he would mess it up and didn't want another murder on his conscience. Rangdev told him he would have to think about it and would let Bhupathi know in a few days,' Akhandanath faltered. His expressions were cagey and tense.

Saralkar guessed his own role in the affair was coming up and he was anxious to present it without indicting himself. 'Go on,' the senior inspector said encouragingly.

'Err ... Rangdev told me this one day and inquired if I knew any supari killer who could do this job. I was taken aback and told him I didn't know anyone. That was the end of the topic. Rangdev didn't discuss it with me again. A few days later, I was instructed to stop meeting Bhupathi and end the dealings with him. When I called up Bhupathi to inform him that there would be no further dealings, he told me he himself had refused to work further unless Rangdev Baba did what he'd asked him to do. I asked Bhupathi cautiously if it had anything to do with his wife. He just grunted and said if Rangdev tried to act smart and rat on him to the police, he'd make quite sure that Rangdev's goose would be cooked too. Thereafter, I had no further contact with Bhupathi.'

'But what about the phone call you made to him ten days before Sanjay Doshi's death?'

Panic made a comeback on Akhandanath's face. 'I didn't call

on my own, sir. Rangdev asked me to dial Bhupathi's number on my cell, then took the phone and talked to him in private. I have no idea what they discussed,' he explained anxiously. 'That's why the moment I heard about the murder, I began wondering if Rangdev had got it done through some supari. Then when you came and I was taken into custody, I naturally assumed I was being trapped in a deal Rangdev had struck with you. My phone had already been used to call Bhupathi earlier. Rangdev had also made a couple of other calls from my cell phone immediately after talking to Bhupathi that day. What if one of them had been to the supari killer? I didn't want to go back to jail for a crime I had nothing to do with. I—I thought I was being set up. All these thoughts ran through my mind and I panicked, so I just made a break for it. The thought of being jailed once again was too much to bear, sir.'

He paused abruptly as if suddenly aware of having exceeded some imaginary word limit. His head and face glistened with sweat like that of a marathon runner.

To Saralkar, Akhandanath's account had sounded quite probable even though it had taken him by surprise that Sanjay Doshi had approached Rangdev for help in getting rid of his wife. That possibility had never struck him. Was that the solution to the mystery behind the murders?

'But if Rangdev had arranged for a contract killer at the behest of Bhupathi, only Anushka Doshi should have been murdered. How come Bhupathi also was killed?' PSI Motkar put into words what Saralkar had just been thinking of.

Akhandanath shrugged helplessly, then said, 'Sir, maybe Bhupathi got killed by mistake because he was also present when he actually shouldn't have been.'

PSI Motkar looked at Saralkar doubtfully. Saralkar did not react. Instead, he said to Akhandanath, 'If it is confirmed you are Shivappa Goud, we'll talk further. But if you are lying, you've had it.'

'I'm not lying, sir. I'm prepared to undergo a lie detector test if you want,' Akhandanath pleaded.

Saralkar nodded curtly and left the interrogation cell, followed by Motkar.

'Sir, it doesn't make sense that Doshi got killed by mistake by the contract killer.'

'Strange things do happen, Motkar. This case only seems to get murkier and twisted,' he said thoughtfully. 'Wonder what kind of ugly truth we are going to end up with.'

29

CONSTABLE SHIRKE HAD ANTICIPATED THAT THE FOUR PETTY criminals from Belgaum, who had impersonated Sodhi in the land deals, would remain tight-lipped during questioning. Even after being confronted with evidence, they volunteered no information. It was pretty standard tactics from that class of habitual criminals. If they were busted, if the police had proof, it was neither their burden to co-operate and confirm the evidence nor to offer additional leads to complete the investigation circuit.

They knew they were generally only inconsequential cogs in offences which were usually not very serious. A few slaps countered with stoic denial that they had any information would get the cops off their backs sooner or later. A short stint in the lock-up or a few months in jail, and they would again be free. It was a low-risk existence and keeping quiet was the best policy to minimise damage from both law-keepers as well as those up the criminal hierarchy who had used them.

Therefore, Constable Shirke's question, 'Who hired you for the impersonation jobs?' elicited no response from any of them. Their faces were blank when Shirke mentioned the names of Sanjay Doshi, Anushka Doshi, Shaunak Sodhi, Bhupathi, Rangdev Baba. Nor did they react to the photographs of these people. But all that finally changed when Constable Shirke informed them it wasn't just a case of impersonation and forgery but also of murder. Their faces suddenly clouded with anxiety and concern. They hadn't bargained for murder.

Each of them began showing withdrawal symptoms, pleading they had nothing to do with murder and only with posing as someone else for a land deal. They hastily provided details of the travel to Pune, the places they stayed at, the measly amounts they were paid to do their part. But while two of them were still reluctant to give information about who put them up to the job, one of them finally revealed a name, begging Shirke not to let anyone else know he had leaked the information.

The name by itself meant nothing to Constable Shirke, but it was troublesome because of who the person was and his position. A little later, the name was confirmed in whispered tones by the last impersonator too.

Constable Shirke knew he needed to consult PSI Motkar or Senior Inspector Saralkar for instructions on the next move. On the pretext of taking a short break, Constable Shirke moved out of the cell and then out of the police station.

'Sir,' he said as PSI Motkar took his call. 'All the impersonators are in hand. Two of them are saying that they were hired for the job by a police officer called ASI Murgud, posted at Belgaum Crime Branch. What do you want me to do?'

PSI Motkar promised to call back in a few minutes after discussing with Senior Inspector Saralkar.

'ASI Murgud!' Saralkar exclaimed, and slapped his forehead with a why-didn't-I-think-of-it before air of disgust. 'Tell Shirke to ensure that the impersonators don't get an opportunity to call or pass a message to ASI Murgud,' he instructed Motkar quickly. 'Also arrange for their transit remand documents immediately. You can requisition a few constables from the nearest Maharashtra Police Station near Karnataka border to accompany Shirke back here with the impersonators.'

'Yes, sir. But who is ASI Murgud and what is to be done about him?' Motkar asked.

'ASI Murgud was the Bangalore Homicide Unit officer assisting Inspector Hegde in the Rahul Fernandes murder case. He was transferred to Belgaum later,' Saralkar explained. 'All along I've had this feeling that Krishna Bhupathi and Shaunak Sodhi could not have remained fugitives unless they had help from criminal associates or someone else. Perhaps it has been ASI Murgud who helped them escape and remain below the radar all these years. Or maybe it's not just Murgud but Inspector Hegde too! After all, we know that Sodhi and Bhupathi escaped with a lot of cash, taken from Rahul Fernandes. Enough to bank roll them for life and buy the assistance of crooked police officers.'

PSI Motkar nodded slowly. 'But if we move the impersonators to Pune, ASI Murgud is bound to get to know about it, since he works in the Belgaum Crime Branch. He'll immediately sense it's got something to do with the Doshi murders.'

Saralkar pinched his chin into a cleft. Motkar was right. The only way out was to arrange a simultaneous detention of ASI Murgud. He made a decision. He had to go by his instinct and trust Inspector Hegde, hoping he was not hand-in-glove with Murgud. And then he needed to go somewhere quiet and do some serious thinking. There were just too many strands and developments pointing in different directions—the anagram, the idea Motkar's play had given him, Akhandanath's revelations about Sanjay Doshi and Rangdev's involvement, ASI Murgud's role, and, most importantly, to make sense of it all.

'Has this Meenakshi Rao turned up for questioning?' he asked Motkar.

'No, sir.'

'Well, she has to be traced and questioned today, at any cost. And if she's missing, then send a request to forensics to carry out facial reconstruction on Anushka Doshi's skull.'

'Sir?' Motkar asked, taken aback, wondering what his boss was implying.

'Yes, Motkar,' Saralkar said wearily. 'If Meenakshi Rao does not show up today, we need to determine if the dead woman was really Anushka Doshi or was it Meenakshi Rao, her face destroyed by acid so that she could pass off as Anushka Doshi.'

He reached for the phone and began dialling Inspector Hegde's number in Bangalore.

The woman waited for her 11 a.m. appointment with her doctor in Panjim, Goa. She'd been here several times before. It was the place that had changed her life, five years ago. It had not been an easy change, wreaking confusion and rage in her heart and mind and flesh, as if two masters ruled her whole being—each trying to vanquish the other and gain complete dominance.

Perhaps it was like that terrifying punishment of medieval ages when a man would be ripped apart while tied to two horses pulling in different directions. But she had survived the excruciating transformation, and it was almost like being reborn as a different creature, except that this time the labour pains were your own. And the pangs never seemed to end. As if the newborn self had gone into one long manic spell of post-natal depression, itching to unleash its wrath on anyone.

'Ms Anushka Doshi,' the receptionist's voice cut through the woman's thoughts, 'Dr Dhingra will see you now.'

Anushka Doshi got up and walked towards the doctor's examination room, knocked and entered. Dr Dhingra wasn't one of those affable doctors who greeted patients with a wide smile and hearty, gushing bonhomie. He was a serious man filled with self-importance. At fifty-five, he was at the top of his specialisation—a life-changing job that wouldn't have been possible if he hadn't the essential gravitas, the aura, the confidence-giving manner that encouraged people to take that leap of faith.

In fact, surprisingly, what would have been a distinct disadvantage for other men—beady eyes, crowned with hooded eyelids—had turned into an advantage for him. It lent an air of dark, sombre respectability and competence, like that emanating from a suitably eerie Dracula, if you wanted to trust someone with the macabre arts.

'Come in, Anushka,' he said quietly and beckoned her to take a seat. He watched her as she pulled back the chair roughly and sat down. 'How's your condition now?'

Anushka Doshi glared at him. 'How much longer am I going to be in this half-way stage? It's been four years. There seems to be no end to the agony and torment. You had told me it would all be smooth!'

Dr Dhingra's face remained expressionless. 'Anushka, we have had this conversation before. I had told you quite clearly the risks and problems involved. It's just taking unusually longer in your case. You can never be one hundred per cent sure of how a particular body reacts. Even in an organ transplant operation, sometimes the body just rejects the new organ inexplicably.'

'Well, do something about it! I have paid you many times over. You are supposed to be one of the best in your field, so what happened? What went wrong with me? Fix it, damn you! You better fix it!' Anushka Doshi demanded, her voice shrill with rage.

'Calm down, Anushka,' Dr Dhingra said gently, rubbing one of his hooded eyelids. 'Tell me exactly what symptoms you are experiencing. Let me examine you. I'm here to help you see this through.'

Anushka Doshi's eyes glowered as if the doctor's words were having exactly the opposite effect on her, enraging her rather than calming her down. Then, without a word, she got up in a huff and began stripping away her clothes, as the horrified doctor looked on. A moment later, she stood before him stark naked, without a stitch of cloth on her.

'Look ... look at your bloody handiwork,' Anushka Doshi screamed. 'It doesn't work one bit! It's useless! None of it makes me feel like a woman. Either make it work top class or give me back what I had, otherwise I'll ruin you, Dhingra. I swear I will kill you.'

Dr Dhingra felt chilled with fear. He had been threatened before in his life, by unfortunate human beings driven to despair and misery. But never had those threats been more than pathetic outbursts. Anushka Doshi's eyes and tone conveyed a different, sinister menace.

'But we have done everything that can be done ... there's

really nothing more.'

Anushka Doshi appeared beyond the power of reason. 'I don't care. Fix it one way or the other, or I'll make you pay!'

Dr Dhingra felt a sweat break out all over him. 'Let me examine you, please,' he pleaded.

Anushka Doshi continued staring at him with hate and fury, then moved toward the curtained partition which screened the examination table. She lay down on the table, still fully naked.

Dr Dhingra composed himself, walked over, and began examining her. He had done a good job. Even after four years, the three procedures he had performed were fault free. As always in such cases, the problem lay elsewhere—in the patient's mind, in the unpredictability and inherent contradictions of the human psyche, and the anatomical eccentricities and peculiarities of individual human bodies.

'Have you been taking the oestrogen hormone injections and medication regularly?' he asked nervously.

'Of course, I have!' Anushka Doshi hissed back. 'And now I suppose you'll ask whether I am doing the vaginal dilation exercises adequately. How many times to do that in a day? Twice? Thrice? No bloody sensation; nothing, you bastard. I feel like a raving, throbbing lunatic.'

'Anushka ... please understand, there is really nothing wrong with the surgical outcomes. There is nothing more that can be done physically; it now depends entirely on lifelong oestrogen therapy and ... and psychiatric counselling. You know, in many cases it takes up to seven or eight years for the person ... to make the physical, mental and emotional adjustments to the profound changes ... to become the individual you wanted to become.'

'When ... when ...? I don't believe you anymore, Dhingra,'

Anushka Doshi exploded and sat up on the examination table.

Dr Dhingra recoiled, but before he could take any rearguard action, she had grabbed him by his collar. He let out a little gasp, his hooded eyelids doing a backflip, while his beady eyes popped out, as he felt the frightening strength of the naked woman's grip. He was about to scream but instead only a croak emerged from his lips. 'Look, Anushka!'

'You listen, you bastard. You've not made me the person I wanted to be, so give me back what you have taken. Return me what I had, what I was.'

'But, Anushka, you know it's irreversible. I had told you repeatedly,' Dr Dhingra whimpered, now almost debilitated by fear.

Anushka Doshi's eyes bored into him, filled with bitter loathing. She said in a vicious rasp, 'I don't care what you do but if you don't get me out of this condition, I'll do something terribly irreversible to you and someone you love, do you understand.'

What she told him next, made his blood run cold. Dr Dhingra wished he'd never set eyes on Anushka Doshi.

Inspector Hegde had shown no signs of hesitation or stalling when Saralkar had spoken to him about ASI Murgud. He had called back an hour later with some details. ASI Murgud had been taking frequent leave for two to three days in the past two weeks under the pretext of court appearances for personal property-related cases. Policemen rarely got frequent leave but sometimes they managed to use accumulated leave on critical or compassionate grounds. Murgud had claimed having to travel to Mangalore, his hometown.

Hegde said he would have it checked whether Murgud had really been travelling to Mangalore or elsewhere. He had also intimated Murgud's superior at Belgaum Crime Branch, who had agreed to ensure that Murgud would not hear about the arrest of the impersonators, either officially or unofficially.

ASI Murgud was due back on duty the next day, so Hegde decided against recalling him under the pretext of urgent official work to avoid arousing his suspicions. A colleague of Murgud in the Crime Branch would instead just casually call him up to ask for some minor assistance in a case and double-check whether he was coming back the next day.

'You know, Saralkar, while interrogating Bhupathi at that time, sometimes I would get the feeling he knew exactly what leads we had,' Hegde reflected. 'Once or twice, I wondered how uncannily he called my bluffs. As you know, this does not usually happen, except with really hardened criminals, which Bhupathi wasn't. Now it makes sense, if Murgud was helping. In fact, Murgud was on my team because he had also assisted during the investigation of the recruitment scam. So, I thought he would be useful to have because he'd dealt with Sodhi and Bhupathi before. Anyway, I'll do everything to nail Murgud personally, if he's been helping these fugitives all these years.'

'Thanks, Inspector Hegde. One more thing. Is it possible for you to grill Sherly Fernandes again on one point? She was not forthcoming with me about what kind of torture and suffering her husband, Rahul Fernandes, subjected her to. She kept saying she'd told you everything, mostly to ASI Murgud, and was not interested in repeating it. There was nothing much I could do officially to force her to reveal it, but I've not found anything in her testimony or statements in the case documents. Perhaps you could speak to her?'

'Sherly Fernandes? But what's her testimony got to do with Bhupathi or Murgud?' Hegde asked. 'What bearing will it have on the case?'

'Just indulge me, please. It's a wild theory, a possibility my mind has conjured up.'

'Well, I am a bit tied up with some important cases. Tell you what, I'll call Sherly Fernandes to my office, warn her she must co-operate with you, and then you can question her on the phone. How's that?'

'Suits me,' Saralkar replied, and thanked him.

His eyes strayed towards the lab reports on the vials found in the Doshi refrigerator which he had sent for testing. Hormone dosages. Oestrogens and anti-androgens. The pieces of the bizarre jigsaw which had been floating around in his brain for some time were beginning to fit into the slots, even if he was nowhere near sure what exact picture was emerging. He had to look harder, closer, check the patterns and the pieces. He needed to think, to look for other pieces in places that needed more careful scrutiny.

'Sir,' Motkar said, walking into his room, 'Akhandanath's identity has been confirmed. He's Shivappa Goud as he says, and he really did serve his sentence in Bangalore for rape. Most of what he's told us is true.'

For Saralkar, it had been a foregone conclusion. He'd long abandoned the theory that Akhandanath was the elusive Shaunak Sodhi. 'Okay, so let's get to work on Rangdev now. Summon him right away.'

'Yes, sir. One more thing, Meenakshi Rao hasn't turned up. Her mobile is switched off and she's untraceable. But the facial reconstruction on the corpse will take some time so we can't right away make any judgement that it wasn't the body of Anushka Doshi, or that it is definitely Meenakshi Rao's body either.'

'Never mind,' Saralkar said. 'It's Meenakshi Rao, all right. There's a simpler way to ascertain. Check the size of the undergarments found on the corpse. Chances are they'll match with samples found in Rao's house and be different from the size of Anushka Doshi's undergarments, even if they were roughly of the same build.'

Motkar was surprised by how the commonsense methods of policing had so quickly been taken over by an excessive focus on technology and forensics, that even policemen like him needed to be reminded of simpler methods of testing suspicions and doubts. 'Should've thought of that myself, sir,' he said.

For once, Saralkar was gracious enough not to take another dig at him, possibly because he was too preoccupied.

30

ASI DHARMESH MURGUD WAS A MAN OF FEW WORDS AND even fewer scruples. Policing was the perfect vocation for him. He could catch crooks, while also allow full play to the essential crookedness of his own nature—enjoy the best of both worlds. That's just the way he was made. The black in his nature had always coexisted alongside the white. In fact, the white nurtured the black, as if all his vices were legitimised by the single virtue of sometimes discharging his duties as a policeman.

Money was, of course, the big reason why he had helped two absconding murderers for the last seven years. He had helped in every possible way, even extraordinary, unimaginable ways, using his position and contacts as a policeman officially and unofficially to enable the fugitives to forge new identities, documents, conduct legal and illegal activities, and remain undiscovered for so long.

Money was also the reason he was abetting Anushka Doshi even now in yet another murky crime and in making a final bid to escape justice. But there was another motive beside money—the sheer thrill of criminality that coursed through his veins in doing something ugly, something wicked, something that gave the black in his nature a massive kick. It was almost as if he couldn't help doing it, as if some inner part of him gained terrific pleasure in doing acts decent human beings would dare not do.

Anushka Doshi—Murgud reflected with amusement—had been known to him by another name in another avatar. A killer then, a killer now, he was sure she could kill again if Dr Dhingra did not resolve her problem. Murgud, of course, would have nothing to do with murder, just as he had nothing to do with the other murders committed by Anushka Doshi in this or any other name. His task was limited to assisting before and after the act to the extent possible with resources, resource persons, logistics and information. This time he had agreed to provide supervisory services too. He had played his part in helping Anushka Doshi lure and ensnare Dr Dhingra's buxom mistress, Geeta Chaudhari, at Tirupati. Anushka Doshi had bumped into and befriended her, then baited her with her 'past life regression' trap about her liaison vis-à-vis Dr Dhingra.

The end result was the poor woman lay abducted and drugged at a farmhouse near Dharwad. A couple had been entrusted to look over her and Murgud had agreed to visit every alternate day to make sure everything was all right. He was at the farmhouse now because Anushka Doshi was to meet Dr Dhingra and to arrange for Geeta to scream into a phone, when Anushka called, in case the doctor showed any scepticism about his mistress's abduction.

But that had not been necessary. Anushka had not called. Perhaps Dhingra did not require convincing. Instead, another call came through now on his official cell phone from a colleague. Murgud had half a mind not to take the call. He was on leave; he could ignore it. But much of police work depended on networking, and when a colleague called, it was always better to respond.

'Yes, Naik!' Murgud said. 'Anything I can do?'

'Arre, Murgud, wanted your help, yaar! Where are you?'

'I am on leave today, Naik,' Murgud said cautiously. He couldn't think of any immediate assistance Naik might want from him. 'What's it you require?'

'Leave? Long leave or what? I just needed your help on an extortion case. Thought you'd be the right guy. When are you back?'

'I'll be in office tomorrow. Just came to Mangalore for my property case court date.'

'Perfect. So, what time can I drop by tomorrow morning? Ten?' Naik asked.

'Okay. At ten in my office.'

'Great. Thanks. See you,' Naik said, and disconnected.

Minutes later, Inspector Hegde was informed of the conversation with Murgud and that he could be detained the next day. Hegde, in turn, lost no time in informing Saralkar.

'Want to go down to Belgaum, Motkar, to grill Murgud? No drama practice excuses now,' Saralkar asked his subordinate.

Motkar flushed red. 'Raring to go, sir.'

'Good,' Saralkar said, then looked at the wall clock. 'Where's Rangdev?'

'Already in the interrogation cell, sir. I had just come to call you.'

Two minutes later, they were face to face with a visibly jittery Rangdev Baba. His face was drawn tight, the veins lining his forehead puffed up like tubes about to burst through the skin.

'Saralkar, sir, I heard Akhandanath was arrested. Did he ... er ... admit he was involved in all the illegal activities at my ashram?' the god-man asked at once.

Saralkar ignored his question and stared him down in silence. 'What is it you charlatans possess that makes blind devotees out of otherwise sensible people?' he asked.

Rangdev Baba had the grace to blush with shame and look away. He was hardly going to attempt to answer the question. In any case, Saralkar knew the answer—the terribly scarce commodities of hope, compassion, support and guidance in the garb of blessed spirituality. That's what the likes of Rangdev supplied—the most basic of human nourishments—which is why withering, despairing souls got drawn to them.

'Akhandanath says all the illegal activities at the ashram had your sanction and, in fact, you forced Sanjay Doshi to continue multiplying the money for you,' Saralkar spoke.

'I—I deny it, completely. I am a man of God—'

'Spare us that crap,' Saralkar interrupted him. 'Just ten minutes with two of my constables using old-fashioned methods and you'll admit to just about everything, Rangdev. That's a guarantee. I don't have time to humour you, so you better start spitting out the truth.'

Rangdev Baba's face was now dark and scrunched with fear. He was ready to capitulate.

Saralkar charged at him. 'Did Sanjay Doshi ask for your help in getting rid of his wife, Anushka Doshi?'

Rangdev Baba flinched, and went ashen-faced. 'People ask me for help with all kinds of difficulties. It doesn't mean I oblige.'

If it hadn't been so pathetic and defensive, it would've been cheeky and funny.

'Are you telling me people often seek your help to kill? They think you are some kind of Killer Baba?' Saralkar asked.

'No, no. I mean there are people, you know, who think a

god-man can use some kind of black magic to help them get rid of a spouse or a brother or a mistress or a tormentor.'

'Is that what Sanjay Doshi approached you for?'

Rangdev Baba took his time before nodding tentatively.

'You expect us to believe a criminal like Sanjay Doshi asked you to perform black magic to bring about his wife's death?' Saralkar scoffed.

'Yes, believe me, Saralkar sahib. You don't know how deep superstitions run. Whether it's ordinary people or criminals or the highly educated,' Rangdev said, sounding almost like a lamenting rationalist.

'What exactly did he say? Why did he want you to perform black magic on his wife?' Motkar asked.

Rangdev Baba pulled at his robe, on the crest of his shoulder, then smoothed it down his chest self-consciously. 'He ... he uhh said his wife ... he said his marriage was living hell, that his wife was a sexual pervert, that she tortured him, and made him do sick things he didn't want to because of her impulses. He said he was afraid he would never be free from her clutches and that he was terrified she might kill him some day,' Rangdev Baba paused, and clasped his shaking hands together. 'He ... he said he would lose his mind one day and go mad. He then pleaded with me ... asking if I could do some puja or ritual or anything that would end his suffering, that could lead to her death, otherwise she would kill him one way or the other.'

'Did he specify what kind of sexual perversion or why he thought she would kill him?'

'No. He just said he could no longer take it ... her sleazy demands. He said he had committed terrible sins and that guilt and fear and shame and disgust were driving him crazy. He said she would kill him because he'd been her partner-in-crime,' Rangdev Baba replied reluctantly, like a man afraid of being sucked into deeper waters.

'So, you knew very well he was an absconding criminal, probably guilty of heinous crimes,' Saralkar said pointedly.

'But I never denied that, sir. I—I told you being a god-man I can't turn anyone away, even sinners, criminals,' Rangdev Baba croaked.

'Even when a criminal comes and asks your help in getting rid of his wife? What a true saint you must be, Rangdev! What was he going to give you in return?' Saralkar's tone had suddenly shifted to a higher gear.

'He ... he offered money for me to perform black magic. I immediately turned him down and told him to leave. Believe me, sir.'

'You are bluffing, Rangdev! Doshi didn't ask you to perform any silly black magic to do away with his wife. He asked your help to actually eliminate her physically. In return, he said he would launder and multiply all your money for free. So, you arranged for a contract killer to get Anushka Doshi killed. But something went wrong and Sanjay Doshi got killed too. Isn't that what happened, you bastard?' Saralkar said, turning the screws on as Rangdev Baba seemed to become speechless with fear, his face and expressions doing all the talking.

'Speak up, you scum,' Saralkar bellowed at him again, and Motkar was aghast to see his hand rise up with lightning speed and strike Rangdev across the face. Once, then again, in quick succession. 'Or was it the other way round? Did you team up with Anushka Doshi to stage a double murder—of Sanjay Doshi and an innocent woman to pass off as Anushka Doshi?'

Motkar gaped at his boss, even as Rangdev Baba cowered, bushwhacked by Saralkar's unexpected assault. Speech, which had been knocked out of him by the force of Saralkar's words earlier, seemed to make a comeback now, rushing forth in a torrent of words. 'No, no, Saralkar sahib! That's not true. I didn't help anyone kill anyone. Not Sanjay Doshi, and I didn't even know his wife. I didn't arrange for any contract killer, I swear. Yes, I knew Sanjay Doshi was a criminal and ... and I did use him for illegal activities to multiply the ashram's money. Yes, he asked me to help him in getting rid of his wife but I ... I just played along, without doing anything! When he asked me again, I said what I could do is try some black magic, that's all. I don't know who killed the Doshis. Sanjay Doshi and I agreed to part after a dispute about the share he wanted of the money generated from betting and my other activities. We both knew we had each other's secrets, so it would be a folly to try and create trouble for each other. After that, there was no further contact.'

Rangdev Baba stopped, now reduced to the state of a common criminal, bracing himself wretchedly for more blows that might follow. Motkar was shocked as Saralkar obliged with another resounding slap. 'That's another bloody lie. You made Akhandanath call up Sanjay Doshi a few days before he was killed. What did you discuss? That you'd found a contract killer for him?'

'No, no!' Rangdev Baba spoke, almost on the verge of tears, shivering uncontrollably, his voice a whine. 'Please believe me, I had nothing to do with their deaths. I made Akhandanath call Doshi to persuade him to come back and work for me. I just dangled a carrot ... that I might know someone who could help with his problem. It was just to lure him back.'

'How did Sanjay Doshi react?'

'He was drunk, said he'd think about it. Then said he had to get her, his wife, before she got him. Then he started sobbing. He was a ... complete mess! He said he'd be grateful to me for life, but I didn't actually do anything, sir ... please believe me, I've told you the whole truth,' Rangdev Baba looked ready to grovel, his body tense and twitching in anticipation of being hit again.

Saralkar gave him a long glare, then wagged a finger at him. 'If you are hiding anything, Rangdev, I'll personally come back and set to work upon you. You won't be able to stand on your two feet again.'

In response, Rangdev Baba simply burst into tears. His humiliation and surrender were complete. Yet another human being had tasted spirit-destroying indignity, Motkar reflected. Not that Rangdev Baba didn't deserve the treatment for a life spent taking advantage of gullible human beings, but Motkar almost always felt sorry when it happened. Physical intimidation always seemed to work, but he wished there was a better way of getting people to reveal the truth than stripping them of dignity. It was soul destroying for policemen, too, brutalising their outlook, hardening their consciences, regarding all human beings as fair game for ill-treatment in the quest for answers.

As he followed Saralkar out of the cell, Motkar's thoughts remained unspoken. But perhaps his face was full of question marks, for no sooner had Saralkar glanced at him, the senior inspector scowled. 'Had to be sure it's not him, Motkar. Wipe that god-damned accusing look off your face. It's time to start eliminating all other theories and find the truth.'

Dr Dhingra poured himself another large peg of whisky. His hand shook, as if even the weight of the nearly empty bottle was too much for his fingers. There was no more ice and there was no more soda. He would have to make do with water, but his legs were unsure of getting up and making the short journey to the refrigerator across his consulting room. He toyed with the idea of sipping it neat, then decided to wait for a bit. Maybe in a few minutes, his body would gather the resolve to fetch the water. He shut his eyes and tried to make himself more comfortable on the sofa.

He hadn't gone home. He doubted he would be able to go home now, unless someone came over to pick him up. But what was he going to tell his wife or his sons? Why was he still in his clinic at all, that too drunk like that? He had kept his nerve all day—through two surgeries, scheduled consultation appointments, and his evening rounds of patients in his hospital. But, in the evening, the deep anxiety was back to haunt him like some ghostly creature of the dark.

He had taken a peg to steady himself, then another and another but that had not made it go away. What was he going to do now? How was he going to thwart Anushka Doshi from her horrible plan? How was he going to deal with her dangerous delusions? How was he going to be able to save Geeta's life if he couldn't persuade Anushka Doshi that it wasn't surgically and medically possible to reverse the procedures?

He had been scared but incredulous at first. But there was no doubt now that Anushka Doshi had not been bluffing about having abducted Geeta. A few days ago, when Geeta had suddenly cut off communication after reaching Tirupati, he had not known what to make of it. He had wondered and wondered what happened. He'd gone to her house. But it was locked.

He had kept trying her number, growing more and more anxious when all he heard was the recorded message that it was switched off. He had even briefly contemplated lodging a missing person's complaint but, of course, he couldn't do that. It would all be out in the open then that the well-known Dr Mahendra Dhingra had a paramour, who'd gone missing. It would create no end of trouble for him in his personal and family life. But not doing anything wasn't an option either. He really did care for Geeta. She was his love, even if illicit. He had set about looking for a discreet private detective agency which could help find her whereabouts.

That's when Anushka Doshi had come for her appointment and told him where exactly Geeta was and what would happen to her if Dr Dhingra did not comply with her wishes. She had played out a recording of Geeta, blindfolded and trussed up, pleading in utter terror to help her or these people would kill her. Anushka Doshi had given him forty-eight hours to decide exactly what he was going to do or she had promised, 'Geeta is going to die a horrible death and I'll make sure your whole sordid tale comes out, with you as the prime suspect in her murder.'

The wind had been knocked out of Dhingra when he'd heard that. His mind had almost ceased functioning. What alternative did he have? What was he going to do? His life was about to fall apart. Going to the police would not only mean a threat to Geeta's life but also to his family life. On the other hand, it was just not within his power to satisfy Anushka Doshi and do what she wanted. And failure to satisfy her would again mean the same thing—the end of Geeta and end to his life as he had known it.

Dr Dhingra opened his eyes. The whole world seemed to

be swimming around him. He reached for the whisky glass, staggered across to the refrigerator, afraid his legs would buckle any moment. Somehow, he managed to pour water into the whisky and slumped back into the sofa. He took a long swig, feeling no better than he had so far. In his liquor addled brain, he had even briefly considered the possibility of suicide, rather than face the consequences of the unfolding scenario. That thought now made a comeback with force. Instead of experiencing the humiliation of his reputation being ruined, the shame and disgust of his family, carrying the sense of helplessness and guilt of being unable to save Geeta, whom he loved, would it not simply be better to end it all?

It seemed the only way out—write a note to the police explaining all. Maybe his death would save Geeta's life, once Anushka Doshi realised he was dead and there was nothing to be done about it. Or perhaps once the police got the suicide note, they would nab Anushka Doshi before she could harm Geeta. And then even though he would be exposed in front of his adoring family, he at least wouldn't have to see the scorn, hate and disrespect in their eyes. Yes, Dr Dhingra thought as he took another big sip, that was the best course.

And then another idea materialised from the flickering recesses of his brain. What if he told Anushka Doshi he would reverse the procedures, get her on the operating table, and then turn the tables? Threaten to kill Anushka right there itself if she did not immediately release Geeta unharmed. What choice would Anushka Doshi have then? Vulnerable on the operating table and in imminent danger of being killed by a desperate doctor! Such was the startling audacity of the idea that, for a moment, his intoxicated senses experienced sudden clarity. Would he really be able to pull it off, Dr Dhingra asked himself, threaten to take the life of another human being and really mean it?

And what if Anushka Doshi dared and challenged him? Would he be able to take her life then, even if it meant Geeta's fate would also be sealed? Would there be any point if, in the end, it would only bring humiliation and fatal consequences? Dr Dhingra's mind began swimming again.

31

'Saralkar,' Hegde's voice boomed over the line. 'We'd activated our informer network to find out what Murgud's been up to. He's been going to Dharwad, not Mangalore, and has been spotted frequenting a small farmhouse on the outskirts of Dharwad—last week and even yesterday. I've requested for a watch on the farmhouse but it might be difficult because of VIP duty.'

Saralkar clicked his tongue. 'Sounds just like the kind of place a fugitive might hide.'

'Crossed my mind too that if Murgud has been helping Bhupathi's killer, then it's possible the person is hiding in the farmhouse,' Hegde said. 'But who exactly would that be, I am wondering. Shaunak Sodhi?'

Saralkar cleared his throat. He wasn't sure it was the right time to share the theory that had been growing in his mind with Inspector Hegde. He hadn't even told Motkar yet. It was too hypothetical and convoluted to explain over the phone any way, apart from possibly provoking incredulity. Instead, he decided to share the other alternative theory he had thought of, which, although equally full of suppositions, at least fell into the bounds of plausibility.

'Ahem ... look, the woman found dead along with Bhupathi

in their apartment ... is not his wife, Anushka Doshi, as we'd first thought she was. It's someone else's body. So not only is Shaunak Sodhi missing, but also Anushka Doshi, Bhupathi's second wife. That means Murgud is either helping both on the run after they murdered Bhupathi, or maybe it's just Anushka Doshi because as yet we've found no evidence of Shaunak Sodhi's involvement,' Saralkar struggled to explain. 'It's possible Anushka Doshi and Murgud have together planned and executed this whole crime. It could also be that Shaunak Sodhi is a phantom, who's left the country or disappeared on his own long ago.'

There was a ruminative silence at the other end as Inspector Hedge tried to digest what Saralkar had told him. 'I see,' he said at long last. 'Let me understand correctly. Your assumption is that Bhupathi and Sodhi might have parted ways long ago. Murgud was in touch with both or at least with Bhupathi. So, when Anushka Doshi married Bhupathi, Murgud and she decided to get rid of Bhupathi for the money and property he possessed and have liberally sprinkled Sodhi's name around to mislead us. Right?'

'Yes, it's possible Shaunak Sodhi is nowhere in the picture and his name has just been used to send us on a wild goose chase,' Saralkar said.

'Hmm ... you might have something there, Saralkar. Bloody diabolical if that's what has happened,' Inspector Hegde conceded. 'So, this means its Anushka Doshi who might be holed up in the farmhouse?'

'Yes,' Saralkar said, much relieved that Hegde was not sceptical.

'Okay. Send a photo of Anushka Doshi to Dharwad Crime Unit. I'll ask them to start surveillance on the farmhouse as soon as they can,' Hegde said, and gave the number of the concerned officer. 'Let's also see what Murgud says during interrogation. Bloody shameful for the Karnataka Police if he's neck deep into this.'

'Thanks for all the help. My assistant, PSI Motkar, will be there for Murgud's questioning,' Saralkar said, 'By the way, what about Sherly Fernandes? When can you get her to speak to me?'

Inspector Hegde's tone became a little tentative. 'She's refused to cooperate for any further questioning by you or us. Says that there is no legal obligation for her to comply with our request and that we can go to hell.'

'Come on, Hegde, it's bloody important. I have to speak to her. Please apply some pressure.'

'I've tried that, Saralkar. She's defiant. She says she will go to the National Human Rights Commission and State Women's Commission and complain about police harassment. She's technically right. I can't force her to answer us because it's not as if fresh evidence has come up in the case, or as if she is a suspect in the Rahul Fernandes murder. Anyway, what's so important? What has she got to do with your case?'

Saralkar hesitated and avoided the question. 'Can you just give me her number? Let me try. I just need her to answer one question.'

'If you insist,' Inspector Hegde grumbled, and gave him the number. 'But don't drag my name into it. I don't want any witness harassment complaints.'

Saralkar thanked him and disconnected. PSI Motkar, who'd been seated across, listening patiently, said, 'Sir, what do you need to ask Sherly Fernandes?'

'Just a question that might put at rest a freaky little theory my brain's been bothering me with.' He scowled at Motkar, then said, 'And all because of that drama performance of yours.'

Motkar's eyebrows shot up, then dived down to shape into a frown. 'I don't understand, sir.'

'Never mind, Motkar. I know you often find some of my theories downright crazy, isn't it?'

Motkar neither agreed nor disagreed. It was one of those questions. In reality, he'd always found his boss's theories brilliant, although he viewed them with extreme circumspection.

'Well,' Saralkar said, observing his reactions, 'this time the difference is that even I find the theory being cooked up by my brain so weird that I dare not share it with you first.'

Without another word, he began dialling Sherly Fernandes's number with one hand and gesticulated at Motkar to leave the room, with the other.

Geeta Chaudhari strained her ears to try and hear what was being said in the brief conversation going on in the next room. But except for some random words, she wasn't able to pick anything up. She wasn't sure whether it was the caretaker couple talking to each other or if there was someone else too. She thought she could discern the harsh, hoarse voice of the woman they called 'Madam'—the woman who had laid out the trap for her in Tirupati, into which she had walked with gullible willingness.

The woman had introduced herself as Meenakshi Rao from Pune. They'd met at the hotel she'd been staying in, and got into a casual conversation. Geeta had been drawn to her friendly, compassionate nature. Somehow, the subject of past life regression had come up and the woman had talked about how our previous births cast long shadows in our present lives, causing a lot of pain and problems. She'd inquired if Geeta had ever tried past life regression to ease her own pain and resolve her problems. When Geeta Chaudhari said no, Meenakshi Rao had startled her by asking point blank if she was stuck in a relationship with a married man, someone who loved and cared for her but could not marry her.

Her insight and sympathy had broken through Geeta's initial reserve and she had found herself confiding in Meenakshi Rao the state of her passionate three-year-long affair with Dr Dhingra, which could not progress to marriage and living happily ever after, since Dr Dhingra was married. Geeta had told her new confidante about her intense depression arising out of not knowing what was going to happen—whether the relationship had any future. She'd come to Tirupati as she did every year, hoping the deity would resolve her situation, show her the way, calm her emotions, bless her with peace and equanimity to face things as they were.

That's when the lady she knew as Meenakshi Rao had cast her bait. The deity might do its job, but past life regression was a wonderful way to make peace with oneself, to understand who our soulmates were, what relationship we had with them in our previous births. Would she like to try it?

Like an over-eager fish, Geeta had taken the bait and the next thing she'd known was waking up in captivity—disorientated, terrified, gagged, bound and trussed up. She'd quickly lost count of the days. Possibly she'd already been there a week now. Long, long days of intense, pounding fear, of not knowing where she was or what fate awaited her. Days on end of acute mental and physical agony—cramped body, sweat, grime, headaches, hunger, thirst, mosquito bites, and swinging in and out of consciousness.

The designated couple brought her some awful food from time to time and took her to the toilet thrice a day. Geeta had tried to resist and shout a couple of times, only to be immediately slapped or beaten viciously. The man had also threatened rape if she did not behave. Meenakshi Rao had visited just twice. Both the times she had said nothing to Geeta, just given her painful injections, the effects of which she was unable to process although it felt something inexplicable was happening inside her body. Another man had also come and gone, but his face was a blur and Geeta Chaudhari had no idea who Murgud was or why he had come.

The door to her room clicked open now. A torch or the beam of a cell phone shone her way in the dark, blinding her. Geeta could hear the rustle of someone walking across towards her. Her heartbeats quickened, like a car that accelerates to high speed within seconds. Every single time someone came into the room, the pathways of her mind were filled with fear that someone had come to take her, kill her, end her life.

The rustle stopped near her but Geeta's palpitations continued. Her heart was again in her mouth. She could make out the outline of the figure now. Was it Meenakshi Rao?

A pitiable, wretched mumble escaped Geeta's gagged mouth. It was an abject plea for mercy—nothing mattered more to human beings than life when it came to the crunch—not love, not pride, no finer principle or lofty emotion. Just life.

Meenakshi Rao's icy voice cut through the surrounding inkiness. 'Soon you'll know how much Dr Dhingra really loves you, Geeta.'

A cold, clammy sensation gripped Geeta's being. This was the first time since she'd been brought here that she'd received a ghost of a hint of why she'd been abducted like that, although the thought had crossed her mind before. She tried to speak again. Her mind screamed to ask questions, to know why, to plead!

She heard a chair being dragged and her captor sit down within arm's length of her. 'You want to know what's it all about, don't you?' Meenakshi Rao asked in a wicked, teasing tone.

Geeta emitted guttural, pleading sounds. Who was this woman? Why had she kidnapped her? What did she have against her or Dr Dhingra? Was she doing all this to punish her for having an affair with Dr Dhingra? Was she Dr Dhingra's wife, having discovered her husband's adultery? Was she by any chance a former paramour of Dhingra? Or was she a criminal holding Geeta for a big, fat ransom from Dr Dhingra?

Above all, Geeta's tortured mind wanted to know—would Dhingra pay up or do what the woman wanted? As her captor had asked—did Dhingra love her enough? Suddenly, Geeta wasn't so sure.

The next moment, her fear magnified hundred-fold as she felt the chilling touch of her tormentor's fingers and palm on the nape of her neck. Geeta wanted to howl in terror, as the touch travelled down from her neck to the cups of her firm breasts inside her blouse, fondling them, squeezing the nipples hard.

'Nice. Genuine. Guess Dhingra likes the real thing,' she heard Meenakshi say with menacing sarcasm. Then, the woman extricated her hand from Geeta's blouse and placed it on her exposed midriff, feeling the soft belly, pinching it, one finger circling the navel, then taking a quick dip inside it.

Every fibre of Geeta's body screamed with fear, as if her skin and flesh knew her captor's hands could slice and rip through her, if she so decided.

Anushka Doshi was groping at Geeta's buttocks now, pinching, pulling and patting but mercifully the fabric of the saree spared Geeta the direct touch of her loathsome fingers. But that relief was short-lived, for Anushka Doshi's hand reached Geeta's feet now, and then joined by its companion, both her hands entered the folds of her saree—ten spidery fingers riding up her ankles, calves and thighs.

What do you want, you sick, pervert woman? Geeta wanted to cry out. Meenakshi Rao's touch felt slimy, filthy and evil. The fingers of one hand inevitably entered Geeta's panties now, tugging at the folds of her most private parts, then slowly, insidiously, slid into her cavity.

'Perfect ... how does that feel, Geeta?' came the question in a hypnotic, low-pitch echo. 'I too wanted to be like that, experience such sensations, feel like a woman all over. I trusted Dr Dhingra, trusted him with my body ... and he fooled me and betrayed me! He said, 'Anushka, you'll feel every pleasure, but he's a liar! I don't feel a damn thing!'

She abruptly withdrew her fingers from deep inside Geeta. Geeta tensed as she felt her captor's mood change. *Who was Anushka? She had said her name was Meenakshi. What was happening?*

'Tomorrow is his last chance. I've told him if he can't make me feel the way I yearn to feel, then he should give me back intact what he took from me; he better do that! So pray he loves you, Geeta, or today might be your last night on earth.'

The voice was almost maniacally calm and chillingly, matter-of-fact. As if the thin line of sanity had been erased in Anushka

Doshi's mind and everything she thought of appeared perfectly reasonable.

Geeta heard her walk away in the darkness. The door of the room opened and shut behind her, leaving Geeta shaking uncontrollably.

Outside, the lone constable watching the two-storey house was almost nodding off, blissfully unaware of the conversation between the kidnapper and her hapless victim.

Sherly Fernandes had slammed the phone down on Saralkar twice. Then when he had called again for a third time, she had threatened to file a complaint against him with NCW, NHRC and Maharashtra state police authorities. When he still persisted firmly but politely, she had resorted to abuse.

That's when Saralkar decided to take the bull by the horns. 'Listen, Mrs Fernandes, did the torture Rahul subject you to have anything to do with gender reassignment?'

There was stunned silence at the other end of the line. Saralkar waited, unsure what she would do next. Would she disconnect? In which case he was sure she wouldn't take another call from him. Or would she answer—confirm or deny—that he had hit bullseye? 'Please, Mrs Fernandes,' Saralkar spoke again, 'trust me, I will not make any information public. You will not be dragged through any muck.'

He was surprised by the deep empathy palpable in his own voice. Had it got across to her?

He heard little sniffles, as if Sherly Fernandes was crying. 'The sick bastard ... used me as a guinea pig,' she said, her voice full of indignation and tears. Then her words gushed forth in a torrent.

32

ASI DHARMESH MURGUD SENSED HE WAS IN TROUBLE THE moment his ex-boss, Inspector Hegde, entered the room with his current boss, along with a Maharashtra state police officer. It was clear to him that he had been baited by the phone call from his colleague the previous day to ensure his presence. The point was, how much did they all know?

The allegations and questions came thick and fast, but he knew all about interrogation techniques and feints. For God's sake, he himself had used them so often! Murgud almost relished parrying and refuting all suggestions of wrongdoing. He denied everything. He denied ever having helped Bhupathi or Sodhi; he denied being in touch with them over the years; he denied helping them get new identities; he denied knowing Sanjay Doshi and Anushka Doshi; he denied getting petty criminals to pose as imposters for land deals in Pune; he denied being Anushka Doshi's accomplice in Sanjay Doshi's murder or knowing her whereabouts now.

He kept proclaiming his innocence, claiming hotly that he was an upright officer now being framed for reasons unknown to him. Murgud had no illusions. He knew he wouldn't be able to keep up the denials forever. But he certainly could limit the damage by first assessing how much they knew. Most people who committed crimes sealed their own fates by implicating themselves during interrogation. The trick was to make the policemen lay their cards on the table—a technique only habitual criminals used with a fair degree of success.

Only when he had some idea of the limits of the information and hard evidence available with them, would he start framing answers. He dared not underestimate the cops in front of him, of course. The Maharashtra cop, PSI Motkar, had slipped in a few surprise questions already and Murgud also knew Inspector Hegde to be a wily man, capable of giving suspects a frightening grilling. They would eventually press the right buttons or tie him up into knots. But he was fairly sure they wouldn't resort to third degree against one of their own ilk, that too so soon.

Just as he thought the first round of questioning was drawing to an end and that he would get through without being seriously pinned down, the unexpected happened. His other cell phone, the one in his pocket, began to trill. His official cell phone had already been taken from him and switched off temporarily by the interrogators. The rings from his pocket alerted them to his other cell phone, since he had not been searched so far.

'Take the call,' Inspector Hegde ordered him. 'Put it on speaker.' The stiffening of Dharmesh Murgud's body and the momentary look of alarm on his face had roused Hegde's instincts immediately.

Murgud slid his hand into his pocket and drew out the phone slowly, hoping the rings would stop while also wondering whether he should disconnect instead of taking the call. He knew he was damned either way. Why hadn't he put it on silent mode? But how was he to have known he would be in the midst of an interrogation.

'Murgud, quick! Take the call,' Hegde repeated sharply.

Dharmesh Murgud did as he was told and put the phone on speaker mode.

'Dhingra's mobile is switched off,' Anushka Doshi's voice came through. 'You think he might be up to something?'

Hedge gestured to Murgud to reply. Murgud cleared his throat. 'Maybe he's just in a surgery or something. Try again after some time.'

'Hmm ... I don't like it,' Anushka Doshi said edgily. 'Could he have gone and contacted the police?'

Murgud looked at the three cops in front of him nervously. If the conversation went on, he was bound to implicate himself in Geeta Chaudhari's kidnapping—a matter that his interrogators had not raised so far and perhaps did not have an inkling about. If they got to know about it now, he knew his goose was cooked.

He could make out from their shrewd glances that they had scented they were onto something. Hegde silently whispered instructions into his ear.

'I—I—I'll call you back in an hour's time. I can't speak much now,' Murgud stuttered into the phone as instructed.

'Okay. But if that bastard Dhingra tries anything smart, I swear Geeta won't go back in one piece,' Anushka Doshi rasped viciously before hanging up.

The remark landed a sucker punch on Dharmesh Murgud's prospects, blowing a big hole in his claims of not being involved in heinous crimes with Anushka Doshi. He felt sick. His interrogators were now going to make mincemeat of him.

It wasn't long before Murgud was telling them all they wanted to hear, to save his own skin.

It was late morning, and Dr Mahendra Dhingra had still not left home. Mercifully, he hadn't scheduled any surgeries that needed cancellation that morning, but he'd asked his receptionist to cancel all his appointments and also ring up other hospitals he was attached to, to excuse him for a day or two.

He'd driven home at 2 a.m., drunk and terrified of crashing his car into something or someone. No sooner had he reached home, he'd staggered to the bathroom and thrown up. His household had woken up, staring unbelievingly at him, shocked and wondering why he was in a state in which they'd never seen him before. His wife was relieved, concerned and indignant, all at the same time; his teenage children puzzled and embarrassed.

Dhingra, who was in no position to offer an explanation, just crawled wretchedly into bed—spent, humiliated and scared to death. When he woke up in the morning, his head was splitting, his body aching and feverish. The problem had, of course, not gone away. It loomed even larger, as if it had grown bigger during the night. What was he going to do? How was he going to save Geeta's life? What was he going to tell Anushka Doshi when she called? He frantically looked at the wall clock. It was past 10.30 a.m., he realised with panic. She was supposed to have called at 10. What if she had already tried calling, while he had still been sleeping?

Dhingra reached for his cell phone and doubled up with fear when he saw the missed calls at 10.01 a.m. and 10.10 a.m. What would Anushka Doshi have concluded when he hadn't taken the calls? How would she react? Would she take it as defiance? Would she be enraged? Would she immediately have acted upon her threats to harm Geeta?

An intense wave of nausea hit Dr Dhingra again, and he felt

mentally and physically drained. Yet, he didn't make any effort to call back on the number and try speaking and placating Anushka Doshi. What was he going to say, anyway? His brain had arrived at no solution. Instead, he sought refuge in the bathroom and turned on the shower. Maybe that would soothe the drumming inside his head and stem the sick, unhealthy feeling creeping all over his body.

He suddenly began to sob and retch, his body wrecked by the effects of last night's drinking binge and mind devastated by the burden of the situation he was in. Dhingra stepped out of the bathroom a few minutes later, no better in mind or body but feeling just a little less fragile. The rings of his mobile rattled him again and he felt curiously torn between the urge to answer the phone on the one hand and to ignore it on the other.

It was an unknown number, not Anushka Doshi's. Was she calling him from another phone to check what Dhingra would do?

'Hullo,' Dhingra answered timidly.

'Dr Dhingra, this is Senior Inspector Saralkar from Pune Homicide Squad, Maharashtra Police,' a crisp, authoritative voice spoke, stunning Dhingra.

'Yes, yes,' he managed to say, his blood running cold with the thought that the cop was calling to report they'd already found Geeta's body.

'Dr Dhingra, we have information that a patient of yours called Anushka Doshi has abducted your paramour, Geeta Chaudhari, and has threatened to kill her if you don't fulfil her demands,' Saralkar quickly summarised. 'Is that right?'

'How—how do you know?' Dhingra asked, his mouth sticky with dried saliva. 'Who told you?'

'Crimes have a way of surfacing, Dr Dhingra. Never mind. What have you decided about her demands?' Saralkar asked. 'Reversing the gender reassignment procedures you carried out on Anushka Doshi four years ago?'

'It simply can't be done, sir!' Dr Dhingra replied. 'The procedures can't be reversed. I mean, the breast operations can be but the penile inversion into a vagina cannot be undone. She's crazy. I've tried to explain this to her so many times. Nowhere in the world has it been successfully done.'

'I see. So, what was going to be your answer when Anushka Doshi called today? Say "no" and let Geeta die?' Saralkar asked sharply.

'No. I—I don't know what I was going to do ... try and reason with her again, maybe. I even had this crazy idea of saying I'd do the reversal surgery. Then once she'd be on the operating table, I would threaten to, uhh, kill her ... if she didn't release Geeta.'

'Why didn't you approach the Goa Police?' Saralkar cut in.

Dhingra spluttered to a halt, then replied defensively. 'Anushka warned me against it. Geeta's life is in danger, so ... so I am really scared. I didn't know if I could trust the police.'

'So would you prefer to continue handling the situation on your own?' Saralkar mocked.

'No, no! Please, please help me. Anushka Doshi already called twice this morning but I couldn't take the call,' Dhingra wailed.

'Couldn't take or chose not to take the call?' Saralkar asked.

'No, no. Please. I was so drunk last night. I just woke up. Tell me what to do, sir?'

'When did Anushka Doshi call?'

'About an hour ago. Two calls, at 10.01 a.m. and 10.10 a.m.'

'Okay. Here's what you will do, Dr Dhingra. Call back on the number. If Anushka Doshi picks up, tell her you have a solution. That gender reassignment surgery can only be reversed at an advanced research facility in some foreign country by a certain team of specialists who've done pioneering work in the field.'

'But, inspector, there isn't even a single successful ...' Dhingra felt compelled to interrupt.

'Dr Dhingra, hear me out,' Saralkar said forcefully. 'We have to concoct a convincing solution to lure and snare Anushka Doshi. So, you need to tell her what I have suggested. With your knowledge of the field, I am sure you can fill in authentic details of which country, which medical research institute, and the leading specialists, etc. You have to further tell Anushka that you are prepared to pay for all the expenses of the surgery, including travel, and that you will arrange for references and even documents to enable her to get a visa on medical grounds. You can even offer to accompany her. Then plead with her to come and meet you for a detailed discussion or show your readiness to meet her wherever she wants to. You have got to be persuasive. Do you understand?'

'But why not simply tell her I'll operate and ask her to come over?' Dhingra asked doubtfully. 'That's what she wants.'

'Dr Dhingra, do you have any idea who you are dealing with? Do you know Anushka Doshi's background?'

'Well, her original name as a man was Shaunak Sodhi, when she came to me five years ago. Her documentation and legal compliances were all in order, including psychiatric evaluation from two well-known psychiatrists. Why? How's the question relevant?'

'That's because she's not some crazed psychotic transgender who wants to become a man again,' Saralkar said. 'Anushka Doshi is a dangerous, volatile criminal who's killed at least three people so far, one as a man and two as a woman, and she will have no compunctions killing again if she suspects you are bluffing her.'

Dhingra gasped, feeling clammy and weakened. 'My God!' was all he uttered.

'Exactly. So, are you confident of explaining to a psychotic murderer why suddenly, overnight, you are in a position to perform a reversal surgery, which you said wasn't possible two days ago?' Saralkar asked. 'Should we take that risk?'

'No! No!'

Saralkar continued driving home the reasoning. 'Whereas, if you hold out hope convincingly by telling her you can help get it done abroad, at least we buy enough time. We have some idea where Geeta is being held, but we need to make sure we are in a position to rescue her unharmed. Or at least make sure that Anushka does not get into a murderous frame of mind. Also, it'll be a good reason to explain why you hadn't been able to pick up the phone earlier by saying you were busy speaking to the concerned specialists at the medical facility abroad.'

'Okay,' Dr Dhingra acceded as the officer's logic began making sense to him. 'Where is Geeta being held? Is she all right?'

'At a farmhouse near Dharwad, about 150 kilometres from Panjim,' Saralkar said. 'She's unharmed, as far as we know.'

'But Dharwad is in Karnataka state, so how come you are from Maharashtra Police?' Dr Dhingra asked.

'It's a joint operation. In fact, we'll also be coordinating with the Goa Police. Anyway, let's not waste any more time. You need to call Anushka immediately. Ring me back as soon as you finish talking to her. Then we'll devise the plan of action. Do you want me to repeat the instructions and what you need to say?'

'No,' Dr Dhingra said, now feeling a lot less weak and helpless.

He disconnected the call and then took a few seconds to compose himself. Ideally, he would've liked to show his face to his wife briefly, but he knew there was no time to be lost. He braced himself and began dialling Anushka Doshi's number. His fingers shook, something that never happened to him when he wielded the surgical scalpel.

33

'WE NEED TO PREPARE FOR BOTH POSSIBILITIES,' INSPECTOR Hegde said, as the four police officers conferred on a con-call. PSI Motkar and Murgud's boss sat beside him while Senior Inspector Saralkar was at the other end of the line, 300 kilometres away in Pune. 'If Anushka Doshi agrees to meet Dr Dhingra at his clinic in Goa, then it might be simpler. We set up a police team at the clinic, in wait for Anushka to show up. Meanwhile, we send Murgud to the farmhouse where he is let in by the two caretakers. Then our police team follows, makes them surrender with Murgud's help, and releases Geeta Chaudhari. Ditto, if Anushka calls Dhingra to some other location. On the other hand, it's going to be very tricky if Anushka calls Dhingra to the farmhouse in Dharwad. She will then have two hostages instead of one. Assuming we send in Murgud and surround the farmhouse, how do we know for sure Anushka and the two henchmen will surrender without a fight?'

Saralkar, seated in his office in Pune, grunted into the receiver. 'True.' He refrained from mentioning that what was really giving him the jitters was the third possibility of Anushka Doshi simply turning down Dhingra's proposal. Then they would be left with no option but to plan a rescue operation within hours.

'What do we know about the couple at the farmhouse? Are

they history-sheeters or just petty criminals?' he asked.

'Not comforting at all,' Hegde replied. 'Both the man and woman have a record of violent crimes. But Murgud says they'll do exactly what he tells them to.'

'Including surrendering meekly and getting arrested if there is a police raid?' Saralkar asked sceptically. 'I doubt that.'

'Mmm ... I am also not all that sure, after seeing their records.'

Motkar interjected. 'The two also have arms with them, sir. Two country-made revolvers at least, Murgud told us.'

'That's bloody great,' Saralkar grumbled. 'Is that guy, Murgud, just bloody rotten or also crazy to supply gun-toting henchmen to a murderer for a crime like this? It can't be just money.'

'Everything in this case seems bizarre, Saralkar, and everyone sounds crazy,' Hegde replied. 'I mean, this guy, Sodhi, undergoes sex change, becomes a woman and lives as Anushka Doshi with Bhupathi as husband. Later, she suddenly wants to reverse the change and wants to become a man again, so she kills Bhupathi and another woman to pass off as herself. Then she kidnaps her doctor's paramour to force him to conduct an impossible reversal surgery. It's too twisted even for someone like me who's seen it all. And to top everything, a police officer is involved neck deep in the crimes.'

Saralkar took a deep breath. It was now time to take them into confidence and lay bare his startling conjectures and conclusions. 'That's not all, Hegde,' he said. 'There's still something Murgud hasn't told you.'

'What?'

'That it wasn't Shaunak Sodhi who underwent sex change to become Anushka Doshi. It is Rahul Fernandes who transformed into Anushka Doshi. It was Shaunak Sodhi who was killed by his partners Fernandes and Bhupathi all those years ago. It was Sodhi's body you found with its head severed. So, it's Rahul Fernandes we are dealing with.'

There was a bewildered silence on the con-call for a few seconds, as if the three cops in Belgaum had collectively held their breaths or had the plugs pulled out of them.

'Anushka Doshi is actually Rahul Fernandes?' Inspector Hegde repeated slowly, grappling with the new information. 'How do you know? Did Sherly Fernandes tell you this?'

'No. She doesn't know Rahul is alive and exists as Anushka Doshi today. What she confirmed was that Rahul Fernandes married her to use her as a guinea pig.'

'What do you mean?'

'Look, it's bloody convoluted. Can I explain later? There are a lot of conjectures and leaps of reasoning from my side, as of now. Only when we have Anushka Doshi in hand can we get the whole picture,' Saralkar said. 'But I am quite sure of one thing. And that's that we are after Rahul Fernandes, not Shaunak Sodhi, who's long dead.'

He knew it must sound unsatisfactory to his colleagues in Belgaum and they would be itching to ask more questions. Mercifully, his cell phone rang at that moment. 'Just hold on, Dhingra is calling on my cell.'

He took Dhingra's call, listened to what the doctor had to say, asked a few questions and gave instructions.

'We're on,' he relayed to the Belgaum team after completing the call. 'Dhingra says Anushka Doshi has agreed to come and meet him at his Goa clinic tomorrow morning. Let's get started with the preparations.'

'Okay. In that case, Murgud should be getting a call from

Anushka any moment now,' Hegde responded. 'Are you going to Goa, Saralkar, to nab Anushka when she shows up at Dhingra's clinic?'

'Yes,' Saralkar replied. 'Anushka Doshi alias Rahul Fernandes.'

Anushka Doshi combed his hair. She'd dreamed of having long tresses but even now they were barely shoulder length, something she'd managed to grow even as Rahul Fernandes. She kept the comb down, picked up the lip gloss and began applying it on his lips.

Bitterness seared through her soul as she looked at his face in the mirror. He should've known she would never completely look feminine or pretty. Rahul peeped out from too many features. The threaded eyebrows were feminine but not the eyes. The lips were luscious and full like a woman's, but the tent-shaped nostrils were far from delicate. The less said about her body, the better.

Life had duped him, playing an almighty hoax—deceived him into believing that he could lead a life as a person he was not born as, merely by making changes to his body and become the woman he had always felt frolicking inside him. Well, the body had not become the organ she'd wanted it to. The only music it made was off-key—no harmony, no melody, just an unbearably hair-raising, screeching sound, like the scratching of nails on a slate.

If he couldn't be Anushka Doshi, he wanted Rahul Fernandes back. She didn't know why, just as he hadn't known why he had desired to become a woman earlier. It was some compelling, unstoppable impulse that ran riot through his mind and body.

Then and now! It was ruthless in its desire, even manic. He'd killed before for it, she'd killed even now, and it would make him kill again, if forced to. It couldn't be thwarted. A heart wants what it wants! And if it knew it wasn't going to get what it desired, it could also be vengeful.

Someone had to pay. Someone always paid. Sometimes, the not-so-innocent like Shaunak Sodhi and Bhupathi, and sometimes the completely innocent like Meenakshi Rao and Geeta Chaudhari!

Anushka took one last look at himself in the mirror, then opened her bag to double-check the contents. Everything she needed for that one last gamble was packed—money, clothes, documents for Anushka Doshi as well as for Rahul Fernandes. She zipped it up and walked across to the next room for one interface with his victim.

Geeta Chaudhari cringed and shrank pitiably on her bed. Pain and fear were the only two emotions that coursed through her veins now. Everything else had been drained out since the previous night when Meenakshi alias Anushka had suddenly appeared next to her, surgical knife in hand. Before she had even realised what was happening, Geeta had felt the sharp blade slice through her firm flesh, twice, in quick succession. The raw agony had been indescribably excruciating as the blood spurted out and she lost consciousness.

She had woken up some time later, her fresh wounds throbbing and hurting like hell under the two bandages covering them. The searing pain had continued all night with her muffled moans as the only antiseptic against the skewering of flesh and numbing fear.

'Don't worry, Geeta. I just came to say bye,' Anushka Doshi

said, with menacing pleasantness. 'I am going to meet your lover now. I hope he can make me happy for your sake. I can't remain unhappy all my life and let others remain happy, can I?'

She paused and regarded her terrified victim, running her eyes over Geeta—lingering and lascivious. 'Sorry if that hurt a little last night, but I've got a right to be a little spiteful. Let's see if your lover can fix that for you, since he's supposed to be such a great cosmetic surgeon. I'd love to see the look on his face when he sees my handiwork. Maybe he might like your lopped off looks?'

Anushka winked and grinned. 'You never know, Geeta. Men are so kinky. I'm keeping these as mementoes.' She held up the two soft, button-like pieces of pinkish, brownish flesh she'd sliced from Geeta the previous night.

Geeta held her breath, too paralysed by fear to think. What was Anushka going to do to her now? That was the only question drumming in her mind.

'Oh, and one last thing,' Anushka Doshi said, coming closer. The movement made Geeta's flesh creep, and when she saw Anushka's hand emerge from behind, holding a syringe and a needle, her heart beat like a machine gone crazy.

Anushka had given her two injections earlier. Both had generated weird sensations in her body. She tried to plead desperately by shaking her head. But Anushka Doshi had already jabbed the needle into her, with no effort whatsoever to minimise the pain. The needle sunk into Geeta's flesh.

'This might pain, just a bit,' Anushka Doshi said with relish as she pumped a final dosage of malice and venom into Geeta's body.

'Saralkar, Anushka Doshi has just left the farmhouse in a white taxi, Karnataka registration. Our plainclothes team will be tailing her in another taxi, but we don't want to make her suspicious,' Hegde intimated Saralkar.

'That's fine. I am relaying the cab details to the Goa Police. They'll start tailing her when she crosses the state border,' Saralkar replied. 'I just hope the rescue operation of the hostage goes off without any snags. You don't think Murgud has any last-minute tricks up his sleeve, do you?'

'I don't think so, Saralkar. What's he going to do? Enter the farmhouse under our watch and then join the goons? Threaten to kill Geeta Chaudhari if we don't allow him safe passage?' Hegde asked, articulating Saralkar's precise fears. 'I doubt Murgud's that crazy. He knows if he helps us, he has a chance of turning prosecution witness and get a lighter sentence. If he does anything else, he's gone. No, don't worry on his count.'

'Okay. All the best. Let me know once it's done,' Saralkar replied, still unable to share Hegde's confidence. He disconnected. There were nearly three hours to go for Anushka Doshi's scheduled meeting with Dr Dhingra. Preparations were in place. He had tutored Dr Dhingra on how to handle Anushka, what to say, and how to draw her into incriminating herself. He had told the doctor about what to do in case Anushka Doshi became violent or aggressive, or happened to be armed. The Goa Police team would, of course, be close at hand to deal with the situation, but he wanted to ensure that Dr Dhingra didn't say the wrong things or act in a way so as to endanger himself.

Rahul Fernandes alias Anushka Doshi had so far shown himself to be wily, dangerous and unpredictable. It was best to expect the unexpected while dealing with him, rather her.

Saralkar's mobile pinged. It was a message from his wife. *'You could've at least taken me to Goa with you. Have fun.'* A smiley followed. Instead of lightening his mood, he felt irritated. *'No bloody fun,'* he wanted to respond.

His head had been throbbing all morning, probably the after-effect of the overnight journey from Pune to Panjim. He wondered if he could ask Dr Dhingra for a pill to set it right. Even gender reassignment specialists were bound to know enough basic medicine to cure a headache.

Just as he began striding towards the doctor's chamber, Saralkar suddenly felt giddy and, for a second, everything went black, as if someone had just shut off all daylight. He was ambushed by a frightening sense of disorientation, as if he was hurtling down a great height—free falling all the way. Saralkar desperately tried to open his eyes and re-focus, but the blackness cloaked him again. He heard a thump, then realised that it was the sound of his own body slumping and hitting the floor. Pain shot through his right side which had taken the impact. He heard voices and exclamations. Somebody called out his name, probably one of the Goa Police constables.

He briefly opened his eyes but everything was swaying and swimming around, so he shut them again instantly. Saralkar felt himself being lifted by a few hands and transferred to the doctor's examination table. Even as the giddiness continued gripping him, he felt incredibly angry and foolish for having made a spectacle of himself like that.

Next, he heard Dr Dhingra's voice addressing him, even as he felt the stethoscope lightly press against different spots on his chest. His pulse was also being taken simultaneously. Then he heard the familiar ripping of Velcro, an armband being wrapped around his upper arm and the sphygmomanometer being pumped for taking his blood pressure readings. The rapid tightening and loosening on his arm followed twice in quick succession.

The swaying and swimming had ceased now, so Saralkar opened his eyes gingerly. Apart from Dr Dhingra, the faces of Goa Police personnel stared down at him. Saralkar felt his humiliation was complete.

'Do you have a history of hypertension, Inspector Saralkar?' Dr Dhingra asked grimly.

'Not really,' Saralkar lied instantly, then added, 'although a couple of days ago it was slightly high.'

'Are you on any medication?'

Saralkar had no wish to admit he'd been advised to undergo tests, which he had been avoiding.

'Why? What's the problem?' he counter-questioned grimly.

Dr Dhingra said, 'Look, your blood pressure is too high right now. We need to get it normalised. And you require bed rest.'

Those were the precise words Saralkar didn't want or care to hear. 'Oh, come on, doctor, it can't be all that serious,' he said gruffly. 'Just give me something to lower my blood pressure; I'm okay otherwise. You know we've got a job to do.'

Dr Dhingra looked at the posse of Goa Police, then back at Saralkar. 'Perhaps some other officer should handle it. You've already explained to me how to tackle Anushka Doshi; I don't think it'll be a good idea for you to.'

Saralkar felt enraged but just as he was about to fire back at the doctor, darkness blanketed his eyes again and the giddiness and nausea returned. 'Okay, doctor,' he mumbled, his eyes still closed. 'Do what you have to. But I need to be up on my feet again in an hour's time.'

34

ANUSHKA DOSHI ALIAS RAHUL FERNANDES WATCHED THE highway zipping by. An hour to go before he entered Goa. He had been a fugitive from justice for too long now to not have developed an unerring instinct for picking up its faintest signals. The moment Dr Dhingra had changed his tune from insisting sex-change procedures were irreversible to claiming that it could be attempted at an institute in Europe, Anushka Doshi's sensitive antennae had sensed a false note.

When Dhingra had offered to pay for the procedure, even arrange medical documents to support and arrange her visa applications and also accompany her, Anushka Doshi was near certain that the doctor wasn't acting alone. Either he had got in touch with the police or with a private party, which was trying to set up a trap for her to walk into. Without prolonging the conversation, she had accepted the offer of meeting Dhingra at his clinic in Panjim.

Anushka had then mulled the situation, getting surer by the minute that it had been a ruse—to buy time so that she wouldn't harm Geeta.

The confirmation came when he'd called up Murgud. He'd known Murgud long enough to know something was up, from the way the cop had spoken. There had been a strained quality in his voice, pauses where there should've been none, as if he was parroting a script or being prompted. And, most significantly, he'd asked too many cautious questions—something highly uncharacteristic of Murgud.

Moreover, what had been a dead giveaway was when Murgud had twice told her not to harm Geeta in the course of the conversation. That kind of overt concern was most unlike Murgud. Right at the outset, he'd warned Anushka that if Dr Dhingra did not yield, she was free to do what she wanted to do with Geeta Chaudhari but no blood should be spilt in Karnataka state, his domain. Nor would he or the two history-sheeters help. Anushka would have to take the hostage elsewhere on her own and Murgud would have nothing more to do with the matter. She could release the hostage or kill her, but somewhere far away in another part of the country, with no trail that could lead back to Murgud.

It was therefore most odd that Murgud had exhorted him not to harm Geeta Chaudhuri, especially when his own people were on guard at the farmhouse. And so, Anushka Doshi had made the shift to Plan B, to do what he did best—disappear!

For disappearing was the key to being free. And remaining free was a requisite to having any chance of finding some happiness in her wretched life. She permitted himself a brief smile. Thank God, he had been born in Goa!

Saralkar had been dimly aware of somebody calling out his name and shaking him gently. The voices had now become louder and the shaking considerably more vigorous. He stirred and tried to open his eyes. It was a Herculean effort, as if his eyelids had been glued together with adhesive. When they finally became unstuck, the visuals were hazy and his mind completely befuddled, wondering where he was. For a moment he felt like Rip Van Winkle, before memory began trickling back. Mercifully, the world wasn't swimming and although his head was still heavy, it felt much better. Probably Dr Dhingra had given him a sedative and medication to lower his blood pressure.

'Sir,' a young Goa Police officer was addressing him, 'PSI Motkar is on the line. He needs to talk to you urgently.'

Saralkar noticed the officer was holding his own cell phone. He took it from the officer, without getting up, because he still wasn't quite confident of even sitting up. 'Yes, Motkar.'

'Sir, are you feeling okay?' Motkar asked.

Still feeling embarrassed, Saralkar replied tersely, 'I'm alive, Motkar. Go on, what's the update? Has the hostage been rescued?'

The slight hesitation in Motkar's reply was enough to send alarm bells ringing in Saralkar's mind. 'What is it?'

'Sir, we rescued Geeta Chaudhuri from the farmhouse as planned, without any hitches. Murgud played his part without mischief and there was no resistance from the two caretakers. But the hostage is in pretty bad shape. We are not sure if she can make it yet.'

'What? Why? Explain.'

'Sir, Anushka Doshi has damaged Geeta Chaudhuri quite badly. It could be fatal.'

Saralkar finally sat up. 'Motkar, tell me clearly what has happened?'

'Sir, Anushka Doshi sliced Geeta Chaudhuri's nipples off both breasts last night and, worse still, she's been injected with a nearly lethal dose of testosterone.'

'Testosterone? You mean the male hormone?' Saralkar said slowly, feeling unreal.

His eyes strayed towards Dr Mahendra Dhingra who was staring at him anxiously, his ears pricked at the mention of testosterone.

'Yes, sir. The dose injected was several times bigger than normal. Doctors think she most likely won't survive,' Motkar replied.

'Oh, my God!'

The alarm bells were clanging in Saralkar's mind now. Why would Anushka Doshi have done that to the hostage while agreeing to meet Dhingra? Something was wrong. Those weren't the actions of a kidnapper who expected to get her demands met. Why would she want to endanger her bargaining chip so perversely? It would've been understandable if she'd done it after her demands had been fulfilled, not at this stage. Something wasn't right.

'And that's not all, sir,' Motkar said. 'Anushka Doshi also gave the Karnataka Police tracking team a slip somewhere near the Goa border.'

Saralkar could almost feel the sedative inside his body, physically trying to restrain his blood pressure from shooting up. 'How the hell did that happen?' he growled.

'Sir, the car stopped at a food plaza along the highway. Anushka Doshi had already gone in by the time the team following her reached the place. They waited while one of the plainclothes men went in to have a look. She was nowhere to be seen. They are not sure of what exactly happened, but she didn't return to the car. The driver of her taxi knew nothing. They think she probably changed her get-up in the restroom and fled in another car that must've already been waiting outside the food plaza. The plaza has two CCTV cameras, and the footage is being checked.'

Expletives and abuses had been rising to Saralkar's lips and for once, he would've liked to scream 'serenity now' to see if it really worked. 'Look,' he said to Motkar, holding back his exasperation, 'she's probably changed into Rahul Fernandes to escape detection ... and I think he might've jumped into some waiting luxury bus, not a car. Check if there were any luxury or state transport buses that he might've got into.'

'Yes, sir. I'll get it done. You think Anushka Doshi knows that she was being lured into a trap, sir? That Murgud might've somehow leaked the information to her?'

'She certainly suspects something, that much is clear, unless she's just taking precautions to double-check she's not being followed. But what she did to Geeta is pure vengeance, so I'm doubtful she'll turn up at Dhingra's clinic now,' Saralkar said, then caught Dhingra's eye and immediately regretted having mentioned Geeta. 'I just hope we haven't lost him again. Rahul Fernandes has shown himself adept at disappearing.'

He disconnected and braced himself to tell Dr Dhingra, fearing the worst but hoping for the best.

Anushka Doshi alias Rahul Fernandes neither showed up at Dr Dhingra's clinic nor was nabbed either by the Goa or the Karnataka Police in the days that followed. Geeta Chaudhuri just about managed to survive after battling with death for three days.

Saralkar fretted in the waiting room of the pathology and diagnostics laboratory, a week later. He had finished the blood test and urine sample, and now he was supposed to go the whole nine yards with ECG and sonography, and double echo tests. All because of that stupid bout of giddiness in Goa!

His wife had finally put her foot down. She sat next to him now, reading a newspaper, throwing hawk-like glances in his direction every now and then, as if she expected him to fly away any minute.

Saralkar's thoughts went back to Rahul Fernandes. Not that criminals hadn't outsmarted him before but Anushka Doshi had made him feel like a complete fool. He wondered if he'd been too clever by half in suggesting an elaborate ruse to Dr Dhingra. Would it have been better to have kept it simple? Would it have worked if Dr Dhingra had been instructed to simply tell Anushka that he was accepting her demand? In a bid to make it convincing, had Saralkar overplayed his hand and alerted Rahul Fernandes to some kind of a trap?

He had to admit to himself, if not anyone else, that perhaps that's what might have happened. He was not alone, of course, in making a mistake. The annals of crime were full of misjudgements made by policemen that had led to criminals escaping. So, there it was—another over smart policeman who had let a smart criminal get away. Saralkar bridled at the thought. 'How long do we have to wait for the damn ECG?' he grumbled to his wife.

'Don't fret like a kid,' Jyoti rebuked him, looking up from the newspaper. 'You like Remo Fernandes?'

'Who's that?'

'Come on, don't tell me you don't know Remo, the Goan

popstar! Remember *Jalwa*?' she replied, referring to a cult Hindi movie, the title song of which had introduced Remo Fernandes to the larger Indian public.

'Hrrmp,' Saralkar said. 'What about him?'

'He's in the news. It seems Remo had adopted Portuguese nationality several years ago, like many native Goans whose parents and grandparents lived under the Portuguese colonial rule till 1961. This fact's just come to light because of some recent accident his family member was involved in,' Jyoti replied, showing him the news item.

Saralkar read the item. Like native descendants from the former French colony of Pondicherry in South India were eligible for French citizenship, it seemed eligible Goans too could apply for and get Portuguese citizenship, which ensured they had access to nearly a hundred and seventy countries without a visa. A buzzer went off in Saralkar's mind. He knew exactly how and where to look for Rahul Fernandes and stop him from fleeing India, if he hadn't already done so.

'You can come for the ECG now,' a nurse came up and announced.

But Saralkar paid her no attention. He was too busy calling up PSI Motkar to order him to get in touch with the Portuguese embassy in India.

Portuguese passport holder Rahul Fernandes was nabbed seven days later as he showed up to board a Malaysia-bound flight at Chennai airport. Saralkar's hunch had hit bullseye.

35

SARALKAR REGARDED ANUSHKA DOSHI, AS HE AND MOTKAR entered the interrogation room. She looked back at him full in the eye, without flinching. It was a cruel, cynical face—not yet feminine but no longer manly.

It curled into a defiant, sly smirk almost immediately. 'Shouldn't a woman cop be present too? Technically I'm a female suspect, you know. I could claim you tried to molest and rape me in custody.'

The voice had that peculiar quality, of sounding as if it could have belonged to either sex. Perhaps Rahul Fernandes had also undergone voice feminisation therapy.

'Well, that's been your tragedy, Rahul Fernandes. Anushka Doshi has always remained an unfulfilled fantasy, hasn't she?' Saralkar mocked.

The smirk vanished from Anushka Doshi's face and bitterness surfaced in each feature. 'Do you know what it is to feel the way people like me do? To be a man outside and throb like a woman inside, every minute! To live like a totally different being than what you are born as, to feel a stranger in the body you have not chosen for yourself, year after year? To want a vagina, where there's a penis? To be bloody trapped! And then when you change into a woman, to feel cheated, deceived, left stranded! To want to go back to being a man, if you can't really be a woman ... it's hell. Damn it, it's a living hell.'

Anushka Doshi blazed all her hatred and fury for the world at Saralkar.

'So first you had the urge to become a woman and became one. Then you wanted to return to being a man again,' Saralkar said in the same scornful, mocking tone that pricked like a needle. 'But looks like one urge remained constant throughout—the urge to kill. Whether as a man or woman, eh Rahul, sorry, Anushka?'

Anushka Doshi's eyes flashed in response. 'You would have done the same thing if you were in my place. Anyone who feels threatened and trapped can kill. It's a basic instinct.'

Saralkar gave a derisive chuckle. 'You know a good headline I can think of, Motkar? Unsuccessful Transgender, Successful Murderer,' he looked at Motkar deliberately, then back at Anushka Doshi. 'By the way, you proved that saying right—the female of the species is deadlier than the male. You just murdered Shaunak Sodhi when you were a man. But as Anushka Doshi, you slaughtered Krishna Bhupathi, Meenakshi Rao, and almost killed Geeta Chaudhuri. *Three and a half Murders!* Bravo! Kudos to woman power! Tell me, which slaying did you enjoy the most?'

Anushka Doshi didn't respond. She looked away and PSI Motkar wondered whether his boss was going about this grilling in the right way. Perhaps it was time to step in with a different approach. He glanced at Saralkar, unsure whether the senior inspector would like him to interfere. But Saralkar was in fact staring back at him, as if waiting for Motkar to take over.

'You think I'm just a depraved pervert, don't you?' Anushka Doshi spoke suddenly, before Motkar could begin. 'Some kind of a despicable, weird, murderous sexopath on a killing spree?'

'Sexopath? There's no word like sexopath, but I like it,' Saralkar sniggered, 'although you flatter yourself, you freak! Perverts and psychos can't control themselves. You are just an ordinary, cold-blooded killer.'

Anushka Doshi exploded. 'I'm not an ordinary, cold-blooded killer. I fooled the law for seven years. I almost got away even this time.'

'Ah, not just a cold-blooded killer but vain too, with delusions of grandeur. So, you think you are a criminal mastermind, is it?'

Anushka Doshi looked at him nastily. What she said next took Motkar's breath away.

'You are a fool, Inspector Saralkar. You have in front of you a criminal mind with extraordinary motivation, and instead of giving respect and cajoling and coaxing me to reveal more, you scoff at me, thinking I'll talk. I might or might not be a criminal mastermind, but you surely are one stupid, dumb policeman.'

A shocked, ominous silence, crackling with tension, prevailed for a minute. Motkar dared not look at his boss, except from the corner of his eye. Saralkar's expression was stony-faced, as if molten age had condensed into rock. Anushka Doshi was eyeballing him, cocky and defiant, kicked with herself for heaping the insult and awaiting a reaction.

Motkar fervently hoped his boss wouldn't lose it. He was relieved when Saralkar spoke in an even tone. 'You do have a point, Anushka. You might not be a run-of-the-mill killer, after all, but I am still not sure whether you ought to be classified either as a psychopath or a mastermind. Whatever it is, I must say you do have balls, sorry guts, because your balls must've been removed by Dhingra, right? Yes, it's a rare criminal who's had the guts to call me a fool to my face.'

Motkar watched Anushka Doshi's face. A satisfied expression had started creeping over it, as if she'd managed to put the policeman in his place.

'And frankly, in my long career, I haven't seen too many fugitives who've given cops the slip for as long as you have,' Saralkar acknowledged in a brilliantly modulated grudging tone of sneaking admiration.

Motkar marvelled at his boss's ability to sound and appear convincing, even as he made subtle and not-so-subtle course corrections midway through an interrogation. He had witnessed it a few times earlier too. He could see the effect it was having on Anushka Doshi now. She was looking smug.

Saralkar was silent for a second, as if brooding, then said, 'So tell me your story from the beginning. My professional curiosity has got the better of me ... I'm swallowing your insult.'

'Maybe you should apologise to me first, Saralkar,' Anushka Doshi responded with a crooked, triumphant grin.

Saralkar fixed her with a look. 'You know I can have you thrashed black and blue, so that you'll soon be begging to tell us all, but I think you've suffered enough in life and your future doesn't look bright either. So, I'll indulge your vanity. Sorry. Now your turn to convince us whether you are a mastermind or merely a—what did you say?—a sexopath.'

It was the kind of manoeuvre and manipulation that could've gone straight into a textbook on interrogation techniques, Motkar thought.

'I told you I am nothing of the kind,' Anushka responded disdainfully and glared, and then began her narration. 'I knew there was a hardware software mismatch in my body since I was about nine or ten. All the things I was attracted to were girl things—dressing up like them, dancing to cabarets and girly numbers, jewellery, cosmetics—but I had to do only boy stuff. We lived in Goa, in a village near Vasco—my mother and I. My father had died a few years earlier. He'd been a clerk in the colonial Portuguese administration and later, after liberation, in the Indian administration. He had married quite late, when he was nearly forty. I was born almost six to seven years after their marriage. Immaculate conception, I bet, knowing the kind of woman my mother was.' He paused and gave a cynical, mirthless chuckle. 'She was a long-suffering hag, afflicted with religion and superstition. She lost her mental balance completely by the time I was fifteen. So, I fled.'

'You mean you deserted her, abandoned her,' Saralkar observed.

'Call it what you will. I couldn't handle her unique cocktail of religion and looniness, not with what was happening inside me. I went to Panjim for a few years, doing odd jobs. My English was good, so it helped in tourist trade. When I went back to Vasco, she was gone. Neighbours had found her dead in the house one day.'

'Sure you had nothing to do with that?' Saralkar asked wryly.

'I didn't murder my mother, inspector. I'm no Norman Bates from *Psycho*,' Anushka Doshi replied. 'Anyway, I collected all her stuff which the local pastor had kept in his custody for me, if and when I turned up. Fortunately, all my father's documents, my birth certificate, some money and jewellery were intact. We didn't have any close relatives, except my mother's brother, who wasn't the least interested in me. I returned to Panjim. Soon after, I started becoming seriously conflicted—I couldn't completely understand my abnormal urges and impulses. I would get angrier and angrier, even as my lust hormones seemed to go wild. I began to think I was gay, because why did I feel like being a woman otherwise? I also had a few bad sexual encounters, and it all added to my confusion and torment.'

Anushka Doshi paused, closing and rubbing her eyes as if to erase the memory from her mindscreen.

'It must've been hard,' Saralkar said, almost gently.

Anushka Doshi responded to the tone earnestly. 'By God, it was hard! You know what I did then? I began gymming and bodybuilding, trying to aggressively make a man out of myself, trying to screw every girl willing to sleep with me. Nothing helped ... nothing could drive away that girlie self in me. It was as if all my apparatus was wrong. By the time I was in my early twenties, I knew exactly what I was—a man who had to somehow turn into and live as a woman to find peace and happiness. Being in Panjim, I had met many foreign tourists, with different sexual orientations, and had learnt a little about sex change and stuff.

'I tried to find out more and realised there were surgeries and therapies by which I could actually become a woman some day. That's when I decided to make money, get rich by hook or crook, enough to be able to change my sex and live as a woman for the rest of my life. I knew big money would never come just like that, working as a tourist guide and driver, so I turned to petty crime. Nothing serious, but anything that earned me a few extra bucks.'

'But you don't seem to have a crime record in Goa. How come?'

'I didn't stay long enough in Goa to get caught for anything, inspector,' Anushka Doshi replied. 'I pissed off a local gang lord by mistake. You see, I'd also taken to indulging my fantasies by dressing up like a hot chick sometimes and going off for dances in night clubs and other seedy dance bars. I'd do some dirty dancing with men; it was a form of titillation for me, but sometimes drunken men wouldn't realise I was a man, and they'd get horny. That's exactly what happened with this gang lord, so when he finally realised that I was really a man dressed as a woman and that he'd been aroused by me, he felt humiliated and infuriated. He came after me with his gang the next day and I just escaped by the skin of my teeth. I had no option but to flee Panjim for some time ... and that's how I landed up in Bangalore.'

'When did this incident happen? When did you reach Bangalore?' Motkar spoke for the first time.

Anushka Doshi gave him a slightly surprised look. 'Signs of life! So you are not mute after all. Just the strong, silent type, I guess, because your boss does all the talking?'

She turned to glance at Saralkar spitefully. Saralkar said nothing.

'Answer the question, Anushka,' Motkar spoke again.

'Well, let me see. I think it was 1995 or 1996. But it was just the right time to be in Bangalore. The city had just begun exploding into a real metropolis. Real estate was booming—the biggest respectable scam on earth—and I jumped in. I was soon making more money than I had made earlier. I took to Bangalore like fish to water, learnt Kannada and Tamil with surprising ease. The city was my lucky charm. I made the right contacts, got my foot into all the right money-making rackets—betting, chit funds, dance bars, escort services. All the businesses had legitimate and illegitimate sides. I realised that if things continued that way, I could actually manage to get rich enough in a few years to be able to attempt undergoing sex-change procedures.'

'Had you consulted doctors?'

'Yes. I had gathered information and first went to consult a surgeon in Delhi. I was put off by the shadiness of his practice but he had told me the entire procedure involved. To start with, certification by two psychiatrists of my dysphoria—'

'Dysphoria?'

'Yes, inspector. Haven't you done your homework? Dysphoria is the compelling psychological and physiological urge to change one's sex,' Anushka smirked. 'Two qualified psychiatrists need to certify this condition of any individual who wants to change his sex. This is to be followed by hormone therapy for a year or so, then compliance of legal formalities for undergoing surgery and, finally, the actual series of surgeries. I came back to Bangalore and thought the matter over. I had several doubts. How was I to be sure that it was worth undergoing gender reassignment? What if something went horribly wrong? What if the surgeries failed? It was a big risk, plus the shadiness of it all. I needed to find the right doctors, people I could trust ... So, I began looking all over India. I even wondered if I could get it done abroad.'

'Is that when you first thought of getting a Portuguese passport?' Saralkar asked.

'No, no, that was later. It hadn't even crossed my mind then,' Anushka Doshi said. 'I was just hunting for the right doctors and the money I would require to live the rest of my life as a woman later on—the investments I needed to make to lead a comfortable existence—when I realised I needed more money-spinning avenues. And that is when I got this idea of recruitments abroad; I thought it would really bring in money faster. I, of course, couldn't run it myself, so I thought of Bhupathi who I had met during some land deal. He seemed just the right guy to run the scam. He agreed to become my partner but, in turn, suggested that we needed one more partner, and that's how Shaunak Sodhi came into the bloody picture.'

Anushka Doshi paused, a look of disgust on her face as if contemplating how different her life would've been if there had been no Shaunak Sodhi. 'Headstrong, educated nitwit!' She spat out the words and picked up the narrative again. 'I didn't want him—too white-collared for my tastes. All crime requires blue-collar instincts. Shaunak was a novice in scamming and crime, he was very unstable, but Bhupathi convinced me he was the right guy for the racket, especially because he seemed corporate and street-smart at the same time. When Bingo Recruitments became a success, my initial reservations faded. But when things began to go wrong, after the suicide of one young man, whose death created a furore, Shaunak was the first to panic and began flapping and clucking like a complete idiot. In jail he turned Bhupathi's head also, and by the time they got out on bail, they got it into their heads that I was somehow double-crossing them and getting away scot free.'

'Weren't you?' Saralkar took a dig. 'They went to jail, you didn't. You successfully managed to portray yourself as the innocent partner, who knew nothing about the racket. Then one after the other, you swiftly liquidated properties bought by three of you, which were all in your name, and you salted away all the money. Why blame them for suspecting your motives and intent?'

Anushka Doshi sniggered. 'All part of the game, inspector. Come on, you know it. That's how things work. What did they expect? That I would try and get myself implicated in the scam too? Does that make sense? I told Bhupathi and Sodhi repeatedly that it would all blow over soon. Even if there was enough evidence against them in the scam, they would soon be out on bail and we'd get good lawyers and defend them. Bhupathi understood the ways of the crime profession, but this idiot Sodhi was just unnerved by jail and that damned asthma he suffered from ... he just wouldn't listen to reason. Yes, I'd sold off a lot of property but he got it into his head that I was double-crossing them. And then they began demanding a much higher share from the proceeds. His logic was that they were undergoing all the hardships of jail, so I should hand over the lion's share of what I had liquidated, as compensation. When they got out on bail, Sodhi was completely out of control. Abusing, demanding, threatening. I could see Bhupathi, too, had started supporting his views, although hesitantly. He had also developed a sense of grievance that I was cheating him.'

'So, you hatched a plan to invite Sodhi and Bhupathi for a compromise meeting, pretended to agree to their demands, got them drunk, killed Sodhi and threatened Bhupathi with dire consequences if he did not go along with your plan of establishing your death—the death of Rahul Fernandes—and propagate the false myth of Shaunak Sodhi as the absconding murderer.'

'No, no. I had not planned to kill Sodhi. I wanted to resolve the issue amicably,' Anushka Doshi said. 'But the two just wouldn't be reasonable, especially Sodhi. They kept accusing me of cheating them and demanding more. Sodhi was drunk and abusive. He insisted we go to my farmhouse immediately and hand over all the cash. I agreed. I also tried to explain that

I had already fixed ASI Murgud so that he would slowly weaken the evidence and case against them, make witnesses turn hostile through bribes or threats. It would take some time but they would eventually be able to fend off a long sentence. At my farmhouse, I gave them about Rs 15 lakhs each, but they wanted more. Sodhi turned even more aggressive and threatened that he would testify against me and ensure I also got dragged into the case and went to prison.'

Anushka Doshi paused and looked at the two policemen intently. It was a look Motkar recognised, the look that many criminals gave, yearning to be understood as they prepared to reveal what had been their personal tipping points, which triggered them to commit heinous crimes for the first time.

'It was the threat of a prison term that really spooked me.' Her voice was down to a harsh yet vulnerable whisper. 'Going to prison would dash all my hopes, of ever undergoing sex change and living life as a woman, of being happy and at peace. The bastard shouldn't have threatened me with that. Shaunak Sodhi dug his own bloody grave with that threat because I knew he was serious. That's when I lost it. I couldn't bear the thought of living life as a man for years together, that too in a bloody prison. So, one moment Shaunak Sodhi was alive, ranting at me, the next he was dead. I shot him at point blank range; Bhupathi saw me do it and he immediately capitulated with terror. He thought I would shoot him too. I knocked him unconscious and then just sat thinking. A plan soon formed in my mind. I revived Bhupathi and warned him I would spare his and his family's life if he did exactly as I said.'

'But how come you didn't kill Bhupathi too?'

'I needed him alive if my plan was to work. Otherwise, who

would tell the story that Rahul Fernandes had been murdered and Shaunak Sodhi was absconding?' Anushka Doshi replied coolly. 'I convinced Bhupathi that it was the only way out. We then severed Sodhi's head and dismembered him; it wasn't all that hard. Once you've killed the person, he's like any other inanimate object that has to be cut up. After that, we took the torso and buried it at a spot along the Mysore highway, drove further on towards Mercara and threw Shaunak's head into the valley. From there, we split. Both of us had cash. Bhupathi went back to Bangalore to take his family. I warned him that if he got caught, he better stick to the version I had said or I would make sure that his wife and son would meet the same fate as Sodhi. The rest of the story you already know. Bhupathi got caught before he could flee Bangalore and he told the police exactly what I had told him to. Even better, he couldn't lead them to the place where we'd buried the body and so I, Rahul Fernandes, became established as the victim and Sodhi, the fugitive, even though he was dead. In turn, I used this as the perfect cover to change my sex and assume the identity of the woman I always wanted to be.'

'So that means you had already made preparations to undergo gender reassignment before Sodhi's murder?' Saralkar asked.

'Yes,' Anushka Doshi replied. 'I told you I wanted to be sure about gender reassignment. So, I'd started looking for good specialists and one of them was Dr Dhingra who had a practice in Mumbai but had also set up a weekend consulting clinic and surgery in Goa, where he had plenty of clients from abroad too. Later he completely shifted to Goa, probably to be close to his paramour, Geeta Chaudhuri. I had got to know about Dhingra because by chance I had met Sherly, my wife, at a party. My mind was blown when I got to know that Sherly was a transgender, who'd successfully transitioned from being a male to a female, following gender reassignment procedures. I knew this was the perfect opportunity for me to see for myself and make my mind up about gender reassignment. So, I proposed to Sherly and asked her to become my wife. After some hesitation, she agreed. Living with her for three years gave me full confidence that becoming a woman through gender reassignment was perfectly viable sexually, emotionally, psychologically, physically, behaviourally ...'

'Yes, Sherly told me you used her like a guinea pig, experimenting and subjecting her to mental and physical torture,' Saralkar remarked.

'Oh, come on, inspector! I needed to find out for myself that Sherly was not faking things and that gender reassignment worked in every way, that's all. And I rewarded her handsomely, didn't I? Left her most of Rahul Fernandes's investments and flat. Anyway, it helped me make my final decision. Two years after marrying Sherly, I started my treatment and hormone therapy. Psychiatric counselling had already started. When the recruitment scam blew up, I had already decided to undergo the surgery in a few months and had been taking concrete steps to prepare myself for a new life after the surgery. I was so bloody close to fulfilling my lifelong dream, and Shaunak Sodhi threatened to ruin it all ... that's why he had to die.'

'So where did you escape? When did you get the surgery done?' Motkar asked.

'I moved from place to place across India for about three months, and then reached Goa. I squared up with ASI Murgud fairly early on, since I knew I would require him to get things done, and to make sure Bhupathi didn't squeal or crack under pressure. He did a good job by getting Bhupathi off the hook and ensured that the investigation floundered so that no chargesheet could be filed. Bhupathi got bail and fled. I was now quite sure the police had no scent of the truth, so I decided to get my gender reassignment done at the earliest. I would then have a new identity as a woman and that would help me flee justice forever. Since I had learnt about the fact that Goan citizens whose parents or grandparents had been living under Portuguese rule could gain Portuguese citizenship, I lost no time in applying for it. Portuguese nationality would also make it easier to travel and settle wherever I wanted, and it would also be simpler to switch to my new identity as a woman later, legally, since these matters are easier in Europe.

'But when I decided to go ahead with the surgery, Dr Dhingra told me I would require regular follow-up for at least two years, apart from the continuing hormone therapy. He also told me that the best way to make the transition was to also be in a relationship after about a year. That's how I decided that it would be best to stay with Bhupathi as a couple, and we became Sanjay and Anushka Doshi.'

'Ah, so you did to Bhupathi what you had done to Sherly earlier. You used him as a guinea pig to experiment with your newfound womanhood,' Saralkar said.

Motkar felt himself hit by a wave of nausea. And yet, this was the crude and sordid truth of the life of the person in front of them. A person who had an urge so different from normal that he needed to plumb the depths of sadism.

'Well, I had to keep an eye on him, didn't I? So, what was wrong ... if I ... I mean, I had become a woman, I was not a man any longer, so why couldn't we have a relationship? It wasn't as if Bhupathi could've got into bed with many women except hookers or maidservants; I was better than that.'

'Then why didn't the cosy arrangement work out? Why did you have to kill him?' Saralkar asked.

'I had to; I had no choice. If I hadn't killed Bhupathi, he would've had me killed or revealed our secret and got us arrested. He had become a complete alcoholic, forever teetering on the verge of full-scale breakdown. It was only a matter of time. He hated me and was shit scared; he knew I had murdered Sodhi and he thought I would kill him some day. He was freaked out by my sex change and by staying with me. He was repulsed by my demands. He didn't want to have intercourse with me ... he had become a complete mental wreck. He had also started getting into unnecessary problems, with that agent Somnath Gawli and even my maidservant's son, Hrithik Dhond, and had lost the ability to tackle things on his own. And then, he began visiting and working with that Baba Rangdev. I began to sense trouble. I realised someone had blackmailed him into money-laundering and betting activities.

'That meant someone had recognised him or perhaps he had blurted something out while in a drunken state. I began checking his text messages and call logs. Sure enough, something was going on. Then sometimes, he would blabber things in his drunken stupor, which clearly indicated sooner or later he would collapse and get us into trouble. Side by side he also seemed to be planning something, maybe getting rid of me. In one particular conversation, I even overheard him talking to Rangdev about black magic and giving a supari. He thought I was still in the bathroom, but actually I had already stepped out. It was a very hush-hush, short discussion but I heard it. All this rattled me and I knew I needed to act fast. Meanwhile, even after four to five years of the gender-reassignment surgery, things were completely frustrating. Nothing was satisfactory. I didn't feel like a woman, got no pleasure or peace whatsoever. I felt I had been duped. I felt angry all the time, deeply, unbearably frustrated and disappointed. Whatever Dr Dhingra did, all procedures, all therapies, nothing seemed to help. Earlier I had felt like a woman trapped in a man's body; now I felt like a freak of nature imprisoned in an artificial dungeon. I had just escaped one trap to land into another. My frustration was turning into rage. If I couldn't be a woman, I wanted to go back to being a man.'

Anushka Doshi stopped and suddenly burst out into a volley of expletives, as if out of control, trying to purge her body of the accumulated poison. Motkar felt his revulsion rising, but Saralkar did not react.

'Go on,' he prompted dryly after a long minute.

Anushka Doshi gave him a hostile look, grimaced, then picked up her narrative again. 'I was scared that if Bhupathi made a blunder, I would be caught and would have to spend the rest of my life as this ghastly freak. I wanted to escape, so I began planning to get rid of Bhupathi and fake the death of Anushka Doshi with the finger of suspicion pointing to Shaunak Sodhi again. I knew, eventually the police would trace the case back to my earlier crime. Rahul Fernandes would still remain dead, Bhupathi would die, but Shaunak Sodhi's phantom would still remain alive. With Anushka Doshi's identity taken care of, there would be no possibility of linking it back to Rahul Fernandes. I would coerce Dr Dhingra to help me become Rahul Fernandes again, and then I would flee India on my Portuguese passport. That's how I planned it. ASI Murgud had helped me trace

Dhingra's lady love, Geeta Chaudhari, so I decided to abduct her from Tirupathi, where we knew she went every year. Snaring her was easy with my past life regression spiel.'

'But didn't it cross your mind that sex-change surgical procedures were irreversible? That no matter what you did or tried, Dr Dhingra wouldn't be able to help?' Saralkar asked.

'How was I to be sure that it was irreversible? Perhaps there was some technology to reverse it. If women can undergo sex change to become men, why can't a woman who was earlier a man become a man again? I mean, they use our own tissues and skin grafts to create the organs,' Anushka Doshi said fiercely. 'Can't you see? I just wanted to stop being and feeling like a freak. I had spent my life in this hell, never feeling the slightest pleasure or happiness, always feeling the wrong person in the wrong body, always knowing something was weird and abnormal in me. Bewildered, tortured, as if I'll explode at any moment, devoured by my cravings that I hadn't asked for, a body and urges I didn't choose to be born with ... and Dhingra had assured me everything would be all right. Then whose responsibility was it to make sure I really became a woman? Felt like one? He had failed, and he either needed to make up for it or pay with something valuable to him ... and I was bloody well going to make him pay.'

Anushka Doshi regarded them with a strange expression, as if sanity had retreated momentarily and naked, irrational emotion had completely taken over. Was that what happened with most murderers when they committed the act of killing, Motkar wondered. When they were so blinded with an emotion that it obscured everything else—a return to man's most primitive self in which all other brain functions shut off, leaving just one active impulse that suffused human beings with the will to kill, to harm, to destroy?

'So, that's the reason you planned to pump so much testosterone into Geeta Chaudhari? So that she could start turning into a man?' Saralkar asked harshly. 'You knew that would kill her.'

'That's because you interfered. I was planning to keep her for a few weeks till some signs of masculinity spoilt her feminine features that had so bewitched Dhingra. I had planned one shot a week, as they do during hormone therapy ... that would have been some revenge,' Anushka Doshi gave him a horribly spiteful smile, as if her soul was twisted beyond redemption.

'And what about Meenakshi Rao? What sick justification do you have for that?' Motkar asked abruptly, with unexpected fury. In a long time, he had never felt so angry.

The look on Anushka Doshi's face didn't change. 'Would you have preferred if it had been Kunika Ahuja instead?' she said in a mocking tone, which was suddenly loaded with vehement bitterness. 'God makes innocent victims out of so many of us, nobody calls him a pervert or a sadist. So why can't I victimise? I needed somebody to die as Anushka Doshi. It happened to be Meenakshi Rao's fate. Anyway, their lives were hardly worth living: Meenakshi or Kunika—the wretched bitches born and endowed as women and look how they were wasting that womanhood—living like pathetic, teary, long=suffering virgins.'

Suddenly, PSI Motkar could bear the ravings of this sad, irreparably damaged, demented, human being no more. He got up and strode out of the cell, filled with loathing and disgust, without excusing himself even from his boss.

'Feeling better, Motkar?' Saralkar asked, joining him at the police canteen, half an hour later. 'First time I have seen you react like that.'

'Sorry about that, sir. Couldn't take his disturbing bullshit anymore,' Motkar replied. 'How don't you ever get affected?'

'Who says I don't get affected, Motkar?' Saralkar grunted. 'How do you think I got this hypertension and all?'

They sat silently for a few seconds, each weighed down by their own thoughts. Motkar fidgeted with his empty teacup.

'You know what he—I mean she—said to me?' Saralkar spoke again.

'What, sir?'

'That the same God who'd blessed us with common sense, had cursed him with this self-destructive kink,' Saralkar replied. 'It got me thinking ... poor bastard.'

'You feel sorry for him—er—her—sir?' Motkar asked, not a little incredulously.

Saralkar was quiet for a disconcertingly long second. 'No. Feeling sorry for a murderer is betraying the victims. But she's got a point. I wonder how many of us would commit murder if we carried fatal kinks in our beings or lacked good sense.'

'But she knew exactly what she was doing, sir. Both as Rahul Fernandes and as Anushka Doshi.'

'Exactly, Motkar. Which begs the question, why was he unable to stop himself then? Answer: the kink in his system coupled with the absence of good sense,' Saralkar said, then shook his head. 'It seems nearly forty per cent of those who undergo sex change regret it, want to go back to being their original selves.'

Motkar shrugged. 'That's still no justification for murder, sir. I think Rahul Fernandes ought to be hanged.'

'Well, you are on the same wavelength as Anushka Doshi, then. Says it'll be a relief to die—an escape from hell. But I doubt she'll even have that pleasure any time soon, given the pace of law,' Saralkar replied. 'Anyway, our job's done for the moment, Motkar. Let's order some more tea.'

'Sure, sir. How about mixed bhajjis, to go with the tea?'

Saralkar's face lit up briefly, but then a shadow settled over it. 'No, I can't have bhajjis. I have been advised to cut down on fried and salty foods. But you go ahead.'

He retreated into a moody silence and Motkar excused himself awkwardly to fetch the tea. Just as he reached the canteen counter, Saralkar bellowed out to him. 'Motkar, get a plate of bhajjis for me too. Who bloody wants to live forever anyway?'

Minutes later, he attacked the hot, sizzling bhajjis with gusto and slurped his tea contentedly. Motkar, on the other hand, chose to sip and nibble his.

www.ingramcontent.com/pod-product-compliance
Lightning Source LLC
LaVergne TN
LVHW010308070526
838199LV00065B/5479